Carol Birch was born in 1951 in Manchester and went to Keele University. She has lived in London, south-west Ireland and now Lancaster. Her first novel, *Life in the Palace*, won the 1988 David Higham Award for Best First Novel of the Year. In 1991 she won the prestigious Geoffrey Faber Memorial Prize with *The Fog Line*. *Little Sister, Come Back, Paddy Riley, The Naming of Eliza Quinn* and *Scapegallows* are also published by Virago.

Turn Again Home

CAROL BIRCH

virago

VIRAGO

First published in Great Britain by Virago Press 2003
This edition published in 2004 by Virago Press
Reprinted 2005, 2011, 2013

Copyright © Carol Birch 2003

The moral right of the author has been asserted.

A CIP catalogue record for this book
is available from the British Library.

ISBN 978-1-86049-978-4

Typeset by M Rules in Bembo
Printed and bound in Great Britain by
Clays Ltd, St Ives plc

Papers used by Virago are from well-managed forests
and other responsible sources.

MIX
Paper from
responsible sources
FSC® C104740

Virago Press
An imprint of
Little, Brown Book Group
100 Victoria Embankment
London EC4Y 0DY

An Hachette UK Company
www.hachette.co.uk

www.virago.co.uk

For Joe and Richard —
and for Martin

Acknowledgements

Certain people proved invaluable in the writing of this book: thanks to Rosemary Martlew, Lee Hilton, Martin Butler, Steve Power, John Euers (for the tiger), Margaret Shennan, and the greatest thanks of all to James Stuart Rowe.

. . . *such a tide as moving seems asleep,*
  Too full for sound and foam,
When that which drew from out the boundless deep
  Turns again home.

TENNYSON, *Crossing the Bar*

Prologue

In spring, in Rome, the petals of the cherry trees drifted all over the Via Malagassia, pink and rippling like the small waves that roll in at the edge of the sea. When the small breezes blew, the gorgeous ice-cream softness shifted and spooled, lazily turning upon itself. While it lasted, which was not long, Jack Caplin would wade with slow steps through the pink froth every morning on his way from the Metro to work. It was a day like any other, traffic squalling and brawling, slick windows smelling of sun, the bitter brown aroma of coffee from the awning on the corner of the street into which he turned. The tables outside the Taberna Amalia were newly washed down from the morning dust of traffic, and a woman in a black pencil skirt and top sat reading the newspaper with a small dog at her feet.

Jack had a cubby-hole in the Archivo di Classica Mythologica, on the second floor of a tall, venerable building overlooking a small piazza. To reach his hole he had to run the gauntlet of the bright raking smile of the librarian, whose black-rimmed eyes and thin carmine lips always made him think of the death's-head woman in *The Rime of the Ancient Mariner*. His cubby-hole was a small brown room that closed all around him on all sides like the round woven straw of a dormouse's nest, full of his own smell and substance, where he could bury his head under his paws and curl up tight and drift and drift. It was hot and airless. Pigeons crooned along the ledge outside. A depiction of the horned god Cernunnos the abundant, the fertile, sitting like the Buddha on an Italian rock carving from the fourth century BC, was pasted on the wall over his desk. Books and files to the ceiling, mountains of mythology, Roman and Greek, Eastern European, Scandinavian, Finno-Ugric, Celtic (his own speciality).

Several rare and valuable manuscripts, protected by faint yellow plastic coverings, awaited his attention, held down by a big glass paperweight in which a seahorse hung suspended.

Jack sat down, rubbed his eyes with the heels of his hands, opened his notebook upon the strewn desk, put his head down sideways upon it and closed his eyes. He was working on the Celtic sack of Rome in 387 BC, but that was not why he succumbed to lethargy: he was always like this. He yawned, showing healthy pink gums and sharp incisors. His large arched nostrils flared. He could sleep any time. The sounds from the street lapping away. Anywhere. People walking, talking. Slide away. But instead of sleeping he pulled himself together and blinked. He set to handling the rare manuscripts in a totally sensual, totally indulgent way. *Dies Alliensis* was never forgotten by the Romans. So close an infringement of the Capitol itself could not go unavenged. Never again would Rome be found sleeping.

'You're in a dream,' said the librarian, Signora Mancini, one large thigh and a squashy haunch flattened along the side of his desk. Her black hair was taken back into a knot.

'Life is but a dream,' he said, smiling.

'Someone was trying to get through from England,' she told him. 'It could have been for you. Maybe they'll try again.'

His mother was dead. He just knew.

'For me? From England?' 'When?'

'Half an hour ago.'

My mother's dead, he thought, that's what it is. People don't call me here at work from England. Early morning there. He sat back, folding his arms. 'I bet my mother's popped her clogs,' he said in English. One hand, long and languid, pushed back the mousebrown hair above his high, tapering brow. 'I have to make a call,' he said.

She withdrew. It's the same, he thought. A call when there shouldn't be a call, the same as when his father died. Same feeling. He listened to the telephone ring in his mother's house. No one answered. A cold seepage of guilt stole over him. The old lady. The way she lived.

He rang his sister Georgia. No answer.

His sister Joanne. No answer.

He sat, gazing at the horned god, eyes big with a kind of humour, a kind of bemusement. Something big happening. Airwaves a-quiver. Shouting and laughter from the street outside.

The phone rang.

'Jack Caplin.'

'Is that you, Jack?'

Who?

'Yes. This is Jack.'

'Is that you, Jack?' Slurred voice.

'Uncle Bob?' Uncle Bob? Uncle Bob never phoned.

'It's Nell,' he said abruptly, and coughed. 'It's your mam, Jack.'

'Mum dead?'

Mum dead.

'No, Jack, no. She's had a stroke.' Voice full of gin and beer, always the same.

Pause.

'How bad?'

'Bad, Jack.'

Jack sighed deeply, making it audible down the phone, all the way to Manchester.

'She's in hospital. I think she's going, Jack. The girls are there now, I said I'd ring you.'

Go on to automatic. Think.

'Is she conscious?'

'No.'

'When did it happen?'

''Bout eight o'clock must've been. Standing on the doorstep talking to a neighbour from up the road.'

Motorcycle revving out in the street.

'Oh, God, Uncle Bob,' Jack said.

'It would've been quick, Jack. You know your mam, she would-n't have wanted you getting upset.'

Auntie Eva said something in the background and Uncle Bob sniffed hard. 'It would've been quick,' he repeated, before his voice trembled away into tears. 'Sorry, Jack. I can't believe it. Our Nell. She was always a good sister to me.'

She'd adored him. He could do no wrong.

'I'll come home,' Jack said.

He stood blank for a moment, then packed a few files and books into his bag. His mouth was dry. He'd come a long way. *A long way from St Louis, and baby, you sure got a long way* ... Jazz tunes, as always, meandered in his head.

She wasn't so old. But she'd reverted to type, smoked like a chimney, drank like a fish, put on weight. In his mind he was struggling with the idea that somehow she'd let him down, changing from the mother she once was into that old woman.

A bird flew from a balcony where purple flowers hung. Voices sang from the children's dance school. And he was back in the pink blossomy froth, wading. It made him think of the dead leaves, red and orange and brown, crackling along Green Grove in the mornings in Manchester when he was a scrubby scuff-shoed child walking hand in hand with his big mother. Made him think of glistening rainy Manchester; of sunny bright Manchester in long summers when he steered his raft along the stinky brook that meandered past the allotments and through the dim high cutting overhung with white death-lilies, their gaping mouths hungry in the deep green banks of ivy; of three-foot snows into which he fell from the front steps of his house. Oh, to be in England now that April's here. *You came a long way from St Louis, but baby, you still got a long way to go.* The bridge under which he walked, where the spray-gunners had gone to town, echoed his dream, though he couldn't for the life of him remember what it was. Out the other side. A rainy Manchester night shivered through his bones in the bright teeming Roman morning.

And on the plane, high over the Alps, paralysed and parched with terror, he finally fell into a kind of sleep that was not a sleep, in which his spirit went out from him walking on the clouds, looking down between the gaps at the horrible distance, the empty miles between himself and reality, reeling in terror and elation, and he dreamed again, though he was still not asleep, that he was an angel, Lugus, the

Shining One, and he rose up and up and up like bursting, till he could look down on the earth from impossible heights with a god's eye and see it all laid out below as far as any sense could reach in any direction, and that included time too. He got lost. Oh, but it was what he was for. He wandered in the clear blue, one spring, one gorgeous honeysuckle rose-petal long-grass bumbling-bee day in spring, the sweet spring, in England, once, like a filament of a dandelion clock floating with swingboat motion on the small breezes.

Down it went down with deadly precision to where it had to go. To little Nell.

PART ONE

Old Folks at Home

1

In Linden Lea

There she sits. She is twenty years or so off giving birth to her only son, Jack. There in Gorton Nelly sits on the stairs, top of the stairs in the shadow, in a brand new council house on Sutton Estate in 1930, a little timid round-shouldered girl with glasses and a plain face. Brown hair cut square with a short fringe. A squint. Baby Bobby's sick. Scarlet fever. Scarlet fever has a beautiful sound. But baby Bobby might die. Baby Bobby might die. Violet's having a weep on the doorstep. Downstairs the serious voices, Mam and Dad, the tousled sleepy bed made up for Bobby on the sofa in the small dark curtained room, by the empty grate. Smell of sickness in the room.

They were sending her away on her own.

Bobby shouting: 'Tongue hurts, Mam!'

His hair, the colour of crumbly white cheese, now darker, wet, stuck on his forehead.

He's three now. Had his birthday last week. Dad brought Yo-Yos home.

Mam came out of the room carrying the sick bowl. 'Oh, don't be so bloody stupid, Violet,' she said, 'of course he's not going to die.'

Violet hugging her skinny knees.

Nelly went out on to the front. Kitty O'Neill was pushing a doll's pram up and down over the road. The wheels squeaked. The privets had just been planted but they had not yet grown up. Violet said you could die of scarlet fever. Bobby was all red. Mam said, 'Don't be so bloody stupid, he'll be right as rain in a week – you see.' But Dad's face was grey and long, and they were sending her away up to Morland to Granny and Grandad's. And that was a good thing, a sweet flowery feeling in the pit of her stomach. Morland was Linden Lea.

Kitty O'Neill's hair was red, rich orange-ginger, curly and wild. A soft light shone around the edges.

'My baby's poorly,' Nelly said.

'Your little Bobby?'

'Yes.'

Dad didn't like the Irish.

'My grandad's coming for me. I'm going up to Morland.'

'Where's that?'

'Oh, it's a long way away. I'm going on the train. My grandad's coming. He's at my uncle Edmund's. He's a headmaster.'

'Your Violet's crying,' said Kitty, looking over her shoulder.

'He might die,' Nell said.

'Oh, Nelly!' Kitty said. 'Not your Bobby!'

The siren sounded. Kitty went in. Grandad turned the corner at the top of their street. He has always been old, old and wise and venerable. A heavy salt-and-pepper moustache all but obscures his mouth altogether. He doesn't look big coming down the road: he looks little, and old, and shambling. But Grandad is a great man. He writes poems. His stature grows as he comes near, till he is wide and large and hairy and formidable. He stops before Nell and leans down towards her till his face is close. Hairs sprout from his nostrils. His eyes behind his wire-framed round glasses are old, full of frayed red veins, a stern, hurt look about them.

'Now then, la lammy,' he says. 'Coming with your grandad?'

She nods shyly, in awe. He takes her by the hand and they walk up the garden path. Violet jumps up from the step, smiling and crying.

'Now then,' he says, 'it's not that bad,' lets go of Nell's hand to kiss Violet, and then Dad opens the door at the bottom of the stairs and through it Nell sees Mam rising, a heavy woman putting one hand on each big round knee beneath her pinny and pushing herself up to a stand with a great weary sigh.

'Run up, Violet,' Dad says, 'run up and get Nelly's things. This is good of you, Dad.'

'Not at all, Sam.'

Mam comes out to straighten Nell up. 'Now you be a good girl for your granny and grandad and do what you're told,' she says, in a scolding voice.

'Of course she will, Bessie.' Grandad's moustache moves in a way that means he's smiling.

Vi comes down with Nell's bag and Dad runs in the back for a bag of cough candy for the journey. Nelly starts to feel sick, all quivery with excitement. She looks at her small, thin dad, his striped shirt soft with wear, braces undone. Tears fill her throat. She doesn't really mind about Mam and Violet, it's Dad she doesn't want to leave. And Bobby. And while the grown-ups are standing talking on the path, she sneaks back in and goes into the forbidden room and stands by the sofa where he lies. He's awake. His eyes are crusty, his hair dirty. The skin is peeling on his fingertips.

'I'm going now,' she whispers.

'Nelly,' he says, 'when you come back will you bring me some chocolate?'

'If I can.'

Mam caught her in there and played hell. She was like that, Mam, still moaning as she stood at the gate waving Nelly off with a martyred air. Dad walked down to Belle Vue and got on the town bus with them, sitting her on his knee to look out of the window at Hyde Road passing, West Gorton, Ancoats. At London Road station he bought her a bag of chestnuts; she clutched them so tight the neck of the bag grew limp in her palm as she leaned out of the window of the Penrith train to give him a kiss.

'Good girl, Nelly,' he said. 'You have a lovely time and don't you worry about old Bob. Right as rain this time next week, just you wait.'

But there were tears somewhere in his eyes, she could see, not at the front of them but somewhere; and she cried as she waved him off in the steam.

'Now, la lammy,' Grandad said. 'Now.'

But then he couldn't think of much to say to her, because Grandad only really knew how to talk to other grown-ups. So he read his book, a detective book with a man in a mac lying face-down in a pool of blood on the cover, and Nelly looked out of the

window at the steam streaming past the window and thought of
Morland in Westmorland, with the mountains all around, and the
big fells, and the wild flowers nodding all along the lanes. Morland
is Linden Lea that her grandad sings about, accompanying himself on
the piano. Morland is Heaven. Dad said the earth was Hell. All of us,
he said, are already there. But Morland was Heaven, and Morland
was on earth. In Morland the maids carried their pails on yokes
across their shoulders to the village pump, just like in her nursery-
rhyme book.

She fell asleep to the rattling of the train.

Grandad is at the piano. His large gnarled hands play cleverly and he
sings in a deep throbbing voice, his moustache going up and down as
he sings:

> Within the woodland flow'ry-shaded
> By the oak tree's mossy moot,
> The shining grass blades, timber-shaded,
> Now do quiver underfoot,
> And birds are singing overhead
> And water's bubbling in its bed,
> And there, for me, the apple tree
> Do lean down low in Linden Lea.

Dust sparkles in the window light beyond the old man's head. She
sits on the high-backed cane-bottomed chair at the open back door
of Granny and Grandad's house in Morland in Westmorland. She's
been here for six weeks. The scarlet fever turned into something else,
some other bad thing. They were very far away in time, Dad and
Mam and Bobby and Vi. She saw them down a long tunnel like the
one Dad saw when he was shot and nearly died in the war. It went
towards a brilliant white light, he said, and who should be there at the
end of it but his own granny and grandad, and his cousin who'd died
ten years ago, standing in a beautiful garden full of flowers. The most
beautiful garden you could ever imagine, he said, and he wanted to
go to them, but they waved to him to go back because it wasn't his

time. So he'd come back instead and married Mam, and here they all were.

Heaven. Or at least the garden at the beginning of Heaven – but Nell knew that the most beautiful garden in the world was Granny and Grandad's, with the two trees yielding sour little crab apples, and the mass of dog-rose and all the sage ranks of tall purples and yellows. Small red rambling roses with hairy stems and deep red thorns grew all over the wall at the front. If she looked one way Nelly could see Granny tying up beanstalks, her long hair falling down from under her big straw hat in white ringlets at the back, her white hankie coming out of her sleeve. If she looked the other she could see Auntie Lal, who was up from London, sneaking a drink from the place behind the curtain under the sink. Lal had a liking for the drink too, Mam said. Oh, they all do, she said, it's in his family. Dad's family. Lal always kept a bottle of whisky hidden around the house somewhere where nobody would find it. She carried a hip flask. Yesterday when they'd gone for a walk, as they passed the pump she'd turned aside and had a little drink from it, discreet and ladylike. She was very genteel, Auntie Lal, even though she had an enormous baby in her belly that, in spite of the shapeless sacklike thing with no arms she was wearing, made her look like a snake that had swallowed an egg. Sweat shone on her upper lip. 'Ssh!' she mimed to Nell, finger on lips. Her face, small and hawk-ish, mild-eyed. Her brown hair had lost a pin and was coming down at the side.

Grandad played the piano in a rumpled shirt, open-collared, with the sleeves rolled up and his waistcoat hanging open. The weather was fine, clear and calm, and the scent of Morland in summer, and the droning of bees, came in through the door. On the big stuffed chair lay one of his lurid-covered murder mysteries. Stiff and grey and stern and kind, he sang throbbingly:

> *For I be free to go abroad*
> *Or take again my homeward road*
> *To where for me the apple tree*
> *Do lean down low in Linden Lea.*

13

And the music ceased.

There was a brief pause, birdsong from the churchyard.

Grandad fetched his pipe and pouch from the mantelpiece, sat down heavily in his chair, lit up and shook open the *Westmorland Gazette*, puffing on his pipe. Lal came in from the kitchen, pulling all the rest of the pins out of her rich brown hair and sitting up as neat as a fairy in the stuffed chair in spite of her belly. Both Dad's sisters were tiny, but Lal was the tiniest. And Auntie Molly had been tiny too. She'd died having her baby, like Violet's mother. Lal's belly stuck out before her like a weird mushroom that had sprouted on her.

'Iphigineia,' Grandad said, 'if I put the kettle on will you make tea?'

Lal was Iphigineia, which was from ancient Greek, though Grandad was the only one who called her that. Grandad knew all kinds of things because he had been a headmaster and was a learned remarkable man who wrote poetry that had been printed in newspapers. They had a cutting from the *Isle of Man Times*, 9 December 1909: 'On Those Who Perished In The Ship "The *Ellen Vannin*".' By S. J. Holloway. Samuel Joseph. Grandad.

'Yes, Dad,' said Lal.

Grandad lumbered into the kitchen and put the kettle on, then poured hot water from the range into the bowl. When the sink was steaming, he reached down his white pinny from the back of the kitchen door. Lal sat down with her tiny slippered feet up on a pouffe, frowning, hair-clips sticking out of her mouth, delicately dabbing at her locks with her big tortoiseshell comb. Her hands were child's hands.

'Auntie Lal?' Nelly said.

Lal took the clips from her mouth.

'Yes, love?'

'Do *you* think the world's Hell?'

Lal put her head on one side and thought for a moment. Then she frowned and said, 'Where've you got that from? Your dad?'

'Child's been listening to things she doesn't understand,' said Grandad gruffly, from the kitchen, turning from the sink with a cloth in his hand.

'Look at that lovely sunshine out there,' Lal said, getting up and

14

stretching her narrow back. 'Does that look like Hell to you?'

'No.'

'Well, there you are, then.' And she followed Grandad into the kitchen and reached the tea caddy down with her hair flowing about her shoulders.

Nelly looked out at the lean-to, the trailing branch of the big ash tree at the side; the privy at the bottom of the garden, and the bean and lettuce and radish rows, and tiny Granny, old Hannah, pulling a lettuce in her big straw hat and dusty blue dress; her withered, miserable old face with the collapsed mouth downturned, her one tooth in the middle at the top, the pickle-stabber they called it behind her back. And she looked at Grandad washing the pots with his pinny round his big stomach and the back of his thick red neck sparsely sprinkled with small snow-white hairs. Things familiar and safe. But terrible things *did* happen. Poor murdered people, and little Freddy Slack who got run over on Cross Street, whose head was hanging by a thread, as the women said, over the fences; Freddy Slack whose mam went mad. And the way Dad's hands still shook because of the war. And maybe Auntie Lal would die having her big baby because she was too little. And maybe Bobby would die. Baby Bobby. Big boy now running about. Pushing her, her pushing him. Bobby who everyone says got all the looks, blond and pretty with a dimple in his chin, a deeper version of Dad's cleft. When Vi walked on the front with him when he was a baby, she was always being stopped by people wanting a look, a poke, a tickle. Bright red Bobby with the scarlet fever that sounds so pretty.

She watched the postman come up from the church, walking and pushing his bike. Granny spoke a few words with him, wiping the back of her hand against her long skirt, not bothering to smile. He handed her a letter and a postcard. She glanced at the letter and slid it under the postcard, which she read closely.

'Post,' Nell said.

Granny fingered the big yellow brooch that held her blouse together at her throat, wiped her eyes on her sleeve, took off her hat and fanned herself for a moment before gliding slowly up the path. She came in, blinking from the sunshine.

'Card from Benny,' she said.

Lal dashed from the kitchen, grabbed it from her and read it. 'Well!' she said with a smile. 'Gay Paree!'

And the feeling in the room turned, as it always did when anything came up about Auntie Bennet. Granny and Grandad didn't talk about her any more. Mam said she was the black sheep of the family. Baa Baa Black Sheep. It sounded nice. No one ever knew where she was.

Nelly could see on the postcard not a black sheep but three fluffy black kittens all snuggled up in a row in a little basket with some big silk roses. Grandad came out of the kitchen, wiping his meaty hands on his pinny, a look of deep contained concern on his face. He took the card from Lal, glanced at the kittens, turned it over, read it once and tossed it on the table where it fell among the breadcrumbs and sugar grains.

'Silly girl,' he said.

'A very wilful girl,' said Granny.

Nell stood up and stole over and read what it said on the card:

> Dear Old Mam and Dad,
> Guess who I saw walking down the STRAND? John Barrymore! Off to GAY PAREE soon! but keep a welcome in the hills for,
> Your loving Daughter,
> Bennet.

She broke her dad's heart, Mam said.

And the letter?

'Well, well, we're to lose you, la lammy' said Grandad, looking at her and frowning with his forehead but smiling with his eyes. He looked back at the letter in his hand, sitting down with his big knees apart under the pinny. The kettle began its long throaty hum, preparing to shriek. 'I'm pleased to say your Bob's better. Oh, that is good! You'll want to go home and see him now, won't you? See your mam and dad and Vi again?'

But the first thing she thought was, I have to leave Morland. The oak tree's mossy moot. Back to Manchester. Back to Gorton. Then

16

she felt ashamed of the pang she felt because, more than anything in the world, she wanted to see her dad.

'Granny?' she asked. 'Can I take some chocolate back for Bobby?'

2

Auntie Bennet

Morland was heaven, Gorton was home: the greyhound racing at Belle Vue, the buses going up and down Hyde Road, the Essoldo and the baths and the trains at Gorton Tank and the Beyer, Peacock's siren going off every night at six; and Ryder Brow and Old Hall Drive and Sunnybrow Park in the valley, with the swings and the roundabout and the witch's hat, and the old ladies with fat legs sitting on benches; and small yellow caterpillars with beady black dots on their backs moving everywhere over the wrinkled, nearly black bark of the creaky old trees round the sides. You collected them and kept them in a jam-jar with leaves and twigs and watched them crawl about.

Over the railway, into the wilds – where gypsies camped on Mellands, the big fields that went on into open country of beck and gorse and hillock all the way to Reddish. In the daytime boys played football and girls played rounders on the edge. If you walked by their camp, the rough dark gypsy men and little dirty children all looked, the women with hair piled on top, tied up with bits of bright rag. The skinny brown dogs barked at Jock. After dark you saw the camp-fires. You smelt the horses and the smoke.

They weren't allowed to play on Mellands when the gypsies were there, but they did. Mam had a rhyme: *My mother said that I never should* ... but the gypsy kids weren't friendly anyway. Still, Nell liked to see them there with their painted wagons and cooking pots, and all their lovely great horses grazing. She'd have given anything to have a horse to ride. But she wouldn't hobble her horse. That was cruel. The gypsy kids rode bareback and barefoot and roamed the roads, instead of staying in one place like everybody else. Auntie Bennet roamed about too. But Nell had only ever lived in two places, first when they were all in one room together, Mam and Dad and Violet and Nell, and Bobby when he was a baby. Then here. When they moved in, the estate was so new it was still being built on cleared back-to-back slums like they still had in West Gorton and Longsight. They moved in – a real house! A semi with a front and back garden and a path up the side – and the builders built on next door for the next family.

By now the houses had settled into their foundations. Grass grew up between the flagstones.

They ate boiled egg and soldiers, the family at the table, kitchen door open, flies buzzing around the fly-paper hanging there. Jock sat staring up at Dad with his ears pricked. Violet was at work, Saturday shift at the chocolate factory. Mam sliced the tops off the two eggs smartly, a no-nonsense chop. She and Dad had the tops with their bread and marge. Bobby and Nell got the good bits, the strong orange yolks to salt and dip their soldiers in and dunk up and down, the whites to scrape till the shells were completely clean but still intact, so that they could turn them upside down in the stripy egg-cups and pretend they were as good as new. It didn't work unless the shells were clean. You had to make sure the yolk didn't run down the shell. Dad hated that. He was very fastidious.

'I don't want my egg,' said Nell nonchalantly.

'Neither do I,' said Bob.

'Oh, an egg for me! Look, Sam, our Bobby's giving me his egg!'

'Oh, what a good boy!'

'You can have mine, Dad,' said Nell, pushing her saucer towards him. It worked every time.

'Oh, that is kind! A nice fresh egg!'

Reaching for it, Dad's hand shook.

Mam and Dad made a great show of delight, cracking the lovely white eggs with their teaspoons; they made an even greater show of

18

their disappointment, staring with open-mouthed disbelief at the shattered shells, faces falling in mock despair. The children shrieked with laughter. The little fluffy black dog ran about all over the place with its daft stump of a tail wagging like mad. Jock was a kind of Scottie who considered himself of equal status with the children. Dad stood, chuckling, a small man with even features, slight and pale with dark curling hair. He stood very erect because he was once a soldier, used to marching about and standing up straight on the parade-ground. Upon the sideboard was the big framed picture of him taken in civvies when he was first discharged, Private Samuel Bruce Holloway of the Labour Corps, with the ends of his moustache waxed, wavy hair slicked back and a cigarette in one hand. He sang a song to the tune of 'What A Friend We Have In Jesus'.

> *When I get my civvy clothes on*
> *No more soldiering for me ...*

it began, and it ended:

> *Then I will tell the sergeant-major*
> *To stick his medals up his arse.*

There weren't any photos of Mam.

Mam started nagging again as she cleared the table. 'I don't suppose you did their beds,' she said, 'did you?' Mam's face was round and rosy, broad-nosed, with flat cheeks on which the veins were beginning to crack.

'I've put them in a bucket,' he muttered mysteriously, reaching for his cigarettes on the mantelpiece.

'You've what?' Stout in her flowery pinafore, she straightened; the tops of her arms wobbled.

'The sheets and pillow-cases. I've put them in a bucket. They're soaking.' He struck a match.

'Well, what's the bloody use of that if you haven't put fresh sheets on?'

'You sound like a parrot.'

'I'll give you parrot, you cheeky bugger. Get upstairs and change them sheets now.'

'Give us a bit of peace, woman,' Dad said, crossing his legs. 'I've only just sat down.'

'It's all right for them as can!'

She stamped into the kitchen.

And so they went on, backwards and forwards as they endlessly did, until Dad stood up and gave Mam a look, raising his eyebrows and jerking his head towards the ceiling, and they both fell silent for a second.

Then she said, 'Bugger off.'

But they went upstairs anyway, for a lie-down.

Mam's litany: Don't touch the stove. Don't touch the plugs. Violet'll be home in a minute. And don't you pick on that lad!

'I don't pick on him!'

'You do,' said Bob.

'I don't!'

'You do.'

'Don't start,' said Mam, and closed the door on them.

Bobby could act daft till the cows come home. He lay on the floor and wrestled with Jock, then got up on to his knees and pretended to be Al Jolson singing 'Mammy' to Jinty the cat, which had got on to Dad's chair and was just settling down. Jinty completely ignored him.

'Ssh!' Nell said, kicking Bob. 'You'll have Mam down.'

He laughed and kicked back, turning his attention to Jock.

'Mammy!' he throbbed. 'Doncha know me? I'm ya liddle baby!'

Jock began to bark.

Bob hurled himself flat and wailed: 'Mammy! My liddle mammy!' Jock jumped on and off his head, shivering, till something beyond anyone else's senses distracted him and he started running frantically backwards and forwards between the door and the table, whimpering.

'Vi,' said Nell, getting up and opening the front door.

The gate was ajar. Jock ran out and sat there wagging his tail, staring at the place at the top of the street where she would appear. When she did he was off like a bullet. Down she went with her arms out to catch him and wrestle his head. Vi had a drawn appearance round the eyes, hollow cheeks with prominent bones, a thin mouth. 'Good boy, Jock!' she cooed. 'Good little lad!' putting her hand down into her bag and bringing out a chocolate to pop into his mouth. She brought home bags of mis-shapes from the factory, dusty and delicious, making sure to get in a few of everyone's favourites: soft centres for Nelly, hard centres for Mam, Turkish Delight for Dad and soft caramels for Bob. Nobody liked coffee creams so they gave those to Jock.

Violet was in charge now. Vi was not their proper sister; she was only half. She threw herself down with her legs sprawling. 'Make us a cup of tea, Nell,' she said. It was good to have Vi back. She was so funny she could make them wet themselves laughing, with her funny faces and silly voices. She was no looker but her eyes had great humour and her hair was soft and dark and sat about her face in big sausagy curls. She turned the wireless on and sat tapping her feet and humming, playing with Jock and waiting for her tea, which she took black. 'Ooh, ta, love.' Then she started laughing over some daft thing at work, but she couldn't tell them what it was because it wasn't quite suitable; only she would anyway because they wouldn't understand. Anyway: this girl, her little brother comes to meet her at the gates when they clocked off, and he's been to the dentist and had a tooth out so he's all bleeding round the mouth, poor little soul, and he's got this white thing over his mouth to catch the blood with two loops one at either end, and he's got the loops one over each ear, and it's a –' she leaned forward and whispered loudly '– an ST!'

Nelly laughed.

'What's an ST?' Bobby asked.

'You're too young,' said Nell.

'Oh, definitely!' Vi confirmed. 'Much too young.'

He flicked his fingers at them as if they were a couple of witches and aimed a kick towards their shins. Violet grabbed him and tickled him mercilessly, face set with glee. He screamed piercingly and Dad thumped on the ceiling.

They subsided in a flurry of shushing and giggling.

'Do a dance, Vi,' they begged, 'go on, do a dance.'

Violet twiddled the knob of the wireless till she got fast, jazzy music. Wide-eyed, side by side on the settee, they watched her skinny black-stockinged legs, twisting and writhing crazily in the frenzy of a made-up dance.

'More!' they cried, each time she stopped, and she'd laugh and start all over again. When she was too exhausted to go on, she decided all at once to take them out. She'd been taking care of them for years, wiping their faces, hauling them around with her, putting on their coats and bonnets, pushing them up and down the street in the old pram, airing them and getting them out of the one-room lodging in which they all used to live.

So she checked their hands and noses automatically.

Granny and Grandad had six sons and three daughters, and three of the sons lived on Sutton Estate: Dad, Uncle John and Uncle Edmund. Why, with an erudite, educated father who'd been a head-master, had Sam and his brothers ended up living on public assistance in grim old Gorton? Maybe it was the war. Maybe it was the things they hardly ever talked about. The Somme. Passchendaele. The trenches, the frostbite, the shaking hands. Or maybe it was the Holloway weakness: they all have it one way or the other, Mam said, not just a fondness for the drink, something more. They never could keep a job down, any of them, even when there *was* any work, and there wasn't any now anyway. Dad used to work on Gorton parks. Used to leave his things out all ready for the morning down to the last detail, down to the one match wedged out of the matchbox all ready to strike his first cigarette of the day.

They didn't see so much of Uncle Edmund because Mam said Auntie Isabel was an old witch. Uncle Edmund and Auntie Isabel had nine children, Uncle John and Auntie Grace thirteen at the last count. Sutton Estate teemed with Holloways.

'Whenever you see Grace,' said Mam, 'she's got one at the breast and one in the belly,' and it was true.

Auntie Grace sat by the fire, newly lit for the evening, suckling a small bald head, baby-white trails of shawl dangling milkily. 'Sit down, chuck,' she said, looking up. 'Your uncle John'll get you some tea in a minute.'

22

There was always a welcome at Uncle John's. The table was set and Uncle John was counting heads. The kettle shrilled on the hob.

'And how's that grand lad?' said Uncle John. Auntie Grace's small snub face beamed. They were all mad for Bobby. Everyone was. His hair grew white-blond and the dimple in his chin had deepened and his face was so impish and cheeky that it could make you laugh just to look at it, and everyone wanted to pick him up or ruffle his hair or sit him on their knees. And when being naughty got him an indulgent and slyly proud laugh as well as a telling-off, and his waywardness garnered more admiration than censure in the grand scheme of things, Bobby decided to lark about as a way of life. Doing it got him adored, swaddled and coddled; and, always, allowances were made.

'Now then,' said Uncle John, picking up Auntie Grace, chair, baby, big round belly and all, lifting her to the newspaper-covered table; on every plate there was a thick slice of bread and marge and a banana. 'Now then,' he said again, turning to take the kettle off the hob and pour the steaming stream of boiling water into an enormous stained brown teapot. 'Seen anything of your auntie Benny, have you? Isabel said she was round our Edmund's last night.'

'No,' said Violet, 'I thought you might have.'

The mention of Bennet brought a quickening of excitement. Auntie Grace made a tutting sound and shook her head.

'Oh, well,' said Uncle John, 'no doubt she'll make her appearance in due time.'

He lined up the cups and jam-jars, took down from the top of the cupboard a big roasting tin, the one he always made his sponge cake in.

'Benny only comes when she wants something,' Auntie Grace said, cutting her piece of bread and marge with her free hand.

'True enough.' Uncle John carved out slabs of cake, meticulous. He was like Dad, small and thin, exact in his movements.

'And what she wants,' Auntie Grace continued, 'like as not, is a bed for the night. So she won't come here.'

'There you are, lamb.'

Violet sat with her cousins, Ruby and Berenice, and was given a

23

proper cup, but Nell and Bob drank hot tea and condensed milk out of jam-jars. Uncle John's sponge cake was always delicious, moist and warm and golden with a dark crust round the edges.

'Oh, well,' said Uncle John, sitting in to the table, 'if you see her, tell her not to be such a stranger.'

'Well, she's got a bloody cheek if she thinks she's showing her face round here again after last time,' Mam said.

'Shut your bloody mouth, woman. You're so mean you wouldn't give a dying man the pickings of your nose.' Dad sat polishing his brasses.

'Ugh!' said Bobby, ceasing for a moment from popping his blown-up cheek with his finger. 'As if he'd want them.'

Nell and he, sitting together in one chair, giggled. Violet was getting ready to go round to her friend Josie Spedding's, standing in front of the fire looking into the mirror and tinkering with her rolls of hair. She pulled one of her daft long faces in the mirror at them, and they giggled the more.

'Dirty bugger!' said Mam, her round face punished and aggrieved.

'What did she do last time?' asked Nell.

'You mind your own business.' Her mouth went into a line.

'What did she do, Dad?'

'She didn't do anything.'

Mam could click her tongue so loudly to express disapproval it was like a big dog lapping. She walked heavily into the kitchen and the atmosphere plunged. Dad looked down at the brass dog he was rubbing with Dura-glit and scowled, his hollowing face drawn and drooping. Bobby went back to popping his cheek and Violet pinched a little colour into her wan face. She had a mannish face, like Dad's. It wasn't fair, Nell thought, that Violet resembled Dad more than she did. *She* wanted to look like Dad. She was nothing like him. But he was hers more than anyone else's because no one else could love him as much as she did. Wells of tenderness rose inside her at the sight of him, because he was the one she had studied when she was very small, not Mam, who was always out cleaning. He was the one who was always there, because he was hardly ever in work; he was the one who got them dressed and fed them and bathed them in turns in the tin tub with his fag hanging out of his mouth. 'Dad!' they'd cry. 'Dad! Your smoke's going in my eye!' So she knew what was going on in his mind just as if she was in there with him, knew when he was happy or sad or worried or just trying to pluck up courage to ask Mam for an extra fourpence for a packet of Woodbines.

Right now he was thinking of his sister Bennet: beautiful Benny Brown on the Hippodrome playbill, his childhood playmate, the charming young lady with the dazzling smile and cloud of dark hair on the lid of the chocolate box. She'd had her picture taken for calendars. The music-hall star Harold Whelan had proposed to her, the one who came on stage pulling on a pair of white kid gloves and whistling his signature tune. Mad for Auntie Bennet, he'd been, but she'd turned him down.

'You be back here by nine,' Mam snapped peevishly at Violet, stomping in from the kitchen.

'Oh, Mam!' Violet's face fell. 'It's Saturday night. I'm only popping round to Josie's.'

'Don't you oh-Mam me. Nine o'clock.'

Violet sighed.

'*You* tell her, Sam.' Mam went back into the kitchen and started banging about in the pantry. You could hear her grumbling to herself.

'Dad!'

'You can't argue with your mam,' muttered Dad, with a defeated shrug. If it had been either Bob or Nell he'd have stuck up for them and got into a row with Mam over it, but he wouldn't stick up for Violet.

'It's not fair,' said Violet quietly.

'Life's not,' he said, lighting his cigarette.

'Oh, well.' She straightened her jumper. 'I don't mind coming back early if Auntie Benny's here.' She smiled. 'Are these two staying up?'

'Aw, go on, Dad, can we stay up for Auntie Bennet?'

'No, you bloody well can't.' Mam was in the kitchen doorway. 'You can get to bed your normal time.'

'Oh, God, I'm off,' said Vi.

'Violet!' Dad said sternly. 'You will not take the Lord's name in vain.'

The argument between Mam and Dad simmered on and off all night till Nell and Bob were in bed. Nell was reading *The Yellow Fairy Book*. She loved reading and she loved the fairy books by Andrew Lang. But it was hard to concentrate because Bobby was scratching like a demon on the other side of the big double bed they shared, and she was listening all the time to the different footsteps coming along their road, listening to see if any of them sounded like high heels, if any stopped at their gate. But they never did. Then she was scratching too.

'Shout down,' said Bobby.

'Dad!' she shouted. 'Dad!'

'I've got a flea!' called Bob.

Up came Dad. Slowly, methodically, he began the trawl through their nighties, his old union shirts that were thick and warm. 'Got you, you little bugger,' he said.

Pop! went the flea between his two thumbs.

Then he went through the bedclothes and sheets and pillows, frowning with concentration. Dad knew all about fleas and lice because of the war. You never saw anything like the fleas in the trenches, he said. And that was the least of it. The rats used to run about all over you, cheeky little buggers, not a bit scared, they'd eat the laces out of your boots while you were wearing them. Just run over you, he said, as if you were an old sack. You got used to it.

Mam stood in the doorway with her moaning face. 'They don't catch them here,' she said. 'It's that school. This house is spotless. Even if I do have to spend all the weekend on my hands and knees as well as slaving in other people's houses, and all the sheets and pillow-slips are washed without fail once a week no matter what, so you can't blame *me*.'

'Nobody's blaming you,' Dad said.

'Dirty buggers they are round here, some of them.'

When she changed the sheets she dabbed their hair with paraffin. It worked pretty well and was safe enough so long as they didn't go anywhere near a naked flame for a bit.

'It's that dog,' she said.

'The dog never comes up here. Why don't you take that face off you, woman?'

'What face?'

'You know.'

'Well, it's all right for some, isn't it?' she exploded, going red. 'It's not as if she even lets on when she's arriving, she just turns up like Lady Muck and I don't know what she thinks – we're all just sitting there waiting for her to walk in? How'm I supposed to know whether or not to save a bit of dinner?'

'It's nowt to do with you.' Pop, another flea. 'I'll make stew. It can keep warm.'

Mam's eyes were hurt. 'Make me sick!' she spat, and flounced off downstairs.

'Your mam,' Dad muttered, 'she wouldn't just cast the first stone, she'd be there handing them out.'

They tittered and Dad chuckled, tucked them up and turned off the light, and for a long time they just lay there talking while Dad and Mam moaned away at each other familiarly downstairs.

'Tell me a ghost story,' Bob said.

'There was a big ball of red worms all wriggling about.' She didn't know where she'd seen it but she knew she had.

'Yeah?'

'And it was in the corner of the room. Downstairs by the front door. Only it's invisible, and it rolls about like a big ball catching at people's legs and they don't know it's there. And sometimes it rolls about the house in the night and it rolls up the stairs and up on to the bed ...'

'So what?' said Bob. 'That's not ghosts. Tell a proper story.'

Auntie Bennet didn't turn up. Vi came back about ten and Mam played hell. Nelly heard their voices nagging backwards and forwards, Mam shrill and Violet complaining; then she heard Vi go to bed, and Mam and Dad go to bed, and then it was quiet and everyone was asleep.

Bennet came on Sunday evening when the church bells were ringing, walking down their street with that proud head-in-the-air walk, sending echoes from the houses opposite with her dainty little heeled shoes clicking and clacking as her tiny feet side-stepped this way and that through the manure from the rag-and-bone man's horse.

Mam sighed. 'Violet, you can get in with the kids,' she said.

'Hiya, Benny.' Dad stood on the doorstep to welcome her. The kids crowded behind him.

'Hiya, Sam.' She put her hands up and kissed him. Her perfume wafted in, sweet and flowery, like the roses that grew in Granny and Grandad's garden in Morland. She came in and kissed everyone, and there was another smell from off her breath, sour and not very nice, like the smell on Dad's breath first thing in the morning when he'd come home drunk the night before. Nell always felt clumsy beside her dainty aunties. 'Do you know?' Bennet said, sitting down by the fire. 'It is *the* most glorious evening. Makes you wish you were out in the country.'

She'd been very beautiful, Auntie Bennet. You could still see it, something to do with the way she moved, delicately. And she spoke very sedately, never common or dropping her aitches like everybody else. They had a picture of Molly sitting on a chair with Bennet standing beside her with her hand on the back of the chair. They were both very young in the picture. Molly was actually the prettier of the two, with short, boyish hair, wide-set eyes and teeth that were very slightly buck but nicely so. Bennet had thin features and a faintly bird-like look. But Bennet was the one who knew what to do and went for the glamour in a big way, the hair, the make-up, the smile, the vivacity. She still had it, though there were lines now in the corners of her eyes and around her mouth, and the skin of her throat had a drawn, sinewy look. Nelly was never sure how she was supposed to feel about Auntie Bennet. Something had gone wrong with her and she didn't live like everybody else, but she was exciting: no one else she knew had an auntie who'd been on the stage and could sing and dance and juggle.

'Well well well, my chickadees!' she cried gaily, taking off her hat and fishing for a cigarette in her bag. 'How you doing, Violet, love?'

Violet was her favourite because she had been taken to Morland when she was a baby, after her mother died having her. Dad and his

28

brothers were fighting in France in the big war, the terrible war. Vi had been Benny and Molly and Lal's baby doll. 'I'm smashing, Benny.' She beamed.

'Working?'

'Oh, aye, same place.'

'How are *you*, Bessie?' Auntie Bennet asked Mam, flashing her a smile. 'Keeping well?'

'Can't complain.' Mam was civil if unsmiling. She went to put the kettle on. Bennet and Dad sat one on either side of the fireplace. Bennet put her lovely fine-boned feet up on the fender and waggled them about playfully in the dainty shoes, the kind she always wore to show them off.

'I saw our Lal in London,' she said, waving the still unlighted cigarette about. 'Little Victor's a picture. Oh, a charmer!'

London was worlds away. Lal lived in London with her husband and baby. London. Paris. Bennet got about. Dad hung on her words. Lal was doing fine. Looked well. Bennet threw back her cloud of black hair, still fluffy like it was on the picture they had, the one from the calendar, where she was showing her shoulders. She put the cigarette between her lips and seemed about to light it but withdrew it instead. 'Now,' she said teasingly, smiling around, 'I wonder what I've got in my bag.'

Three pokes of pineapple rock, one for Nell, one for Bobby and one for Violet, 'because I know you like it, Vi, even though you're not a child any more'. And a book for Violet too. With lots of pictures. *Tales from Shakespeare* by Charles and Mary Lamb. Then Bennet eased off her shoes and lit the cigarette, stretching her throat right back to blow smoke up to the ceiling. The way she smoked was like sucking candy and made you want to have some.

'Had your tea, Benny?' Dad said, leaning down to poke the fire.

They could hear Mam banging about in the kitchen. 'Violet!' she called sharply. Violet looked at the ceiling and went.

'I've had a bite, Sam,' said Auntie Bennet. She was so thin, like a bird, she looked as if she never ate. Drank like a fish, though, Mam said. That was what had gone wrong with Auntie Bennet. The drink, Mam said. That, and men. Nell didn't really know what that meant. Such a proud and pretty creature, so bright, and yet she seemed so nervous too.

'Tell you what, though, Sam.' Suck suck. 'Couldn't let me bed down on the floor in here tonight, could you?'

Mam was leaning in the doorway, plump arms folded over her flowery pinny.

Dad didn't say anything straight away. He scratched his ear. 'Where've you been staying?'

'Here and there,' she said quickly. 'Just for tonight, Sam.' She smiled briefly but her eyes were scared. Then they weren't scared any more, they had never been scared, they were merry and defiant. 'Ah, go on Sam,' she said softly.

'And what about tomorrow night?' Sam asked. 'What about that one and the one after, Benny?'

She laughed. 'Consider the lilies of the field,' she said, 'take no thought for the morrow. Or something.' And she laughed again till tears came into her eyes.

'It's OK if our Benny stops, isn't it, Bessie?' Dad looked over his shoulder, but Mam just shrugged and went off to boss Violet in the kitchen.

'Sure,' he whispered gruffly. 'Sure you can stay.'

'One night, Sam. I've got a start in Liverpool. No kidding. Hey, listen, Sam, what do you think of this for a coincidence? This is how I know it's genuine. My friend Polly Harkin, you won't credit where she's living. Erskine Street! Erskine Street! Oh, Sam, do you remember? Well, I thought, Erskine Street, I can't turn that down. I ran into her on Deansgate and she gave me her address and I couldn't believe it! She was going back there. To Liverpool! Oh, Sam! And she knows this fellow, you see, who has a very nice little club apparently, very pleasant, she says. Well, she says, you must come ...'

She went on, prattling, gaining poise with every turn of her head.

'Are you going to stay the night, Auntie Bennet?' asked Bob.

Violet was bringing in the big wooden tray with the tea things. Mam followed, blank-faced, carrying the sugar bowl.

'You'd better ask your mam,' Auntie Bennet said, smiling.

Mam plonked the sugar down. 'Our Violet can go in with these two,' she said.

'That's it, you're a sport, Bessie.' Bennet, grinning all over her face, took the cup and saucer Vi fondly handed her. Her thin hands were shaky and there was a slop.

'Well, that's that, then,' said Dad, pouring the sweet red tea into his saucer.

Late that night, when everyone else was in bed, Sam and Bennet sat up talking and smoking cigarettes.

While Bobby slept with his hands thrown back above his head on the pillow as if he were being held up at gunpoint, Nell and Vi conversed in whispers so as not to disturb Mam next door. She was terrible for coming in if you talked, standing there in the light from the door in her long white flannel nightie with her stomach sticking out and her hairnet on. 'Shut your bloody mouths,' she'd say. 'Have you seen the time? Christ!' Don't say that, Dad would scold if he were there. Our Lord is not a swear word!

Later maybe Bennet produced a bottle from somewhere, because she started singing. She sang 'Just Like The Ivy', and Vi and Nell were quiet, holding their breath, till they heard her stop and laugh softly before starting on 'Two Little Girls In Blue'. Stifling laughter, they crept out on to the landing, tiptoed half-way down the stairs and sat side by side to listen. Dad sang 'McCafferty' in his stern voice, as he always did, and then they both sang together: 'Lily of Laguna' and 'Sonny Boy' and 'Little Pal, If Daddy Goes Away', which was Vi's favourite and always made her cry. Then came the spirituals, beginning with 'Poor Old Joe', Nell's favourite: *Gone are the days when my heart was young and gay ...*

Sitting half asleep on the stairs, the sound was heartbreaking, floating in the dark. Dad's was his usual bass growl but Bennet had a lovely voice. Clear as a bell. Bennet didn't just sing the words like everybody else, she made you feel them, like little sharp knives pricking you into tears, so that when she softly called: *I'm coming! I'm coming!* a wondrous wistful rising lilt, you saw cottonfields and a high sun, and a chariot swinging down from pink and gold clouds like a swingboat at the fair; and you were poor black Joe whose head bent low, yearning for the golden shore.

31

Dad and Benny were closest together in age of all their brothers and sisters. Their voices together were like a twined thread, used to one another. They sang: *Way down upon the Swannee river far, far away* . . .

They sang of golden days gone by, gone for ever, yearning never satisfied, never filled, and all the closest bed-warm days of brother and sister, and sister and sister, and anyone and anyone wrapped up warm together—

Gone.

Nelly drooped against Vi, who sang under her breath, while a tear tracked slowly down her cheek:

> *All up and down the whole creation*
> *Sadly I roam*
> *Still looking for the old plantation*
> *And for the old folks at home.*

Dad told them how they used to sell the poor slaves away from their families: the idea of someone taking you and selling you away from everyone you knew. Away from Mam and Dad and Bobby and Violet and everyone. *All the world is sad and dreary, everywhere I roam ...*

Their voices soared.

Then Dad recited his favourite poem, the one he did sometimes after he'd got back from the pub. In her mind's eye, Nelly on the stairs saw him linking his fingers over his chest as he lay back in his chair, eyes glazing over as he gazed at the ceiling:

> *Sunset and evening star*
> *And one clear call for me ...*

Bennet didn't get up till after ten, long after Mam, who cleaned from nine till four for half a crown, had gone off to work. She didn't eat any breakfast, just sat in front of the fire and smoked a few cigarettes while Dad cleaned up. She was off for the Liverpool train, she said; then she kissed the children and put on her coat, and Dad shoved a couple of bob into her pocket as he kissed her goodbye on the doorstep. She seemed sad. Then she was gone.

Nelly remembered she hadn't told her about not being such a stranger to Uncle John. Too late. Anyway, maybe she didn't go there so much because she couldn't afford to buy all those packets of pineapple rock.

There was a row when Mam came home. There always was after Auntie Bennet's visits. Mam found Bennet's dirty tea-cup from this morning still down by the side of her chair next to the fireplace. She'd been working all bloody day, she said, and she wasn't coming home to a pig-sty. She wasn't used to those kind of filthy conditions even if some others were who could rot in bed all day while decent people got up and went out scrubbing bloody floors on their hands and knees to put food on the table.

Dad was dishing up sausage and mash, dollop, dollop, dollop. Dad did all the cooking. 'Shut your bloody mouth,' he said. 'Can't even get through the door without your bloody moaning.'

'I've got a right to!'

Two sausages apiece, but Dad always pretended he didn't want his and popped one on Nelly's plate and one on Bob's. Poor old Violet, of course, didn't qualify for an extra one because she was near enough an adult, or at least not a proper child any more.

Mam and Dad went on at each other all through tea and right on into the evening. The kids went and played out on the front like they always did. They were on Dad's side. No matter what, all of them were always on Dad's side whenever there was a fight, and there were always fights. It was still going on when they went back in. Mam had found out about the couple of bob he'd given Bennet and was screaming that she didn't go out slaving all day to put money in Benny's pockets, let her put money in her own pockets, she can do, you know what she is, we all do, she'll not go short. Then he slapped her across the face and she kicked him and punched him in the chest, and they set to for a while till Mam broke a plate on his head and made it bleed.

'Dad's bleeding,' Bobby said.

'Serves him bloody right!' said Mam. 'Violet! Go and get your dad a plaster.'

33

3

Bessie

Bessie wasn't from around here. She was from somewhere out towards Lymm and had been in service in a big house in Altrincham during the First World War, a buxom broad-nosed young woman in black with a white apron and mob cap. She shared a small room with another girl, and could fold linen and lay a table beautifully, having been a maid from the age of fourteen.

As a girl Bessie had a round, flat, good-natured face, a filthy tongue and a quick temper. When she danced she smiled, showing her teeth; she couldn't help it. She loved dancing and was fast and light on her feet in spite of her sturdy frame. She danced alone or with imaginary partners, in the kitchen sometimes. Mrs Stevenson, the Irish cook, laughed and called her Twinkletoes, unless she was feeling steamy and bothered, when it was: Will ye stop that, for the love of God! Bessie would have danced in her room but the floorboards were too light and it would have made too much of a racket. Best of all, of course, was to go to a proper dance at a dance hall, which happened sometimes but not often enough because she got hardly any free time; but that was how life was, you worked and you worked and you worked and now and again you played, and you got dressed up for it and everything was special. You danced with everyone who asked you to dance and, who knows? One of them might turn out to be your future husband. And if no one asked, you danced with your friend, Maud Rowley, also from Lymm, who was in service in Sale. You laughed while you danced, all out of breath.

Most of the time Bessie did as she was told and got along. She scrubbed and polished vigorously and never answered back, at least not to her employers. Downstairs she was cheeky, told filthy jokes and laughed herself silly at the punchlines, clenching her eyes and weeping real tears. She didn't have gentlemen callers. The young men she danced with from time to time didn't ask. She wasn't particularly good-looking, too rosy, on the heavy side, and her nose had a snub, bulbous quality. But she was cheerful enough. One day she'd get married, most people did. She'd had a beau before the war, a young man called Bill Amberley apprenticed to a draper in Timperley. She'd walked out with him three times, gone to a dance (two if you counted the one where she met him) and a matinée at the Alexandra. Bill Amberley was killed in his first week in France. She thought it was funny when she didn't hear anything from him, he'd promised to write, so she'd gone up to his house thinking maybe he'd lost her address and there'd be a letter for her there. His mother answered the door, a little thin woman with a wart at the side of her nose.

'I'm a friend of Bill's,' Bessie said. 'I was just wondering were there any letters sent here for me?'

'Oo, lass, our Billy's dead,' the woman said, and started to cry.

Bessie cried too. She hated to see this poor mother wiping her eyes with her apron. Bill's mother told her he'd been shot in the head. It was horrible to think about. His mum invited her in for a cup of tea but she didn't want to see where he'd lived and have to think about that too, so she declined quickly and nearly ran off down the street, so eager was she to get away and put the whole thing behind her. Poor Bill with his nice fair hair. Horrible, horrible.

'He was only eighteen,' she found herself saying in a bewildered way throughout the days that followed. Fairly soon she was forgetting parts of his face and even the sound of his voice, which had been plain and flat and low. All that remained was the sad fact that he was only eighteen. Maud Rowley and Mavis who shared her room, and even Mrs Stevenson, were very nice about it and looked upon her, she felt, with a new kind of reverence. At odd times during the day, even as time passed, her pale blue eyes would fill with tears and a heavy feeling would grow inside her, and after a while she wasn't sure what it was for, whether it even had anything to do with poor young Bill Amberley or whether it wasn't something else entirely, something she had no words for.

Bessie got her fair brown hair bobbed at the insistence of Maud

Rowley, who was no longer at her old place but had got married to a large swarthy boilerman called Joe. They had a room over in Rusholme, but Maud and Bessie would sometimes meet in town for a pot of tea at the Kardomah. Now that she was married, of course, Maud couldn't go out dancing any more with Bessie, and Mavis was no fun at all to go with, so when Maud turned up one day saying there was a nice position going on Plymouth Grove in the house where her friend Freda worked, Bessie jumped at the chance. It was in a doctor's house, and there was a big garden all tangled and overgrown all round the side and back. Bessie went along on the Saturday evening and spoke to Dr Fowler's wife. Mrs Fowler told her to come as soon as she'd worked her notice. She'd have her own room. So elated was she when she came out that she stood still and took a few deep breaths, overcome with realisation of the looming change. She'd have to go home and see her mother and father and tell them she was moving again. Suddenly she felt like walking. It was a crisp autumn evening and the lamps had just been lit. The leaves had a smoky smell and crunched under her feet. She walked slowly and dreamily along past all the grand houses on Plymouth Grove, then happily further on around the area where she would be living, and beyond, into streets that began to look poor and sad, out on to a main thoroughfare that wasn't the one she'd come by, full of shops and places of business. A tram trundled by, all glowing.

She panicked. Suddenly it was dark. She shouldn't have come this way, she should have gone straight back the way she'd come to Stockport Road, she knew exactly where to stand there for the London Road tram. She could turn round and find her way back to Stockport Road, which would take ages, or she could try to get to London Road from here. She looked around for some sensible woman she could ask. She felt lost. All the people looked very wrapped up in themselves. She wanted to cry again. Why did she always want to cry? She stopped an elderly couple and they said she'd be best getting a bus for Piccadilly and walk from there. But when she found the bus stop, she found that her money had all gone down through a hole in her pocket and she had to stop and try to fish it all out again, standing there stupidly in a closed shop doorway pulling up her coat and ripping the lining more to locate the money, and the more she fished, getting hot and beginning to swear bitterly, the redder her eyes and cheeks became, and her nose began to run.

There was another hole, or rather a large rent, in the lining of her coat. She'd lost a shilling. She'd have to walk to London Road, and what if she missed the train? She *would* miss her train. Oh, what a stupid fool she'd been!

Bessie set off walking as fast as she could in the direction of town. She was tired now and her feet ached, but she just plodded on and on, only stopping to ask directions, growing more and more terrified with each minute that passed. If she missed her train she had no idea when the next one went. What if there wasn't one? She'd have to go and ask a policeman what to do.

There was a man selling chestnuts on London Road. The hot burst of air as she passed the brazier made her mouth water but there was nothing she could do. She crossed over the road and ran for a very short distance, but she was stout and cumbersome and soon out of breath. There was a stitch in her side by the time she reached the station. She'd missed her train but there was another one due in an hour. She went to her platform and sat upon a bench and waited, and the pigeons stalked about around her feet, which would have been cold if they had not ached with such a fierce ache. There were a few people on the platform, all quite respectable. She sat near a fatherly looking old man in a tweed jacket for safety in case any peculiar men came along, you never knew these days; or any fresh young men up to no good seeing her on her own. When a train came in and the old man got on it and left her unprotected, she stood up and moved through the smoke to be near a posh-looking middle-aged woman in a blue fur-collared coat, who seemed to be constantly telling off a disgruntled-looking girl of about fifteen. This meant she had to stand for twenty minutes. She moved twice more before her train came and she was able to get on and flop herself down in a corner of a carriage occupied by two miserable old ladies. As the train gathered steam and chugged off into the darkness she closed her eyes. The wheels clattered a rhythm. The movement rocked her. She opened her mouth and yawned loudly, not caring, as lights rolled over her eyes.

When she woke up, with a start as if someone had just clapped their hands next to her ear, her heart was racing and her mouth and throat were dry. She'd gone blind. Nothing. No light anywhere, not even a chink, as if she were deep underground, buried alive. A terrible cackling sob of terror came from her throat, deep and horrible in the emptiness.

It was not that she feared a ghostly touch from the darkness, that kind of thing had never bothered her. It was not even that she feared the knife of a madman or the hands of a strangler or the breath of a pervert. Bessie's terror was miasmic, clinging as fog, spreading like the chill of death through her helpless limbs. It was a kind of ultimate refinement of loneliness. She was lost in the universe, alone. She couldn't even think to say her prayers, which anyway she didn't really believe in. She was dead, and eternity was just this, blind panic, finding that you alone are all there is, for ever.

Then, slowly, like being born, something dawned very dimly in the black night, a patch of dark not quite as dark as all the rest: the train window.

The world fell into place around it. She could smell soot. She was on the train, just where she had been when she fell asleep. But why was everything black and silent? Why weren't they moving?

Bessie sat forward. Her hands were frozen. Her feet burned. She couldn't see anything out of the window, just darkness with shapes in it, and a glimpse of lighter darkness, the sky. Not a sound. And she was cold to the bone. She tried the door, fumbling around. It was locked, she was locked in. Buried alive in her coffin and couldn't get out, and she began to call in a thin sad voice, with tears streaming down her wide cheeks, 'Help! Help!' but no one heard, no one came. After a while she sat back and huddled herself up in her arms against the cold, crying stolidly. This was the situation. She had fallen asleep and somehow been overlooked when they closed up the train and shunted it into the siding. She had no idea of the time. Her coat was not good enough to keep out the cold, which had taken on a vicious, enduring quality that penetrated straight through to the marrow and felt like a thin grey filament passing down the middle of her body. No one would come now, not till morning. Didn't they have a night shift? Surely they had a night shift? But there was not a sound. Not a sound.

Throughout the long night, the longest night she had ever known, Bessie wept from time to time, or sat silently gazing at the still grey rectangle of window. Her mind was wide awake. She didn't even try to sleep. She thought harder than she had ever thought. She was twenty-one. She hadn't had a beau to speak of for three years. Well, what was it like with all the nice young ones away fighting, giving up their poor young lives? Dr Fowler's eldest son had lost an arm at Loos. His youngest was in Egypt and they hadn't heard a thing in weeks. Maud's brother John dead. Last time she'd seen him he'd been a little lad, poor little scrap of a thing with adenoids. She was knitting socks, her and Freda, like a couple of old biddies, knitting away every night. How was she supposed to find a man? It wouldn't have bothered her too much, she wasn't romantic, but she knew she had to get married. What else was there? Being all alone like this, all alone. No one would miss her. No one would even notice she was gone. Not that swine Freda she worked with, not Maud Rowley either. *She* wouldn't care. She'd be glad. Maud wasn't bothered with her now she'd got a man. That's the way it went. And the men didn't like it, didn't like their wives going out and seeing their old friends, not really. Even Mavis was courting now. But then I've always been on my own, Bessie thought. Always. Nobody cares for me, nobody, nobody, and it's not fair. And she wept and sighed and waited for the darkness to lift.

Hour upon hour more of the same, till she started to make out little dots in the darkness and the rivets on the window-frame appeared, then a neighbouring carriage, and the sky turning bleary and pale. Next came sounds, distant and meaningless, banging on her exhausted brain like tiny mallets. She heard whistling and blew her nose vigorously. She started to hammer on the window.

The man whose startled face appeared was old and stout and pink. He wore a peaked cap. 'What are you doing there?' he cried, shocked by her dirty, tragic face. 'Wait there!' as if she could do anything else. He dashed off and returned minutes later with two other men to unlock the carriage.

'I should have got off at Altrincham!' she shrilled, as one of them helped her down the step. She was tottering. 'I fell asleep! I fell asleep! Don't you look in the carriages before you close them?' She burst into tears all over again.

'Now now,' a bear-like man with a beard said, 'you're all right now. That's right, just this way, my flower. A nice hot cup of tea, that's what you need. We'll soon have you right as rain! Well! You'll have something to tell the grandchildren!'

Bessie wept harder. Her feet were killing her. 'Where are we?' she sobbed, limping along between the carriages on the arm of the nice man.

'This is Knutsford,' he said.

Knutsford! Where she was born a bastard in the workhouse. Knutsford, the place of shame. She'd never seen it.

'There!' said the bear-like man. 'I can see the blood coming back to your cheeks already!'

After the war, though there were nice young men around again, at the dances and in the music halls and picture palaces where she went with Freda, somehow Bessie didn't click with any of them. She felt her years passing, one, two, Freda got married and moved away, three, four, still an old maid. She lost touch with Maud Rowley. Sometimes she had no one to go out with at all.

She went alone to the Hippodrome one night, having fallen out with Lucy, the latest parlourmaid. Lucy kept saying she wanted to go dancing at the Midland, even though she knew that Bessie couldn't go back there after her terrible embarrassment the last time. In full view of everyone, Bessie had been up on her feet dancing. She wore a white dress. When she returned to her seat Lucy leaned across, red in the face, and whispered behind her hand: 'You've got blood on the back of your dress.' Bessie had to walk past everyone to the toilet, and it was true, there was blood on the back of her white dress, and she felt mortifyingly, horribly ashamed. She got her coat and went home.

'So what?' Lucy said now. 'No one'll remember.'

'How do you know? I can't go back there.'

'Oh, don't be so daft.'

Bessie insisted on the Hippodrome. There was a variety bill on. Lucy just went on and on about wanting to dance. She said she'd already arranged for them to meet Theresa Clukas outside the Midland, she hadn't a notion that Bessie would have minded, they couldn't just leave poor Theresa standing there waiting all on her own, could they?

'Well, you should have thought about me, shouldn't you?' Bessie countered. 'What right have you got to go making arrangements on my behalf without asking me? I'll have you know that was a very embarrassing experience for me.' Her eyes filled with tears. She'd just had her hair done in marcel waves and now she supposed she'd just have to sit at home and do nothing.

'Oh, come on, Bessie!'

Bet she *wants* me to look a fool, Bessie thought. She's never really been a friend.

'I bet no one even noticed,' Lucy said.

Well, she would say that, wouldn't she? Ugly bugger, no one ever looked at *her*. Whereas Bessie, when she was dancing she was so good that surely somebody noticed, somebody. How dare she say that? As if no one ever looked at Bessie, no one ever fancied her, as if she just didn't exist.

'Piss off, Lucy,' she said distinctly, threw on her coat and grabbed her bag and hat and stormed out and went to the Hippodrome all on her own. She had never done such a thing before. She was only just in time. She had to stand with the crowds at the back because it was full. The lights dimmed. The band struck up and the gorgeous shimmering curtains swished back.

Sam Holloway was also out on his own, not out of pique but because he'd taken on himself something of a roaming persona since the end of the war. Truth to tell, in a funny sort of way he missed the war. Well, not so much the war, the army really. And yet he couldn't wait to be discharged. And when he was, there was nothing at all for him. He'd got used to taking orders, not having to think, just do and do, whatever they said, you just did, easy; and now – now that he was free and the longed-for return was real, he was like a balloon let off a string. Drifting. John and Edmund were in Peacock's foundry in Gorton, but he couldn't be doing with it, the heat stifling, the sweat pouring; so he'd worked on the parks instead. The parks, the brick-works, the brewery, the biscuit factory, and now the parks again. And the times in between. And what, I'd like to know, was that decent education for? Johnny Acock had been blown to bits right by his side. All that was left were his puttees with the feet still in them. It sounded funny. Young Billy Deare under the mud. When they pulled, out he came with an almighty sucking sound. Head to toe mud, all of them, and Billy's legs gone. Well, with what was left of life, you might as well enjoy it. Time enough for the grind. He liked a drink. He liked a smoke. He liked to saunter around alone just looking at the dear old streets he'd never thought to see again. And he had a reason to be here in the Hippodrome, though he could have wished he hadn't left it so late and got down the front. As it was, he was in the aisle seat on the back row, and he had his eye on this young woman standing in the crowd. She was chuckling in a vulgar way at the comic on the stage, a deep, throaty cackle that promised a bit of fun. Her cloche hat framed a beaming pink face. Why was she on her own? He thought she looked tired, the way she stood with one leg taking all the weight, sagging sideways slightly.

'Excuse me, Miss,' he said quietly, standing, tipping up his seat more noisily than he'd intended to and catching her attention.

She turned her still smiling face towards him and her smile fal-tered.

'Would you like to sit down?'

Well, she looked tired, poor girl. She had nice blue eyes. 'Oh, thank you!' she said brusquely, and sat down in the seat he'd prof-fered. He stood just behind her. A country girl, she looked. Well-endowed. Didn't look the frivolous type. There was something solid and sensible about the set of her shoulders.

Bessie, of course, was conscious of him standing just behind her and she was making plans. She'd only caught a glimpse of him, but it was enough. A small slim man with dark blue, almost indigo, eyes and a heavy black moustache. Unless he turned out to be a lunatic or something, she'd have him if he was on offer. Enough of living in other people's houses and never knowing where you'd be five years from now, how you'd live, where you'd go; enough of getting older and still not married. She'd *got* to get married. Everybody else did, apart from sad things like poor old Florrie, the withered prune of a lady's maid from her last but one job; or those horrible old teachers everyone was scared of. Already she was thinking many steps ahead. Yes, if he offered, she'd have him.

There was a magician, a dance act, a comedy double act, very smutty stuff some of it. Bessie didn't mind, she liked a good laugh. Her uncles, farm boys and labourers all, had been full of smutty stories, she'd grown up with it. They used to come and sit round the back door for the bread and cheese her mother made. Sweaty and high-smelling, pinching her cheeks.

Then a lovely girl came on, a flowery vision in white, with white roses against the jet black hair that flowed from her brow and temples in great waves, framing her sweet pointed face. Against her backdrop of painted pink roses, cascading much like her hair from flattened casements and classical pillars, she sang 'Roses Of Picardy' in a strong pure voice, smiling dazzlingly when she got to the end. She told a couple of jokes while she juggled with ninepins, doing a backwards and forwards little tap dance at the same time and never losing her smile. Then she sang again as she danced with her parasol, and everyone sang along with her:

Oh by the light of the silvery moon
I love to spoon
To my honey I'll croon love's tune …

Bessie sang, smiling. She loved this one.

When the girl left the stage, her hair swung out behind her, lifting like a shawl in the wind and settling again all over her back, down almost to her waist. Bessie was surprised by how enthusiastically the young man who'd offered her his seat applauded, a deep booming hand-clap that offended her ears. When she glanced round she saw that he was very nearly tearful with emotion, mouth set in a fond smile, eyes proud and soft and glued to the spot at the side of the stage where the pretty young girl was taking her curtain call. Instantly she was jealous. He'd forgotten all about her. So peeved was she by this that when the lights went up for the interval and he leaned down sharply and spoke at the back of her ear – 'Excuse me, but I wonder if you'd like to come for a drink in the bar' – she put on a couldn't-care-less-if-I-do-or-I-don't sort of an expression before she turned to face him.

'I don't mind,' she said, not smiling.

He bought her a sweet sherry and had a pint himself. 'Come, landlord, fill the flowing bowl,' he said, smiling, as he set them down on the table. He had a shaky hand.

He noted that she was plump and short and well made; she that he had a cleft in his chin and a ridge dissecting the end of his nose. The hair that showed from under his cap was black with a bit of a curl to it. They talked. He seemed respectable enough, quietly spoken. He said he lodged with his brother and his brother's wife, that he'd fought with the Cheshire Regiment, and that Benny Brown, the beautiful girl on the stage, was his sister. Bessie was impressed in spite of herself. The stage, the bright lights, the colour – all of it a different world, not a world the likes of herself could connect with. She looked down at herself. She was wearing brown, like a sparrow. She shrugged about her own past. *He* had a whole raft of brothers and sisters beside the vision on the stage, and all she had to talk about was her sister whom she never saw since she'd married out towards Wigan, and her mother and father, and *they* could never agree on her. Lately she'd begun telling herself a story – that her father really was her true father, and that he'd really loved her true mother only he couldn't marry her because he was already married to Mam. That's why Mam and Dad had adopted her. Mam knew Dad really loved Bessie's true mother. That's why she'd never liked her.

But she wasn't telling him all that. Not yet.

Sam asked Bessie very politely if she fancied going and seeing the brass bands at Belle Vue next week.

'Don't mind if I do,' she said, with a little sniff.

That was how Mam and Dad met.

Many a time Dad told them, as he chopped carrots for stew or

44

wiped down the tiles round the fireplace, or getting them ready for bed, Nelly already in her nightie, Bobby in the tin tub in front of the fire. Dad kneeling with his eyes narrowed against the smoke from the cigarette stuck on his lower lip.

'Dad! Your smoke!'

The dimple in Bobby's chin was so deep that when Dad washed his face he had to stick his finger right in it and scour it out with the flannel as if it was an ear.

'I gave her my seat at the Hippodrome,' Dad said, a wicked glint in his eye. 'Worst bloody mistake I ever made.'

On the third or fourth meeting, Sam told Bessie about Violet.

His wife had died in childbirth during the war, he said, and he didn't see Violet properly till she was four. She lived in Westmorland with his parents. He didn't say that she wasn't intended, that when he finally got the letter out there on the salient in front of Ypres and heard he was a widower and a father (Again. The other was a long time ago. A boy. Five now. He didn't think about it any more) he experienced a sinking in the gut, less at poor Olive's death than the fact that his parents had taken in the baby. 'We have named her Violet Mabel,' his father wrote. 'Rest assured, Sam old chap, she is as bonny a baby as can be imagined, and we will do right by the mite. Bennet is besotted and forever carrying her about, as of course are Molly and Iphigineia.'

That was a bloody terrible time. He'd read it in the dug-out, soaked through, lying back with his greatcoat over him and his head against his kit-bag, the end of a cigarette burning the fingers that protruded from the ragged finger-ends of his gloves. Far away, the dull thudding. Everything steamed. Poor Olive. Poor kid. Just a faint grey memory, she was. He was sure she'd got herself pregnant on purpose. He'd never have married her otherwise. He tried to remember the wedding. Out here, memory played tricks: the real world was black bread and plank roads and the arms and legs and heads of the dead rising up out of the wasteground like corpses on Judgement Day. He couldn't remember a thing about his wedding but the resignation in him, the awful blank resignation, and the growing hardness and desperate longing to get out of civvies and be gone again, on a train somewhere with the wheels rattling and the lads singing in the dark. Poor Olive, though. Poor kid. He couldn't see her face. His eyes misted. It seemed you could love and not love someone both at the same time. But as for the child – over that his mind closed. He didn't feel as if it were his. He was twenty-two. Soldiering was what he did. He'd been a clerk before the war, but that didn't count. His dad had been on at him to go in for dentistry but he'd been too lazy. Out here it all seemed laughable somehow. Dentistry! Poking about in other people's dirty smelly mouths. People were filth and stink. He'd seen their guts spilled out before him like slugs. They smelt worse than shit.

What did a man on his own want with a child? Olive's mother should have had her.

Seven years on he'd still hardly seen Violet.

'She's seven now,' he told Bessie gruffly, leaning forward with his elbows on his knees. 'She's nothing like me.'

Bessie was captivated. She'd have him and she'd have his child. He was a nice man, gentle, moody from the war, of course, as so many of them were, but that was to be expected. He had nice hair and eyes. She wasn't stupid. He'd not get anywhere near her till they were married. She'd get out of service, be married with a child. A little girl. She'd have her own house and she could teach the little girl how to lay a table and cook and sew and make up a fire so it would light first thing in the morning. Once they were married she'd tell him the truth – about Knutsford workhouse and being illegitimate. Well, maybe she'd tell him. Maybe not.

'Well, that's nice,' she said, smiling. 'A child should never be a burden. They don't ask to be born.'

She thought of Violet, motherless. Or no, not motherless. Mothered by a name she'd never put a face to. Poor little Violet. She'd have her. She'd never say, as her own mother had of her, 'And this is our little orphan. We took her in when she was six weeks old,' so that they looked at you with pitying eyes. She'd never say that about Violet. She'd just say, 'This is my little girl.'

*

She was good-natured, Bessie, Sam decided. A little prone to sulks, but nobody's perfect. She liked a laugh and a lark and she could dance anyone under the table. As he got to know her better, she started bossing him about. He liked that.

They went up to Morland on the train to see his parents. She hated trains. She'd hate them for as long as she lived. She insisted on getting to the station an hour before the train left (just in case) and sitting there on the platform with a set mouth and her hands anxiously clutching her bag before her on her knees. Every five minutes she checked the time. At Penrith, they were collected by Sam's father in an old blue cart drawn by a big brown horse.

'Remember,' Sam said, 'don't mention my sister.' He had three sisters but he meant Bennet, of course. Bessie was just about getting his family sorted out now. There was Edmund and Isabel, with whom he lodged in Levenshulme. Edmund was OK, quiet. Isabel was sharp and snotty. There was John and his lady-friend, Grace, with whom she and Sam often went to Belle Vue and rode on the Ocean Wave, or went dancing on the boards in front of the Firework Lake with its fantastic backdrop of palm trees and tropical lagoons. There were Sidney, Joseph and Thomas, all married and far away, one in Ireland, one in Cambridge, one in London. There was poor Molly who was dead two years now, and Lal the baby, whose real name was Iphigineia, and Bennet, who must not be mentioned. Well, she was hardly likely to mention that one, was she? How are the mighty fallen, thought Bessie. She'd met Bennet by now, twice. She looked older off the stage, not so perfect. It's all make-up, she thought. Make-up and hair. She's not so special. What she did have though was an inborn grace. The set of her head on her neck had it, the way her hands fell, everything. As if everything flowed together just the right way. Oh, but Benny on the booze! The second time, she'd turned up at Edmund and Isabel's blind drunk in the middle of the afternoon. Disgusting! Effing and blinding she was in front of the children. And crying. What had she to cry about? She had a nice family, didn't she? Her fault if she chose to go off and live like a tramp. Later, when she'd had some tea and calmed down a bit, she came out to where Bessie was sitting on the doorstep in the sun keeping out of the way.

'I'm sorry, Bessie,' she said, 'only you don't know what I have to put up with.'

'We all have a lot to put up with,' replied Bessie.

'I'm not saying you don't.' Bennet spoke rapidly, raking her fingers through her thick hair. 'I'm sure everybody has a lot to put up with, Bessie, only I don't know about everybody else, I only know about myself.' She sat down next to Bessie on the step. Her dress was palest green organdie, sprigged with roses, very flimsy. She made Bessie feel huge.

They were alike, her and Sam. They had a look of one another. They had melancholia. And *he* was keen for the booze too, Bessie thought. 'Well, I don't know, Bennet, I don't know what you've got to worry about. You've got a good family, you know.'

Bennet gave a hoot of laughter. 'I know, oh, I know! You ought to try living with Mam and Dad. Long as you do what they say – wonderful.' She ducked her head into her hands but looked up again immediately, smiling. She was still drunk.

'What is it that's upset you?' asked Bessie.

Bennet laughed again. 'I don't know! I just get terrible feelings, Bessie. Terrible feelings! Some people don't seem to feel like that. Terrible feelings and I don't know why. Like there's no God. Like there's no anything and it's all pointless.'

'Well, we all feel like that sometimes,' said Bessie briskly, 'but we just have to get on with it, don't we? That's what everybody else has to do, you know. You're not different.'

Bennet rose with tipsy elegance and stood with her hands behind her back, looking off down the narrow terraced street. 'Anyway,' she said sulkily, 'it's not fair. Why am I always the one that gets into trouble? Look at our Sam. He was a right little devil when he was a kid, we both were, but did he ever get into trouble? No, he did not. Not like me anyway. Got on Dad's pip, you see. Me being a girl. It's all right for a boy to be bad, shows spirit. A girl's not supposed to have spirit.' She swung from side to side like a child. 'He has a drink – fine. It's just "Our Sammy likes his pint, nowt wrong with that." I have a drink – oh, mercy!' She tossed her head and slung the back of a limp pale wrist against her forehead, and her eyes rolled back in her head. With her dark mass of hair that had come loose from its coils hanging down behind her, Bessie thought she looked barbaric, like a woman in a painting. 'And men!' said Bennet, sitting down again. 'Bloody men. That's what did it for my daddy, the men. Oh, mercy, give me a snout, Bessie. You don't smoke. What is my old Sam doing with a woman who doesn't smoke? No, don't take offence, I'm only joking. Don't smoke, don't hardly drink. I wish I could be like you. But, seriously, doesn't it get boring? The men, you see.' She shrugged. 'I always did get on with boys. Having all those brothers, I suppose. So if I'm indiscreet –' Suddenly she sang, with professional ease: 'Another season, another reason, for making whoopee.' Then jumped up again. 'But *him*, dear old precious Sam! Let him spread his seed where'er he will! Hey nonny bloody no! He had to get married, you know. I say all this because I do believe in being honest. And if you and our Sam have got designs on each other you ought to know the truth. Did you know he always chooses the same woman? One with no connections. You're the same but you want to make yourself different. Don't give him an inch. Oh, yes, he had to get married. And there's another one too.'

'You what?' Bessie was horrified.

'Well, there *was* another one. Oh, ages ago. She had a little boy. Frank, she called him. He'd be twelve. You're dead wise, you are. Don't give it away, not to our Sam. I've *got* to have a cigarette.'

And she was gone.

Well, she'd had it out with him straight away, as soon as she got him on his own. At first he tried to make out it was just Bennet talking rubbish because she was drunk, but then he admitted that, yes, there was a child, a boy, Frank. But he wasn't really convinced that it was his. No, he wasn't in touch. It was nothing to do with him, he'd only been seventeen at the time. It was when he first came to Manchester looking for work and Edmund got him taken on as a clerk at his own place in Salford. All day he checked bills of lading for the ships on the Manchester Ship Canal. She was older than him, it was her fault. She worked in a mill. Anyway, it probably wasn't his. She'd got married to a sailor.

Well, he was a good-looking man, Bessie thought. These things happened. But she'd make him behave now. Oh, how she'd make him behave! She slapped him across the face.

'It was years ago!' he protested.

She slapped him again.

Sam's father got down from the cart and greeted her very graciously, a large, somewhat formidable old man with pained eyes that drooped sharply down at the outer corners, overhung with skin like an old dog's. Bessie felt sorry for him because of his eyes. Riding back in the dark, the horse's hoofs clip-clopping along the lanes, the air sweet and moist and as different from Manchester air as wine from water, she knew this would be a ride she'd take again. And again. Sam's dad was talking to her over his shoulder, telling her the local layout as if she was on holiday and he was her guide. She'd never been on holiday. This is Eden, he said, and chuckled. Morland lies between Penrith and Appleby in the Eden Valley. To our right is Shap and Haweswater and the Lake District, to our left Cross Fell.

But you couldn't see anything because it was dark, only smell that glorious sweet, moist air, like drinking it, like smelling flowers. For a moment Bessie felt happy. A strange unknown feeling, vaguely remembered from – what?

The house was in the village, not far from the church. There was a low wall in front, a big tree at the side.

A door opened and against the light a little girl cried out: 'Mam! It's our Sam! Our Sam and Bessie!' But it wasn't a little girl when they got into the low room, it was his sister Lal, a girl of twenty-two but the tiniest thing. And his mam, a small, dry-looking woman with an unforgiving mouth and thick grey hair. And, of course, there was the child, Violet, and though she was very plain there was no mistaking that she was Sam's. She had his long upper lip, his prominent cheek-bones, his dark hair, his eyes. She sat in a big chair with her legs sticking out in front of her, wearing a lavender-coloured smock and white stockings. Sam kissed his sister and mother but not Violet, though she gazed wonderingly at him from the moment he entered, a frail smile on her thin lips.

'Violet!' his mother said softly. 'Get up and say hello to your daddy!'

'Hello, Violet,' Sam said.

She stood nervously before him. 'Hello, my daddy.'

He put his hand sternly on top of her head, like a priest making a blessing.

Bessie shared Lal's room. In the dark Lal told her about Molly, how lovely and nice she'd been. 'Molly was a lamb,' she said. 'Molly never fell out with anyone. She was just one of those people, you know? Molly got married to a lovely bloke. He was heartbroken. She had her baby, oh, the most lovely little girl, the sweetest baby you ever saw and so good! We would have had her like a shot, Molly's little girl. Like when we had our Violet. But her daddy took her. They're in Borrowdale but he's brought her to see us. Such a sweetheart! Broke my dad's heart when our Molly died. Look! I'll show you.'

She jumped out of bed and lit the candle and carried it, tiptoeing in her long white nightie, to her dressing-table, opened a violet-adorned basket there, and searched about. 'Look!' She showed Bessie a piece of paper with a poem written on it in beautiful handwriting.

Bessie read it by the light of the candle, which flickered slightly.

To His Daughter Muriel Who Died In Childbirth Aged 23.

O, loved one, still in death
Why must we see thee thus depart?
What cursed power has stopped thy breath,
And stilled thy gentle heart?

The dark and silent tomb,
Where thy still form is laid to rest
Is but the symbol of the gloom
That shrouds my troubled breast.

How few thy earthly joys!
How brief thy span of mortal bliss!
Go, wing thy flight through yonder skies
To fairer worlds than this.

Go seek some world of light,
Some distant, bright, celestial sphere,
Some radiant home of spirit bright,
Far in the ether clear.

Thou hast no art in death,
O, guileless spirit, pure and free,
And gentle as the zephyr's breath
That whispers o'er the lea.

Though passed from mortal view,
I cannot mourn thee now as dead:
I see thee sweep the empyreal blue
On fairy wings outspread.

By S. J. Holloway.

'Aw,' she said, 'what a shame.'

'Broke his heart,' said Lal. 'And then with our Benny too ...'

They were good enough people, Bessie thought. Better class than her own, all her labouring uncles and her dad just a labouring man, and her mam with her dirty rhymes. Yes, they were good enough, even, she thought, quite swanky in a way. No money, though. Come down, they had. They'd had a servant once, he'd said. When he was a boy. But then they'd moved around such a lot, and down somehow they had come. Where'd he said they'd lived? Liverpool, Lincoln, Stowmarket, Berwick ... but back here in the end, back here where they'd started, so this must be home. Yet still, well-educated the lot of them, readers. Sam could quote from Tennyson and Browning. Fancy his dad writing a poem like that. Imagine any of *her* forebears sitting down and writing a poem. Well, it's all very well, she thought, poetry, for them as have the time. And she thought of her uncles in their sweaty shirts.

'What about your mam?' she asked. 'Did she take it bad?'

'Oh, Mam!' said Lal, yawning, 'She never lets on about anything. Just keeps going, our mam does.'

Meals here were silent. No one spoke, except to say pass the salt or something. When they were children Sam and Bennet always got the giggles. Stern and solemn at the head of the table their father would sit. The big stick next to him ready to be seized and thwacked down hard on the table at the slightest infringement of the respectable hush of muted chewing and the clink of cutlery. Your heart would jump. It was awful, they only had to catch each other's eye across the table and they were off, bursting and shaking with the effort of keeping it in. First it was the thwack on the table. If they carried on, their knuckles got it. But something always happened, a fly would land on someone's forehead, someone's stomach would make a funny noise, anything to set them off, it didn't matter.

Bessie wasn't used to it. At dinner at home they'd always talked. Dinnertime had been when her mother and father argued and her sister told stories on her and she protested her innocence and everyone went red in the face and sometimes she cried because it was rotten and unfair. Her dad stuck up for her. 'Oh, give over picking on the lass,' he'd say.

She was walking down the lane with him once when she was about ten and she'd said, 'You are my dad really, aren't you, Dad?' She'd just said it, she'd been meaning to for years even though he'd told her he wasn't.

He'd actually stopped still and looked down at his feet for a few long, thoughtful seconds, pursing his lips. Then, 'No,' he'd said kindly, 'no, Bessie, I'm not your proper dad. But it doesn't matter.'

Only it did matter. Because he was, she knew he was really her real dad, so why was he pretending not to be? So now when she looked at Violet sitting there across the table from her, she felt moved. Poor child with her plain peaky face, can't keep her eyes off her father sitting there not taking any notice of her. Cruel man! Yes, there was

53

some cruelty in him. She saw it now. He's not doing right by that child, she thought. Well, we'll have to see about that.

'I'm not eating that,' Violet said.

The silence buzzed. Sam's dad looked up sharply through his bushy grey eyebrows. 'I *beg* your pardon?'

'I'm not eating that.'

'Eat it up now, Violet,' said Sam's mam. 'It's good for you.'

'I'm not eating it. It makes me sick.'

'Enough now.' He no longer kept the stick by the table but he hated this disruption. 'Violet Mabel, you will eat that fat this minute. Now.'

Sam's mother picked up the fat and attempted to put it into Violet's mouth. Violet lashed out and flung it from her as if it were a worm, jumped up and started screaming. 'I'm not eating it! I'm not I'm not I'm not!'

'Sit down!'

Violet hit the air in front of her, her face went red and tears flooded down her cheeks. Lal jumped up and grabbed her and tried to calm her, but Violet struggled away and stood on the hearthrug and shouted, 'I'm not I'm not I'm not!' till her face turned a polished purple, quite alarming.

'Oh, Violet, sit down,' Sam's father said, standing up still chewing, his big square cheeks working under his whiskers. 'Come on now, sit down. The blasted fat's gone on the floor now anyway, it's blasted inedible. Now sit down, do.'

Violet sobbed and stamped her foot.

Spoilt, that child, thought Bessie.

Sam's father reached out and drew Violet to him. 'There, there, la lammy,' he said, 'no need to cry. Grandad's not angry.'

'She should have eaten the good food,' Sam's mother said, taking up her own knife and fork again with an air of dismissal. 'It's nourishment she needs and it's nourishment I'll get down her whether she likes it or not.'

'That's enough,' Sam's father said. He pushed Violet, still snivelling and scowling in her exaggerated way, gently back towards her own chair. 'Now, please may we finish our repast in peace?'

Sam had gone on eating throughout all of this, looking sternly down at his plate, saying nothing.

'We'd never have got away with that,' Lal said later, as she and Bessie went for a walk up and down the village and out through the fields.

Bessie had never seen anything quite so lush as this before: the mountains with a sheen like breath on them, the meadows frothing with flowers. Bright little birds flitting in and out of rampant hedges. The church was old and grey and hushed, set high in its graveyard full of weathered stones and ancient, spreading trees. A dark narrow path ran alongside, bordered by tall foliage and a wall twice her height that was covered in tiny flowers. Lal had an apple, she was tossing it up and catching it again in her hands as they walked as if it were a ball. 'It's funny,' she said, 'soft as anything with Violet, he is. You should have seen him when *we* were kids.' She took a bite of her apple and chewed. 'You didn't move! Believe me. Oh, he used to lock horns with Bennet he did, though! Not that she'd have said anything at the table, she wouldn't have dared, but she had a cheeky look, you know, our Benny did. Insolent. She only had to look at him with that face on her and he'd go all red, face like thunder, you know. He doesn't half miss her, you know. Poor Dad! Funny, ain't it? She was the only one who'd answer him back and yet really she's his favourite out of all of us even now. Oh, I don't know, though! I don't know why I say that, really. Now, our Molly wouldn't answer him back. Oh, no, not Molly! And I wouldn't either.' Lal bit thoughtfully into the speckled russet skin. 'Violet, though.' She chewed and swallowed. 'Violet gets away with murder.'

Violet cried in the privy at the end of the garden. They were giving her away. She didn't want to go with her dad and Bessie. She wanted her dad. He was *her* dad, she loved him; he was always away fighting the ruthless Teuton bands in the war. She wanted him but she wanted him to come and live here with her and Granny and Grandad and Auntie Lal. Everyone went away. It was horrible. Auntie Bennet went away. Auntie Molly went to Heaven. Auntie Lal was going too, she said, when she got married next year to her young man James; all the way to London, which was miles away, and she'd maybe never see her again, she never saw Auntie Bennet or Auntie Molly any more. It wasn't fair. And now she herself was going away and it was all being planned out for her and no one was telling her anything, only she heard things, she knew, she heard them arguing in the room, her daddy and Granny and Grandad. They were saying things that made her feel sick in her heart. It's not that we don't love her, Grandad said, we do, but we're not getting any younger and it's a tremendous strain on Mam. As you know, Iphigineia's going to be married to young James. How we'd manage it without Iphigineia I don't know.

Daddy said: She's not an easy child. I'm not used to children.

She should be with her father, Granny said.

Manchester. Big, grey and red, fancy. Big roads. Playgrounds. Funny square hedges. She'd been there. Uncle Edmund lived there, he lived near Crowcroft Park. Croaky. That's what they called it, Croaky Park. Where she first saw her dad. She had a memory of being taken there to meet him once when he came home from the war. Somebody said, 'Here is your daddy,' and he came walking towards her in khaki with his poor hands bandaged from the frostbite he'd got in the trenches, on the Somme.

Here is my daddy, she thought. My daddy.

'Lal,' said Granny, 'Lal, go and get that child. She's sulking in the toilet.'

But Lal was not there: she'd just popped upstairs for something.

'I'll see to her,' Bessie said, getting up and going out into the garden, walking down through the foxgloves and ox-eyes and veronica. 'Violet,' she called through the door, 'aren't you coming out?'

No answer.

'Come on, Violet, I've got to go for a walk out to post a letter, and I need you to show me where the postbox is.'

No answer.

'Oh, come out and don't be so soft! What's your daddy going to think if you sit around sulking all day?'

The latch fell and Violet came out.

'You are a silly girl. What good's sitting in there going to do? You come with me, I'll get my letter.'

'Who's it to?' asked Violet.

'It's to *my* mam and dad,' replied Bessie.

Thin as a stick, Violet walked alongside her. 'Don't you live with your mam and dad?'

'No.'

'Why not?'

'Because I'm grown-up.'

'Are you going to marry my dad?' she asked.

'Yes, I am. So we'll get to know one another.'

'*My* mam's in heaven.'

'That's right,' said Bessie, 'but I'm your mam too.'

'Are you? Are you my mam?'

'Yes, I am. I'm your other mam.'

Nelly came along when Violet was nine, Bobby two years later. Dad lost his job on the parks. Mam went cleaning for an old lady who lived alone in a big house with just her dog. And Violet discovered that she loved babies. Baby Nelly in the old highchair with the chipped blue paint, sitting on a cushion with her legs sticking straight out from under her dress in scuffed shoes and long socks. An anxious baby from the start, with a short-sighted stare. Nelly and Bob were Violet's little darlings, her cuddly toys. She would sing and dance like Auntie Bennet in front of the mirror that hung over the fireplace, Bob on her shoulder, Nell at her heels. She'd stick them in the old pram, one at each end in their white dresses, take them with her wherever she went. People always stopped to admire Bobby with his blue eyes and white-fair hair and sunny toothless smile. She took them on errands, put the shopping in the pram with them. The day before dole day she went on an errand with Nelly in the pram and found a ten-bob note lying on the pavement. She bought a pound of bacon, a big tin of tomatoes and a woolly hat for Nelly. 'There!' she said, satisfied, tying the bow under Nelly's chin. 'There!' and trundled her home in the pram.

Mam was moaning. Dad had been drinking. His eyes twinkled. He giggled. 'What's this?' he cried, seizing up Nelly and snuggling her in his arms. 'Who's got a nice new hat? Hey? My little lamb?'

Dad's eyes were gentle when he looked at Nelly in a way they never were for Violet.

'What's this?' Mam cried, in a sharp voice. I should have known, she was thinking. I'd never marry a drinker again. Remembering Bill Amberley, who had grown in her mind into something he'd never been in life: a beautiful boy with waving golden hair and kind brown eyes, a seemly and courteous suitor who'd worshipped the ground upon which she walked and had vowed to marry her when he got his first leave.

He was very keen on me, she said in her mind. He was. Very keen on me.

'I found ten bob!' shrilled Violet. 'In Darras Road, a ten-bob note! I've got change! Look!'

She poured out the pennies on the table.

'You good girl!' Mam said firmly. 'Good girl, Violet!'

Instead of corned beef, that night they had bacon and tomatoes for tea. And later, Dad and Mam went out and left Violet in charge, and she danced.

'Dance for us, Vi!'

'Go on, Vi!'

Violet's skinny legs in black stockings, leaping and kicking. Violet making them laugh. Pulling her faces and doing her voices.

4

Hey, Nelly, Ho, Nelly

Nelly sat among the rough, scruffy kids of Gorton in Standard One of Old Hall Drive School, always wishing she was somewhere else, at home with Dad, or in Morland where she went on holiday to Granny and Grandad's. She hated school. She hated that grim cold grey playground. When they did PT Miss Battman made them do the splits; she came round pressing down on the top of your head, trying to force you down till it felt as if your legs were going to break. They teased her because of her squint. Then when she wore her glasses they called her Specky-Four-Eyes. She hated the teachers, iron hair, hatchet faces. People were rotten, everybody except her and Bobby and Dad and all the rest of the family (well, most of them but not Auntie Isabel, Mam said Auntie Isabel was an old witch) was rotten. In Singing they sang 'Sweet Lass of Richmond Hill' and 'The Ash Grove' and 'Billy Boy' and 'Nelly Bligh', and Miss Flower came round sticking her ear right up against your mouth to make sure you were really singing, and she'd point and boom: 'THIS – GIRL – CAN'T – SING!'

> *Nelly Bligh*
> *Piped her eye*
> *When she went to sleep,*
> *When she wakened up again*
> *Her eye began to peep.*
> *Hey, Nelly! Ho, Nelly! Hearken unto me,*
> *I'll sing to you, I'll play to you*
> *A cheerful melody.*

'Nelly Bligh' was the worst, because when they got to the words 'Hey, Nelly! Ho, Nelly!' everyone turned and looked at her and laughed, and sometimes they sang it at her in the playground, in a jeering stupid way: 'Hey, Nelly! Ho, Nelly!' Anyway, they were all scabby and snotty and horrible. Or there were the nice little girls, the ones who flirted like peacocks, the ones who had dancing lessons and put their heads on one side. All the teachers were nice to them. They wore pretty dresses, with ribbons at the sides of their faces. Nelly wanted to wear a nice dress for school but her mam wouldn't let her. She had to wear a black gymslip. Some of the children in her class didn't have any shoes. Their feet were dirty and stank. There was a girl who smelt strongly of soup. When she had a day off school, it was noticeable, the absence of the smell of soup.

When Bobby started, the rough kids left her alone. If anyone thumped his sister he'd bloody kill 'em, pile in roaring, terrifying, bowling down the playground all fists and fury, mad, small and fearless, bawling, 'That's my bloody sister you're hitting!' The Holloways had rage. They had voices that carried. Mam could squawk like a parrot. Nelly had an enduring memory of being very, very small, holding Mam's hand in town. It was a hunger march; big crowds, muffling voices, men's shoes. People shouting. Mam's grip on her hand hurt, and a low, meandering stream of swearing was issuing from her tight lips. 'Bloody stinking crowds,' she was saying to herself, through gritted teeth, 'bloody move aside.' Gorgeous big brown horses, like racehorses, appeared before them in a line. Nell wanted to go up to one and stroke its legs. The cracks in the pavement shifted under her feet in her brown boots. Then a scream. Everyone running, pelting along, men shouting, women screaming; she was dragged, hauled by one arm off her feet, the toes of her brown boots skimming the ground. Thunder. Hoofs. Big brown horse like death going by, thunder. And over it all, louder than anything else, louder even than the siren that was going off somewhere, Mam's shrieking parrot voice: 'There's children here! There's children here!'

Nelly, quiet, awkward Nelly, could snap without warning, do the parrot. Nelly's temper was a force that burst up like a geyser, shaking her, clenching her teeth. Jack-in-the-box! Force it, batter it back down, hammer hammer ham, quick and clip the box lid down on its horrible grinning head. Scary thing. She threw Violet over the hedge for teasing her. Violet still couldn't believe it.

So the bullies gave up messing with the Holloways.

'You're as good as any of them,' Dad said. 'Don't you ever forget it. You're as good as any bastard in this world.'

Dad was wise and good and gentle. Dad was there, in the night, in the fever, it was Dad. Always. First and always. He was Nelly's and she was his. When she looked at his eyes she saw something looking back that knew her beyond anything. A knowing like that was holy.

★

'Mam, Mam, they've been picking on me!'

'Stop picking on that lad!'

'We haven't!'

'Yes, you have! He's just said. Bob! Bob! Come to your mam!'

'Mam! Ma-a-a-a-am!'

'Now, hush!'

'Honestly, Mam!' Violet was going out, she wore a two-piece of donkey brown. 'We haven't touched him! He's a right little liar!' Her friend Josie Spedding, also in donkey brown, was walking up the path to call for her.

'Well, what's he crying for, then?'

'What's to do, old Bob?' asked Dad gently, lifting him up to sit on his arm. 'What's to do, son?'

'Honestly!'

Violet was off, walking down the path and away down the road with her friend. Donkey brown was all the rage this year.

'What do they look like?' said Dad, standing at the door with Bobby in his arms, watching them go. 'Two lumps of shit walking down the road.'

Nelly laughed.

Violet was not one of them. It mattered. She was not their full sister, not blood. She and Bobby were the same blood. Blood mattered. Dad said so. Really, you'd have thought Dad only ever had two children.

As vice-chairman of the Sutton Estate Social Centre, Uncle Edmund organised children's outings. They went to see the Rose Queen crowned at Belle Vue. Nelly knew one of the cushion-bearers and a couple of the petal throwers from school. Kitty O'Neill who lived over the road was there, Kitty O'Neill from her class, with her nice red hair. They all looked shiny and spanking brand new, their hair and skin and the gorgeous satin of the dresses, the bouquets all perfect curls of stiff petal arranged just so. They were transformed, as if they came from fairy castles and never sat there in the classroom in their black gymslips and white blouses, picking their noses and scuffling their feet. The retiring queen came on all smiles and took the crown from the crown-bearer and put it on the new queen's head. Everyone clapped.

The Rosebud Queen lived down Darras Road and went to Old Hall Drive.

'I don't think she's very pretty,' someone said.

She wasn't really, but she was one of those that always wore nice ribbons and went to dancing classes. It wasn't really prettiness that counted, it was something else. Nelly didn't know what it was but she knew she hadn't got it. Nelly could never be like that, lovely, popular, on the stage. She was nothing like. Nothing like. Plain as anything, her and Violet. She was not a chosen kind of person. Team games. Mary in the nativity play. An angel. Rosebud Queen. Anything. She just wasn't the kind. Anyway, she wouldn't have wanted it, not really, standing in front of all those people, all looking at her. She'd have felt daft. Sometimes they were horrible, those girls, nice as they looked. Once she'd stayed at Granny and Grandad's at the same time as Cousin Faye, Auntie Molly's little girl. They'd had to share a bed. In the night Faye picked her nose and wiped it off on Nell's leg with her finger. And she stole Granny's chocolate. Granny had chocolate squares and water by her bed. 'Go on,' Faye said, 'go on, she'll never notice.'

She felt left out. She didn't make friends easily. It was us against the world, always us against the world, other kids were hostile, different, not quite right. Not us. Violet went out, though, Violet knew people. Nell got to thinking about Auntie Bennet again, up there in her lovely dresses, singing and dancing and juggling. Bennet didn't dance any more, though. Not on a stage anyway. 'Maybe on a table sometimes,' Mam said with grim satisfaction, shaking open a newspaper, 'when she's had a few.'

No one else had an auntie who could juggle. She'd tried to teach them once but it was hopeless. 'Like this! Look, it's easy.'

The balls danced in the air. She had on her professional smile.

Nelly couldn't catch a ball for toffee. That's why no one ever wanted her on their team.

On the bright stage, the dance troupe performed. Then a couple of girls came on and sang 'For Me And My Girl' and 'Felix Keeps On Walking', with actions.

Anyway, beauty didn't do well, beauty was dangerous. Look at Auntie Bennet.

Mam stood by the sideboard, counting food tickets.

'Where is he?' she shrilled. 'Where is he?'

Violet was out. Why doesn't she ever stop moaning? thought Nell, sitting on the sofa with her white dress pulled over her knees. Violet was out, Dad was out, Bobby was out. She wished she'd gone out too now but she'd wanted to read her book after tea, and now she was stuck here with Mam moaning, moaning, on and on. Bobby had gone off playing with Ralph Brigg. It was starting to get dark and Mam was worried, he hadn't come back. She walked rapidly backwards and forwards between the window and the back door, freckled hands clasped at her waist.

'Where is he?' She was nearly in tears. 'Where's Violet? She can go round to the Briggs and see if he's there.'

'I'll go, Mam.'

Mam shouted and her face went deep red: 'No, you will not! You'll vanish too! Stay there!'

Nelly sighed.

Mam paced.

'She knows damn well she should have been back by now! Where the hell are *you* going?'

'I'm only going to the gate.'

She left the door open and went with Jock to look out for Violet, but instead saw her dad come walking along the street with the jaunty walk he had when he'd been drinking, cocky and rolling, now and again banging his shoulder against the hedge. Jock ran to meet him and clung around his knee.

'Well, my little chickadees,' said Dad, embracing them both. He pulled out his fob watch and checked the time.

'Bob's not come back and Violet's not come back and Mam's going mad,' Nell said.

'She went years ago,' muttered Dad. His eyes were merry. 'Where's our Bob gone then?'

'Ralph Brigg called for him.'

Nelly saw Mam's face in the window, bleak and bespectacled, the mouth a wan O.

'They'll have gone up the brook,' Dad said.

Violet came round the corner smiling, her smart hat tipped down over her forehead. Jock ran to her and down she went on one knee. 'My good likkle boy!' she cried.

Mam flung open the door and came storming down the path: 'What time d'you call this? Our Bobby's not back. Get round to Briggs and see if he's there.'

'He'll have gone up the brook,' Dad said again, 'he's a bad little bugger. Or over Jackson's.'

'I'll go,' said Nell. It was exciting. The dark was growing.

'You'll get in that house!' Mam shrieked. 'Or you'll get a good hiding!'

'It's not our Nell's fault.' Dad frowned and lit up a cigarette, sucking his gaunt cheeks gaunter. 'I'll go down the brook. Vi, nip over Briggs.'

Nell was left stuck in the house in case he came back, with Mam sitting biting her lips, now jumping up and going to the window and standing there heavy and stiff, looking down towards the end of the street. 'I'll kill him,' she said, 'I'll kill him!'

Nelly wasn't worried, she didn't know why. Bobby was always late, and Mam was always going mad. He'd be here in a minute.

'Where *is* he?' Mam worried, sat and worried. 'Where *is* he?'

'He'll be all right, Mam.'

'*You* don't know.'

She was up again.

He wasn't here in a minute. Violet came back with Ralph Brigg's dad. Ralph Brigg wasn't back either. No one had seen where they'd gone. Then Dad came back from the brook and he and Ralph Brigg's father went off and looked all round everywhere, asking all the other kids if they'd seen either of them, and then they split up and searched, and Violet and two of her friends searched, and Kitty O'Neill's dad came out of their house and said he'd go over and have a look on Mellands, the gypsies were there again; and he set off puffing on his pipe with his red hair glinting from under his cap. Kitty O'Neill and her mum came out on the front. Kitty's hair was red like her dad's, a lovely glinty red. She looked like the sun standing next to her plain brown mother. Kitty hopped over to their gate. 'Your Bobby's lovely,' she said.

Nell said: 'Ahum ahum, Kiss my bum.'

Kitty stuck out her tongue and hopped away. She didn't care. Nell felt sorry.

'Something's happened,' Mam said, in a terrible voice. 'Get the police, something's happened.'

'Now now, Mrs Holloway,' said a woman from round the corner, who happened to be passing by and seemed to know all about it, 'you mustn't think the worst.'

'What else is there?' wailed Mam. 'He's not here. Something's happened.'

Uncle John arrived with Dad and Ralph Brigg's dad.

'Sam, you're getting the police,' Mam said, in an aggrieved voice, as if he'd already refused to do so. 'You get down that police station now.'

And as Dad was turning to go they heard the voices, boys' voices tunelessly singing,

> *Romanee-e-e!*
> *We saw the campfires gleaming …*

and around the corner they came, Bobby and Ralph Brigg weaving raggedly from one side of the pavement to the other, arms companionably slung about one another's shoulders. Mam dashed forward and gave Bob an almighty whack across the head. 'Where've you been? Where've you *been?*'

Bobby laughed.

'You!' said Ralph Brigg's dad. 'Here!'

Behind the boys came Kitty O'Neill's dad grinning all over his face.

'They're drunk!' said Dad, and everybody burst out laughing, apart from Mam.

'They were like this coming along Melland Road,' Kitty O'Neill's dad said.

'We've been with the gypsies,' Bob said. 'This man had a guitar. He let me have a go.'

'They had a big fire,' said Ralph.

Mam swiped a blow at Bob's head again, but he ducked and ran in laughing. Nelly ran after him, and Jock.

'What was it like?' Nell cried. 'Did you go in one of their caravans?' She was jealous. Bob went to the tap and stuck his face under it, drinking. 'Tell me!' she pleaded.

'I had a smoke,' said Bob, turning, dripping, eyes all red but sparkly. 'It was all right. They let us sit round their fire. They were dead nice.'

Mam came in, grabbed him with both hands and shook him till his teeth rattled. Dad followed, and Violet.

'You bloody fool!' Mam screamed. 'You bloody fool!'

'You don't do that again, son,' Dad said. 'We were off to the police.'

'They'll take you away,' said Mam, letting him go. 'Big policeman'll come and take you away. Put you in a home.'

'Let them,' Bobby said.

'Go on, tell us,' Vi said, all smiles. 'What was it like? Did they sing?'

'"Romanee-e-e-e! We saw the ..."'

He skipped aside from Mam's hand.

'It's all right now,' Dad murmured. 'All's well that—'

'And you can shut up too! You've got no more sense than him. You're his father. Why aren't you saying owt? Because you're soft as pigshit, that's why! Soft as—'

Dad made his hand into a mouth, thrust it into her face going yak-yak-yak. Nelly and Bob leaned together, giggling painful silent giggles. Violet stood behind Mam and pulled a ridiculous face, elongating her long upper lip even more, straining the skin over her high cheekbones, making her eyes perfectly round and owlish.

Mam slapped Dad, wheeled round and turned on Bob. 'Get up them stairs now! Now!'

He dashed up, Nell ran after. In the bedroom they fell upon the bed shoving the blankets into their mouths, shaking; tears ran down

Nelly's face. Downstairs they heard little bumps and thuds, and the sound of Mam's moaning voice droning on and on and on till she'd moaned herself out. Then Violet putting the kettle on, calling cheerily, 'Hey, Dad, guess who I saw tonight ...'

'You go down, Nelly,' Bob said. 'I'm getting into bed. You can tell her I'm sorry.' He'd be good now. All sweet blue eyes and fat lower lip, till his mum ended up kissing his dimple and rolling him in her round arms, telling him what a little precious he was and how she could eat him all up.

When Nell went down, Mam was in the kitchen. 'There's no point arguing with your mother,' Dad was saying, in a low voice to Violet, 'you'll never get anywhere.'

'Time after time I tell him: "You walk away. You walk away from trouble, Bobby." What does he do? Walks straight towards it.' Mam was banging about with a duster, a turban on her head. 'Sick of it, I am.'

Nell was sick of it too. Dad had taken Bobby up to see Granny and Grandad in Morland, and she was bored. Jock scuttled under the table. Nelly sat tight, quiet, reading again her postcard, very nicely written in Dad's long, sprawling handwriting: 'To Miss Nelly Holloway, 15 Wembley Road, Sutton Estate, Gorton, M/Chtr. My dearest Nelly, hop you are a good girl. Got your letter this morning. Best love from Dad and Bob xx.' And there was the old Forge Bridge in Morland, lovely and shady. She thought about Bobby there. Smelling the wild roses. How would he do at dinnertime with no one to catch his eye and make him laugh? Meals in Morland were silent, not like home. She and Bobby always got the giggles, it was awful. They'd shake, burst, convulse, screamingly, streamingly silent, while Grandad sat stern and solemn with his grieving eyes at the head of the table.

It was lonely. Just with Mam moaning and Violet going out all the time. Nell looked out to see Violet and Freddy Gumbold standing at the gate. Mam said Vi had to be in by nine every night, even though she was seventeen and working. Freddy Gumbold had shiny hair parted at one side. One front tooth completely wrapped over the other one, and Nell wondered if it got in the way when he kissed Violet. She could imagine it sticking into your lip like a toothpick. Like Granny's pickle-stabber. Violet was no beauty, was she? Did OK for boys, though.

Mam flung open the door and stood, arms folded, on the step. 'What time d'you call this?' she shouted.

'Sorry, Mrs Holloway,' the boy said sheepishly. 'It didn't finish till half past eight.'

Mam said Violet wasn't going out on Saturday, she wouldn't give her any money to go to Belle Vue with Josie Spedding.

'Oh, Mam!' said Vi, who never had any money of her own because she had to give all her wages to Mam. Even Dad did when he was in work. Mam managed everything.

'It's hard bringing up a family,' Mam said abruptly, sitting down on one side of the fire, lips compressed. 'You'll find out one day. And your bloody father's no good.'

Nell hated this.

Vi went into the kitchen to make a pot of tea and look for a biscuit. 'Hey, guess who I saw?' she called back. 'Edie Mulcahy who used to be at Peacock's. Her brother's working in the Co-op. Put the cups out, Nell.'

She stood in the doorway, gave an unearthly yodel and beat her breast. 'That's what Tarzan does,' she said. 'Isn't it funny without our kid?'

Mam didn't dance any more. She used to, Nell remembered, when they were little. She used to dance round the living-room table to the music from the wireless. Sometimes she danced with Dad when he got back from the pub. Nell used to follow the steps. She was on the front showing Kitty O'Neill how to dance the Charleston when Dad and Bob came back, turning into their road with their bags on their shoulders. Jock ran to meet them. Violet came smiling down the path. 'Dad,' Violet said, 'Dad.'

He ruffled Nell's hair, soft-eyed. 'How's little Nell?' he asked kindly.

She knew it was bad the way he was different with Violet than

68

with her and Bobby, but it didn't matter, she just loved Dad whatever. Violet's eyes filled with tears but she went on smiling. That's how she was. Laughed easily, cried easily. Cried when she laughed too much, cried when she was happy, cried at films and songs, then laughed again, at herself, ended up humming, saying something daft, making a face.

'Where's your mam?' Dad asked her.

'Upstairs changing the beds.'

They went inside. Mam came clattering down the stairs, beaming, red cheeks glowing, crying: 'Where's that lad? Where's that lad? Have you been a good boy?'

'Of course he's been a good boy,' Dad said, 'our Bobby's always a good boy.' Which he'd continued to believe unwaveringly against all the evidence, as he also thought Nelly could do no wrong.

Dad brought big news. 'Our Bennet's got married,' he announced, not pleased.

'Benny?' said Mam. 'At her age?'

'What d'you mean, at her age? She's still a good-looking woman, our Benny.'

'Who's she married?'

'I don't know. Some bloke. He's a lot older than her. Called Walter. Getting on for sixty.'

Mam clicked her tongue. 'Oh, well,' she said, 'I suppose it's about time. Still, there's no fool like an old fool.'

Poor Auntie Bennet! All that lovely hair, and the singing and dancing and pretty little shoes, all that – ending up with some old bloke. Sixty! *Sixty!* It was horrible.

'She could've had anyone, our Benny,' said Dad.

'Well, she's no spring chicken herself, is she?' Mam said.

5

Beautiful Benny Brown

She was no spring chicken. Pushing forty if she was a day when she met Walter Moss, though she didn't look it at all. She'd hit hard times but hard times glowed on Bennet, made her shove her small pointed chin up higher and glare the world straight back in the face. She had to find a berth. She was in from Liverpool on the train, there was no work any more, not now, not with all the old halls closing and these new-fangled places opening up. Her friend Polly Harkin had married a coalman. Dora with the snakes had gone off to Paris with an escapologist. And the men, oh, the men had come and gone and come and gone and come and gone and gone. Last year she'd been sitting pretty in Yarrow Street with Mr Sigerson taking care of the rent. Well, she knew it wasn't going to last and so did he: both of them had always laid their cards on the table. From Day One. That had always been Bennet's way.

She did her hair and make-up on the train, took out her compact and powdered her face carefully and cleverly, with a skill born of many a year of day-in, day-out practice. Not too much, don't want to look like a tart. Don't clog the wrinkles, only draws attention. Just enough. The gentleman in the opposite corner is glancing from time to time, well, kiss my bum, you can look. Her bright red lipstick was worn down into the socket of its tube by her finger. She smiled into the mirror to make her eyes bright, and lit a cigarette.

Manchester was just as cold as Liverpool. Bloody teeming down. She put up her umbrella and stood on the concourse. So many times she had stood so, somewhere, anywhere, careless, careless of the next night and the next day; find digs; near theatre; look someone up; elbow in; carelessly standing on the brink of another new thing, the old repetitive uncertainty exhilarating, peaking, a slow down-fade like the house lights at that moment of supreme expectation. Begin again. Anew. Breathe in, breathe out, *step out*! *Again*. Never say die.

This time was different. Why? An aching in her bones. Now it felt more like fear. A miserable, cold, howling sort of fear, like the freezing winter weather cutting through your coat while you fish in your purse for your bus fare, your gloves getting worn, see, another soft pang. Here's the fare to get on the bus and go and find some old friend with a sofa for the night, or perhaps not bother, perhaps just go round to old Sam's, him and his old battleaxe Bessie. Dear old Sam would never let her down. Never. None of her brothers would. Good lads, good lads all!

Yes, she'd go to Sam's, but first she'd go down Deansgate, where Dreena Bostock and her brother Al lived over the top of a tobacconist's shop. Dreena and Al were old pros who knew everyone. They might know of a job, a possibility, a pointer. Nice little berth somewhere.

Dreena opened the door in a green silk kimono decorated with golden-eyed salmon-pink dragons, very faded. She was ancient, short and fat with carrot-red hair that stuck out from her balding scalp in violent corkscrews. Dreena had worked with them all – Dan Leno, Marie Lloyd, Florrie Forde, all the legends. Her perfectly round face was powdered dead white, crazed with a hundred tiny cracks like an old china saucer. A thin crimson mouth and two thin black eyebrows had been painted on, making her look surprised.

'Benny, my darling,' she croaked, waving a cigarette in a stained white holder, 'what a *gorgeous* surprise!' and reached out with her soft plump hand to draw Bennet across the lobby and into the hot smoky living room.

'Benny dear!' cried Al.

They were drinking whisky, Dreena and Al and a man whose eyes met hers as soon as she entered, with a desperate purpose, both insolent and pleading; it seemed absurd at such short notice and a little bit frightening. He was old. *Completely* grey.

'Walter, this is Benny Brown,' said Al, a mild and jovial elephant with scraped-back hair. 'I'm sure you've heard of Benny Brown.'

'Indeed I have,' said Walter, 'oh, indeed I have,' and rose politely from his seat. He was not tall. His voice was wonderful, deep and serious, and he was so nicely spoken. 'Walter Moss,' he said smoothly, and bowed. 'I'm delighted to make your acquaintance.'

'Why, thank you.' She flashed him her smile, the big one.

His face fell in three big folds, tight to the bone, strange. It was as if age hadn't got to all of him at once. He was still slim and trim, and his lips were not wasted like an old man's lips but firm and full, brown lips; and the hair, though grey, was a dark iron-grey, vigorous and wavy.

'Are your boots wet?' asked Dreena sympathetically.

'No no.' Bennet sat down, smiling. She wondered if Dreena had been doing Walter Moss's feet. She had a way with feet, she'd been doing them for years. When you danced a lot in tight shoes you had trouble with your feet. Which reminded Benny: she thought she might be getting a bunion. Her big toe was starting to look a bit peculiar, she thought, must do something about it. She shook her coat off her shoulders, took off her hat. She was staying. The pelt of a snow tiger lay across the back of the sofa, shot, Dreena always maintained, by her first husband. The walls were covered with photographs of herself and Al when younger, she like a white chicken or a wedding cake in her frills and flounces, Al just Al; he'd always looked the same. A rug bearing the Black Watch tartan covered his massive round knees, and his bare feet dangled below its fringe like a child's, not quite touching the floor. As if stabbed, a ventriloquist's dummy slumped by the side of his chair, the rictus of death on its dark fawn face.

'Working, Ben?' Al asked cheerily.

'Not at the moment, Al. I just this minute got back from Liverpool. Thought I'd have a little breathing space, look around sort of thing. Only popped in on the off-chance you might know of some *staggering* opportunity that was just *made* for me!' She laughed and rolled her eyes, accepting a cigarette from Al and swaying her shoulders in a dance of expectation as she waited for a light.

'Oh! What were you doing in Liverpool?' asked Walter Moss, leaning forward and speaking very distinctly.

She decided he was drunk. His eyes were terribly soft and sad.

'Summer season,' she said, with a smile, testing the front of her hair for raindrops, holding out her hand for the whisky glass Dreena proffered. 'Ta, Dreena.'

'Nothing doing round here, darling,' Dreena said. 'OK for a kip?'

'Thank you very much but I'm visiting my brother, Dreena,' said Bennet. 'Our Sam, you know. He's got a lovely family.'

She drank.

She stayed longer than she'd intended.

Walter, it turned out, had a little house, a two-up two-down in Fallowfield. He was an actor, though he wasn't working any more because of his health. 'The old heart,' he said, with a sweet, regretful smile, 'could pull the rug on me any time. And yet in these dire times I find I am in gainful employment. So I really can't complain.'

'Oh? What do you do?'

'I grind knives.' He said this with such a pleasant, self-deprecating smile, and laughed when she did, as if it were some wonderful joke. And later, when she rose to go for her bus, he stood up too. 'I believe it has stopped raining,' he said, raising his eyebrows at the darkening window. Such an expressive forehead. 'Miss Brown, I wonder if you'd permit me to accompany you as far as Piccadilly.'

It might have sounded pompous, but not the way he said it: quiet, smooth as silk. Aha, she thought, putting on her hat; so that's the way of it, is it?

'Don't go out of your way, dear,' she said lightly.

They strolled. It wasn't quite dark but the lights were on and shone on the wet pavement. His black suit, she saw, was old but cared-for. He was a clean old man. Sixtyish, she guessed. Not *so* old. Older than her other gentlemen, granted. She didn't know if she could ever do it with a man this old. But, goodness, she thought then, with the same sad, quick pang as before, I'm not young any more. Am I? And thought again of those lodgings, those old cold lodgings, again. Walter walked oddly, slow, with one foot pushed out to the side, his hands behind his back. He wore a grey muffler. He talked about his career. He'd been in Shakespeare. Enobarbus in *Antony and Cleopatra*. He'd done Lennox in *Macbeth*, Barnardo in *Hamlet*, Trinculo in *The*

Tempest. You could tell he was classically trained, the way he spoke. 'I do not presume,' he said, and it was like listening to spoken verse or, indeed, an actor reading lines, 'to consider myself a Great. That genius was not to be mine, alas. I merely did my best, and gave creditable performances.'

And at that he looked at Bennet and smiled into her eyes.

So posh and polite. It was the eyes that did it for her. Like the most sad old dog, one that adored you faithfully for ever and laid its big hairy old head on your knee.

There was some big do on in Piccadilly, crowds of people, policemen.

'What's this?' she asked.

'Mosley,' he replied.

It was the Fascists marching. They were diverted down a side-street. Someone was making a speech. She felt his hand upon her elbow. Both of them were drunk.

'How'm I supposed to get to my bus stop?' she said imperiously. 'This is ridiculous.'

'We must go down here,' he said.

Away from the crowds.

'You are not interested in politics?' he asked.

'Oh, politics!' She snorted.

'It's a young man's business,' he said, 'all this marching. I keep out of it.'

'Well, I'm Labour me,' Bennet said. 'Always have been and always will.'

They were by the canal. She thought of her dad who always voted Labour, always had and always would. She hadn't seen her dad for so long. Wasn't her fault. Wasn't her fault she couldn't do as he said.

'So sure,' he said, and laughed, then suddenly seized her hand, stared hard into her eyes, and gave the performance of his life, speaking low, intense:

> *Fie, wrangling queen!*
> *Whom everything becomes — to chide, to laugh,*
> *To weep; how every passion fully strives*

74

To make itself, in thee, fair and admired.
No messenger but thine; and all alone
Tonight we'll wander through the streets and note
The qualities of people.

Bennet was transfixed, her lips parted with delight.

"'Come, my queen—'" He lowered his face. "'Last night – you did – desire it.'"

This last he whispered close in her ear so that she squirmed and laughed.

'You're a funny chap,' she said, skipping away, 'a knife-grinder who spouts Shakespeare.'

He smiled. His lower lip, licked, gleamed in the light from the street-lamp.

6

Hop-Along Lil

Whenever Granny and Grandad came down from Westmorland, there was competition over where they'd stay, even though no one had room. Uncle John and Auntie Grace's was out of the picture completely, of course, owing to sheer weight of numbers. With another one due in March and Joey not yet out of nappies, it was getting that way at Edmund and Isabel's too. This time, then, to everyone's but Mam's satisfaction, it fell to Dad to go and meet Granny and Grandad at the station and bring them back on the bus.

They came up the path very slowly, going at Granny's pace.

'Now then, old Hannah,' said Grandad, holding her arm when they reached the step, 'up you go.'

'Thank you, Samuel,' said the tiny old creature, lifting her long skirt. The children came forward and kissed her through the veil that hung down from the hat she always wore for travelling, a wide-brimmed black straw boater with a bunch of false grapes at the side. Through the veil her skin was soft and cold.

'Come and sit down, Hannah,' Mam said.

Dad took her coat and Granny sat on one side of the fire, lifting the veil to uncover her withered, wrinkled old face with the loose jowls and collapsed mouth.

'How are you, Samuel?' Mam fussed about, poking up the fire.

'In the pink, Bessie,' said Grandad, lowering himself into the chair opposite, 'in the pink.' Very smart he looked in his thick grey three-piece suit. You could hardly see his mouth at all but his brindled moustache went up and down when he spoke. 'Mam's not been so good, though. She's been getting a pain in her left side. Haven't you, old Hannah?'

Granny took off her hat and touched her hair. She was vain about her hair. It was done in long shallow waves at the front and all its weight pinned in a bun at the back. 'Just a stitch,' she said.

'I've told her,' said Grandad, straight-faced, adjusting his wire-framed glasses, 'it's all that running up and down the fells that does it. But can I stop her? Can I billy-o. You want to slow down, old Hannah.'

Granny smiled. Her pickle-stabber edged over her lower lip.

After tea, Uncle John and Uncle Edmund came over. The children put on their nighties but no one sent them up to bed, and they stayed on in the warm room listening to the grown-ups talk.

'With regard to the Devil and Christ,' said Grandad, stern-faced, puffing on his pipe, 'they are both sons of God.'

This was the way the conversation often turned when Grandad came.

'As a pictorial depiction of good and evil,' Uncle John said, 'both serve. But it doesn't answer my question. Why did a good God allow certain things to happen?'

'You're using the wrong word,' said Grandad. 'God did not *allow* ... Look at it this way: all Archangels are sons of God; and Christ also was a son of God.'

76

Dad was in reverie, his head bowed and a frown on his face. When the firelight flickered in his bones there was an old look beginning, a drawn, weary look. He was remembering the war. She always knew. Nell didn't know how she knew but she did.

'Satan rules this world,' said Dad.

Grandad sat forward. 'Now this is interesting,' he said eagerly. 'Now you know how Christ speaks of Lucifer in the Bible. Prince of this world. God of this world.'

'This is Hell,' said Dad. 'Our world. Anyone with half a mind can see it. Look at the world. The things that happen, the things people do. It's not down there. We're *living* in Hell.'

'Well, Sam,' said John, 'this little corner of Hell isn't all that bad.' Edmund laughed.

Mam told Violet to go and put the kettle on.

Nelly was all snug in a corner of the settee, hoping no one would remember and send her up to bed. He'd said it before, that this world was Hell. But this was home and safe, with everyone that mattered here. Jock's eyebrows twitched in his sleep. Jinty the cat purred on the arm of Dad's chair. The fire blazed on Granny's old eyes, making them bright liquid. Tiny flames leaped in them. What was she thinking with her one tooth and old, old eyes? You couldn't imagine she'd ever been young. That her hair had ever been anything other than snow-white. Auntie Bennet once said it was because of Granny they'd moved about so much when they were growing up, Morland, Liverpool, Lincoln, Bangor, Berwick, Gloucester, Morland again ... because in the end Granny always got jealous of one or other of the lady schoolteachers Grandad worked with.

Auntie Bennet hadn't been round for ages. She was just somewhere off in another part of Manchester with her old husband.

'And that is why,' said Grandad, 'Christ had not as much power as he would have liked to have when he was down here. He was in the dominions of his reprobate brother, you see. Prince Lucifer.'

Stalking with cloven hoof down their street. Uncle Sydney was coming home late one night and met a man walking towards him and asked him the time. The man said, 'Time for the living to be in bed, and time for the dead to walk.' And when Uncle Sydney looked down, he saw that the man had a cloven hoof.

'If you read the Book of Job,' said Grandad, 'you'll see that Satan, Prince Lucifer, speaks to God in a friendly way and just treats him as an equal. It's a very, very complex matter.'

'Those bairns should be in bed,' said Granny.

'You can't take the Bible literally, Dad,' Uncle John said.

'You certainly can not! It's been translated and transcribed hundreds of times. Full of mistakes. I think there are about four hundred mistakes in the New Testament alone!'

He was so clever, Grandad. He knew everything.

'It's Hell,' Dad said, 'it's the only explanation. God knows what we've done to deserve it but we're here. All we can hope to do is earn our way out of it.'

'Here's some tea, chuck,' Mam said.

Nell drifted, with the voices mingling and fading, winding in and out and together like strands of wool. The strands felt as if they were inside her head. She saw the fire glow inside her eyes, in the dark; and then the darkness writhed and out of it came a tangled knot of bright red wool, all fast and wriggling about like a ball of worms. She jerked.

'That child's falling asleep,' said Uncle John.

It was the same old dream, the one that came back.

Yet she couldn't sleep when she went up, the room was all strange, with truckle beds and Mam and Dad's things laid out on the big chest. Bobby fell asleep straight away. Nell started to think about all the creepy things she'd ever heard. Uncle Sydney asked the Devil the time. Dad's auntie went out to post a letter and met herself coming back. She died three days later. And Nell remembered the music hall, red curtains, crowds, women in big hats, and a woman in a green dress. Yet she'd never been to the music hall. When she told Mam, Mam had paused in her flurrying about and gasped. 'Oh!' she said. 'That was when I was carrying you. It'll be that green dress with the frill I had, I remember that night. Oh, there was a lovely singer on. What was she called? Oh, she was a lovely singer! "Only A Rose" she sang.' Then Mam had sung 'Only A Rose' in a high, quavery voice.

How could she have seen all that from inside Mam's stomach? And what about that other thing? That – *thing*. Dad was coming up the stairs. All the lights were on and everything was normal. Dad came into the room like he always did, just dear old Dad in his crumpled white shirt and black waistcoat and fob watch, and walking right behind him, an after-image: himself repeated blood-red, only evil. It was staring at the back of her dad's head and it wanted to kill him. She closed her eyes and tried not to think about the Devil, listening to the grown-ups' voices rumbling on into the night downstairs. Soon Violet would come up, and then Mam and Dad. It would be just like the old days again, all of them together in one room.

Granny and Grandad stayed for a week. They talked about Joseph in Cambridge, Sydney and Thomas and Iphigineia, but they never mentioned Bennet.

'What exactly did Auntie Bennet do that was so bad?' Nell asked Violet.

'She went against her father,' Violet replied very seriously. 'She broke his heart. She shamed her family.' There was pride and love in her voice.

'Yes, but what did she actually *do*?'

'She went on the stage,' said Violet.

'You should have settled for Harry Whelan,' Dreena always said.

Harold taking off his gloves, whistling in that sophisticated way.

Maybe I should have. Maybe I should have, thought Bennet. What have I done? I've married him. Too quick, too quick. A lifetime for what? To change it all in a couple of weeks to this, because that's how quick it happened, a couple of weeks, and now I'm married to him and that's that. He asked me and I said yes. Six months ago. I was sort of in love with him at the time, though now saying it makes me shiver.

She shivered, walking down London Road. A few little drops of rain fell. I can't help it if I have a lot of friends, she thought. And if some of them are men. What am I supposed to do? Lie? They're like that, some of these men. They like you because you're pretty and free

79

and then they try to stop you being like that. He's driving me up the wall, talk about faddy. Won't pee down the drain in the garden like any normal man. Oh, no. And what's this thing about toilets? Listens outside when I'm in there, now what sort of a way is that to behave? With his dreadful sad eyes following me here and there like the eyes of an old dog, growing now baleful, now hard, now empty, but always, always following me. Wherever I go and whatever I do.

I'm not free. That's what he's done to me. Some men are terrible like that.

Bennet sat down at London Road station and chewed her thumb. Thought about getting on a train to Penrith and going to see her mam and dad. I'm always getting on and off trains, she thought. It seems that all I've really done for years is get on and off trains. What would I say to them? What would they say to me? Yes, Dad, you were right. I did come to grief. I suppose. I suppose that's what this is. But then I did have some bloody good times, Dad, too. And Mam? Mam just never shows anything. Anyway, Walter's not all bad. He's a kind man. He's kind to *me*. Oh, yes, there's nothing I can't have if I want it, he's not tight with his money, I'll give him that. And he likes a drink like me. Oh, I do like a drink! Pop in the Nag. Pop in the Nag before I go home. He's mad by now anyway. In for a penny. Anyway, he can't live for ever. You might not do too bad out of this in the long run, Ben, you know. It's his own house. Oh, yes, there's been money in that family somewhere. Shocking the way he's squandered it. Seedy old sod. Yet there's something fascinating about the man, the dreadful old ham, yet he does it so well. So bad it's good. Oh, he should have been in films, that's where he should have been. Poor old Walter. When he's nice he's nice. A *lovely* smile. And he does love me, there's no doubting that.

In fact, that's the trouble. That's the trouble. He loves me. Adores more like. Yes. Unhealthily adores. That's how I'd put it.

Walter going round the streets with his knife-grinding paraphernalia. When he appears in the street, out they come: the young wives and old ladies and eldest girls, and he woos them all with his sad eyes and speaks to them so beautifully. His stones go whirring. 'My dear Mrs Lawson, how are you? Mrs Read, have you brought me the

Great Sickle? Splendid! There, my dear, sharp as Brooks of Sheffield.'
   'He's barmy, him,' they said.

Dad said you didn't need to go to church to be a good person and believe in God. They never went to church, none of them, except in Morland when they stayed with Granny and Grandad, who were very religious. Sunday, the savoury smell of Dad's broth all over the house and out of the house in the garden. Mam was in a bad mood because she'd had to go cleaning even though it was Sunday, and she'd had to wait ages for a bus coming back and her feet were killing her. A boy had come round with a message a couple of days ago. Mrs Holloway's not to come her usual time because Miss Peverill's had a burglary. Please could she come Sunday instead. Sorry, but it's all a bit awkward at the moment. Miss Peverill would pay time and a half. So Mam had gone, not wanting to fall out with Miss Peverill who she'd been cleaning for for a long time.

   'She's been burgled,' she reported. 'Stole a priceless diamond necklace apparently.'

   'Serves her right for having it,' Dad said, stirring up the broth with the big ladle. Dad's broth was ambrosia. First he steeped the dried butter beans and peas overnight. Then he simmered them all day with a pestle and every kind of vegetable he could get his hands on, small amounts of each cut as small as possible. Dad was a marvellous cook. His food was highly perfected: he did certain things and he did them well. Stew. Pea soup. Chopped-up salad. Sausage and mash. Corned-beef hash. Broth. Broth and bread. It filled you up and made you warm. Afterwards you felt happy. Dad was a fine chopper. That was his secret.

   After tea, replete, Bobby lay on his back on the floor, half under the table, one leg crooked over the knee of the other, the foot tapping on air. Every fifth or sixth tap caught the end of Nell's toe. Violet stood in front of the mirror, patting her thick dark hair.

   'Mam, tell him,' said Nell. She was trying to read her book.

   'Bobby!' Mam said warningly. 'And where do you think *you're* going?' This last to Violet, who for the past half an hour had been quite obviously getting ready to go out.

'Oh, for God's sake, Mam!' Vi said, turning from the mirror.

'Violet,' said Dad, 'I will not have you taking the Lord's name in vain.'

Violet scowled. 'Don't worry, I'm doing the pots before I go.'

Nell and Bob started giggling, then they began pushing one another about. The dog growled. Mam threw them all out into the back, Nell, Bob and Jock. Bobby had got a ferret from Stanley Mulcahy, a white ferret with a pink nose that ran up and down wildly in front of its wire mesh. Next door but one in the old hutch were his rabbits, Mutt and Jeff. Jock bounced in the tussocky long grass at the end of the garden. A train hooted from the railway line over at Ryder Brow and Bob commenced a lonesome wailing like a train whistle, like Jimmie Rodgers doing a hobo song. 'I'm going to get a guitar, Nell,' he said, sitting down cross-legged on the ground in front of his ferret. His knees were rough and red and scuffed like old sandals.

Stanley Mulcahy called. Violet went with him.

Mam came out and set to sharpening the big knife on the back step.

'I'm going to get a guitar, Mam,' Bobby said.

'That's right, love,' she said. 'You will when you're older.'

Uncle John came over and went into a huddle with Dad in the lobby. They heard Dad say, 'Oh, Lord Christ!' so then they knew it must be something very serious. Mam looked up and her hand stopped sharpening the knife.

'Ssh!' she said.

The voices rumbled on for a little while, then Uncle John went without staying for a cup of tea and Dad sat down by the fire. Mam went in. Nell and Bob looked at each other, scared and excited, and followed.

Dad's eyes were stormy. 'It's our Benny,' he said, 'she's been run over.'

'Oh, Sam!' cried Mam.

'It's her legs,' he said, 'her legs are bad.'

He reached up to the mantelpiece for a spill to light his cigarette.

'Don't give me such a fright,' said Mam, 'I thought she was dead.'

'I didn't say she was dead, did I?' He sounded angry, as if it was all Mam's fault. 'I said she's been run over. Car hit her on London Road.'

'Well, what does it sound like, run over?' Mam was aggrieved. 'How bad is she?'

'Bad enough. I don't know, it's her legs, John doesn't know, he's gone round to our Edmund's. Someone's going to have to get word to Morland.'

The children were silent. Nell thought of Auntie Bennet's dancing legs, her lovely little feet in the dainty shoes; all crushed.

'Had she been drinking?' asked Mam.

Dad hurled his spill into the fire. 'How the hell do I know?'

Bennet walked again but only with pain. She didn't get around much and never came visiting; her brothers went to see her now and then, but whenever Violet asked if she could go with Dad, he made an excuse and put her off. Violet felt it more than the rest. She loved Auntie Bennet. Violet was sentimental. All family attachments were for her stirring, lifelong; even the mention of Auntie Molly's name could fill her greeny-brown eyes with mist, and she'd hardly known her. 'Auntie Bennet's poor little legs!' she'd say sorrowfully, hugging herself and shaking her head. 'Poor Auntie Bennet!'

Dad said she wasn't doing so well. He was always depressed when he came back from seeing her, and Mam always moaned. On Sunday she ended up scraping his burnt dinner into the pig bin and slamming round in a foul temper while Violet cleared the table. Bob and Nell went out to play. Kitty O'Neill was on the front with her little brother Neil. It was very windy and Kitty's dress was plastered against her legs. They had a bottle with a bit of fizzy red mineral sloshing around in the bottom, passing it backwards and forwards between themselves as they walked up and down.

'Where'd you get that from?' Nell asked.

'Our dad brings it,' Kitty replied. All round her mouth was red. 'We always have mineral on the weekend. Don't you have it?'

'Course we do,' Bob said.

'Course we do,' said Nell.

They never had mineral, Mam said they couldn't afford it.

'Give us a taste,' Nell said.

Kitty handed her the bottle as if she couldn't care less. Nell wiped the top fastidiously, raised it to her lips and tasted for the first time the glorious sweet bite of Tizer. It tickled her throat, which she now realised had been dry.

'Can I have some?'

Kitty looked at Bob and shrugged. Nell passed him the bottle.

'It's too windy,' Kitty said, standing on one leg and pointing the other one out straight in front, 'I'm going in.'

Dad came round the corner, head bent into the wind. This was the weather he hated. I'd rather anything, he'd say. Let it rain and pour, let it snow, I don't care. I bloody hate windy weather. Loathe and hate and detest it. He swore through gritted teeth as he went down the street against it. And now he'd walked in it all the way from Fallowfield, all across Mellands where it was wide open. His face was grim. 'What kind of a mood's your mam in?' he asked.

'Moaning,' said Nell.

'As per usual. It'd take a bloody good 'un to please your mother.'

'I've had some mineral, Dad,' Bobby cried. 'It's smashing!'

Dad straightened his shoulders and walked in.

'Your dinner's ruined,' Mam said sourly, not looking up from the newspaper she was reading. 'It's in the pig bin.'

Dad sat down on the other side of the fire. The kids trooped in to hear the news of Auntie Bennet. 'I've had a pie,' Dad said. 'No matter. I'll get some toast later.'

'I'll get you some toast, Dad,' Violet said, standing in the kitchen doorway with the tea-towel in her hands.

'I tell you what, Vi,' Dad said, easing off his black shoes, 'I wouldn't mind a cup of tea; a cup of tea and a bowl of red-hot water for me feet.'

And while Violet boiled up a kettle and the big pan, he started telling how sad he'd found Bennet because she was sick of going nowhere; how bored she was, she who'd always been so lively and gone about here and there as free as a bird and had a good time. And none of her so-called friends came near from what he could tell, but he reckoned that was because of Walter. Smarmy piece of work.

Nell sat on Dad's knee, Bobby on Mam's.

'She just sits there in this rocking-chair,' Dad said.

Violet brought him a bowl and he lowered his feet down very carefully into the red-hot water, gasping, 'Aaah!' at the heat. 'I'll fetch your tea,' Vi said, and was off again, boiling up another kettle to pour in for him when the water started to cool down.

'She's started knitting,' Dad said. 'She just sits there in this rocking-chair knitting. She's making something for John and Grace's youngest. And *he's* a funny bugger too. Sitting there like a wet week-end. Shifty. Talks like he thinks he's better than you. I hate that.'

Violet brought Dad his tea, and he poured it into the saucer and blew on it to cool it down. Mam clicked her tongue.

'It's a bad marriage, Bessie,' he said.

'Aye, well,' Mam sniffed, took off her glasses and started cleaning them, 'there's plenty of them about, i'nt there?'

Later Uncle Edmund came round. He said he'd been to see Bennet and Walter a month ago, and they'd started having a row right there in front of him. 'Effing and blinding,' he said, 'you should have heard it. You think, If that's what it's like when I'm there, what goes on when they're on their own? Here, here, I said, that's enough! She starts crying. "Showing me up in front of my brother," she says. And he just sits there like a big baby looking at her, just about sucking his thumb. I don't know, he's weird-looking, looks like a little monkey.'

Dad shook his head. And later still when Edmund had gone, Nelly heard Dad say to Mam: 'It's worse than I said. He's knocking her about. So help me I'll swing for the bastard.'

'What do you mean?' cried Mam righteously. 'She's an injured woman!'

'Dun't make no difference. She told me after he'd gone out. She said he's slapped her once or twice. "Mind you," she said, "I get him back, oh, I do, I get him back." She won't take it, our Benny.'

'She's made her bed,' said Mam.

Dad told her to shut her mouth and it turned into a row, which turned into a fight that grappled and staggered all about the room and round the children who were sitting at the table doing a jigsaw. Then

Dad went down the pub, and when Nell looked round a bit later, Mam was sitting looking into the fire with a mournful face, and you could tell she'd been crying.

'You're as good as any of them. You're as good as any of them,' Dad said. He was drunkenly dissolving cubes of red jelly in hot water. Nell and Bob watched, fascinated, as he stirred. 'That's the way,' he said gruffly, 'now the cold.' The jelly slopped and glistened like a jewel in the bright kitchen light. Dad poured in the cold and stirred, round and round slowly and carefully with the wooden spoon. He'd washed out a couple of old sauce bottles, soaking them for hours in hot sudsy water to get rid of the sauce smell. They stood clean and shiny on the draining-board. He's doing this because he loves us, Nell thought. Dad's eyes squinted against the smoke from the cigarette sitting crooked on his lower lip.

'There we are,' he said; all his movements were deft and delicate as he poured a fine stream of thin red liquid into each bottle, screwed on the caps and gave each one a shake. 'There!' Handing them one each. 'Now you take these out with you and you tell them you've got mineral too.'

Bennet didn't come for so long that they'd nearly forgotten all about her when she did, unannounced, getting dropped off in front of the house from a car driven by a man no one knew. He wasn't her old husband, Walter.

Dad was planting pansies in the front garden, hoping to get them in before the rain, Nelly standing by to help. The front door was open. In the house Mam was singing some of her dirty songs to Bob, making him laugh, and Violet was cuddling Jock on the sofa. Mam's songs were all about shit. Nell heard her dirty fruity laugh, and then she was off again: 'Shine a light, shine a light, shine a light a minute ...'

'Who's that bugger?' Dad muttered, standing up straight and rubbing the earth from his hands; then he was rushing off down the path to open the gate for Bennet as the man drove off. She had a stick.

'Hello, Sam!' she said brightly, smiling her big smile, but she was different, a faded little bird, and when she came walking up the path one foot dragged along while the other did all the work.

'Oh, my little chickadees!' she cried, as they all appeared on the steps and Jock came running, shaking his hindquarters. 'You're enormous! Violet! Look at you!'

Her kisses were boozy.

She sailed in like a beautiful ship standing high out of the water, crossed her dainty ankles in button boots one over the other on the fender and made a big fuss of Jock. 'Well, I was just in town,' she said, 'and my friend said he was passing this way so I thought, What a good idea! See my old Sam and his little chickadees.'

Mam made tea. Bennet drank a cup and accepted a slice of seed cake, holding it prettily between small pointed fingers. 'Look at your poor old auntie!' she said gaily, looking down at her feet. 'Hop-Along Lil! Hey, a new act! Can you see it? Hop-along Lil, the dear little songbird with a broken wing. Go down a treat at the old Hippodrome. Come and sit down, my love. Look, your auntie's brought you some pineapple rock.'

Bennet sat with her back ramrod straight, her head with its pile of hair like a large and gorgeous hat poised with swan-like grace above her slim white throat. Her eyes were bright and laughing. Dad sat down opposite her, got out his new pipe with its black stem and red bowl and contemplated it.

'Any time you want, Ben,' he said, 'you can come here, you know. Any time you want.'

'I know that, Sam,' she said emotionally, 'I know I've got some bloody good brothers.'

Mam was in the kitchen. You could feel her there, listening. Violet put the radio on. An orchestra played 'Stars Fell On Alabama' and Bennet hummed along. It began to rain, long silver stripes lashing against the window.

'Ooh, this is nice, sitting by your lovely fire,' said Bennet, crinkling her eyes at the warm.

'Take your coat off, Benny,' said Dad gently. He got out the Dura-glit and started polishing the fire brasses. Mam came and sat next to the sideboard. It was like a lot of afternoons. The rain came down, hush hush hush. Dad and Bennet were given to reminisce on such afternoons. Mam sent Violet out for biscuits. Dad remembered their maid, Mary. This was wondrous to Nell. The very idea of having a maid. 'Oh, in those days,' Dad said, 'it wasn't so special. Didn't seem so special, did it, Ben?'

'Oh, no!' She shook out a match and threw it into the fire. Blue layers of smoke formed, delicately spreading in the dim air above the fireplace. 'It's not like we had a house full of servants or anything, not like where you used to work, Bessie.'

'I know that,' Mam said.

'It was only Mary,' Dad said. 'She was only a young thing herself, I suppose, but she seemed grown-up to us, didn't she, Ben?'

The boys had a spyhole bored out in the floor of their bedroom and could spy on her as she sat in the kitchen at night. She cooked eggs for herself. 'We can see you cracking goggies!' they shouted down through the spyhole. Uncle John and Uncle Edmund sacked her for telling them off one night when she'd been left in charge of them. Put her into the gig with all her things, drove her down to the station and left her there in tears.

'Poor Mary!' Bennet said. 'Fancy being left in charge of us lot! Dad had to go dashing down the station to get her back, and she was so upset she refused to come. She did in the end, though, and he made them apologise to her. Oh, he wouldn't have you being rude to Mary, our dad. They got thrashed for that.'

Violet bought ginger biscuits and ran back through the rain, not wanting to miss anything. They were remembering Molly.

'Do you remember Erskine Street, Sam?' Bennet asked.

Erskine Street was Liverpool.

'Molly brought that little cat home.'

Dad puffed away at his pipe and clouds appeared. 'She was a devil for bringing things home.'

'She loved that little cat,' Bennet said. 'It used to keep me awake at night with its purring. Sitting on her bed washing its paws. Mam used to go mad. I had to jump up quick first thing when I heard Mam coming and chuck it out of her bed for her. She'd never wake up. Every morning the same, it'd have got in the bed and be lying

there with its head on the pillow as if it thought it was a real person.'
Bennet laughed and belched, putting up her hand to her mouth.
'Oh, pardon me!'

'Soft-hearted she was.' Dad tapped the bowl against the fireplace.

'Oh, we had some good times there, didn't we, Sam?' Bennet's
voice thickened and wavered.

'Now now, Benny,' he said gruffly.

Mam sighed palely in the back of the room, wearily rose to her
feet and went into the kitchen.

'Now, you know me, Sam,' Bennet said, lighting another cigarette,
'I was never a one for getting down in the dumps, but now you
know, sometimes, Sam, I'm getting really scaredy-cat these days.
Every little thing's got my nerves on edge.'

Mam stood in the doorway with the kettle in her hands. 'You
want to go to the doctor's, Benny,' she said. 'You've never got over
the accident.'

'It's not that, Bessie,' she flashed a smile, 'it's that I'm not used to
it. Being in, I mean. He's a funny man. Doesn't like me going out at
all, you know the way some men are? He gets ever so jealous, I've
never known anything like it. It's not that he's not a nice man or anything, he is, he's an extremely kind man, he really is, but he's jealous.
Terribly. And it does you in after a while, you know.' She sniffed. 'I'm
sorry, Sam.' She turned her peaky face towards the children and gave
a chill smile. Her eyes were red. 'It's OK, pets,' she said, 'your auntie
Bennet's just got a bit of a cold.'

Of course Bennet moaned about her husband. Husbands and
wives always moaned about each other. Mam and Dad did, Kitty
O'Neill's mam and dad did; Uncle Edmund moaned about Auntie
Isabel; Granny moaned about Grandad; when the Proctor house on
Forber Crescent caught fire and Mrs Proctor, coming home from her
sister's, heard that her husband was still inside the burning building,
she cried: 'Let the bugger burn! Let the bugger burn!' People laughed
and called it out to each other in the street. Mr Proctor got out.

That's how things were. The only married couple Nell knew who
didn't moan about one another was Uncle John and Auntie Grace.
She tried hard to think of another.

'What's she go and marry that old bloke for anyway?' she asked Mam in the kitchen.

Mam jiggled the knitted cosy on to the teapot. 'I suppose she wanted someone to take care of her in her old age,' she said.

'How old is Auntie Bennet?'

'Oh, now,' said Mam, and had to stand and think. The kitchen window reflected in her glasses. She counted on her fingers. 'About forty-three,' she said, 'probably.'

That was terribly old.

'That's what happens to them as are too choosy,' Mam said grimly, straightening her pinny, 'they end up having to make do with what's left.'

'Where have you *been*? Where have you *been*, my queen?'

'Oh, I called at our Sam's.'

The old ham. Sharpening the kitchen scissors there by the range.

'Bennet, you know I love you.' Out of his silly mind. Drunk again. Looking at her with that fixed, hostile, needy stare, as if his eyes were bleeding all over her. Look, she wanted to say, I'm with you, aren't I? What more do you want? You dirty old bugger, you ought to be glad to have a woman like me. The skin below his bleary eyes hung low, so that the red fleshy sockets were revealed, raw and naked as genitals. The red matched his large lower lip, pendulous, shiny.

'Ah!' she cried, lowering herself down carefully into the rocking-chair. She was exhausted.

'How's your precious leg?' he cried, laying aside the sharpened scissors, falling to his knees at her feet. 'Shall I remove your boots? Oh, let me. Yes, yes.'

He was reeling, rolling, eyes hooded. Poor old Walter. Slurring his words, stumbling over them with his tongue as if they were boulders.

'You must not go out in the cold, my little darling, no, no, you must stay here in the warmth of our hearth, with your husband. Your *husband*, Bennet!'

'Oh, leave off, Walter, do!' Bennet turned her face to the wall and rocked, sighed, closed her eyes. She was drunk too. She'd been in the Red Lion on the way back, she'd had a few stouts, her head was moiling and beginning to ache a little. Her own words slurred. She hated that. It's not enough that I'm an old drunk, she thought, I have to sound so obviously like an old drunk too. Just at those times when you're most confident, most bright and glorious and shining, that's when your stupid voice lets you down, when it catches its feet, one behind the other, and trips you up on your arse in front of everyone.

'Oh!' she said, and thumped her hand upon the arm of the chair.

Just sitting here and her leg aching away down there, aching all up her side. What was the point of going out if you came back feeling like this? 'I am a prisoner here,' she said, her eyes filling with tears.

'No no,' he said, 'I am *your* prisoner.'

Absently she stroked his head upon her knee.

'No no no. You can go out whenever you like. I can hardly bloody walk.'

'Poor little leg!'

'Oh, stop it, Walter! You do overdo things.'

He was like a weeping sore. He raised his thick-haired, grizzled head tragically. 'Where did you go?'

'I popped into the Red Lion,' she said, and yawned. 'Oh, where's my knitting?' She laughed. 'Look at me, old granny sitting with me knitting! Heigh-ho!'

'Was there many in there?'

'Not really. A few. Dolly Bridges was there. We had a couple of stouts together.'

'Dolly!' He went into performance mode. Lower lip out-thrust, eyebrows raised, voice carefully modulated: 'Oh, well, if Dolly *Bridges* was there.' But his eyes glossed over and hardened.

No, she thought, tired, not now.

'Well, she's a fine one for my wife to be sitting talking to, isn't she? Do you know what they call Dolly Bridges in Platt Fields? Fallowfield Fanny. Fallowfield fucking Fanny. And you're sitting in the pub,' the voice deepening, plateauing in seriousness, 'in full view of everyone, drinking stout with the likes of Dolly Bridges! I suppose you were approached. I suppose you know that if you sit drinking in broad daylight with a woman like Dolly Bridges, who hasn't got a brain in her fat head and spreads her fat arse for anyone who'll buy her a pint of stout—'

'Don't you dare speak to me like that! How dare you? I wasn't brought up to listen to such stuff!'

'Well, Bennet, you know what you can do with it, don't you? Your gentility? You know exactly where you can put it, my love. Exactly where I am about to put my hand now ...'

She gave a great kick and he sprawled against the range with one knobbled brown hand splayed against his heart, the other holding her dainty brown button boot. He looked at it and smiled fondly. She was so beautiful, Benny Brown against her backdrop of flowers, old roses, honey-honeysuckle, flashing eye and prancing hair: Beautiful Benny Brown.

'You know, Walter,' she said thickly, 'you really are the most incredible old fool. Give it up, love. Give it up.'

He smiled the smile of an enemy. That's the kind of love it was too, an enemy's love, real, of course: she saw it all so clear for a second. It was the look that came on his face, the look that told you this was love, or something, but a bitter love, the kind of love that wished you harm. 'You're sick, Walter love,' she said, 'you sick, barmy old thing. That's what you are. Aren't you?' Something in her head dived and swooped like the Bobs at Belle Vue. 'You're a sick, barmy old thing. Aren't you lucky I love you? Aren't you? God pardon me for my sins, but I do.'

He was disgusting. Pity she felt. Such pity. If someone had to pity me like that, she thought, I'd die. God, what strange shapes love takes. He cuddled her boot. God, what are you playing at? You make us so easy to break.

'Poor old Walter,' she said.

'Bennet.' He moved, he kind of crawled from the base of the range.

'Poor old Walter.'

He was here again, leaning with his elbows on her knees like a child, making the chair rock. Trouble in his eyes. As if a lifetime of everything that could go wrong with a person, all the small injustices and fears and stabs and kicks and anything else, as if all of these had fallen down a deep, deep well and festered there, and turned into a slimy thing, a serpent, a loathly worm like in the ballads her father used to sing, the laily worm at the foot of the tree, that crawled out into the light of day and laid waste all the land for many a league. 'My sweet love,' he whispered, raising his lips, his seamed and longing face, for a kiss.

She pushed him away.

He struggled towards her.

'Oh, give it up, Walter!'

She wasn't going to give in. She wasn't kissing his big dried-up mouth. She wasn't giving him the satisfaction of winning, even if he hit her, and he would. He'd done it before, twice. He said it was to keep her from getting hysterical. 'I have to look after you, my love,' he'd said, weeping.

But instead of forcing it, he sat back on his heels, his face folded into a twinkling smile, and he began to sing at her:

> *Poor old Dicey Riley*
> *she has taken to the sup,*
> *Poor old Dicey Riley,*
> *she will never give it up,*

She threw her knitting at him. 'Stop it!'

> *For it's off each morning to the pop*
> *Then she goes in for another little drop,*

'Stop it!'

> *Oh, the heart of the roll is Dicey Riley.*

'Shut up! Shut up!' she screamed. 'I've had it to here!'

Walter stood and paraded by the range.

> *She walks along Fitzgibbon Street*
> *with an independent air,*

Oh, and then it's down by Summerhill
and as the people stare,
She says it's nearly half past one,
Ain't it time I had another little one?
Oh, the heart of the roll is Dicey Riley.

He sat down, arms opened, expansive.
'I hate you!' she shouted. 'I hate you!'
Up he jumped, with the kitchen scissors in his hand.

7

A Day Out

That was a great day out they had in Blackpool, before the strange evening that followed.

Violet and Stanley Mulcahy, Violet's friend Josie Spedding, Nell and Bob. First it was just Violet and Josie taking the kids, but Stanley somehow got included on the way to the station. Stanley looked like Mr Punch, rubbery-faced, big-beaked. All the Mulcahys did. Stanley was OK, though. Hardly said a word but smiled a lot, big rubbery smile. He was mad about Vi, you could see, the way he hardly ever took his eyes off her, smiled at her all the time, laughed when she acted daft. And she was always clowning, always easy with him. With everyone, really.

'Come on, you lot,' she called, beckoning from the end of the pier in her short jumper and tweed skirt. 'You two! Stop wandering off!'

The pier was noisy and crowded, the day overcast and a bit breezy, too cold to go in the great grey sea that rolled and swelled biliously beneath their feet. They went for a walk along the prom, went on the Big Dipper and the Dodgems and the Ghost Train; Stanley bought them candyfloss, and a toffee apple each. Nelly stroked the velvet nose of a white donkey called Merry. The sun came out and everyone cheered. Bob and Nell started giggling, tagged one another, ran round and round in circles.

Stanley bought a beach ball at one of the shops along the Golden Mile and they went on the beach and played catch, all apart from Nelly, who couldn't catch or throw for toffee and couldn't be bothered either. She sat and read her book, but was distracted by Josie's snorting laugh and Violet's high tee-hee, and the fact that every time Bob ran by he kicked up the sand at her with his big shoes so that it sprinkled on the pages of the book. Wet sand too, cold sticky clods of it. He was like that. Thought he was a big man now, swaggered like a man in his baggy trousers and Cousin Teddy's jacket that was too big for him, the sleeves hanging down nearly to the ends of his grubby fingers. Scruffy kid. Laughed like one too, forced and raucous.

She jumped up and thumped him and they ran miles and miles down the beach together before turning back.

Violet was putting down a Stuart tartan rug. Granny was a Stuart.

'Sandwiches!' Josie called.

Dad had packed egg with mustard and cress, and there was an apple each. Nell put her headscarf on because her ears were beginning to ache with the breeze. Violet crossed her legs on the rug, dark brown stockings and heeled sandals with little tear-shaped holes punched in the leather. Josie Spedding pulled out her camera and took a picture of them eating their sandwiches. And later, after the band had started playing jazz on the distant pier, and Stanley, still wordless, had waltzed gallantly with first Violet, then Josie; after it had started spitting rain and they'd packed up and started heading back along the beach in the direction of the station, Stanley got bold and put his arm about Violet's waist. She smiled and leaned against him coyly. Nell and Bob got silly, giggling, chasing about.

'Oh, shut up, you two. You pulled my arm then, our Bobby! Just stop it!'

Stanley just smiled at everything.

'Vi! Stanley! Look at me!'

Josie with the camera, beaming.

Vi and Stanley posed with their arms around each other's waists.

'Aw, that's nice. That's lovely,' Josie Spedding said, peering through the lens, preparing to press the shutter, but not before Bob and Nell had dashed up and ruined the shot, giggling, mugging at the camera, Nell sticking her laughing bespectacled face out from behind Vi, yanking down on her arm and shoulder; Bob getting practically right in front of Stanley and bending his head with a goofy grin.

'Oh, no, you two!' cried Josie, clicking, capturing them for all time. Stanley went on smiling. Violet did too, only just. She could have killed them. I'll get them later, she was thinking, but said nothing more than a mild 'Don't start, you two.' She didn't want to seem a harridan in front of Stanley.

Bobby just laughed and ran on ahead. They strung out along the sand – Bob way ahead, then Nell and Josie, with Vi and Stanley, arm in arm, bringing up the rear.

'Ey, your Vi and Stanley, eh, what do you think of that?' Josie kept saying to Nell. 'What d'you reckon of that, eh? What you make of him, Nelly? Your mam said anything?'

'Only the usual. You know what she's like.'

Grinning wildly, Bobby sprawled on his stomach on the cobbles that sloped down below the sea wall, chin cupped in his hands. Cocky.

'Look at *him*,' said Josie affectionately. 'He'll break a few hearts, eh?'

Click. She caught him.

The platform was full of day-trippers going back to Manchester. And the strangest thing happened while they were waiting under the pigeon-haunted girders for the great black engine on the other side of the track to uncouple from its carriages. All of the benches were taken, but Violet and Josie had managed to perch on the edge of a big wooden pallet outside the guards' room along with half a dozen or so other people including a roly-poly red-faced old man with an accordion, who was gazing absently away out of the end of the station towards the great outdoors. All huddled up in a thick grey coat, his arm

96

across the instrument, which appeared to have no case of any kind.

'You two keep well back from the edge,' Violet said.

And then Stanley, who'd only spoken about six words all day, began to talk to the accordion man; and the accordion man, who'd been old and vacant and about to doze off, perked up and chuckled and talked back. They were looking at the instrument, which was all silvery and sparkly on the outside.

Stanley, it turned out, knew about accordions. He and the accordion man talked to each other enthusiastically in accordion language, like people from the same place meeting in a foreign land. The accordion man opened up his instrument and it sang out. His thick cracked fingers moved deftly on the keys, just a few notes. People turned to look. And then he handed it over to tall gawky Stanley, who held it as if he'd always held it.

'I didn't know you played the accordion, Stanley,' Violet said.

'Oh, yes,' he replied. His elbows flexed. Suddenly some fast, jolly, jiggy thing was flying from his fingers, like musical notes in an upsy-downsy string on the air. He played a couple of bars with fluid ease, his face serious as if he was trying to hear something far away, then stopped. Everyone applauded. Nell and Bob burst out laughing, it was so strange, Stanley suddenly being clever. He'd made everyone smile. Nell was delighted and decided Violet could marry him if she wanted to. Violet seemed to think so too because she leaned her head on his shoulder all the way home on the train.

'Oh, you're back, are you? About bloody time too. Thought we were going to have to miss the beginning.'

Mam and Dad were going to the pictures to see Charlie Chaplin. Mam's thick legs clomped about in heavy brogues. Her dress, loose and belted with a pattern of small flowers all over it, emphasised her big hips and stomach. Thin and gaunt and long-faced, Dad stood waiting by the door, cigarette on his lip, flat cap on his greying hair.

'Hey, Mam,' said Violet, 'you ought to hear Stanley play the accordion. Isn't he good, Nell?'

'Fantastic.'

'Can I have an accordion, Dad?' asked Bob.

'Maybe one day,' said Dad. 'I didn't know Stanley had an accordion.'

'An accordion?' Mam cried. 'Oh, yes? Where are we going to get the money for an accordion from? Don't go raising the child's hopes. No, of course you can't have an accordion.'

'You'll have to get Stanley to give you a go on his,' said Dad.

'Now, Violet, you're in charge.'

'Right.'

'You two, you do what Violet tells you.'

'Right, Mam.'

'If she tells you to go to bed, you go to bed.'

'Right.'

Outside, the wind was getting up, and a spattering of drops hit the window. Nell poked up the fire. Bob rolled about with the dog, singing: 'When it's peach picking time down in Georgia, everybody picks on me.' He wouldn't get up, even when Violet gave him a jam butty and told him to sit up or he'd choke; he jammed it into his mouth, chewed, swallowed, pretended to choke, clutched his throat and screamed and arched his body up from the floor. Nell pushed him with her foot. He rolled over, put his hands behind his head and whistled tunelessly, crossing one knee over the other and swinging his foot about with reckless abandon so that it kept catching the edge of Nelly's book.

'Bobby!'

'You're a bloody nuisance, you are,' Violet said. 'He always starts when Mam and Dad are out. Ignore him, Nelly.'

He laughed in that stupid way he had, deliberately to infuriate. The music on the radio had changed to some slow torch song and he sang along with it in a loud, gormless voice, and when that changed to talking he stood at the back of Violet's chair singing 'Little Pal If Daddy Goes Away' and clutching a pillow to his chest. 'Little Pal If Daddy Goes Away' was Violet's favourite song. It made her sob if she was in the right mood. She couldn't stand to hear it desecrated in this way, leaned sideways and gave him a quick push with her elbow. Bobby staggered sideways and fell on the floor clutching his ribs and screaming as if impaled on a lance.

'Ignore him,' Violet said.

He played 'Scotland The Brave' by holding his nose and hammering his throat with two fingers while wailing, a technique that produced a deep, undulous bagpipe sound.

'Ignore him,' Nelly said.

He played 'Scotland The Brave' two or three times then 'Loch Lomond' then 'Scotland The Brave' again. They yelled at him to shut up. He played 'Scotland The Brave' another eight or nine times, then came and stood in their light. As one they sprang to their feet and grabbed him and threw him on the floor and tickled him till he screamed and laughed and cried all at the same time. He started thumping out at them with his bunched fists, then kicking, caught Nell a right one on the arm, struggled free and grabbed the poker and waved it in front of him, laughing raucously at them.

'You put that poker down now!' ordered Violet.

'Ha!' he cried. 'Ha! Ha! Ha!' He swished it about like a sword.

'You wait till we tell Mam,' said Nell.

'Couldn't care.'

Violet bashed him on the head, grabbed the poker off him and threw it down. He flew at her, they grappled. Nell joined in. Between them, she and Violet managed to drag him to the front door, chuck him out, slam it shut and collapse together against it in a fit of giggles.

'Violet!' he yelled.

'You're staying out!'

He hammered on the door. Jock barked and ran madly to and fro. It went quiet.

'Quick! He's going round the back!'

They dashed to the back and shot the bolt just in time. Bob battered and kicked at the back door.

'You're not getting in!' they shouted.

'I'm telling Mam!'

'Tell her!'

'I will! I'm telling my mam!'

He ran back to the front window. 'Violet!' he wailed. 'Let me in! I'm cold! It's raining!'

'Serves you right!'

'Violet! Violet!' he wailed for a while, then his face disappeared.

'What's he doing?' asked Nell.

'God knows.'

They ran to the back. No sign. To the front. There he was at the window, arm raised, a big brick in his hand, the one from the top of the rabbit hutch. 'I'm going to smash the window!' he bawled.

'Don't, Bobby!'

He drew back his arm, testing the weight of the brick, grinning. They screamed. He laughed and made as if to throw.

'He will! He'll do it!'

'Put it down, you fool!'

'Bobby, no!'

He kept bashing the brick towards the window, laughing and mad, always stopping it a fraction before it hit the glass. Each time, they screamed. Violet made a mad dash and opened the door. 'Get in, you bad boy!' she shrilled.

Bobby chucked the brick down and swaggered in smirking; they threw him down on the ground, punched and tickled him. 'Gerroff! Gerroff!' he yelled, rolling and fighting and giggling. In the middle of it all, the door opened and Mam and Dad walked in.

'Mam!' cried Bobby, bursting into tears. 'Mam! They're picking on me!'

'Ooh, you little liar!'

'What!'

'What've you been doing to that lad?' shrilled Mam.

Dad sat down by the fire and began stuffing his pipe. 'Can't bloody go out without all hell breaks loose,' he muttered.

'Get to bed!' Mam screamed, cuddling Bob fiercely. 'Get to bed! All of you!'

A rapping came on the door and she dumped Bob and went to answer it.

'I'm looking for Mr Samuel Bruce Holloway,' said a man's voice.

'Sam, Sam,' called Mam nervously, 'it's a policeman for you.'

Then the policeman was in the room and everyone fell silent.

'Upstairs,' Mam said, 'Nelly, Bob. Upstairs.'

★

When they crept back, after the man had gone, Dad still sat in his chair by the fire, frowning at the flames and puffing on his pipe. Mam was in the kitchen. Violet sat on a chair by the table, pulling at the fringes of the tablecloth, looking down into her lap and crying.

'What's the matter? What's the matter?'

No one took any notice of them.

'I'll swing for him,' said Dad, in a terrible low voice, 'God help me, I'll swing for him.'

Mam came in, eyes pained with sympathy. She gave Dad a cup of tea, then stood with her hand resting lightly on his shoulder, stroking it gently. 'Drink that, chuck,' she said softly.

He put one hand over his eyes as if he was shielding them from the sun.

Mam came over to them, hustled them out and told them to go and put their nighties on, quickly. In the lobby she whispered, 'Your auntie Bennet's dead.'

It didn't mean anything.

'Why?' said Bobby.

'An accident,' Mam said. 'Quick, go on up. Violet'll come.'

They didn't speak as they got undressed, put on Dad's old union shirts and got under the blankets. Violet came running up with big strides and crouched kneeling on the end of their bed. 'It wasn't an accident,' she said, tear-streaked, dramatic, 'it was murder.'

They stared at her.

Murder?

'It was Walter,' she said, 'her old husband. They've arrested him.' She started crying again. 'Her neck's broken.'

Bennet's neck. Slim, white, delicate.

Snap.

It was a row, that's all anyone seemed to know for sure. The neighbours had heard it, the shouting, the effing and blinding, all that; nothing unusual. They were always at it. But then the sudden silence. Oh, well, perhaps they'd made up. No one thought any more of it at the time. Not until the following evening when Walter was seen walking down the street, normal as can be. In fact, he was smiling.

He went into a phone box on Wilbraham Road and reported an accident. Ten minutes later he came back, and the next thing anyone knew was the ambulance, the police all over the place, the curtains drawn and, like a black veil falling over the house, a sense of tragedy and the awe of the word: murder, murder, murder, a Chinese whisper passing down the street.

You heard bits. *'That's twice this family's been touched by murder.'* Mam to Violet, whispering in the kitchen.

Twice?

Nell asked Violet but Violet wouldn't say anything.

Poor Dad. *Poor* Dad. Late at night he sat up, alone, staring and staring into the fire. His blue eyes watered day and night. Nelly and Bob played out on the front. 'Our auntie's been murdered,' they told the other kids.

'She hasn't.'

'She has. She's dead.'

'How did she get murdered?'

'Who did it?'

'Her old husband.'

'What did he do? Did he stab her?'

'Did he strangle her?'

'He broke her neck.'

The other kids looked at them with peculiar respect. Murder was a word from the cover of one of the gruesome novels Grandad liked to read. Murder was something in the paper, in a fairy story like Bluebeard or Mr Fox:

> Be bold, be bold, but not too bold
> lest that your heart's blood should run cold.

Murder was a word dripping red on a black background. It didn't happen to your auntie.

But it had. Auntie Bennet had been murdered. Murdered by her old husband. They whispered. Mam and Dad, by the fire, in the kitchen, in the lobby. And Mam and Violet. Nell asked her again, and again, and in the end Violet took her into the bedroom and closed the door and sat down on the end of the bed and half whispered, half spoke. 'Well, I don't know, I don't know if it's true, it might just be Mam, she might have got it wrong. Dad hasn't said anything.'

'What?'

Violet liked spinning it out.

'I don't know if I should tell you.'

'Oh, Violet!'

'Ssh!' Violet glanced sideways at the door. 'A long time ago. A *long* time ago ...' as if she was telling a story '... before he met Mam ...'

'Yes?'

'I don't know if I should tell you.'

'Violet!'

'Ssh! Don't tell a soul! It was all a very long time ago.'

Nell could hear Bobby in the back, talking to his ferret.

'Dad had another son. When he was very young. He was illegitimate.'

Nelly gasped.

'You know what that means, don't you?'

'Course I do.'

'Well. Anyway. This boy ...' Nelly leaned close to listen. 'This boy was had up for murder three years ago. We're not supposed to know, only Mam told me. He strangled a girl in a tram shelter and they hung him.'

'You're joking.'

'I wouldn't joke about a thing like that, Nelly.'

A brother. A half-brother. A murderer.

'Come on, you little beauty,' Bob said to his ferret. 'Good boy!'

'What was his name?' Nell asked.

Violet shook her head. 'I haven't a clue.' She took a deep breath and sat back on her heels. 'That's all I know, what I've just told you. And Mam said Dad said, "Well, that's it, he's no son of mine," and you're not to say a word, a word to *anyone*, I mean it or I'll get killed and Dad'll go mad. *I'm* not even supposed to know.'

'Why?'

'He doesn't want to think about it. He wants it to be like he never had a son in the first place. Apart from Bobby, of course.'

'No, I mean why did he do it? The boy. Why did he kill the girl?'

Violet sighed, leaning forward again. 'You know what it's like,' she whispered, 'He probably wanted to, you know, *have his way with her*. And probably she wouldn't. She might have laughed at him and he lost control. Men can't stand to be laughed at, you know. Some of them go mad. It's like a moment of madness and everything goes red and afterwards, I suppose, they feel terrible. Sometimes they say they don't even remember doing it. Terrible, isn't it?' She sucked breath through her teeth and shook her head. 'Terrible, terrible.'

I get mad, Nelly thought. I get so angry sometimes I could scream.

'Snowy!' Bob called. 'That's it. Good boy, Snowy.'

They sat in silence for a while, thinking of the boy and girl, two shadowy shapes in the darkness of the tram shelter; thinking of Auntie Bennet and Walter.

'You know he knocked her out of her chair. That's what Mam said. You know what? Mam said Walter's funny in the head. She said he stayed with her body all night and day before he told anyone, and then he tried to make out like it was an accident, like she'd fell out of her chair, but you know what they found? She'd been dead since the night before. He must have picked her up and put her back in her chair because they said her neck was broken, and the back of her head cracked open on the tiles round the fireplace. They know because of the blood on the tiles. And he must be mad, Mam said, because he'd just sat there with her all that time. He must have loved her. They're like that, you know, some of them. They just go mad. It's like they go mad with love.'

God save me from love like that, thought Nell.

8

The Village Pump

Bennet was not buried in Morland, in the shadow of the old church, among the ancient gravestones and the beautiful trees, but in a bleak city churchyard surrounded by mean streets.

Nelly stood holding Mam's hand. The coffin was ready beside the open grave and the priest was saying a prayer. Violet and Mam were crying. Dad's head was bowed, his eyes hidden. A crowd, all sombrely dressed, hushed: the uncles and aunties she knew, and the ones she didn't know so well, Uncle Sydney, Uncle Tom and their wives, Uncle Joseph, and some strange cousins. Auntie Lal was there with little Victor. And there were other people, show people she didn't know; nobody famous, Mam said. Walter did not come, of course, because Walter was in prison awaiting trial. Would they hang him? Like they hung Dad's other son, her half-brother. What was he like? Did he look like Bobby? Did he have the cleft in his chin? What did he feel like when they put the rope round his neck? Nelly put her hand to her own neck. She imagined it, scraping against her throat, scratchy and hard. She felt scared. Poor baby, she thought. Did he cry? How could he bear it? How could anybody? Would they put the rope round old Walter's throat? Would he think about Bennet's little neck that he broke?

Granny and Grandad stood side by side, Granny's face miserable, loose-jowled, a big brooch holding her blouse together at her throat. Grandad's cheek muscles moved as if he was chewing. She wondered if he would write a poem. He always wrote poems when people died. 'Passed beyond the veil', that's how he said it. She saw the veil, like the veil on the straw hat Granny always wore for travelling, blowing gently, mysteriously. The one he wrote for Auntie Molly was lovely. 'Loved one. Wing thy way through azure heights, rest from thine earthly labours.' Because she'd died in labour. Did he love Bennet enough to write a poem for her?

The prayer ended and the men crossed themselves and bent to the task. Nell felt Mam's hand quiver. Bessie closed her eyes and a shiver passed through the core of her. She couldn't watch. All her life she had had this fear: fear of being buried alive. The stuff of her nightmares.

And yet she had to watch. Had to open her eyes and see. It wasn't a very big coffin. She was only little, Benny.

Lovely little Auntie Bennet, thought Nell. No one else had an auntie like her, so tiny and pretty and vivacious. Where had she come from? So bright.

Dad's lips moved silently. He was mouthing his favourite poem:

> *Sunset and evening star,*
> *And one clear call for me!*

And his tears spilled over.

They started to lower the coffin into the grave. And a soft sound came, a muted scrabbling from below, as if Bennet had woken up in there and was fluttering with her soft fingers against the lid. Mam drew in a quick breath. Then a small brown sparrow flew out from under the coffin and tottered on the brim of the grave, scrambled in the grass, toppled, righted itself, hopped in an odd lopsided way, half flying, across the grass till it reached the path. One leg dragged in the dust.

'That's Bennet!' Mam whispered.

Auntie Lal, up from London with little Victor, was doing Nelly's hair. Grandad was at the table in his rumpled shirt. Through the open back door came the lovely flowery smell of Morland in summer, and the droning of bees. Nelly could see Granny in the garden, walking here and there, the white hair falling down from under her big straw hat in ringlets at the back.

Grandad was going through all his old certificates. He'd pulled the drawer right out from the table and had it before him, its contents arranged in ranks. It reminded Nell of the top drawer at home where

Mam kept all the birth certificates and rent slips and things: Dad's army discharge papers with his certificate of good character, Grandad's poems written out on thin blue paper and folded together, sundry bits and pieces, curtain rings, string, darning needles and a bobbin and an old pair of opera glasses, dark wine-red, all snug in a little box just the right shape for them. Thinking of these things made her homesick.

Auntie Lal whistled as she removed the rags from the hair at the side of Nelly's ear. It had never been curled before and felt funny. Nell could see big lumps of hair from the corner of her eye.

'Will it look like yours, Auntie Lal?' she asked.

'It'll look nicer,' Auntie Lal replied.

Funny. All the uncles were still alive but Lal was the only auntie left now. Yesterday they'd gone for a walk with little Victor, who found a chicken feather and stuck it behind his ear. 'I'm an Indian,' he said. Nell liked Indians better than cowboys. She had a daydream where an Indian kidnapped her and carried her away on his horse. As they passed the place where the pump should have been, where the maids used to go with their yokes, as they saw that it was gone and only a scrape of a mark left in the ground, Auntie Lal had had another little drink from her hip flask.

Lal went round the back of Nell to take out the rags there. She was so small, even smaller than Auntie Bennet, so small that standing she was scarcely bigger than Nell sitting.

'Auntie Lal?' Nell said.

'Yes, love?'

'Auntie Lal, is there going to be another war?'

Lal said nothing for a moment. Then, 'Course there isn't! Whatever makes you think that?'

Something she'd heard: 'Another bleeding war!' Dad had said, and he kicked the gate. 'Well, this one's not having *my* lad!'

Lal's kind eyes smiled. But terrible things *did* happen.

Granny came in, blinking from the sunshine.

'I don't quite know how to divide these up,' Grandad said, raising his bushy white eyebrows. 'I wonder if John'd be interested in the science certificates.'

Granny's eye fell on one of his lurid-covered murder mysteries lying on the big stuffed chair. 'You dinged old muck!' she snapped, grabbing it up. 'Leaving this stuff lying around.' She opened a drawer under the cupboard in the corner, shoved the book in, slammed it shut and went mumbling back out into the garden. But Grandad seemed not to have heard. He had come across a photograph Nell knew well, a picture of Molly and Bennet. She knew because of the stain on the back, because of Granny's scrawled spidery words: 'Muriel and Bennet, September 1909'. Two young girls dressed in their best. Elaborate big-buttoned collars. Dark hair parted at one side, swept back. Molly seated in a high-backed chair, Bennet standing with one arm upon its back.

Grandad looked at it for a long time. Then he placed it on one of the piles. 'She was my pride and joy,' he said softly, and continued with his task.

Molly or Bennet?

'Auntie Lal.' Nell lowered her voice. 'Do you think it was right? The verdict?'

Lal's small hawkish face frowning, hair-clips sticking out of her mouth, fiddling with the hair at the sides of Nell's face, delicately dabbing with her big tortoiseshell comb. Walter had got off. Not enough evidence, they said. Mam had gone to the trial. She'd got a bit of a taste for trials since then: she liked to go and sit and watch the drama unfold. She'd gone to Buck Ruxton's and sung to the tune of 'Red Sails In The Sunset':

> *Red stains on the carpet,*
> *Red stains on the knife,*
> *Oh, Doctor Buck Ruxton,*
> *You've murdered your wife.*

She told them about the other trials in great detail but she wouldn't say too much about Walter's. She said he wept all the way through it. He'd loved Bennet, he said. Several times he broke down. They were having a row, he said. Both of them had been drinking. He'd jumped up suddenly and moved towards her, not to hit her, no, no, he said, just to calm her down because she was getting hysterical, but she was startled, she was sitting in that rocking-chair she always sat in and she jerked backwards and the chair went over and she broke her neck and died instantly. When he saw that she was dead his mind gave way and he lay down beside her for a night and a day before his senses returned. He was a broken man.

There was not enough evidence to convict.

Nelly didn't believe it. They'd got Auntie Bennet's chair at home. It was Dad's chair now: he sat in it smoking his pipe and staring into the fire and rocking gently. It was dark brown wood with red, slightly shaggy material on the back and seat and arms, and the rockers made a comforting, sleepy sound, like the ticking of the clock on the mantelpiece. Nelly sometimes sat in it when Dad was out. Sometimes she tried to imagine how it would be, sitting there, and someone rushing towards you with his arms outstretched as if he was going to strangle you; she'd jerk backwards, experimentally. The chair was heavy. You'd have to jerk back terribly hard, she thought, to make it go over, and Auntie Bennet was not strong.

No one really knew what had happened and no one ever would. Except for Walter, of course, who'd gone away; and Auntie Bennet, who was dead. Perhaps her ghost would come back like in a book, all in a long white nightie, pointing her finger at the murderer. Like the picture of Nancy in her book of *Oliver Twist*. And he'd go mad and jump off the roof.

Lal took the clips from her mouth and pushed them into Nell's hair, scraping her scalp. 'I don't know,' she said sorrowfully, 'I just don't know. Anyway, there's nothing any of us can do about it now, so it's best if we all just put it out of our minds and get on with things. Life goes on, Nelly.'

She put her hand to her face and coughed. 'Right! Now go and have a look at yourself in the mirror. Go on!'

The mirror was over the fireplace. Nelly looked and saw her face like a clown with glasses and the dark hair flat on top and sticking out in big sausagy curls at the sides. At first it looked awful and she laughed, but then as she looked she thought her face changed and became older, and it seemed all right.

'Well? Do you like it?'

'I don't know.' She giggled.

Grandad looked over the top of his glasses. 'My goodness me,' he said jovially, 'who's this handsome young lady?'

'Go and show Granny,' said Auntie Lal.

Nell stood at the back door. She saw all these things that were so familiar: the lean-to with the big tree at the side, the privy at the bottom of the garden, the bean and lettuce and radish rows; and Granny, old Hannah in her big straw hat standing holding her side as if she had a stitch. All familiar. All safe. But different because Auntie Bennet was dead; because sausage curls sprouted at the sides of her face; because everyone was older, and the village pump was gone.

PART TWO

Clarinet Marmalade

9

Soldiers

It was the Jew's harp reminded him. Bobby out there in the back twanging away, sitting astride Ralph Brigg's brother's motorbike. Sam had been standing there a while, motionless, gazing out of the back window of his new council house, number 10, Fremantle Avenue, a bigger house than the old one and just around the corner. His reverie was of a young German soldier he'd had to guard, a young lad they'd taken prisoner. It was after Passchendaele. Bitter cold, November 1917. So cold the mud had turned to ice. They'd found this lad all on his own, sobbing in a dug-out in an abandoned trench.

How long had they tramped across that ripped-up wasteland? Him and five others. Johnny Acock playing that Jew's harp. Little Johnny Acock could play anything on that thing, anything at all. Marvellous. Spinks and Barber, and him with the ginger hair. And poor Clifford Clovelly, who'd caught it when the kitchen wagon got shelled. They'd got separated from the rest. God knows how. Rough going. The shell craters overlapped. Not so long ago – how long? – they'd been filled with water, and the rats swam in them, their sleek heads pushing through. Watching them, you thought they were more at home here than you, though this was your world, the only world, the only world you'd been born into, though looking at this you thought you might as well have been born on the other side of the moon. Here and there: things. Something that had been a wagon. A bloated dead horse, great black mound. Tree stumps. Barbed wire, nightmare knots of it, in clumps upon it, things you didn't think about. White. Rimed with frost. A German top boot stuck on a pole.

The trenches were great gashes in the desolation. The Germans had upped and gone. It was like the Mary-Celeste: helmets, rifles, grenades, everything just lying everywhere. Stank to high heaven.

Bodies here and there. They didn't bother him any more, seen enough. Going in for the attack, he'd been running over them as they stuck out of the earth. Arms, knees, khaki-covered, dusted. A booted leg, bent at the knee like a child climbing into bed.

In the trench they came across a German officer, unmarked, just sitting there like a waxwork with his eyes open but gone away, and you couldn't tell why he'd died. His uniform rotting on him. And there was this boy. He'd pissed himself and was in shock. Weeping and moaning. Kid about fifteen, terrified, poor little sod. Should never have been away from his mother. The way he stared at them, his eyes like a cat when it's seen a bird. God knows why he'd been left behind. Probably gone doo-lally when the shells came over, gone all over frozen. He had a bullet wound in his shoulder, but the cold had frozen it up. Cliff Clovelly offered him the water-bottle but he wouldn't take it. Just stared and stared, with a low sobbing moan coming out of his throat.

Spinks and Barber were all for finishing him off, but him with the ginger hair said, 'No, he's a POW, you can't do that'. Him with the ginger hair was like a big schoolboy. Always very serious. But, of course, there was also common sense. Rations were low. Johnny was for just leaving him where he was. Cliff and Sam didn't like it. Maybe if he'd been some great coarse Hun, but this was a kid with freckles on his nose, and he put Sam in mind of Georgie Greenwood, who'd been his mate when he'd first joined the Cheshires and come out with him from Manchester. Georgie was with him in the potato field near Elouges in the blazing heat with the shells bursting all around, hour after hour, waiting any minute to be blown away; and on the Ypres salient, scrambling and sliding and falling off those horrible plank roads in the dark into the mud that even now and for ever after through all eternity would heave and bubble sickly through his dreams. He wouldn't call them nightmares. Nothing that ever haunted his sleep was as bad as what he'd known to be real. Georgie was always terrified he was going to crack. Well, weren't they all? Show it and you're dead. One fool starts panicking and it spreads. They'd shoot you to stop it. So you'd never say anything, only to your best mate, and Georgie must have thought Sam was his best mate because he only ever told Sam how close to cracking he felt. You wouldn't have known it, though. Georgie got mown down by a machine-gun on the second day of the Somme. They'd had the order not to stop and help the injured, but he couldn't have anyway because he never knew the moment Georgie went down. All he remembered was getting knocked sideways into a shell hole and lying there for God knows how long, sipping from his water-bottle and listening to the crying and screaming and wondering if some of it was Georgie. Gorgeous weather it was. The sky so blue. Great waves of battle clashed above, endless. Hours he lay there listening to the poor bastards crying out for their mams. Like being in a hole in Hell listening to the damned. And you knew you could go mad. So you just sat there in your shell hole, resting against your haversack, sipping from your water-bottle from time to time and praying. But it never stopped. And you wondered where God was in all this and realised God wasn't there at all and that you were in Hell and had been all along.

God knows why. God knows what you'd done. And you lit a fag and savoured every last little thing about it because you thought you were going to die at any moment, and when you came out there were bodies piled up everywhere and hundreds and hundreds of big bluebottles buzzing in the heat, and the maggots and rats waxed fat, and someone gave you a bit of butterscotch to suck.

'What's your name, son?' Clifford asked, but the boy just went on with his moaning. He was so dirty, they all were so filthy. Caked and splattered from head to foot in mud.

A babe wet behind the ears. What could you expect from a kid like this?

'You kill him over my dead body,' Sam said. He was a man of few words, so he made those count.

In the end they took the boy with them across the wasteland in which they were lost. He was a lot better when they were on the move, though he never stopped shivering, big milky teeth chattering; and he never stopped crying, lifting his sleeve all the time to rub at his eyes and nose; and he never stopped scratching his head as if he'd rip his scalp to pieces. The wasteland stretched on for ever. Sometimes, very far away, they'd hear a shell explode, and the sound would hang for a while, ebbing softly like an ache.

They came across a sparse wood, just skeleton trees, black, agony in their upthrown arms. All covered in rime. Eerie, the way it glowed as the night came down. A mist hung over it all. And then they came to a farmhouse standing on its own near a blown-up crossroads and a row of dead black trees. Spinks shone his torch around. In the courtyard was a load of rusted wire and the remains of a fire. The people were long gone.

'Go on, Fritz,' Cliff Clovelly said, 'in there with you.'

Of course the house had been looted. Pictures hung crooked on the walls. Old clothes and toys were piled in one corner. Most of the wood had been taken but there were some old drawers they could pull out and break up for a fire. Old photographs fell out, people. One, of two small girls in white, had an address on the back, the Rue Something-or-other in Troyes. Sam and Cliff got a fire going in the grate. Him with the ginger hair found some straw and settled the lad down and gave him a fag. They still had plenty of black bread and enough tea and sugar, but Spinks and Barber started moaning about having to share their rations with him. And then Johnny Acock played his Jew's harp, and a cat came in from somewhere, purring and rubbing herself up against them all. Starving she was, poor bloody creature.

The straw was alive with a million fleas. Through the night they took it in turns to guard the boy. The sleepers tossed and turned. The boy slept heartily, knees drawn up in the straw, but towards morning he woke and sat up, scratched furiously at his head with both hands and coughed pathetically. It was Sam's watch. The boy bit his nails and wriggled about, rocking, feet pulled up beneath him.

'What you want?' asked Sam. 'Go to the lav?'

The boy stared miserably at him.

Wearily, Sam stood. 'Come on.'

It was only just light. A cold sun stood low in the sky. Sam took the boy round the back and waited while he peed up against the wall. Bitter cold. Bitter, bitter cold. Sam yawned enormously and thought about a real bed, with good thick blankets and the hot brown bottle wrapped in a towel that his mam used to lay in it half an hour before he went up. And then he saw that the boy had seen something and was gazing far away, beyond the gap where the farmhouse gate had been, beyond the blown-up crossroads, far, far away beyond the line of dead black trees.

Narrowing his eyes he could just make out the steel helmets.

Stretcher-bearers.

Trucks.

A column of German soldiers in retreat, bypassing the farmhouse, heading away as fast as they could.

For a minute or two Sam and the boy stood and watched. The boy shook all over like a hound that had seen a rabbit. His nose ran and his face was as pale as a duck's egg.

'Go on,' said Sam gruffly, 'bugger off.'

The boy's eyes flickered at him but he didn't move.

Sam came forward and gave him a push. 'Go on,' he said. 'Get back to your mam.'

Another shove and he was off, running, stumbling, his top boots kicking up a rimy dust that shimmered slightly in the freezing morning air.

There were tears in Sam's eyes. Well, this time they're not having *my* lad, he told himself, bad enough when they evacuated the poor little sod. Wouldn't have been so bad if his dad hadn't died, kid could've gone to Morland; but the old man was dead, and old Mam had gone down to Joseph's in Cambridge. So that was that. There hadn't been any money. His dad didn't even have a headstone, but they'd get him one one day, him and John and Edmund, they'd club together, though Joe was the one with the money, he should have done it. Sam felt bitter. Still, what was a headstone? What was worldly show? You were here and then gone, and what came after could only be better. Death held no fears for Sam. You went to your Maker, and your Maker couldn't care less about headstones and money and all the lords and ladies of the world. Your Maker couldn't care less if you were illegitimate. Sam was quite sure his dad was where he'd always known he was going to be, where his mam would soon follow. But when he

117

thought of Morland his heart ached, and when he thought of how Bobby had run away and walked sixteen miles home from Whaley Bridge, Peak District way, after having been evacuated for only two weeks, it came near to bursting with pride and joy. Half-way through a Sunday morning, church bells ringing, smell of Sunday dinners on the air, imp's face at the front gate grinning from ear to ear, covered in grime and sweating; sixteen miles, and there was his big mam on the bench outside the front door reading a book, legs stretched out in front of her, crossed at the ankle.

'Mam!' he cried.

'My little lad!' she shrieked, jumping up and running heavily down the path.

He told terrible stories about a big house and a posh woman, and being made to sleep in a bare loft and not having enough to eat, like some poor orphan in a book.

'He's not staying where he's not wanted!' cried Bessie.

'Oh, well,' said Sam, 'at least if we go, we'll all go together.'

Dangerous noisy thing, Ralph Brigg's brother's motorbike. They all took it in turns riding it up and down Wembley Road. Watching Bob there astride it twingle-twangling on that Jew's harp, Sam wiped one eye with his hankie. The first war had made him; it was through and through him like the writing on a stick of Blackpool rock. Nothing in his life had touched him like that German kid till Nelly and Bob came along.

He stirred the tea in the pot. Bessie had taken Jock to the PDSA to see if she could get something to calm him down. The bombs upset him and he was weeing all over the house. Bessie was going mad. Nelly and Violet were in the front room, Vi bouncing baby Jean up and down on her knees, Nelly doing her lipstick at the mirror over the fireplace, getting ready to go to Belle Vue with her friend, Kitty O'Neill. She wore an open-necked blouse, with a large square brooch of delicate golden tracery made up of the letters of her name. N-E-L-L-Y, all the letters elaborately entwined.

She hated her face in the mirror. It was so plain. Not noticeably squinty like when she was little, at least not so you could see with her glasses on, and it wasn't as if there was anything terribly wrong with it that you could put your finger on. She just didn't like it. It always looked wrong. The upper lip was too long and deeply cleft, that was from Dad. Violet had it too; it was even worse on her. Dad said she looked like a monkey.

Nell wiped a sheen of sweat from her too-long upper lip and bared her teeth to check them. Perfect, even, snow-white, the best thing she had. Fancy ending up married to Stanley Mulcahy. Still, Violet was happy. You couldn't deny that. She had a little house in Chell Street, just off Stockport Road in Longsight. Married into the Mulcahys, a big-beaked family, Dad said. Married when Stan was invalided back from France with a shattered kneecap after getting shot in the leg. He walked with a lurching limp now. Mam had been putting money by for a while towards the wedding. There'd been rows when Dad kept raiding her cigar tin of tightly coiled notes for booze money.

'You'd drink it, wouldn't you? You'd drink away your own daughter's wedding money!'

Violet in tears because she wanted to side with Dad, but it *was* her wedding after all, and she hated them to be rowing over her. She wanted everything to be nice and she didn't want anyone to fall out over it. Anyway, in the end the families went more or less halves on it, and it was a big white do with lovely flowers and Nelly and Berenice and some big Mulcahy girl all dolled up as bridesmaids. And it's a funny thing how none of them could ever have afforded it if it hadn't been for the war. Loads of work at Gorton Foundry at Peacock's, where they made engines, machine tools, armaments. Dad was in the Transport Department. Nelly wanted to go there too but Mam wouldn't let her. She thought it was too rough for a young girl.

'Mam, it's ridiculous! I'm seventeen. They'll be calling me up soon anyway. I've been out of school three years. I'm not a kid.'

There were some nice lads at Peacock's, she'd seen them when she was taking Dad's sandwiches one day.

'Don't you tell me what's ridiculous, you're not too big for a good hiding, you know. You stick where you are.'

'I'm fed up of Utley's. It's *boring*.'

'Everything's boring,' Mam snapped.

119

Fed up of standing there doling out dolly mixtures to snotty little kids, hairnets to old biddies.

Violet sang: "'Ride a cock horse to Banbury Cross ...'" and baby Jean with her floppy head laughed in a hiccuping sort of way.

Dad was thinking not about this but the last war, Nell could tell, gazing as he did with his faraway eyes out of the back window at Bob and Ralph Brigg mucking about on Ralph's brother's motorbike in the long grass.

By the time he's old enough, Sam thought, this one'll be over, please, God. They're not having *my* lad. Please, God, this one would pass over them all.

His back was bad. He rubbed it with both hands, took a deep breath, walked from the back to the front of the house and stood at the open door to look at his small square lawn and the beds he'd carefully planted with pansies and snapdragons.

"'... She shall have music wherever she GOES!'"

And down went Jean between Violet's knees, down to the ground, chuckling and gurgling.

Bessie came along the road. She stood in the gateway with legs apart, feet firmly planted on the ground with those flat, sensible shoes, graceless and portly, wide-faced, chin broad and shiny, nose bulbous. Her hair was kinked and rinsed the colour of caramel toffee, her small watery eyes sad and stoical. Without Jock.

'It was no good,' she said. 'He'd never have got any better.'

Sam scowled at her from under heavy brows. He'd been expecting it. 'He wasn't ill,' he said, 'not really.'

'He was miserable,' she said, coming up the path.

It was too warm in the room. Their eyes all accused her, the misery in them like dogs' eyes, watery and shining. The two girls, realising, set up a wailing as if they'd never grown up. Baby Jean joined in. Hearing the noise, Bobby dashed in from the back. 'What? What? What?' he cried.

'Jock's dead!' cried Vi.

Bobby's face went red. 'No!'

'He wasn't ill,' said Dad.

'Oh, little Jock! Little Jock!' sobbed Nell.

'Why?' wailed Violet.

'Vet said he's had to put down loads.' Mam put her purse down on the mantelpiece. Through the window Ralph Brigg could be seen fleeing down the front path. 'Now, you're not to take on too much,' Mam said, without much hope. 'He said it was the best thing all round. You wouldn't want him to suffer.'

'You knew, didn't you?' Dad said. 'You knew when you took him.'

'*I* would've cleared up all the mess. *I* don't mind!' said Nell.

'You're a bloody murderer!' Bob yelled. Tears poured down his face.

'Don't you dare!' Mam turned on him, one thick finger held aloft. 'Don't you bloody dare, any of you! Someone had to! Someone had to! *Don't – you – bloody – dare!*' And she stormed from the room, slamming the door as hard as she could and ran heavily upstairs and started sorting out the laundry that lay in a big pile on the bed. Her eyes were dry but narrowed, her lips tight. 'Someone had to,' she repeated aloud. Stupid soft things, someone had to. Poor dog, shaking and suffering, like Bonfire Night every night. Too much for him. Best thing. Kinder. They thought they loved it; keep it here they would, in misery, just so they wouldn't have to cry over it. Selfish! Well. She was stronger than that. All right for them. Leave the dirty work to poor old Mam. Let her be the one to take the poor little thing down there, trotting on his lead with his stumpy legs running alongside and his stub of a tail wagging. She who had to sit and wait with him and look him in the eyes.

'He'll be all right, Mrs Holloway,' the vet said. 'Won't know a thing about it. Best thing all round.'

'Always me,' she said sorrowfully now, to the empty room, 'always me.'

'Your Jock? Your little Jock?' Kitty was horrified. 'I can't believe I'll never see his little bright-eyed face again coming to the window whenever I walk up your path.'

Nelly and Kitty were in Kitty and her sisters' bedroom doing each other's legs with cocoa and a black line up the back, to look like silk stockings. Nelly had done her hair in rags the way Auntie Lal had taught her. Kitty didn't need to. Kitty's hair was a lovely shiny dark red with a deep natural wave that swung about her face and on to her shoulders, and wayward curly bits that stuck out here and there somehow just where they should. Nell and Kitty were best friends now and went out together at least once a week.

'I don't feel like going out,' Nell said. 'It's ruined everything.'

'Rats,' said Kitty briskly. 'Do you good to get out. Take your mind off it. No point wallowing.'

Nell was all red round the eyes and the tip of her nose. She had to take her glasses off and touch up her powder. A big heavy weight sat in the middle of her chest and she wanted nothing more than to go home and go to bed and have a good cry, but the atmosphere at home would be terrible. Kitty punched her in the arm. 'Come on, kid,' she said, 'best foot forward,' and they went out smelling lovely, bright red lipstick and pale matte powder, caught the fifty-three to Belle Vue and got off by the greyhound stadium. Vivacious was the word for Kitty. The way she walked, erect, swinging her wide shoulders in her nice little suit. Nelly knew that most of the looks they got were for her. You saw them, their eyes as they slid over you and lit on the full-lipped redhead with the good legs, and stayed there and followed. It's just how it was. But there were always one or two who had eyes for Nell. One or two, and they were usually the quieter ones.

Great swathes of Belle Vue were cordoned off for the army, but crowds flocked to the Speedway, and the Kings Hall was open for the circus. Nell and Kitty went dancing at the Coronation Ballroom and were picked up by two soldiers home on leave, Kitty's tall with very black eyebrows that met in the middle, Nell's a young man called Alan who came from Heaton Chapel. He'd been in Egypt and Crete and was very tanned. His fair hair was cropped short, the tips of it sparkling in the ballroom light, and he danced with her without speaking, humming to the music, smiling somewhere over her head. Kitty's fellow was called Oliver. When the music finished, he suggested they sit down for a drink and the four of them moved over to a table. Nell never knew what to ask for in the way of drinks, she couldn't stand the taste of alcohol, any kind she'd tasted so far anyway.

She hated it when people tried to make her drink. 'Oh, go on,' they'd say, 'just a little 'un, here,' and down they'd plonk a glass of something awful she'd have to force down as if it were medicine. She always asked for tomato juice, Kitty for a Babycham. For some reason, tonight, she didn't ask for a tomato juice. It might have been something to do with the boys' accents, definitely a bit on the posh side. So when Alan said, 'It's a Haig for me. How about you?' she replied, 'Yes, a Haig for me too.'

There was an advertisement: 'Don't be vague, ask for Haig.' She didn't know what it was but it sounded sophisticated. The boys went to the bar.

'Oliver!' said Kitty gleefully. 'What a name! Olly! Yours isn't too bad. Smart chaps, what?' and she laughed, throwing back her head. The girls lit cigarettes. Nell's lips left a bright red kiss on the end of hers. 'Oh, I say!' She laughed. 'Jolly good show!'

You could have a laugh with Kitty. You could have a great night.

When it came, a Haig was a whisky, and it brought tears to her eyes and made her cough. 'Whoops-a-daisy,' said Alan, smiling.

Stupid me, she thought. How did people ever drink this stuff?

Kitty and Oliver chatted chummily. Alan smiled at Nell quietly for a long time. He was a bit parroty. Not grotesquely so, just an amiable hint of it. Very pale blue eyes with a faraway look. Big pink lips. 'You have sad eyes,' he said eventually. She thought that was a nice thing to say.

'Well,' she said, 'that's probably because our old dog was put to sleep today. Just before I came out.'

'Oh dear!' His eyes changed and he seemed seriously concerned. 'You must feel terrible. There's nothing worse than when your dog dies.'

He said he used to have a dog called Boxer. Boxer wasn't a Boxer, he was just called that because he used to sit on his hind legs and box you with his paws. Only in fun, of course. He was a mongrel, a really stupid dog, but you get so attached to them; he knew, he'd cried more when Boxer got lost than ever over anything else, and that included when his grandma died, though it sounded terrible to say it. She asked him how old he was when Boxer died and he said twelve, or thereabouts. Nell found herself describing to him Jock's eager face with the hair hanging over his eyes, and his hard box-like body quivering in your arms, and the way he used to stand at the gate with his ridiculous tail erect, watching the activity of the street. 'He wasn't ill,' she said, 'he was just nervous. Supposing they took that attitude with all those poor men with shell shock?'

And how could Mam be so hard? Never a tear from her!

'She just did it! She just did it without consulting any of us, without – without even giving any of us the chance to say goodbye.'

'... the chance to say goodbye,' he repeated after her, dreamy-eyed.

And at this new and poignant thought, Nell's eyes filled up again, and she sipped the hideous whisky that burned her chest and was like the most revolting medicine she'd ever had to force down. As Dad always said, you can't argue with your mam. Well, who said?

Yes, who said?

She wasn't going to do as Mam said any more. The heat in her chest turned into anger and a fearful burn of pity. She decided she'd go out with this soldier if he asked.

'Are you a working girl, Nell?' She always introduced herself as Nell to the people she met now, never Nelly. Nelly meant Hey, Nelly, Ho, Nelly! in the schoolyard, and not on your Nelly, and My Auntie Nelly Had A Jelly Belly, and all kinds of stupid things. He leaned forward to offer her a cigarette.

She told him she worked in a paper shop called Uttley's. But she was leaving, she said.

'Oh, really? What are you going to do?'

'I'm going to work at Peacock's,' she said, inclining her head for a light.

10

Peacock's

She went to work at Peacock's in spite of Mam, and Kitty O'Neill jacked in her packing job and started with her.

For a hundred years, since the first running sheds had gone up on the farmlands and wild-flower meadows of old Gorton (all that remained was Sunny Brow Park and a few bits of open ground along the railway), Beyer, Peacock on the far side of Hyde Road had been making locomotives and trams at Gorton Tank. Now it made tanks and shells, and engines for the Burma Railways.

Nell took to it straight away, in spite of the heat and the noise and the fact that you scarcely ever saw daylight. She liked the underground feel of it, as if you were a gnome labouring away in a cavernous warren somewhere far inside a mountain. She liked the clang and clamour and hiss, the steam, the echo, the smell of oil, the long, packed benches, the cathedral-sized halls of towering machinery. Everything excited her. She liked going out in the early morning with Kitty, walking down into the crisp-smelling bowl of Sunny Brow Park, past the swings and the witch's hat, and up the other side. She liked clocking on with all the others, smoking a cigarette in the yard on her tea-break, clocking off, the big gates opening, the day shift pouring out. Best of all she liked the boys.

Nell and Kitty were put in the boiler shop. They had to climb up massive steel ladders to the tops of great machines that steamed and simmered, and there they had to check the dials and pull the heavy levers, yank the handles, twist the big wheels, all polished and shiny like the brasses Dad buffed up by the fender.

'Here, love, I'll just hold the ladder for you, you can't be too careful.'

'Nell!' called Kitty from her eyrie alongside. 'Cheeky buggers are getting a right eyeful.'

'Easy does it, pet! Just a little bit more of a stretch, that's it!'

Nell looked down. Grinning faces, white teeth in oil-smeared skin. They were looking up her skirt.

'Ha ha, very funny,' she yelled down, prickling with embarrassment but refusing to show it. She wouldn't have minded but there was that one over there, the one with fair hair leaning against a machine, behind him all those stripes, the pipes of different thicknesses all gurgling and clicking across the battleship-grey wall, grinning cynically but not joining in. She felt herself blush all the way down her neck. What knickers have I got on? she thought. Not that she had any nice ones anyway.

'Clear off!' yelled Kitty.

'OK, darling,' called a bulky Scots man in clogs, who walked up and down the workshop with a bucket all day.

'Throw me a rose, Juliet!' someone else crooned.

'Blimey! A scholar!' said Kitty.

She and Nell giggled.

'This is awful,' said Nell.

'Ey, Nell.' Kitty checked the dial as she'd been told to. 'How's your knicker elastic?'

'Holding up.'

The men were dispersing back to their work. 'We ought to wiggle ourselves around a bit next time,' said Kitty, 'really give them something to look at.'

'Kitty, you're awful, you are.'

Throughout the morning, singly or in knots of two or three, the men hovered persistently around.

'Like flies round a lightbulb,' said Nell.

Kitty could blow really good raspberries. They ended up giggling all the time. Nell felt happy. This was much better than school, the thought of which still gave her a shudder; and much better than always being stuck behind a counter somewhere. Thank God she'd seen the back of Uttley's. Not that she was any better off. Mam still took all her wages and gave her pocket money as if she was a kid, just like she used to do with Violet.

'We're going to complain about you lot,' Nell told the cocky men, as she and Kitty went for their break.

'Lead us not into temptation,' said the fair-haired one, almost as an aside, deadpan, his hair hanging in greasy chunks over his forehead. Another went down on his knees and made as if to bare his breast to her. 'Nell, oh, Nell!' he cried. 'Forgive us our sins.' His face was all black like Al Jolson's.

'That's blasphemous,' she said. She tried not to smile, but couldn't help it. A funny thing she'd noticed: that Kitty was the pretty one and she was not was indisputable, but here, where they were not on the town together, it didn't seem to matter. If anything, she thought, the men were more friendly towards her. They were nice, she thought, you could be mates with them and that was a good way to be with blokes because then those one or two who were going to fancy you could get to find out about it. All that looking up your skirt was just them being fools.

'We can't have this,' she said to Kitty. They were in the big yard and had just finished eating their butties. Kitty's were sugar, Nell's prem with the tiniest touch of piccalilli from Stanley, who worked in the Co-op and got stuff for them now and then. 'Mr Bradshaw ought to stop them. He can see what they're up to, he should stop them.'

Kitty lit the cigarette they were sharing. 'He's as bad as them,' she said.

'These overalls are bugger-all use in a place like this, not when you're going up and down ladders all day.'

Huge iron doors were banging up and down on the other side of the yard, men in brown overalls loading boxes on to a truck.

'Yes!' agreed Kitty. 'We ought to get proper boiler-suits like the fellows. I ask you!'

'Did you see that one with the fair hair?' asked Nell. 'The one that didn't come and look up our skirts?'

'I did, yeah. Jimmy.'

'Jimmy?'

'Yeah. One of the others called him it. Oh, yes, I keep my eyes and my ears open, I do.'

Another thing, thought Nell: with those turbans on she's not got the advantage of all her red hair. It's more equal.

Jimmy.

'Well, anyway,' Kitty went on, 'we can't have this. Are you for coming with me to complain?'

'I certainly am.'

'Right. Hang on, let's do our lipstick.'

Kitty handed the cig to Nell to finish off and got out the lipstick they were also sharing. She did her lips using Nell as a mirror, then off they marched to the offices. In the high, echoing corridor, a door stood open, and through it Nell saw long benches with sinks in, and a blackboard upon which someone had drawn a cartoon of that funny little man with just his fingers and nose and the bald crown of his head showing over the top of a wall. And there were two young men, both not bad, one with golden hair and one with black. And both of them were sitting on high-backed stools at one of the benches, drawing absorbedly and eating sandwiches. One of them looked up, the dark one, round-faced, pale, Italian-looking, and gave her a thin half-smile.

'Here we are,' said Kitty, and rapped on a door.

Next morning they were kitted out with boiler-suits that they cinched in at the waist. With those and the turbans that covered their hair, they giggled together in the wash-room, 'Look at us! Look at us!', and took even more care with the lipstick and eyebrow pencil. The men laughed and whistled when they came in in their boiler-suits, calling them spoilsports.

Nell was going out with Alan, a nice lad, quiet yet easy to talk to. He was OK, nothing special. They went to the pictures and walking in Reddish Vale. He told her about getting bombed in the Mediterranean. He was going to be an engineer after the war and kept wanting to know all about what they were doing at Peacock's, and he laughed because she didn't understand all the questions he was asking.

'Oh, don't ask me,' she'd say, 'I haven't the foggiest what you're on about.'

'You are funny!'

She wasn't sure it didn't get on her nerves, him finding her funny all the time.

'How do you know what you're doing?' he asked.

'I just do the right things at the right times,' she replied, 'I don't have to under*stand* it. That's someone else's job. Anyway, what do you want to know for? Careless talk costs lives.'

He laughed again. They were walking along Hyde Road with one torch between them, its muffled beam illuminating a patch of muddy grey ground that moved before them through the blackness. She was wheeling her dad's bike. Suddenly he stopped and turned towards her across it, dropping his head upon her shoulder. The intimacy of it seemed to her quite inappropriate. She hardly knew him. What a shame you couldn't just go out and have a good time with a boy without all this.

'I like you a lot, Nelly,' he said, 'a *real* lot.'

He did. She wondered why. It was surprising and strange. He didn't have eyes for Kitty at all, only her. And she could take him or leave him like a coffee cream. He kissed her. 'Listen, Nell,' he asked, 'do you like me?'

She steadied the bike and walked on. 'You're all right,' she said lightly.

He laughed again, irritating her. 'Listen, Nell, I haven't got much time. I'll be in Alexandria soon. What I want to know is, will you write to me?'

She was pleased. She could do that. She could write to him. Actually, it might be quite nice, better than having to kiss him. 'Yes, I'll write to you,' she said.

'I'm not brave, Nell,' he said. 'I get scared.'

She stood with one foot waiting to push off. Poor boy. She let him kiss her again but he had to go and spoil it by getting pushy and trying to open his mouth, so she gave him a shove and said, 'See you tomorrow,' and rode away on Dad's bike. She liked cycling through the blackout, particularly when there was a moon. She felt as if she was flying in the dark, down the steep hill of Sunny Brow Park and nearly half-way up the other side before the bike lost momentum and she had to get off and push. On the railway bridge on Levenshulme Road the air-raid siren started up with its great ominous wolf-howl at the bombers' moon, and her heart raced as she crossed the railway and freewheeled down the hill and round the corner into Sutton Estate. Something in her loved the bombs. She couldn't seem to take them as a serious danger to her at all, even when they fell close and the world around her shook. She didn't for one moment think that anything could happen to anyone she knew, and it didn't. Well, there was Stanley's leg, of course, but even that was OK really, it just kept him safe home for Violet and Jean. Her family was charmed. She knew because she'd had a dream where she'd woken up and seen Jesus standing at the end of her bed, his right hand outstretched over her in a gesture of protection. He'd faded and been replaced with Mary, who in *her* turn faded back into him. Mary was like a peasant girl. Jesus was like the statue that stood on the sideboard, given to Mam by an old Catholic lady she cleaned for. Everyone said it was too Catholic. Mam didn't care, she thought it was lovely. 'It's his face,' she said in tender tones, as if a young kitten had come into the house, 'he's got such a sweet face.'

It was funny after the dream, waking feeling very peaceful, going down and seeing Jesus standing there eighteen inches high on the white lace doily on the sideboard, the framed photos on either side of him, the one of Dad as a young man with his waxed moustache, the one of Violet's wedding where Stanley looked like Mr Punch and she like a chorus girl. And Bob, stretched out beneath him on the settee, playing the guitar he'd bought with the first week's wages he'd got humping goods about in a warehouse in Ancoats. She told him about the dream.

'I suppose it was like a vision really,' she said thoughtfully. 'I bet in the olden days they'd have thought that.'

And she showed him how Jesus and Mary had stood with their arms outstretched.

Bobby stopped trying to yodel like Jimmie Rodgers, laughed down his nose and said it looked like the Nazi salute. 'Heil Hitler!' he barked, jumping to his feet and demonstrating.

She dropped Dad's bike in the front garden. Mam was standing on the front step with her gas mask over her arm. 'Where've you been?' she cried. 'I'm worried sick!'

Nell didn't even want to go into the shelter. 'What's the point? If it's going to get us, it's going to get us. You might as well just stay in the kitchen and make a cup of tea.'

'Don't you be so stupid! Get in that shelter now!'

Bob loomed up behind Mam, bigger than her now. 'Mam, I can't find my gas mask.'

'Well, what the bloody hell have you done with it? Sam! Sam! Help our Bobby find his gas mask.'

'Bloody hell, it'll all be over by the time we get down there.'

Bob played his Jew's harp in the shelter. Dad sat, stony-faced, steeled against the bombs, his hands dead straight and quivering a little upon his knees.

'Mam,' said Nelly, wanting to let someone know that she was writing to a soldier. 'Mam.'

But Mam was wrapped up in worry, impenetrable, a look of stoic endurance on her face. The raids were bad for her. She hated confined spaces: all her life, it seemed, they had conspired to enfold her, like the dark in the train carriage, and the fear of being buried alive that still invaded her darkest hours.

She sat like a rock.

Dad lit his pipe. Its aroma was comforting.

A bomb sounded quite near, sounded like somewhere over towards Belle Vue. Oh, all those poor animals, Nell thought. Poor things. Bob leaned against Mam's legs. 'Adiolay-ee-lay-hee-tee,' he sang, like a cowboy. His voice had broken. A fine gold down glimmered on his upper lip.

'Hush! Hush!' said Mam. Her hand on his shoulder, rubbing.

Bob sighed and hung his head.

Nell wondered if Alan had got to a shelter in time, or if he was out there now in a doorway somewhere.

'That lad asked me to write to him,' she told Dad.

Dad smiled weakly, more with the eyes than anything. 'No harm in writing to him, Nell,' he said.

But how was she to know she'd fall in love for the first time that summer? How was she to know that one morning they'd move her from the boiler room to the smithy, and that Jimmy Lee, the fair-haired boy she'd first seen leaning against a machine that first day, aloof and sardonically smiling, had merely been visiting from that infernal place? She was given to him, as it were, to train up.

It was harder, hotter, sweatier work in the smithy. When Jimmy Lee turned from the anvil and raised his sweet, filthy, sweat-bathed boyish face, she felt a fluttering like little wings inside.

'She's an able girl,' said the big Dutch welder, Hans. 'She'll learn fast.'

'Of course she will,' said Jimmy Lee. One long straight lock of fair hair fell over his eyes. He was better, a million times better, than all the other boys she knew. She didn't think she'd be able to talk with him: he was too lovely, she wouldn't be able to concentrate on anything but his face.

'OK, Nell,' he said, 'now, you've worked one of these before?'

'Yes.'

'Of course you have. Rotten work for a girl, Nell. Do you mind?' A quick glance from his soft, mischievous eyes.

'Oh, no! I like it here.'

'You do?' He looked surprised.

He moved away, beckoning her towards a monstrous horizontal wheel, in the centre of which was a blackened furnace.

'Put your goggles on,' he said.

There were two doors, one of which he opened to reveal a bright orange cave burning full of red-hot strips and lumps of metal, glowing like the poker when Dad left it in the fire to do his pokerwork.

'Rule Number One,' said Jimmy Lee. 'Trust me.'

He seized something like the coal tongs that sat by the fire at home, only these were much bigger, and drew from the furnace a luminous imp-red bar of iron, laying it down upon one of the spokes of the great anvil.

'Now, you're gonna hold this down here for me like this, see, with this, see, OK? I'll just show you. See? Like that. And it's very, very important that you hold it still otherwise God knows what might happen. And I'm gonna hammer down on it like this, see, hard as I can with both hands, wham!, see, and then there'll be some impact and you are NOT to flinch or jump or even move a muscle because if you do the hammer will deflect back up to my head, OK?'

He was very serious and slightly nervy.

'OK.'

'And if that happens, it'll make a right mess. See?'

She laughed.

'No, I mean it, Nell,' he said, 'you've got to hold it still. Do you think you can do that even when I bring that hammer down? You don't have to worry or owt, I won't miss, honest. OK?'

'Yes.'

'Sure?'

'Yes.'

'Ready?'

'Yes.'

'OK.'

Nell tensed, held the terrifying thing in place, gritted her teeth.

'Relax,' he said, and raised his arms.

It was fantastic. Fantastic. He hammered out that bar as flat and straight as a ribbon, beating the sparks out of it again and again in spurts, and she never moved a muscle. It was lovely. She didn't think she'd ever enjoyed herself as much in her whole life, not when the bombs fell, not when she went on the Bobs, nothing, nothing came up to beating out a piece of hot iron with Jimmy Lee.

'Smashing, Nell!'

He quenched the strip in a bath that hissed steam.

'Smashing! You're a natural! Now come and see it on a bigger scale.'

She followed him along a row of machines worked by turbaned women, through another room to where a great steam hammer pounded metal on a giant anvil. Hans ambled along with them and stood with his head back, beaming at the colossus proudly as if it were his own creation. There was no talking here because of the noise; dimly in the grime and darkness she saw figures here and there, men working, bursts of bright fiery colour flying from their labours. Jimmy stood next to her looking up. She'd never known before what sort of boys she liked, but now she did: strong and stocky like this, square-shouldered, with a firm, generous mouth and complicated

133

hazel eyes, which had been mischievous at the beginning but were now deep and serious.

They returned to the smithy.

'Now, I'm just going to show you one more thing,' Jimmy Lee said. 'This thing here, see? Do you know what this thing is?'

'It's for the temperature,' she said.

'Right. Now you see this valve? Have you done this in the boiler shop?'

'Something like it.'

'Right, this one's the same thing only bigger. Need to eat your spinach. Have a go. One hand there, one there. OK? Now – *twist* – OK? Bit harder.'

She strained.

'Hang on.' His warm filthy hands gripped hers and he squeezed, tightening the valve with one last smart turn. 'Till it gets to there,' he said. 'Just that last little bit. Like you're wringing something out. OK?'

'What a lovely couple you two make!' Hans exclaimed, red and shiny in the face and smeared with oil, laughing heartily.

Nell's blushes would have been an agony to her if they'd been visible. But as everyone in the place was already red in the face, it hardly mattered. It didn't matter what you did in there, within an hour you were drenched in sweat, and as the morning drew on, the lock of fair hair hanging down over Jimmy Lee's forehead as he laboured over the forge darkened and dripped. Steady drops fell from the end of his nose. He didn't talk to her much for the rest of the morning, just showed her what she had to do. He wouldn't let her go near the molten bath but she learned how to load and unload the furnace, and after her break he summoned her over and gave her a hammer and said, 'Go on, have a go,' and she beat out a small metal strip, avidly and awkwardly.

He raised his goggles. 'You've got good strong hands, Nell,' he said. 'You'll do all right in here.'

They were Dad's hands. Not very feminine.

She took her strip of metal home with her. 'Look at that. I did that. I hammered it out flat. This size, it was.'

'Well, I suppose you're doing your bit for the war now,' Mam said, making the best of it. Dad put Nell's bit of metal on the hob and lit his new pipe, settling back in Auntie Bennet's old rocking-chair.

When Mam sent her upstairs after tea to collect the dirty sheets from the back bedroom, Nell went into her own room and looked at the letter she'd had from Alan:

Dear Nell, here I am at last able to get five minutes to put pen to paper. It's not too bad here. I am in a place called Sidi Barrani and it is very hot, hotter than you can imagine. That's the worst of it, but it's not too bad. I have been thinking about home a lot, and about you. Write soon, won't you? It would mean a lot to me to get one of your letters. We've all been issued with battle dress. I think we may be going to Syria.

She felt dreadful about poor old Alan out there in wherever-it-was. She wouldn't like those hot countries. Her skin went brown as a berry in the sun, like a gypsy. She should stay out of it like Kitty, whose complexion was milky. She felt panicky: she didn't want someone out there under a burning sun waiting for her letter, not poor old Alan anyway, who was really quite a nice boy, she was sure, it was just that she didn't feel that she really knew him at all or that he was anything to do with her. She should never have agreed to write to him, because now she'd promised, of course she'd have to; and she couldn't think of anything to say to him. She'd only gone out with him for about three weeks.

'What you doing up there?' Mam shouted up. 'I'm waiting for them sheets.'

Nell wanted Jimmy Lee to ask her out. She wanted it more than anything in the world, it was all she could think about. Alan had liked her because she'd made him laugh. She didn't make Jimmy Lee laugh. With Alan, it hadn't mattered because she didn't like him that much anyway, but with Jimmy Lee it mattered so much that during those early weeks she seized up in an awful panic whenever she saw him and couldn't say a word. But as the summer passed in the heat and clamour of the smithy, and she continued to work beside him day in day out, a workplace camaraderie grew up between them and drove away the stiffness. She loved to watch him, lost in the job, his face troubled and fierce. He lived near Mount Road, not far from Uncle John and Auntie Grace. He had a little sister, and a friend called Mike Harrowlee, a big heavy lad he went to the stock cars with sometimes. But he didn't go out much. You didn't run into him at Belle Vue of an evening out with Kitty.

Kitty'd been a sod lately. If they were walking down the street and got a wolf whistle she'd say, 'Did you hear that lad whistling at *me*? Cheeky so-and-so!', putting her strong square shoulders back and her best foot forward. Well, it probably was for Kitty but it *might* have been for me, that's what Nell would think; it's not as if I've got a bad figure. And her skin was clear and clean, her teeth pearly.

At nights she dreamed of sparks flying out in the darkness. In the day Jimmy Lee praised her ability to forge metal. She was better at it than him, he said. Hans kept swaggering by with his dirty remarks. He came up behind them while they worked and put an arm round each of them, breathing his harsh tobacco breath all over them. 'Two young lovers!' he bellowed, and roared with laughter. Jimmy scowled; Nell blushed.

When Kitty started going out with Alex Kirby from the labs, Nell found herself tagging along with Violet and Stan now and then while Mam and Dad babysat. It was just as much fun as with Kitty in a funny sort of way. Violet was always a laugh, even if Stanley still never said a word. Which was funny, really, because Kitty said when you went in the Co-op you could hear him chatting away sometimes with the customers. But he never said a thing those nights they all went dancing together, or out to a pub, though you couldn't say he was offish: he always smiled a lot and was perfectly civil. Nell danced with boys from time to time and went out with one or two, but there was no one she specially fancied, only Jimmy Lee. The meat of her life was in those filthy sweaty days when sometimes he hung so close over her by the rotating hearth, while showing her this or that, that she could smell him, high and acrid like a beast, dripping sweat on her.

Christmas at Peacock's, the silver band came and played carols in the yard. Alex Kirby, who was going with Kitty, was on the trumpet; another boy from the labs, Harry Caplin, was on trombone.

After they'd all sung along with 'God Rest You Merry, Gentlemen' and 'Once In Royal David's City' and all the rest, Alex Kirby changed his trumpet for a clarinet, and those two boys stood up on the back of a truck and played jazz. I know who they are! It clicked. They were the two she and Kitty had seen that first day when they'd gone to complain about the men looking up their skirts. The fair one and the dark one. They played a very fast New Orleans–type version of 'I Want A Girl Just Like The Girl That Married Dear Old Dad'. Fantastic! Just like a real band.

Nelly ran in to get Jimmy, who'd just clocked on for his shift. He turned from the fire, a hammer in his hand, and she saw that his cheek was bruised, the corner of one eye puffy and sore.

'What've you done?'

He shrugged.

'You missed the silver band,' she said. 'Come and listen to Alex Kirby and Harry Caplin playing their jazz. They're fantastic.'

Everyone was coming out into the yard to listen. People stood in the doorways of the engine sheds. They played 'Way Down Yonder In New Orleans'. Jimmy Lee stood next to her to listen. Kitty was there. Then Alex got down and everyone cheered, and Kitty whistled and clapped her hands over her head; but Harry Caplin stayed up there and played one more tune on his own, something she didn't know, some fast jazzy piece, smart and rambling, like people dancing on the tops of taxis in the roaring twenties, city lights twinkling, parades, fun, and as the sound echoed round the yards, everyone jigged about, clapping along with the music. Kitty grabbed the boy next to her and jived him up and down the loading bay. Harry Caplin was very handsome, Nell thought, bit on the thin side, with those kind of sloping shoulders she didn't much like on a man. Looks were important. Some of the boys Kitty kissed she couldn't have borne. She was fussy. Now Jimmy Lee had a lovely mouth. Strong and full, with a Cupid's bow. And she bet he'd be a nice dry kisser.

'Good, isn't he?' they were saying all round.

'Good, weren't they?' she said to Jimmy.

'Yeah.' He was smoking a cigarette. His bad eye watered.

'What happened to you?' she asked.

'Had a fight with my old man.' He looked away sideways. The bruise was purplish and brown, like a thumb pushing up under his skin, and his eye above the swelling was bloodshot.

'What d'you want to fight with your dad for?'

Jimmy turned and walked back to work without another word. She thought she'd offended him, but later he came over and asked could she do him a favour because the sweat was pouring into his bad eye and driving him mad? Could she just come and stand for a minute while he beat out this cog? So she came and held a cloth on his forehead to keep the sweat from his face, and as he worked, his poor jaw was grinding and his eyes smouldered.

'I wish this was my dad's face I was doing this to,' he shouted, above the noise, and grinned.

She'd seen his dad. He worked in a butcher's shop, a big man in blood-smeared white, handsome for his age and quietly jovial.

'Never marry a drinker, Nelly!'

Our Bobby drinks, she thought, he's going into pubs already and he's only sixteen, and at the same moment realised that Jimmy Lee looked like Bob. Like Bob only without the pugnacity. Well, that was a funny thing, wasn't it? Both fair and stocky. She looked for the likeness when she got home and saw Bobby lying on his back on the floor playing his guitar, the same little bit over and over again to get it right, he'd do it for ever if that was what it took. His little tabby cat Sukey sat by his head, and his face was stern with concentration. Mam was nagging him from the kitchen. He'd been in a scrap with some bloke on Mellands. 'If I tell him once,' Mam was shrilling to the stove, 'I tell him a thousand times. I say Bobby, you walk away from trouble. Bobby, you just turn round and you walk away from trouble, and what does he do? He goes straight towards it! Straight tobloody-wards it! I'll bloody kill him!'

Bobby was ignoring her.

'Hi, Nell,' he said.

'Oh, not you an' all,' said Nell. 'Jimmy Lee's had a fight with his dad. His dad beats his mam up and Jimmy has to protect her.'

138

Bob shook his head, all the time playing those same few notes again and again. 'Terrible that, Nell,' he said.

'He won't bloody listen!' cried Mam. 'There's a letter for you from that lad.'

Nell's heart sank.

'You know what she's like, Nell,' Bob said, softly and consolingly. 'She's making a mountain out of a molehill. You know I don't go around looking for trouble, Nell, but if it comes to me what am I gonna do? I'm not gonna back off like a coward, am I?'

It wasn't fair. Bobby was going to be gorgeous. He got *all* the looks. He was probably going to be better even than Jimmy Lee. What was she thinking of? Jimmy Lee was never going to go out with her. Jimmy Lee was much too gorgeous. She took the official airmail letter down from the mantelpiece and shoved it into her pocket. She'd read it later. It was awful. She didn't want to write to Alan any more. She could hardly remember him. His letters presumed an intimacy that had never existed. 'I must tell you about the moon tonight, dear,' he wrote.

Dear?

'There's a man down the line somewhere keeps whistling that song you used to like. "When You Wore A Tulip".'

She couldn't remember saying she liked that song. She didn't, particularly.

'Go out and look at the moon for me, dear. It will not be as bright and clear as it is here. The skies are actually bigger here, I swear. But go out and look at it anyway and think that I am under it though very far away.'

Is this to me? she thought. His letters embarrassed her. She remembered how he'd liked his dog called Boxer, and how nice he'd been, easy to get along with in spite of his slightly posh voice. But she couldn't see his face at all, only his pigeon toes. She tried to reconstruct his face. She knew she'd applied the word parroty to him. Poor thing! Parroty and pigeon-toed! Poor boy out there! Then she remembered kissing him. She hated tongues. Horrible wet slobbery things. Ugh!

She put off reading it.

After a few days Mam started nagging again. 'Have you written back to that lad yet, Nelly? It's not fair, you know. If you don't want to write to the poor boy, you'd be better off just telling him straight so he knows, rather than have him always waiting around for a letter from you and never getting it. Anyway, you *are* a selfish sod, you. What's a letter to you? A few lines, you don't have to put much. Those poor lads out there, it means a lot to them to get a letter now and again. I know, I used to have a boy out there. And it's no skin off your nose, is it?'

'Oh, all right, I'll write, I'll write, I'll write.'

She went upstairs and lay on the bed. Gingerly she opened his letter. This one was mercifully fairly brief.

Dear Nell, How are you, dear? I hope you know how dear you are to me. There's a rumour going around we're for Burma. I hope not. They say it's monsoon season out there now. I don't supppose they'll send us till that's over. Can't say any of us fancy it. Heard a lot of those far-eastern troops have been down with malaria. I've been looking out for a letter from you but nothing yet, I daresay the post is chasing us on from Cairo. Don't fancy Christmas in this heat. Seems unnatural. Send me a Christmas card with a lot of snow on it please, Nell. I do hope you have a good one, you and all your family. Give them all my kindest regards for the season. Write soon please. Best love, Alan. xxxxxx

It made her feel awful. Dutifully, she wrote. Pointless twaddle. Poor lad. She paused in the writing and daydreamed idly about moving to the country after the war and becoming a blacksmith's wife, and having a cottage, like in Morland, with wild roses and wild daffodils and a row of round lettuces like Granny used to have. And Jimmy Lee, with his hammer in his hand and his apron on, the muscles along his neck straining under the streaming sweat.

He was like a sacrificial lamb, suffering with his bruised face and swollen eye.

'Here's a health to the jolly blacksmith,' they sang at school, 'the best of all fellows,' those horrible singing lessons when Miss Flower used to come round and stick her horrible shiny red ear right in front of your mouth and tell you you were out of tune. His face all covered in a slick, and she wiping the sweat away from him, with a cloth. Who was it in the Bible – was it Mary Magdalene? – wiping away Jesus's sweat? Jimmy Lee teaching her how to forge metal. Showing her where to bash the hammer down.

It was a terrible time. It went on for months, a time when all she could think about was Jimmy Lee, whose face hung about constantly in the back of her mind, in the back of everything she did or thought. She imagined herself putting a cold compress on his bruised face. She wiped the sweat from his eyes. A whole world was in her head. He was always a pal at work, her best friend apart from Kitty, and took to confiding in her. His dad, he said, had always hit his mam and him, but not his little sister. Once a month or so, either he or his mam, sometimes both, sported a black eye. His dad was a big affable man with lots of friends. His mam never complained about it, she just sort of took it for granted. But him, he wasn't going to take it, not any more, he was facing up to it all now, he was like the policeman of the house, he said, soon as it started up he would get between his mam and his dad, and now he was hitting back, and once he'd even given his own dad a black eye. He felt great about that. Usually, though, Jimmy came out of it worst. His dad was bigger than him, not taller but bigger-boned and heftier.

'I'll probably kill him one day, Nelly,' he said resignedly. 'Or he'll kill me. One or the other.'

He was a moody bugger sometimes. Days when he didn't feel like talking. Days when he slaved away like Hercules, grim-faced, suffering, she thought, a tremendous violence unpent smashing down again and again with his hammer, the muscles in his neck convulsing.

'Come over here, Nelly.' He was the only one at work who called her Nelly. 'Come and look at this, Nelly.'

Standing beside him. Agony.

Along came Hans behind, clapping a hand on each of their shoulders and bellowing, 'Look at this lovely young couple! Made for each other! Go on, lad, don't be shy, ask her out!'

Nell blushed furiously.

Jimmy roughly shook him off. 'Stupid fool!' he muttered.

He didn't ask her out.

Time rolled on, and the war rolled on; Italy fell, Dad left Peacock's because of his back, Mam still went cleaning, Jean started toddling, Kitty finished with Alex Kirby, and still Jimmy Lee didn't ask Nelly out. Twice she and Kitty passed him and his friend Mike Harrowlee in the street, up Hyde Road once, and once just outside the grey-hound track. They all just said hello and walked on. She had another couple of letters from Alan, each one more soppy than the last, till it frightened her and she couldn't stand it any more and wrote quickly, before she could stop herself, that she did not think it a good idea for them to go on writing as it was only fair to tell him she was seeing someone else (well, she was in a way) and it did not seem the best thing to keep on communicating under the circumstances. She hoped he understood, and wished him all the best.

A few days later Jimmy Lee knocked out one of his dad's teeth and chucked him out into the yard. A couple of weeks after that he came in with two black eyes and a fat lip that lasted for ages.

'If I was you I'd be out of that place as fast as I could,' she told him.

'Yeah, but my mam.'

'She should go too.'

''Preciate your concern, Nelly,' he said, 'only it's easier said than done, like.'

He really did remind her of Bob. Not just the looks but some kind of passivity in him. It sounded funny, because look at Bob drinking and fighting and turning the heads of the girls and even the women all along the street when he went out with the crease in his trousers just so and the gleam on his hair; and look at Jimmy manfully pro-tecting his poor mother and knocking out his father's teeth. And yet – and yet – there was this weakness. A kind of what-can-you-do attitude, so that you just knew Jimmy Lee would never get out of that house, he'd just stay there and go on and on fighting with his dad and nothing would get any better and his mother would still get hit. And Bobby, he'd just go on taking the easy way all the time, always the easy way. Still, maybe that was the best thing to do.

'I'd ask you out, Nell,' Jimmy Lee said one day, as they sat smok-ing their cigarettes in the yard, 'but I can't.'

Well, what are you supposed to say to a thing like that? It came after a lull in an ordinary conversation. Afterwards she couldn't remember what it was they'd been talking about before. He just said it, smoking his cigarette and looking out from under his brows across the yard, squinting a little in the sun.

'Why can't you?' she asked.

He thought for a while then flicked away his cigarette end. 'It's the whole thing,' he said, 'my dad and everything. I can't go out with anyone just now, it wouldn't be fair on them. I've got to sort out the situation at home first.'

'Jimmy, do you want to go out with me or not?'

He hesitated.

That was when she gave up on him for ever. It was a shattering moment, a sword piercing home and killing off any expectation that life could ever be anything but second best. She was going to have to live with it. And the people in the yard went on as normal and the sun shone and her cigarette burned down and she felt profoundly depressed.

'Well, I would,' he said, 'but as you know, things are difficult for me at the moment.'

'Sod off, Jimmy.' She turned away, shrugging as if it didn't matter to her anyway. The fellows from the labs came walking through the yard, Alex Kirby and Harry Caplin deep in conversation and laughter.

'Not just now anyway,' said Jimmy.

11

Jazz

*Dearest Nell, We leave for Italy in the morning. I hope I die out there.
With all my love, Alan. xxxxxx*

Only that.

'Oh, Mam!' she said. 'I feel terrible! Look at this letter.'

Mam paused with a window leather in her hand. 'What?' She grabbed and read. Her face softened. 'Poor lad.' Behind her turbaned head the rain teemed down the windowpanes.

'Bad news, Nell?' Bobby stood barefoot in vest and trousers, a fag in his mouth, pressing his trousers on a folded sheet on the table.

'Best thing,' Mam said, handing the letter back to Nell. 'He'll get over it.'

'It's that he's out there. All the fighting and him being scared and ... and now this ... he must feel awful!'

Bobby read it. 'Oh dear, Nell,' he said, shaking his head. 'Still, what can you do? You did the right thing.'

Mam looked out of the window. 'Bloody war,' she said, as if it was just the rain, teeming down endlessly beyond human control.

'I feel terrible,' Nell said, and she looked sick. 'I feel terrible.'

'You will,' Mam said, 'you're not the first. He'll get over it. They always do.'

'He's meant that to upset you, Nell,' Bobby said.

She gulped. 'I feel terrible.'

'Never mind, love,' said Mam, a little later. 'Here, take a basin and go and get a pudding with gravy from Duffy's for your dad, he'll be back in a minute. Here.' Mam slipped her the precious ration book. 'Get something for yourself. Use the sweet ration.'

Nell went out into the crisp day. The feeling of guilt would not shift. It was another of those changing moments, like Jimmy Lee hesitating when she asked him if he wanted to go out with her. Life was hard. It was a truth. You did harm without meaning to. How could she have known he'd make up some fantasy about her out there where he was always too hot or too cold, where his feet hurt and his belly caved in? The comfortlessness of it. Poor boy. She hadn't meant to hurt him. She even felt grateful to him, shadowy as he'd become, for being the only lad who'd ever really fallen for her. Even if it wasn't really her. For how could it be? He didn't know her. It's not as if she could even remember his face.

She didn't suppose she'd ever find a nice boy at this rate. She'd already been a bridesmaid twice, once for Cousin Berenice, once for Violet – Berenice had been matron-of-honour, Nell and Ruby bridesmaids, all dolled up. When the pictures were developed it was shocking, amidst all the confetti and the big bouquets, to see how old Mam and Dad appeared, Mam fat and toothless-looking, though she wasn't, Dad so gaunt and thin and droopy. Twice a bridesmaid and you know what they said. Well, she just wouldn't be a bridesmaid again, not for anyone, not even if Kitty got married and asked her. Never.

The letter haunted her, and after a few days Mam made her throw it away. 'That's that now,' Mam said. 'No point looking back. What's done is done.' Then, when Nell still kept mooning about, she said, 'I don't know what's the matter with you, don't tell me you like him after all? Make your bloody mind up, Nelly. I wish you'd get out from under my feet.' And she made her do her hair and make-up and go down to the Midway with Bob and Vi and Stanley. Bob was becoming quite the dandy and kept her waiting ages while he stood in front of the mirror getting his hair right, combing and combing it back, before they could call for Kitty, who fancied coming along too because she was sort of half going out with Alex Kirby again and his band was on. Kitty said that the worst of going out with someone in a band was that half the time you ended up stuck in the audience on your own or with some other band girlfriends who knew each other but you didn't know them.

'But this is nice,' she said, 'going with friends. I don't mind this at all.' So they all went down and met Violet and Stanley outside the Midway.

The Midway was very bright and grand, with high walls and an ornate gilded ceiling. There were tables all round a large dance-floor, and a long bar glittering on one side. A couple of waiters in maroon jackets went about with drinks on trays and there was a girl going round with cigarettes. They got a table about half-way down one side next to two noisy couples who kept laughing very loudly. Nelly wondered what it would be like to be here with Jimmy Lee. She watched the couples on the floor and thought about dancing with him, and whether he'd be a good dancer or not; probably not, he wasn't really the dancing type, although she bet he could if he wanted to. Anyway, who cared? Alex Kirby's band, the Something Something Stompers, was high up on the stage, the singer singing 'Chatanooga Choo-Choo'. They all wore dickie bows. The singer was awful. It was that very jazzy jazz she didn't like, that jumbly, squealing, messy sort of music that wasn't sure whether it was comic or seedy.

Bobby got the drinks in, a bitter lemon for her. You should have seen how all the girls eyed him up going to the bar, with his square cleft chin and golden hair gleaming with Brylcreem.

'God, look at our Bobby!' sighed Violet, following him fondly with her eyes.

Stanley sat with one arm hooked over the back of his chair. The brown sleeve of his jacket was a little too short for his long arm, and his strong bony wrist stuck out below his cuff. He had a big lump under one eye. Nell wondered what it was, but had never liked to ask. It took over the top of one of his gaunt cheeks. Funny face, Stanley. Mr Punch.

'I remember changing his little nappy!' Violet beamed. 'I do!'

Then the band leader, not Alex, a man with a sharp dark smiling face who played the trumpet, put his hand to his brow and peered out at the audience like a sailor peering out to sea, and cried out: 'I see Harry Caplin! I do! I see Harry Caplin. Harry! Did you bring your horn?'

And there was Harry Caplin from work, with his cheesy grin and round dark head and the gap between his two front teeth, sitting at a table with two other lads, and of the three of them he was by far the best, really very handsome, like a handsome Italian, 'Oh, oh Antonio,' like Kitty said sometimes, 'that Harry Caplin, he's a nice-looking chap.' His trombone, in a black case, lay at his feet like a large faithful dog.

Strange, she knew how Harry was feeling. It was weird. It was like it was with Dad, when she'd just look at him and suddenly know how he was feeling, whether he was angry or sad or moved, even when his face wasn't necessarily doing anything to give it away. And now she knew that Harry was embarrassed, almost unbearably so, but that he was also going to be brave because he was so proud of himself and what he knew he could do, and she knew that that trombone was worth more to him than anything else in the world. He reached down and picked up his case and walked up to the stage with a modest look on his face and did a little run when he got to the steps, and watching him, her heart was in her mouth somehow. Everyone applauded, and some people cheered, deep men's voices, and enthusiastic whistling as if Harry Caplin from work was famous, all togged up in a black suit with a white shirt and a big black dickie bow. He knew all the men in the band and joked about with them while he got out his trombone, while the pianist played some boogie-woogie stuff and everyone clapped along to it. Then Harry played a number with the band. She didn't know it, just some jazzy thing, maybe that last thing he'd played in the yard. Bobby was enjoying himself, his lips smiling round his cigarette. So was Violet. She was clicking her fingers. Harry played a big trombone piece in the middle of the number. It was, it was the thing he'd played in the yard, the one he'd finished up with, when everyone started to dance. He looked nice playing his trombone. Held it straight up in the air as he finished. Then he and Alex Kirby played together, so good, playing just like the old plantations, the drummer using those brushy things to get a soft sound from his drums. And you had to admit Alex Kirby was marvellous on that clarinet. Like water, listening to him play. She liked that. The way a clarinet could sort of curl round upon itself, the sound. Whereas the trombone, now that was a much clumsier sound altogether somehow. Like an elephant trumpeting.

And the word, trombone, that was clumsy too. But still, you could see Harry was good, as good as any of them in that band, easily. And he must be good because the audience went wild with cheering when he finished and wanted him to carry on, but he wouldn't, so the band went back to their fast jazzy jazz and Harry went and sat down. Someone had bought him a beer.

Later, when the band took a break, Nell saw Harry Caplin talking to the drummer at the bar, one foot up on the gold rail. Bobby was at the bar too, he'd met with some friends of his, lads a bit older than himself, out with their girls. Nell was never sure what happened. Vi said it was the other bloke's fault, but you never knew. Get a drink or two or three in Bobby and he was away. It was something to do with a gang of lads a bit further down the bar, and of course the one Bobby picked on was about twice the size of all the others, but then Bobby never stopped to think, that was his trouble. First it was just words, but you could hear Bob from over here: 'Wanna make something of it, do you?' he was saying to this big one, and Stanley got up and started making his way over, and Violet said, 'Ooh, Nell,' and gripped Nell's arm. Bob threw the first punch, but the man parried, and then there was a bit of a tussle, and a loud 'Hoy! None o' that!' from behind the bar, and a couple of big men in suits started coming over. But Stanley calmed everything down. Stanley was great. He stepped into the middle of it, taller than all the others, like a long-necked bird, put one hand on Bob's shoulder and one on the other man's arm and said, 'Calm down, calm down,' in a firm, knowing way, over and over again till somehow everything did.

Harry Caplin was watching.

'Come on, Bob, tek 'em their drinks,' said Stanley.

'Bloody fool,' said Bob.

'Tek 'em their drinks.'

'Bob, you'll get in serious trouble one of these days,' Nell said.

'I'm not having him insult my friends. What am I supposed to do, Nell, someone insults my friends?' Bobby set down the drinks, splashing them, still casting surly glances backwards over his shoulder.

Stanley brought gin and limes for Kitty and Vi. 'Pack it in, Bob,' he said mildly.

'Well, what was all that about?' asked Kitty.

Typical Bob, some garbled tale about this bloke having said something offensive to one of Bob's mate's girlfriends, or at any rate someone had taken offence over something or given someone a funny look, eyeing up someone they shouldn't have, who could tell?

'See, our Bob just thinks he's being chivalrous, Nell,' Vi explained with a fond smile.

'You'll get into trouble,' Nell repeated.

But you couldn't tell Bobby.

Alex Kirby came over and stood at their table with Harry Caplin and the banjo player from the band, who seemed to know Kitty very well. Kitty was like that. She knew people.

Everyone looked because they were talking to the band.

The banjo player was drunk. 'Hey, Goliath,' he said, and punched Bobby on the shoulder.

You never could tell sometimes with Bobby, catch him a bit off-balance, but anyway he just smiled, looking over at Nell. 'It's all right, Nell,' he said. 'You don't want to worry about me, I'm only messing about.'

'You mean David,' said Harry Caplin. 'Goliath's the giant.'

'Yeah,' said the banjo player, 'but Goliath's a better name. Hey, Goliath,' and he punched Bob on the shoulder again.

Alex sat down with Kitty on her chair. The banjo player tried to squeeze on too, which was clearly impossible, but she laughed and pushed him off.

'Bit young for you, hey, Kitty?' the banjo player said, picking himself up off the floor, grinning. 'Goliath here?'

'He's Nelly's little brother,' Kitty said, turning her neck from side to side and shaking her heavy red hair about, then she punched Bob too, on the arm, jogging his drink so that he spilled more.

'Give over,' he said.

'Hi, Nell,' said Harry Caplin. He had lovely deep brown eyes.

'What was that tune you played in the yard at Peacock's?' Nell asked him.

'Which one? "Clarinet Marmalade"?' He smiled, then whistled it. He didn't whistle in an irritating way, the way Bobby did when he was doing it on purpose just to annoy you, he whistled as if he was playing an instrument.

'I like that,' she said.

Nelly was moved to the machine shop, and after that she lost touch with Jimmy Lee. She saw him around, of course. He was always friendly. Always smiled and said hello, sometimes stopped for a chat. But sometimes she'd go nearly a week and not see him at all if he was on a different shift or something. Sometimes still she could have cried, thinking of watching him work, bruised, sweat dripping from his nose and the soaking strands of hair that hung down over his face. Until at Christmas she heard the news, spoken about the place, in the canteen and in the yard and round and about, that Jimmy Lee's father had died. It was mysterious. Jimmy was off for a while, she never got to see him; just this incessant background mumbling that Jimmy Lee's father had died. No one seemed sure how, but that he was dead was certain.

For a moment she wondered if he'd actually done it, if he'd killed his dad, but it couldn't have been Jimmy because it turned out he'd been round at Mike Harrowlee's that night helping him to fix the leaking sink in the back kitchen. Some people said it was the heart that gave out, others that Jimmy's dad just dropped down dead. That's how it came, sudden, like a scythe, like it did for Auntie Bennet. Like a scythe blade on the neck of a bluebell. He was just dead. And Jimmy Lee, beautiful and golden, sweating in the forge, the most gorgeous thing in all creation, he was also just gone, scythed away, just gone, like a big strip of blood ripped from the side of her heart inside, gone.

Because he didn't come to work after that for a while and it was agony, agony. Not seeing him was agony; she thought she'd die of it.

But she didn't die of it.

And with this came a great truth:

Didn't matter how much it hurt, how much you burned, you didn't die of it.

He came back. He was much the same. She saw him sometimes in the canteen. She thought of going up to him and saying boldly, Now

150

your dad's gone, why can't you go out with me? Why not now? Or didn't you ever mean it anyway? And is it really possible that I could have felt so much for someone who felt so little for me?

Yes, I suppose it is.

Well, she wasn't going to wait around for him. He knew where she was if he changed his mind. What else could you do? There were other boys around, GIs who chewed gum and thought a Lancashire accent was cute. Black ones too. Wonder what it would be like with a black man. Some of them were nice. Like Indians, yes, Red Indians, a handsome Red Indian carrying you away on a piebald horse. With those cheekbones. Shiny and dark and different. Couldn't see one of them on Sutton Estate. A whole different world.

Mam was having a general moan. This time it was about Stanley but it could have been about anyone. And a general nag at Dad. 'You're bloody useless,' she was telling Dad. 'What are you good for?'

Dad rocked in the rocker, one leg crossed over the other, taking no notice. His fag sat on his lip, the ash curving down a good inch.

'He's a funny bugger. Never bloody opens his mouth.' She was talking about Stanley now.

He was OK, Stanley. No great shakes. Violet was happy.

Dad's ash fell off on to his trousers.

'He's mad about jazz,' Nell said.

'Who is?' asked Bobby, strumming his guitar in the corner.

'Harry Caplin.'

Harry Caplin. Harry Caplin. Yes, that's the way it was going. Harry Caplin, Harry Caplin and jazz.

12

Harry

Harry Caplin was a catch.

He asked her out one day in the outside yard, a thin boy with flat hair cut high above his ears. Was he good-looking? Who knows? He was nice in a delicate sort of way, slight and pale, with shiny black hair that went back in waves from a widow's peak, so that sometimes, when he was serious, he had the look of a young poet. He looked better serious. When he smiled he had a gawky look.

They arranged to meet at the Essoldo. She arrived a little bit late to make sure he'd be there before her. He'd already bought the tickets and stood there smoking, waiting. 'Hi, Nell.'

And it was so strange, because he was only Harry Caplin from work, and there he was, smiling as if he'd known her for years. She was sure Kitty liked him too, with all that oh-oh-Antonio stuff all the time. He was much nicer-looking than Alex Kirby. Alex Kirby looked a bit like Bob's white ferret.

They followed the usherette's light a little way down the aisle. On the screen were some of our soldiers in the Far East, packing guns, smiling and sticking their thumbs up for the camera. She remembered Alan. Wouldn't it be funny, she thought, if she saw him on a news-reel? Was he still in North Africa? He had the kind of skin that burned easily. Isn't it funny, she thought, as they settled in their seats, here I am in the Essoldo on Mount Road, and when I go home it'll be nice and warm and the fire will be lit and Dad will have put hot water bottles in all our beds? And I can make a cup of tea. And poor old Alan's out in the filthy hot sun, in the desert, or maybe in a tent somewhere, sweating; or is he in the jungle?

They saw *Top Hat*. It was OK. She wasn't keen on Fred Astaire, funny-looking little fellow, she thought, rather effeminate. She thought about Harry, sitting there next to her chuckling and tapping his feet to the music. He was a Jew, she thought. Vi said Caplin was a Jewish name, she said it was normally spelled with a K, some of them changed their names to sound more English. She remembered him standing on his own after Alex Kirby got down off the tailgate. Lovely sound, the instrument all by itself like one person's voice, the voice of the person who's playing it. What was it? Was it 'Come To Me My Melancholy Baby'? Oh, that was nice! 'Come to me my melancholy baby, snuggle up and don't be blue ...' Ginger Rogers was very pretty. Nell wondered what it would be like to go mad and go peroxide. But she'd look stupid in glasses. Glasses and peroxide.

Very much the gentleman, Harry was. He didn't try anything on that night, just rested an arm lightly along the back of her seat. Later as they walked to the bus stop, he said he was going to evening classes in the week to get his metallurgical qualifications. He told her stuff about alloys that went straight through her head. They waited in the bus shelter opposite the greyhound track. She was glad Harry was exempt, that he had an important job and didn't have to go and fight like all the other poor boys and come back dead or all changed and strange. Because it meant he was just like her in a way. You felt funny about all those boys out there, all those boys you'd been at school with. You thought about them picking their noses in class and crying for their mams and wetting their pants and leaving a wet patch on the chair in Standard One.

'Actually, Nell,' Harry said, 'I would have asked you out before only I thought you were going out with that Jimmy Lee.'

'Oh, no,' she replied dismissively, 'I've never been out with him. He's just a pal.'

The bus came. He got on with her. 'Are you coming out again with me, Nell?' he asked, when they'd sat down downstairs, her by the window looking out, him with one leg stuck out in the aisle.

'OK.'

'OK? OK? What does OK mean?' He laughed. 'Yes or no? Do you want to?'

The bus stood there shivering, waiting for stragglers.

'All right then, yes,' she said.

153

'Oh, right,' he said, 'well, I'm glad that's settled.' He put his arm along the back of her seat. She wondered if he'd kiss her. She'd let him. But he didn't try. Instead he asked her if she liked jazz, and she said yes, though she wasn't mad keen actually; then he asked her if she'd like to come and see a jazz band with him some time.

The driver climbed into the cab.

'Yes, I would, Harry,' she said.

A pleasant sleepiness descended as the bus trundled slowly homewards through the dark down Mount Road and round into Melland Road. He got off at her stop and walked her up to the gate.

'See you at work Monday, then, Nell,' he said.

'Right you are.'

Mam was looking through the window.

'There's my mam,' Nell said. 'She'll be out in a minute.'

'Thursday any good for you?' he asked.

'I'm not sure.'

'Well, I'll see you at work anyway. T'ra.'

Quick peck on the side of the face.

'T'ra.'

She went in. Dad was smoking his pipe. Bob was wiping pots in the kitchen, taking off Lord Haw-Haw: 'Germany calling! Germany calling!' Mam was sitting back down to the table where she was doing her pools. Mam was fat. Not soft and flabby, but hard and solid as a ham, broad and stately like a heavy-laden ship. Her eyes were starting to look old and hurt all the time.

'So who's this one, then?' she asked.

'His name's Harry,' Nell said, 'I told you. He's not in the foundry with us, he's in the labs. He looks down microscopes. He's in research. Doing tests on metal. He's got his own desk. He's twenty-one.'

That made him a scientist of sorts, she supposed. Well, that was the sort of thing they did.

The Shalimar, a jazz club in town. If the sirens went off you'd be as well off here as anywhere. They'd had to go down steps to get to where a brassy middle-aged woman in a booth took their money, and then there was another flight. The basement was packed to the seams, full of noisy, almost shouting babble. They'd squeezed in at a table near the front with two men and two women Harry knew, then he'd gone off to the bar and left her there with all these strangers, perfumed women, loud men, swells of laughter that got on her nerves; and she felt suddenly like she used to feel at school, when she first went there and it was all strange and the others seemed to have paired up or gone off in groups and she was just sort of hanging around, waiting. Waiting for hometime, waiting for someone to talk to her, waiting to feel different from how she was feeling. She looked aside. The smoke lay in layers, settling in muggy stratas that stretched and slowly opened their yawning mouths like waking cats. There was a woman with a Yorkshire terrier sitting on her knee. Cruel, thought Nell, bringing the poor little thing in a place like this. It had a red ribbon on top of its head and a thin purple tongue that kept licking and licking away at something the woman had on her fingers.

Harry came with the drinks, a bitter lemon for her, beer for him. Harry didn't mind her not drinking. He was no great drinker himself.

'Hey, Johnny,' he said, 'Paddy Noonan's at the bar.'

Johnny Miller was the quiet fair one. He was nice. He smiled at her across the table, even though it was so noisy that Harry couldn't really introduce her. His girlfriend smiled at her too, the one called Pam.

'Alex Kirby's looking for musicians.'

Fanatical, they were. Fanatical about jazz. That's all any of them ever talked about, even the girlfriends. When the band came on and the music started, Harry leaned towards her on his elbow, sipping his beer and telling her the names of all the members of the band and all the bands they'd played for previously, and then all the names of all the members of *those* bands.

So many people. She was not at home here. That was what Harry was admiring in her at that moment, in fact, that she was simple and a bit awkward in the Shalimar, and that she had a fresh-faced, forthright kind of appearance, her bespectacled face both plain and pretty. She wore powder and lipstick but left her eyes alone. It seemed pointless with glasses, she thought, why bother? Anyway, that was only vanity. In any case she couldn't see to put make-up on.

Harry went to the bar for more drinks.

Johnny Miller leaned over and spoke in her ear: 'Great player, Harry,' he said, 'top-notch.'

'I haven't heard him play that much, only once or twice.'

'You never heard Harry play?' said another man, whose name she never caught. 'And you've known him how long? Lady, you've only known half the man. Harry's a jazzman.'

She smiled. These were real musicians and they respected him. And she was with him. She was with him.

He'd been low when the jazz hit him. His dear old dad not cold in the grave and his mother married the lodger. Couldn't wait. Now the lodger was his stepfather. Stepfather. Not that he ever used the word, not that any of them did. Sid was just Sid. Stupid, the pair of them. Outrageously stupid. Harry kept to his room most of the time. He'd been the boy, he'd always had to have his own room, even when there wasn't a room and his mam had had to hang the curtain up between him and the girls. Our Bud had to have his own room. Our Bud was clever, he was at Central Grammar for Boys. Our Bud had to study.

Our Bud was bitter. Stony-lipped, cold-eyed, stern and dismissive when his stupid mam fussed and flapped around him. To Sid he didn't speak. Let the girls call him Diddy all they wanted. Diddy! What kind of a facetious baby-slop word was that? He'd sit in his room and work, high-minded at the tiny table at the window. His neat sloping handwriting on the page:-d[A]/dt or +d[D]/dt where square brackets denote concentrations. Looking out over the alleys and yards of West Gorton. Couldn't go to the university because there was no money. Couldn't go to art school, though his teacher said it would be a crime if he didn't. He wanted to cry sometimes at the sheer humdrum boring sameness of it all. Fat women in the street in slippers. The rank miasma of boiled cabbage on the stairs. The click of the latch on the toilet door in the yard, the smell of damp whitewash flaking on the walls, the cold seeping into your bones as you sat there. He'd get out. Get away. He wouldn't stay here and rot.

He started on the cornet when he was fifteen because his dad brought it home one night all excited from work. He'd got it cheap from a man. Harry started blowing. It sounded awful and made next door's dog in the yard lift its muzzle to the stars and howl like a wolf. His dad collected tickets on the trams going up and down London Road into town. He did a deal with Fred Slack from Cross Street who delivered coal all round the neighbourhood and went down the greyhounds at Belle Vue every Saturday night. Fred had bought his own greyhound, a white and tan bitch called Madame that he was going to train up and race with the best, 'A magnificent animal, magnificent,' the fat man said reverently, standing by the glass-fronted cabinet in the parlour where Harry's mother kept her daft little ornaments. The magnificent animal was shaking her hindquarters in their tiny kitchen. 'Who's a little beauty?' his mam bleated, hands on knees. 'Who's a little smasher then? Give us a kiss, go on! Ey, give your mam a big kiss! Cheeky! Cheeky!'

Fred wanted time to train up Madame, so on top of his own job Harry's dad took over Fred's Saturday rounds of Abbey Hey and Fairfield, him and Fred's boy to help with the horse, and the money paid for Harry to go all the way up to Victoria Park every Friday night after school and be taught musical theory and practice by an old Salvation Army codger called Colonel Pretty. At sixteen, he joined the silver band and met Alex Kirby. At seventeen, he came back one Friday night to find his dad home early with a pain in his shoulder. Two months later his father was dead. The cancer spread from lungs to liver. He came home to die, shrivelled and shrunk in so short a time. He called Harry from his homework one night and spoke to him.

'Listen, kid,' he said, 'I can read the signs and if there isn't a war coming I'm a Dutchman. I want you to make me a promise now.'

'Course I will, Dad,' said Harry.

'I was in the first war,' his dad said. His breathing was shocking. 'I can tell you this. There's nothing glorious about war. *Dulce et decorum est pro patria mori*, my foot. It's grown men crying and screaming for their mothers, that's all war is. It's bloody madness. You'll never fight in a war. Not if I can do anything to prevent it.'

157

He had to stop then and just breathe for a while, every breath a long fight. 'You mean the world to me,' he said. 'I'm not letting you go through that hell. You get the right sort of job. Then, if the worst comes to the worst, you'll be essential on the home front. You're my clever lad, kid. You know what you're good at. You're a physics and chemistry man. You go in for metallurgy. Hear me? And you stick to your studies, whatever. There's nothing more important than education. Hear me, Harry? Are you with me, kid?'

'I'm with you, Dad,' said Harry, and his eyes filled with tears.

'Got to face these things, Harry.' And his dad patted his hand.

He died next morning, very early, while Harry was still asleep.

'It was the coal dust,' Harry's mam declared, and married Sid.

Harry swept about the house, stern and formidable. His mother quailed anxiously before him. His sisters fawned upon him. Sid fell aside, a little ineffectual man with a jagged limp. They ignored each other completely. Harry became skilled at silence, laden silence, glowering silence. Then one night Harry and Alex went to town and got into a jazz club even though they were both under-age. There was just a pianist on the stage, a tall thin man in a loose grey suit, playing with a fag hanging out of his mouth and his feet rocking up and down. The place was blue and sleazy with smoke. A girl got up on stage and leaned against the piano, singing along in a nasal husky croon: 'Everybody loves my baby, but my baby don't love nobody but me ...' Excitement mounted in his chest. He lit a fag, they were standing way back in the shadows against the wall. 'Someday Sweetheart', she sang, a plump girl in a pale pink dress with a frill at the neck. Later the band came on, just ordinary guys up there, could've been him, me, you, clarinet, trombone, drums, bass, trumpet, piano. They didn't seem to have a name, just some men playing together, low-down bluesy jazz. Alex leaned forward into the light with his fair hair glinting, a smile fixed about his mouth, eyes dazzled, watching the clarinettist take the first break. Alex always said the trumpet was his hobby, the clarinet his soul. Harry watched everything: the way the trumpeter worked the mute when he took the second, the way the drummer slouched, the double-jointed thumb of the bass player. And when the blue soft tone of the trombone took that third break, Harry's fate was sealed. The hairs stood up on the back of his neck and all down his spine as if he were a dog with hackles pricked. A thrill embraced him. Standing in the blue mist, in the shadows, he wept for his father. That's what I'm going to do, he thought. I'm going to play the trombone. I'm going to play that music. That's it. The way the slide slid up and down, so easy.

They said it was called 'Basement Blues'.

They were always there after that, he and Alex, there and all the other little dives and dance halls. Jazz was everywhere. Somewhere they fell in with Johnny Miller. Johnny played fantastic piano in his mam's front room, and she let him bring his friends in, all these jazz fanatics with their records. A bunch of them playing jazz together in Johnny Miller's front room, Johnny at the piano hammering out a regular twelve-bar blues, trying to doodle around over that, Harry wishing he could get his trombone, saving up. Johnny's uncle, Ed, took Harry to a music shop in All Saints to get his first one, second-hand, part-exchange for his cornet. God, what a beautiful instrument! The clear gold reflecting the windows. The warm felty smell inside the case. The clasps for the mouthpieces. The heavy feel of it, the handle in his hand as he walked proudly down the street. Taking it out at home and everyone crowding round to have a look and his mam saying, 'Go on, Bud, give us a tune, go on, K-K-K-Katie! Go on, our Bud!' And the girls wanting to have a go and not getting a sound out of it, giggling.

He then put it to his lips and blew, blew and blew, a bold but ragged tune emerging astonishingly to his ears, even recognisably: 'Stars Fell On Alabama'.

Things improved after the interval. Nell found herself next to Johnny Miller and his girlfriend Pam. Johnny was a small, serious, fair-haired young man with a baby face, Pam dark and round-cheeked, very friendly. He said he played piano. Pam worked in town, something to do with mail order. The band played 'Stars Fell On Alabama'. Harry leaned on the back of Nell's chair and sang along with it, knowing all the words. He was a sentimental man. She could tell by the swerve of his voice. Funny, all this going on all around, and the two of them almost like strangers and yet together. I don't know, she thought, all this with men and women, you never really know why any of it is. It just happens. Like suddenly there it is.

Afterwards, when they found there'd been a raid and all the lights were gone and there were no buses running and some of the streets round Piccadilly blocked off, he walked her all the way home, miles it was; some of the time they didn't speak but that was OK. Her head was ringing a little with the noise from the Shalimar. Arm in arm. He whistled.

'Blimey, Harry,' she said, 'you're well appreciated, aren't you?'

He laughed, looked pleased.

'You should have heard them all saying what a great trombone player you are.'

Men. They loved praise.

'I'm not bad,' he said modestly, 'but I'm not great. Not yet.'

'You ought to join Alex Kirby's band,' she said. 'I bet you're as good as any of them.'

It was nice, walking through the dark with him, arm in arm. He was just about the right height, not too tall but no squirt either. He whistled one of the tunes the band had played.

'My mam'll be going absolutely mad,' Nell said.

It was twenty to eleven.

'I'll see you right up to the front door,' he said, 'let her see you're in good hands.'

Mam was at the middle door, between lobby and living room, the light shining out from behind her bulky figure. 'I thought you'd been bombed!' she shrilled.

'We had to walk, Mam.'

Harry stood on the garden path.

'Well, you took your time!'

'We had to go the long way, some of the streets were blocked.'

'Well, if you'd had a bit of thought for others and left earlier you'd have been back! You know I worry!'

'It's all right, Mrs Holloway,' Harry said. 'We were well out of it. We didn't even know there'd been a raid till we came out.'

'It was right under the ground,' Nell said.

'What was?'

'This club.'

'What club?'

'A jazz club.'

A fretful pause, then: 'Well, what do you want to go to a jazz club for? They're awful places.'

'I wouldn't take her anywhere unsuitable, Mrs Holloway,' said Harry, in his stern, calm voice. 'She was perfectly safe.' Mam looked towards him sharply, momentarily silenced by the supercilious tone.

'Mam, this is Harry.'

Mam opened and closed her mouth a couple of times then said, 'It's eleven o'clock!' There was a hurt look in her eyes.

'Oh, Mam!'

'Are you going to stand there all bloody night?' Dad called from the room behind. 'Bring your young man in, Nelly.'

They went in and Dad stood up from his rocking-chair. His hair was going more at the front, greying evenly. He was swinging his fob watch on its chain back into its pocket in the dark pinstripe waistcoat he always wore.

'Hi, Harry,' he said.

'Hi,' said Harry.

They shook hands.

'Put the kettle on, Nelly,' Mam said.

This was the first boy she'd ever brought home, and she felt he was one she could be proud of. He was really very handsome, she thought. She was nothing much to look at herself, some of the other girls were much prettier, but it was her he'd asked out. When she carried the tray in and set it down on the white cloth on the gateleg table, adjusting the tea-cosy nicely, he was sitting on the chair across the fireplace from Dad. His black hair, going back from his widow's peak in little waves, was very shiny with the Brylcreem. Dad asked him about his work, and Harry was very polite and started talking about alloys and things and how he was going to get all his qualifications at evening classes, even if it took years. None of them had a clue what he was on about. They hadn't an ounce of science between them. Bobby was home from another night mucking about with his mates. He was polishing his shoes for the morning, down on one knee with a brush in his hand. Seventeen years old. Bobby was growing more beautiful, more like a golden youth in an old poem all the time. But he was tough with it, not soft. 'I believe you play the trombone, Harry?' he said genially. 'Nice instrument.'

The Jesus statue standing there on the sideboard like that as if they were Catholics. She loved the Jesus statue by now. But Harry now, what would Harry make of a thing like that? I mean, it's not as if we're Irish Catholics, is it? Sukey jumped up on his knee, and Nell was pleased to see that he didn't push her away, even though she walked round and round with the fur flying from her all over his black trousers. Talking with Bob about Artie Shaw and Benny Goodman and the Duke, and his hero, of whom she'd never heard before she met him, the great Jack Teagarden from Texas. He said in New Orleans the bands used to play from trucks going round the streets, and the trombone players always had to play from the tailgate at the back because that was the only place where there was room enough for the long slides.

'So you playing anywhere now, Harry?' asked Bob.

'Here and there,' Harry replied, stroking Sukey's silky head.

''Ere y'are, chuck.' Mam handed him more tea.

'I play with the D Train Seven. They're OK but not great.'

'I wouldn't mind coming up for a listen some time,' Bob said.

'Why don't you? Come with Nell. We're at the Midway in June.'

She'd like that, Bobby to sit with. Someone to talk to. Everyone'd think she was going out with Bob.

She saw him off in the lobby.

'What a handsome lad your brother is,' he said. He had beer on his breath. He had a large, slightly truculent lower lip, though the rest of his features were somewhat thin. She appreciated the fact that he didn't try to force his tongue into her mouth any more when he kissed her goodnight. She'd soon put him right about that one. She hated it, made her feel queasy, like sharing spoons or someone handing you an apple and expecting you to take a bite out of it when they'd already been slobbering all over it with their spit.

Well, she supposed she'd have to let him do it some time, a bit, but not too often.

He strolled off down the road, whistling with skill and ease, a late-night smoky sound.

13

Stars Fell On Alabama

Harry was serious about her from the off. It had to be serious with Harry. You couldn't go out with him and not be serious. None of this confusing and agonising I'd-ask-you-out-if-I-could nonsense, none of this Jimmy Lee pain. She could rely on Harry. He was high-minded, steady and ambitious, all those kind of things that were completely different from the kind of men she'd always known. Look at Dad and Bob. Not steady, her family. Look at Uncle John and Uncle Edmund. They were lovely but they'd never get on. Stanley was steady, she supposed, but Stanley wasn't ambitious. Stanley was happy enough at the Co-op. And Harry was mad about her somehow; she didn't know why, but he was. She made him laugh. He told her her teeth were perfect.

They were at the boating lake at Belle Vue, watching the bright, dashing little waves and the people out there rowing. Harry wore a fine-weave white scarf, loosely knotted at the throat, dramatic with his black hair. It had been his father's, he said. That was when he told her about his mother marrying the lodger not six months after his father died. He didn't say much more than that about his dad, but she knew how bitter he was from the stern look that came over his face when he said it, as if a tremendous anger was pent up in him.

'It's like *Hamlet*,' Nell said.

'Fancy you knowing that,' he said, in an admiring tone.

'I know Shakespeare,' she said. 'We've got a book my auntie Bennet gave my sister Violet. *Tales from Shakespeare* by Charles and Mary Lamb. It's great, that book. I've read them all.'

'You know, Nell,' he said, 'there's not many girls I meet who'd know about Shakespeare.'

Well, he needn't go thinking he's the only one around here with any intelligence, she thought. My family aren't stupid. And she told him about her grandad being a headmaster and writing poetry and even having some published. Quite a few, actually. And not only that, she thought, but didn't add, I'm a direct descendant of Robert the Bruce.

She could see he was impressed with her grandad being a headmaster. He set great store by education. They walked along towards the turnstiles, hand in hand.

'I suppose you'd better come and meet the old Dutch,' he said.

So next Sunday afternoon along she went to meet his family. West Gorton was all back-to-back two-up-two-downs, cobbled alleys and outside toilets, dead scruffy, but *he* wasn't scruffy. Though his cuffs were sometimes frayed, they were always clean. Their house was small and poky, one of a long terrace. The door was opened by Sid, a thin, weaselly little man with glasses and a concave face. 'Come in, love, come in,' he said eagerly, in a high wheezy voice, kissing her cheek. There was a whiff of beer off him. The door opened straight into the parlour. She caught a glimpse of a glass-fronted cabinet full of dinky ornaments. With a pronounced limp, he led them through, past the dark foot of the stairs and into the back room.

'It's our Bud and Nell,' he announced.

'Come in, Nell,' said Harry's mam, 'sit yourself down, love.'

She was over by the window smoothing the white tablecloth, a small fat sloppy woman in a long, shapeless, red and white striped dress, enormous baggy breasts hanging down to her waist. Bare flabby arms. A double chin. Not at all what Nell had expected, even though he'd painted such an awful picture of her. 'She's not an intelligent woman,' he'd said. 'Whatever I got from her, it certainly wasn't brains.' No, it was his father who'd had the brains, and he was gone. She got the impression of a good, faithful, serious man with a flighty wife, a little dark-haired flibbertigibbet of a thing, carrying on behind his back. A floozy. Him and his dad a bastion of sense in a sea of silly women.

Not this.

'Sit here,' said his mam, indicating one end of the settee and sitting down herself in the armchair nearby. She had small suspicious eyes. She doesn't like me, Nell thought.

There was a twittering in the kitchen, a rustling and whispering. 'It's Bud's girlfriend!' said a high voice, then a shushing and a giggling, and his sisters appeared in the doorway, all smiles. They were very pretty. Such bright-eyed dimpling.

'Marjie and Flo,' said Harry.

'Aren't you going to introduce us properly, Bud?' Flo asked coyly.

'He's done nothing but talk about you, Nell.' Marjie beamed, and they were off in giggles again.

'Listen to them,' said his mam. 'Go and put the kettle on, you silly so-and-sos.' She leaned forward and put her hand on Nell's knee. 'I've got some nice seed cake,' she said, in a loud whisper. Nell looked impressed.

It was our Bud this and our Bud that. How brilliant he was, what a marvellously talented artist, what a musical genius. Harry ignored it all and sat reading the paper. He seemed far more uneasy at home than she'd ever seen him. The girls served tea and offered round a plate of seed cake and arrowroot biscuits. They must have had a few coupons salted away.

'Here you are, Bud, you have that nice bit there.'

Marjie was sixteen, a well-built girl with plump cheeks and thick brown hair. Flo was younger and thinner, a hoyden.

'Is your tea all right, Bud?'

'Fine.'

'I can put a drop more milk in for you if you want.'

'It's fine, Flo.'

'He works hard, our Bud does,' said his mam.

Sid didn't talk much, just the odd time when, in a high, exasperated voice, he'd contradict something his wife said, making her look sheepish and move her head in a slight self-deprecating gesture, tutting at herself with a quick sideways glance at Nell. Later, when he'd limped outside to the toilet and the girls were fooling about in the kitchen and Harry, whistling, had nipped off down to the corner for a packet of Woodbines, she offered Nell a sticky toffee.

'Thank you, Mrs Caplin.'

'I'm not Mrs Caplin,' she said, 'I'm Mrs Harding.'

How could she have forgotten?

'Oh, yes. Sorry.'

'The kids are Caplin, of course. Their dad was Harold Caplin too, and his dad was another Harold Caplin so our Bud's the third. It's a Jewish name, you know. My first husband's father was a Jew but his mother was Irish. I like the Jews. Do you know what my name is? Rosaleen. That's a real Irish name that is. Rosaleen Mary Bernadette. Mick, he used to call me, their dad. "Hey, Mick," he used to say. "Make us a nice cup of tea, Mick."'

The toffee stuck to Nell's teeth so she couldn't speak.

'And what does your father do, Nell?'

'He's at Peacock's,' Nell managed. Oh, God, this damn sweet like a gobstopper, chew, chew, chew. Her jaw clicked alarmingly.

'*My* husband was a ticket collector on the trams.' Harry's mam rose heavily to her feet and started going through a drawer that pulled out of the side of the table. 'There he is, there, and that's our Bud when he was a beautiful little boy.'

Nell saw a small man in a dark jacket and trousers and flat cap, walking along a street holding the hand of a little boy with knobbly white knees between the hem of a chunky black coat and knee-high woolly socks. The boy's round moon face beamed Harry's smile.

'Hmm!' she said, trying to sound admiring while frantically chewing.

'Our old house was bigger, of course,' Harry's mam said.

'Ey, Mam,' Marjie said, in the kitchen doorway with a tea-towel in her hands, 'shall I go and get some of our Bud's pictures? He's a brilliant artist, you know, Nell.'

'Oh, he is!' His mam sat down again, brushing a few crumbs from her cushiony breasts. 'They're good enough to hang in galleries.'

Marjie rushed upstairs.

166

When Harry came back Nell was sitting with his sketchbook on her knees and Marjie and Flo were on the hearth-rug holding up his two oil paintings. Sid was poking up the fire. 'Oh, yes,' his mam was saying, 'he's always had a lot of interests, our Bud. Ever since he was a little boy, you could never keep him in. He won't sit around, our Bud. Oh, no! Always got to be doing. Remember when you used to go boxing, Bud? He's got the gloves and everything upstairs. Ey, Bud, go and get them old boxing gloves. Our dad got them for him.'

'She doesn't want to see a pair of old boxing gloves,' Harry said gruffly.

Stupid woman.

'These are really good, Harry,' said Nell.

Well, of course they were. If he was going to do a thing, he was going to do it to the utmost of his ability. What point, if not? Flo held the still-life with onions, Marjie the portrait of his dad done from a photograph taken in Platt Fields. But Nell preferred his pencil sketches. The back alley. The corner of his room. The girls on the settee. Trees in Gorton Park. His trombone from various angles. And then, as she turned the pages, the nudes from his life-drawing evening class, the big fat woman with the folds of flesh, and of course the girls started giggling moronically.

'They're so real,' Nell said. *She* didn't giggle. She looked at him. Her eyes said, Aren't they silly? She wasn't stupid, not giggly and girly. For one horrible moment he'd thought she was a Catholic, seeing that lurid holy statue on the sideboard in her house, but no. And even if she had been, you couldn't help the family you were born into, could you? Just like he couldn't help being born into a long line of Irish navvies and brought up a Catholic because of his mam, not that she believed, not that any of them did, brought up at the monastery, load of tosh. Confession. Forcing kids to make up sins. He used to go in there racking his brains for a sin. In the end he'd pretend he'd pinched a penny from his mam's purse, just for something to say.

'So, what did you think of the old Dutch?' he asked Nell, as they walked back along Clowes Street.

167

Men were funny about their mothers, she knew. 'She seemed a nice woman,' she replied.

'She's OK,' he said.

But he was ashamed of his mam. There was no getting away from it. She never read a book. Couldn't follow a plot. She'd found her level with Sid.

He didn't have much money, and she only had what Mam gave her after she'd handed over her wages; sometimes they went to the pictures, sometimes dancing, but for much of the time they couldn't do a great deal apart from just sit in the park or go for walks or to Sivori's. He loved walking round town. Just looking at things. He knew all kinds of funny little corners of Manchester; after a while it struck her that the things they were doing, the places they were going, were the very same he'd done and gone with his dad.

'Oh, yes,' he said, 'we were always walking – just me and my dad.'

'You must miss him terribly, Harry,' she said.

'Yes, I do.' His eyes filled with tears and she gave him a kiss, but it made him get all amorous again. Poor Harry. Sometimes there was such a lot of pain in his eyes already and he was only twenty-one. His father, he said, had had a great respect for culture and taken him to the art gallery and museum regularly from when he was very small. He had also taken him to hear classical music whenever possible, though that was not very often as he couldn't afford it.

God, though, she'd think guiltily on occasion, he could be obsessive at times. Poring over the lepidoptera in Manchester Museum. Pointing out architectural twiddly bits as they walked round town, lecturing her on the period. Browsing the second-hand records in Mazel's on London Road for hours on end, looking up occasionally with a grin of pure excitement: 'Look at this! Trummy Young with the Lunceford band!' Squiring her round old churches and insisting on translating all the Latin inscriptions. Oh, yes, he knew Latin, he was clever all right. At least you could sit down in the old churches. The day they'd ended up at that church, the really beautiful one in the back streets, she'd sat down on the steps and taken her shoes off. The Hidden Gem, it was called, he said. There was a stoup of holy water in the porch like at Kitty's church where she'd gone once and sat and waited with a headscarf on while Kitty was in confession. Harry loved old churches, though he wasn't at all religious.

'I despise people with faith,' he said that day, sitting on the steps, while she rubbed her blistering heels. 'Gullible fools.'

They walked on, by the backs of big city buildings, with fire escapes and dark dusted windows, deserted for the weekend.

'Look! Look!' she whispered.

Down in a gloomy area, deep in the shadows underneath some iron steps at the foot of the back of some building or other, some factory maybe, some office block. A family of rats, six, maybe seven of them. Two big ones, some smaller, one darting its head out from under the shadow of the slatted steps. There must have been a hole down there. Someone had chucked something down, an old loaf or something. You couldn't tell what. The weather was warm. They ate the crumbs. Little ones' faces bewhiskered, narrow little eyes stupid and peering and anxious. Wormlike tails shifting.

'Poor little things!' she said. 'They can't help being rats.'

She wasn't pretty in the accepted sense, he thought, but there was prettiness hidden in her face. You couldn't put your finger on it. 'Look at that!' he said. 'Fascinating things! Look, that must be the boss! That big one!'

The way his face lit up. He was soft about animals, like her. She loved that about him.

She went to the Midway with Bob to see Harry playing with the D Train Seven. Marjie was there with one of her friends, and Johnny Miller and Pam, and they all sat together at a table near the front. Nell felt proud to be sitting here with the people who knew the band members, and proud when Harry walked on with the rest of the band and he was *hers*. So handsome. Proud to be sitting with such a fine boy as Bob.

Harry, looking very solemn, took his seat beside the cornet player, his mutes at his feet. There was a saxophone and two clarinets, drums and a piano. The leader played a trumpet and stood in the middle. They all wore black dickie bows. The lights gleamed in the waves of

Harry's black hair. They played so fast. To Nell a lot of it just sounded like a big jangle. She preferred the slow stuff, herself. Like 'Stars Fell On Alabama', which Harry sang so beautifully. If she was truthful she would have admitted that jazz was beginning to grate on her nerves a bit, so much of it, all the time. Some of it was OK, though, and it was such a thrill to see Harry sitting up there on the stage looking so serious. She felt for him. She could never have done that, got up on a stage in front of all those people.

They were doing the Lindyhop on the dance-floor. Marjie and her friend got up and danced together. Marjie looked older than she was, smart and pretty and full-faced, dark red lipstick on rosebud mouth, thick dark hair swept up and back, caught under an Alice band and exploding out behind and all around her face in a big cloud of soft curls.

'Fancy a dance, Nell?' asked Bob.

'You're not going to get me doing that fancy stuff,' she said.

She got up and walked on to the floor with him. Baby brother. She felt a bit self-conscious about her clothes. Bright light. Blaring music. Oh, no, she didn't like being up here. Bob and she danced sedately together, smiling. Bob still had his fag in his mouth.

'You could at least have put your fag out, Bobby,' she scolded.

'Sorry, Nell.'

She could never be angry with him.

They bumped into Marjie and her friend, and there they all were, all smiling at one another on the bright dance-floor. Bob gave his lopsided grin around the cigarette to Marjie. She had a very pretty smile. Deep dimples appeared in both cheeks. Then it was the break, and the band came down from the stage. Harry joined them and had a pint. He was still self-conscious, she could tell, sitting there with a funny little smile on his face. He kept catching her eye with it.

'That was fabulous, Bud,' Marjie was saying, one hand on his shoulder. 'God, I do love to hear this boy play!' She beamed at the world around her. 'My brother!'

'Hark at her,' said Bob.

Harry was embarrassed but pleased too, brushing her off with a lofty air. Ruined he was, Harry. Little king in a kingdom. He smiled at Nell. So soft he made her feel, as if there was a string stretched between them, pulling.

'What's your poison, Marjie?' asked Bob, getting up.

Marjie was only allowed to have lemonade. Harry was making sure of that. Nell was on the tomato juice. Bobby kept wanting her to put something in it, some of that awful bitter-tasting stuff, strong spirits, terrible stuff she couldn't stand. Harry and Bob talked about politics. They were both Labour supporters, like Dad. Nell was Labour too, everyone was. The Conservatives were for the posh people, Labour was for the workers. Churchill called the workers scum, Dad said. 'But they're all a bunch of crooks really,' said Harry, 'politicians, the whole shower of them,' and Bob agreed.

After the break Nell started getting bored. The music was all the same, just jangle-jangle jazz, each number starting and finishing exactly the same and all of them running into one big boring mess. And then, of course, Bob danced with Marjie, and didn't they look lovely together! She was an armful, Marjie, and Bob looked like a film star. When they sat back down, Marjie went on jiggling all about in her chair. She turned her head and snapped her fingers, smiling at Nell. 'Our Flo would have loved this!' she called across the table, across the level of the noise.

'Lovely girl, Marjie,' Bob said, walking home.

'She's a pretty girl, isn't she?' Nell agreed.

'You know, Nelly, as far as Harry's concerned, I think he's a really nice chap. Well, we all do.'

'You like him, then?'

'I do. I think he'll be OK. I mean, I wouldn't put up with it if he wasn't. Don't get me wrong or anything, Nell, I don't mean anything funny, but it's just if he was the type to mess you about or anything, let's say I wouldn't put up with it. You know what I mean?'

'I know what *you* mean. It's all fists with you, isn't it, Bobby? You'll have to watch it.'

'No, really, Nell. What do you expect? You'd expect me to stand up for my own, wouldn't you? It's only what you'd expect.'

Mam was on the doorstep as usual, watching down the road for them, Sukey winding round her feet. 'Oh, get under!' snarled Mam.

Sukey, purring loudly, ran into the kitchen. Dad was sweeping the tiles round the fire with the hearth brush. The room was bright.

'Ralph Brigg's been called up,' said Dad.

'Get away,' said Bobby, sitting, bending down to loosen his shoelaces.

'Got his papers this morning. I was talking to his dad.'

'This bloody war dragging on and on,' Mam said petulantly, as if it was all done as a personal affront to her. 'They'll be taking our Bobby at this rate.'

'I wouldn't mind.' Bobby looked up, smiling. 'Kick out bloody Hitler.'

Mam sniffed, took off her glasses and cleaned them. Tears gathered in the corners of her eyes.

But Bobby didn't go to war, not just yet.

Jimmy asked her in the canteen, sitting there sideways on and not really looking at her properly: 'So, you're pretty much spoken for by Harry Caplin, then, Nell?'

'Yes,' she said.

He nodded. 'Hope it works out for you.'

She smiled, a little sadly. Jimmy Lee was still beautiful. He would always be this beautiful thing in her mind, if she lived to be a hundred. Beautiful Jimmy Lee, beautiful Jimmy Lee, who worked in the smithy.

'Nell,' he said, leaning very close across the table; his eyes shot sideways and his peaky face looked like a child's. He was dirty, his fair hair stood up in tufts.

A bell rang.

'Nell,' he said, looking straight into her eyes, 'do you believe in ghosts?'

'No,' she said.

It was time to go, everyone getting up and straightening their turbans and dimping out their cigs.

'Uh-huh,' he said. 'Makes sense.'

That night when she was going to bed she cried about Jimmy Lee.

172

She had a particular way of crying. Dry-eyed for a long time till the stinging became unbearable and she'd suddenly clench her eyes viciously and sob in a harsh, strangulated, passionate burst that was soon brought under control. She wiped her eyes under her glasses, sat for ages on the edge of the bed feeling awful, then took off her specs, got into bed and curled up in the dark.

Harry came round next day and they went for a walk down to Cross Street. Harry said, Had she heard? 'Your old flame, Jimmy Lee,' he said.

'He's not my old flame.'

Harry said it was all over Peacock's. Jimmy Lee's house was being haunted by the malevolent ghost of his father. The whole family heard him walking about downstairs after they'd gone to bed. 'His father's ghost. *Hamlet* again,' Harry said.

She was surprised he didn't seem more sceptical, him being so scientific, but, no, he actually seemed to believe in all that stuff. He told her a story about something that had happened to one of his aunties, a house she'd lived in where she used to hear an old man breathing wheezily and sometimes coughing upstairs.

They went into a record shop, a great rambling place with an open front and a kind of stage at one side that you had to go up some steps to get on to. The stage and all the floor downstairs and all the pavement in front overflowed with boxes and boxes of records, old ones and brand new ones. About a dozen people grazed like cows in a field. Here we go again, she thought, and hung about stoically reading the posters on the walls while he flicked absorbedly away, in his element, serious of face. After about half an hour, after she'd walked up and down, up and down, smoked a cigarette, shifted her coat from arm to arm several times, he unearthed a prize. 'Mezzrow–Ladnier–Bechet!' he breathed in wonder. Bless him, like a kid with a new toy. He had to rush back home to play it straight away then, he was all excited and couldn't wait, and she couldn't help but laugh at him. He insisted she come with him and listen to it too, so she did. But then on the way back he tried to put his tongue into her mouth and she had to push him away. They were like that, men, all mad for it.

173

Made different. Harry was always getting ardent these days. 'Come on, give me a kiss, Nell,' he'd say, pressing close, and though she loved him and thought he was gorgeous, she wasn't at all sure about this feeling, a state of tension heightened to the extreme. So she'd give him a kiss, that much was lovely, but he'd start all that pushing again and she'd have to keep him at bay. It was hurting him, she knew, even in a physical way, but something about even this appealed to her: no one before had ever had such a need for her. He was completely infatuated. Anyway, soon she'd let him touch her breast. But for now she'd deflect him to her throat, which he particularly liked, where he'd suck like a vampire and leave a love bite that she'd have to remember to cover up next day. What did people want to go sticking all their sticky bits all over you for? Even if they were absolutely gorgeous, why would you want it? Did *anybody* really want it? Why couldn't you just love someone and not have to do all that? What was the point of it?

Babies, I suppose, she thought.

Babies. I don't know. She didn't feel very much drawn to other people's babies. Not even Jean. Jean had a look of Stanley. Sharp little nose. Oh, well, poor Jean, she couldn't help her nose. But babies. She didn't know if she wanted one or not. She ought to. Everyone ended up having one in the end. Apart from Auntie Bennet.

His mam and Sid were out but the girls were at home. Harry wound up the old gramophone and put in a needle and played his new record, and the girls danced together, laughing. They were nice, Flo and Marjie. Flo was a very sweet girl, quite sensible, a lot quieter than Marjie, thinner, much less giggly, with a very nice smile. This music was nicer than the very fast stuff he listened to. He put the record on three times, then played her some Jack Teagarden.

'My hero,' he said.

More fast stuff.

'Oh, our Bud and his Jack Teagarden!' Flo said indulgently.

Then he nipped out the back way to get his boxing magazine and the girls closed in on her.

'Our Bud's mad about you, Nell!'

174

'I've never seen our Bud like this over any other girl. Have you, Marjie?'

'No, never. I'm going to make some tea. I think we've still got some of those broken bikkies in the red tin.' Marjie jumped up and ran into the kitchen.

'No! I know where they are! She's hidden them!' Flo ran after her.

The Jack Teagarden Orchestra played 'Peg O' My Heart'. She liked that. A nice tune, a good old-fashioned tune. Nell stuck out her legs in front of her, stretched her arms and started to hum along happily. She could hear the girls chattering in the kitchen.

'"Peg o' my heart,"' she sang softly, in her deep contralto, '"I love you, Peg o' my heart, I ..."' but there, looking in at her and grinning, was Harry, standing in the back yard. He was carrying his boxing magazine, rolled up in his hand. She felt a bit stupid, laughed. Silly me. The look on his face though, as if he loved to look at her, *her*, Nelly Holloway. She couldn't help but blush.

Bob had started going out with Marjie. Sometimes they all went out for a drink together and everyone got on well and had a laugh; Kitty never came out with them any more because she was going out with some ugly lug called Brian, but anyway they had some lovely times. They went to Chester and took a boat out on the river Dee. They cycled out to Lyme Park. A lamb came and put its head on her knee. She and Harry went for a walk. 'I do like watching you go over stiles,' he said. She laughed. Harry could get his hands right round her waist. And Bob and Marjie, you should have seen them looking so beautiful together, oh, they did, both of them so young and fresh and good-looking. Bob and Harry talked about politics and jazz. Harry wanted Bob to learn to play some jazz guitar, but Bobby said he didn't think he could play it like that: he was more for the classical and Spanish-type guitar. They were kids, Bob and Marjie, just big kids. They did make you feel old. They got off their bikes and rolled down a hill, laughing their heads off. Harry said, as they walked on, the four of them pushing their bikes, he had found out the hard way about the dangers of doing that on a school trip up to the reservoir, when he'd gone off on his own and rolled down a hill (knowing that

175

his dad said he never should) just for the hell of it, and rolled right through a great big cowpat, soft and fresh and disgusting and just about steaming.

'Oh, no, our Bud!' squealed Marjie.

He'd been so terrified of telling anyone, he said, that he'd taken off his shirt, shaken and scraped off as much as he could on to the grass with wildly beating heart and a cold sweat of revulsion breaking out on his forehead, turned it inside out and put it on with the cowshit next to his skin.

It was a really hot day and going back on the bus everyone's going, 'Ugh! What's that 'orrible smell? What's that 'orrible smell?' And some smart-alec at the back saying, 'It's because we're going past the Manchester Shit Canal!' And everyone laughing and taking it up: 'It's because we're going past the Manchester Shit Canal!' And him just sitting there and no one knowing where it was coming from. He got home and sneaked in the back and tried to get clean, but of course his mam found out and went up the wall.

They all laughed. 'You poor thing!' said Nell. 'You poor little thing!'

PART THREE

Far, Far Away

14

East

Off to India, full of hope.

Bobby had been granted his request to join a Highland regiment by virtue of the fact that Granny had been Scottish. He'd wanted the Gordons but they put him in the Drummonds, kilt, sporran, tam o' shanter and all. There was nothing on earth to come near the feeling, marching after the band, the skirling of the pipes, the beating of the drum. The Drummonds had the best bloody band in the entire army.

Going East was a huge adventure. He was a smoker and a drinker and a swearer, just the right sort of lad, the sort never short of pals and always ready for a lark and a laugh. His pay had gone up now he'd got a posting, and the uniform was a pull for the girls.

After the first few days on ship he didn't get sick. The food was OK, and there was plenty of beer. At night, the names of the places he would see on this momentous journey, his first away from his small island (for this, he now realised, was what it was), these names from fairy-tales and the Bible went through his head. The Red Sea, across which Moses led the Children of Israel out of Egypt. The Arabian Sea where, once upon a time, Sinbad the Sailor went about in gold silk trousers and big ear-rings.

East of Suez the heat intensified. The stars were incredible. He and his mates slung their hammocks on the deck at night to get away from the stink of the sick bins down below; lying there under the terrifying immediate glitter of the dome, he realised the earth was a ball, saw the curve of it when he raised himself for a smoke and a look over the rail, trembling inwardly in spite of the heat that never stopped now, not even at night. Sometimes he saw shooting stars.

The officers, of course, didn't have to put up with the rows of bunks and the communal sick bins. They went first class.

'There has to come a change one day,' he wrote on the tissue-thin paper to his new brother Harry, 'and it can't be too soon if you ask me.'

Let them stick that in their pipes.

In Bombay he got tattooed. On one forearm, where the skin was palest and the veins bluest, a snake-shaped dagger; on the other a beautiful crowned woman with shadowy black hair, chosen because she was a lovely-looking girl, but not only that – because she looked serious and intelligent, and sort of wise, as if she was a queen in a fairy story. Eastern women excited him. He loved their hair. He thought of her as his girlfriend in the transit camp where they ended up, where they trained for getting Malaya back from the Japs. They were in a big tent, him and the lads, a whole load of them all tanned like natives, not one of them over twenty-two. Malaya would be a peach compared to some of the places you could end up in. Everyone said. In Singapore there were night-clubs where the women were paid to dance with you and to come and sit with you while you drank your beer; Chinese women with languorous eyes and thick, crackling hair. Everyone said these eastern women, some of them, they'd do things you'd never get a girl at home to do in a million years. On the boat they showed them a film about VD.

He was still in India on VE Day. There was a lot of talk but no one really knew what was going on. His friend Alfie said he'd heard they might not be going to Malaya any more. He said the Yanks were doing well in the Pacific and it looked as if the Japs would soon be on the run. But someone else said, no, the Japs were mad bastards and would never give up. All they knew they got from sitting under the officers' mess windows and listening to the wireless playing inside.

'Fucking hot,' said Davy, a dark, thin-faced Geordie, slapping his sweaty red face. Some biting thing, one of the millions.

Bob was writing a letter to Violet. 'I am writing this,' he wrote, 'sitting under the officers' mess windows. I can smell curry. Tell you, Vi, you really get a taste for it. The people out here make curry out of everything.'

Vi had written and told him Nell and Harry had got a house at last, a little one in Longsight just a few doors down from her and Stan. They're writing to you, she said.

He closed his eyes. With the heat burning his eyelids and sweat crawling down inside his clothes, with the scent of heavy blossom, the aroma of spices, the sing-song tongue of the char-wallahs gossiping round by the kitchen door, Bob thought of words like Irwell and Mersey and Sunnybrow Park.

News came of a massive bomb the Yanks had dropped on a Japanese city, Hiroshima, not a bomb like any other that had ever existed. You heard all sorts of things at first. It was the biggest bomb there had ever been. It killed thousands of people, thousands upon thousands, some said a million, some said sixty thousand, seventy, eighty, one, two, three, four ... then another, Nagasaki. They said they would've been vaporised where they stood. Going down the street on an ordinary day, Mam and Dad and Vi pushing Jean, kids hanging about, kicking around. Out on Mellands with the ferret, under a big blue sky with fluffy white clouds. Ended. These Japs, of course, it was their mams and dads and sisters and kids. Kill themselves rather than give up, but not their mams and dads and sisters and kids. No one could. The Japs caved in. They never gave up, the Japs, they'd rather die than give up. But the Japs caved in.

'It's won us the war,' said Bellman, in a tone of mild sorrow. Bellman was a good leader, little man, snub nose, ginger hair. He knew everything.

Bob thought he'd be coming home, but suddenly it was all up stakes and off for Malaya. He posed for photographs on deck, him and his mates, tall, clever Alfie and dark, rakish Davy, holding their guns and staring seriously at the camera. He handsome and fair, Davy handsome and dark, Alfie not handsome at all. Bob's tattoos came out well. He sent the picture to his mam.

Then off to the military base at Port Dickson.

When Dad talked about the flowers in heaven, that's what Malaya was like. Sometimes it was like drowning in perfume. He smelt Malaya before he saw it, the fragrance a change in the air a day out from its low shores, which eventually appeared, blue out of deep blue water. Then high mountains formed in the sky far away, paler blue

181

still. It was glaring bright as you drew closer to the coastline, and they all crowded the rail. Big sea birds circled between the ship and the shore.

Closer in they saw miles of mangrove swamp, and the mouths of rivers; and further, how tangled it was, and how the mountains were covered in thick, wild jungle. Till at length there were miles of glorious sandy beaches with the coconut palms rearing up like long-necked beasts beyond, and a blue sky with fluffy white clouds.

He loved Malaya, though they were hardly there a minute before they were off to Java. He loved looking out over the Straits of Malacca from the bullet-riddled beach at Port Dickson; loved what he saw of the small towns full of mangy dogs and motorcycles, with their bright Chinese shops and dance halls open to the night and strange little picture houses showing posters for old Hollywood musicals. He loved the garish hand-painted billboards for Tiger beer, and the exotic flowers with their somnolent scents, and the fishing boats, and the tiny kids looking after those bloody great buffalo (though they seemed extremely gentle). And he loved Tiger beer. And the fruit! Bananas everywhere! Great big bunches of them growing on trees! You could just reach up and pull one off. Fantastic. Now you couldn't get hold of a banana in Manchester, not since the war. No, Malaya was great. Beautiful country. With those wild mountains shaggy with jungle steaming away behind everything.

He wanted to stay in Malaya, wanted to go to Singapore where they had all the night-clubs. Why are we here? What's the action? No one really seemed to know. Malaya was only a fleeting dream between India and Java.

Now he was really seeing the world! He began a letter to Nell. 'Life is so different out here,' he wrote, then stopped, groping for words. 'I am on the train to Kuala Lumpur, bound for Port Swettenham to embark for Batavia, the capital of Java. As you know, Java is the Dutch East Indies and there is a lot of trouble there at the moment.'

And what a business that train was, crawling along in the heat smacking at flies, out of the window the wild lallang grass growing tall as a man; then a stop in the middle of nowhere, for nothing, and getting out for a pee and seeing right there in front of him a cloud of shimmering blue butterflies, so big they were like birds, only not birds, like fairies. More than anything else like fairies shimmering. The blue of those wings was kingfisher, the flash of which he'd seen once from the old forge bridge in Morland and never forgotten.

They chugged on through a landscape of rundown settlements, of broken-windowed bungalows, with gardens reverting to the wild. You could see the bullet marks in the sides of bridges and on walls. Here and there you'd come across a pretty house with a terrace of gorgeous flowers and a car parked out front, a line of huge humped cattle in a silver paddy-field; and once, a big stone temple of some sort with monkeys running all over it. Then miles of rubber trees and a station, really just a platform in the middle of the jungle, and a red dusty road down which the people from one of the small villages called *kampongs* came to the side of the train with fruit for the lads – mango, lovely, he wondered if he could take some back home but no, and bananas, of course, and pomegranates, and things he didn't know the names of.

There were still a lot of Japs in the jungle. The villagers were afraid of them. The Japs had chopped the heads off a lot of Chinese, Bellman said.

In Kuala Lumpur he got drunk on Tiger beer in the NAAFI club with Davy and Alfie. Talking about what it must be like having your head chopped off. Kuala Lumpur was safe, and a very fine city too. There were monkeys sitting on top of some of the walls when they went out, but they were wild and wouldn't come near. Going through the streets drunk spending his Jap money, him and Davy and Alfie, finding something very funny, he couldn't remember what, and thinking as they flowed past him in the streets, excited, what a good-looking people they were, these Malays, a very graceful people; and the Chinese, he still wasn't always sure which was which. Some very pretty women. All kinds you saw here, Sikhs in turbans, Indians chewing betel, Europeans and Americans and Eurasians. The three of them, nineteen, in seething, spicy Chinatown, spiky brown rows of dried fish hanging up like laundry on the line. They bought some Chinese tobacco, gave it a go, found it sickly.

183

He had a terrible head getting into the truck next day, and was nearly sick as it swayed along through the rising heat. For one horrible moment he thought he was getting the runs, but it passed. At last they reached the wharf. Chaos. They called the warehouses godowns; those that hadn't been bombed were teeming. They were loading for Java, jeeps and ammo and crates of compo rations and manpower, and no proper troopships to spare so that the men found themselves packed like sardines into an infantry landing craft.

'This?' Alfie kept saying, as it dawned on them. 'This thing? We're going in this?'

Swettenham Wharf. Some of them nobby officers riding up and down in a jeep giving out orders. Then up went the gangplank and it was six days in that bloody tub, with no air. Everyone was sick. Everyone. It got hotter.

Hotter.

They had lifeboat drill, nearly too weak to get up, feeling like dirty wet rags. Nowhere to wash properly. 'The stink of us all,' said Davy, grinning weakly. Alfie wondered about the chances of being torpedoed. Pretty high, Bob thought. They were briefed about Java. They were there to keep the peace, Bellman said. Bellman had a face like a child, a snubby urchin. The situation was tense. The Japs had kicked out the Dutch, who'd been there for years and years, and now that the Japs had surrendered, the Dutch wanted to come back. Only the Indonesians didn't want them. The Indonesians wanted Indonesia for the Indonesians. The Japs were supposed to surrender to the Allies. The Dutch were in concentration camps all over the place and the Japs were protecting them from the Indonesians. They had to liberate the Dutch, making sure the Indonesians and the Dutch didn't all kill each other.

'Sounds like a bleeding mess to me,' Alfie said.

Would they have to fight? They hadn't done any fighting yet. Just training. Always training. Of course they'd fight. They weren't loading all that stuff for nothing. He didn't feel nervous. Not nervous. Just take one day at a time. There might be Jap subs around right now. We could all be gone in a second. Boom! Only like being at home in a bombing raid, really. If your name's on it, your name's on it. You say your prayers like a good boy. Oh, God, don't let it be too much for me. Will we be going into the jungle? They had poison darts in the jungle. There was a haze on the sea, you couldn't see a thing. Slow, very slow, all the way into Tandjoeng Priok, the docks for Batavia.

It could have been anywhere, they just wanted to get off this foul LCI.

The docks were in a right mess, heaps of rubble all over, and a couple of jeeps going up and down. They shivered in the heat, from sickness and fatigue. There were trucks waiting. They drove in a slow convoy into the city. It was like Malaya, the *kampongs* with the roofs of attap palm, the figures bowed under their broad hats in the paddy-fields. And it was lush like Malaya, but the road ran alongside a big canal called the Molenvliet, which stank to high heaven. God knows what was in there. It sat like jelly, disgusting, choked up with rubbish and weeds.

The people seemed quite a bit poorer than in Malaya. In the *kampongs* they turned and looked at the convoy. The soldiers waved and some of the people waved back. But not many smiled.

'They don't seem overjoyed to see us,' said Alfie.

It was hotter than Malaya. Davy, his face the colour of putty, was still being sick.

Along the road they encountered a loose cluster of men in sarongs, who turned and faced the convoy as it approached. One raised a clenched fist. '*Merdeka!*' he cried.

'What does that mean?' asked Alfie. 'Bugger off?'

'Freedom,' replied Bellman, portentously.

There was nothing special about Batavia. There were some big posh houses with verandas, one with a tennis court, but all run-down. It was all bungalows and huts, and its wide streets were teeming, more and more as you got into the centre. Thousands of bikes all ringing their bells. And the girls again, the girls so very beautiful. Davy was keeping himself pure for his girlfriend back home, but the rest of them, they were wondering if they could get a taste of foreign flesh. Succulent. That's what it was. Fruity. You heard it was easy, but it didn't *seem* easy.

They were billeted in the Hôtel des Indes, a grand old place, once the poshest in Batavia, but now shabby and run-down. The Japs had

used it in the war, Bellman said. They were on a long veranda opening out on to a huge garden, where a whole lot of brand new army
tents had been erected among the palm trees and tropical ferns. Bob
was in a room with Alfie and Davy and three other blokes.

'I don't like this,' Bob said. 'We're right on the ground floor, what
about snakes?'

'Doesn't make any difference being on the ground floor,' Alfie
said. 'Snakes can go upstairs.'

Davy said this heat was making him feel really queer.

Thank God they were off that hellish tub. Blessed dry land. Their
faces were drawn and dirty. They went down to the taps and stuck
their heads under the jets of cold water. Ah, the relief! Bellman came
round and told them all to be absolutely sure and take the Mepacrine
and the salt. The Molenvliet canal came right down through the
town, he said, and it was worse than a sewer, dead bodies and all sorts
in there. If you wanted to catch malaria, he said, a little dip in the
canal would sort you out nicely. Funny man.

Compo rations for tea again. Tinned cheese, soup, M&V. Bloody
awful. Fucking compo rations and the char-wallah going round with
the strong red tea.

'When are we going to get some decent food?' the lads were all
saying. 'When are we going to get some decent food?'

The night too hot to sleep, the room stifling, the reek of six
sweaty lads. Bob got out and lay on top of his blanket but it didn't
make any difference at all. Sweat ran all over him, trailing itself slowly
like insects. He slept restlessly in the end, waking to the faraway
sound of gongs. Eerie, the gongs in the darkness and the silence. He
lay awake then, feeling how strange this place was, how even the distance between himself and the gongs was made of different air from
the air of home, and the heat in his nostrils could nowhere find the
fragrant smoky tang that drifted from Gorton Tank of a Friday night,
in late autumn, say, with the beginnings of cold on the twilight.
He'd never known such heat as this, not even in India and Malaya.
Just as well they had a change of clothes that morning then, the first
in ages. His shirt was stiff with countless dryings of sweat.

In the morning, the mail. Got a letter from Nell. A photograph of her and Harry. Did he get Harry's foolscap letter? Harry says the newspapers only print what they want you to hear and they're all in the capitalists' pockets and the British public are all too stupid to see how enslaved they are and will put up with anything, like sheep being herded from field to field. And now this war was over there was still nothing for the common man.

After breakfast there was another briefing. Batavia wasn't safe. You couldn't just wander about, not even in pairs, you had to go in a crowd. The last thing you wanted to do was get taken for Dutch by an Indonesian, though the British uniform usually meant you'd be all right. But you couldn't be too careful. Looting was chronic. And there were these extremists, not just in the interior but here in Batavia, and you couldn't tell an extremist just by looking at him (or her, he said, some of them were women), they could just be the next man or woman in the crowd. They carried guns and knives. The ones with the black hats were not extremists, they were the followers of Sukarno and Hatta, who were supposed to be the Indonesian government, only they didn't have much power. The black hats shouldn't give you any trouble. The big problem was the camps: they were all over Java, deep in the interior, God only knew where, full of Dutch, with a few British and Australians too, unreachable for the present.

They weren't going into the interior, not yet. For now they had enough on their hands with the camps of Batavia, full of thousands of women and children with nothing between them and the mobs but the army and the Japanese guards.

'Some of you may be surprised,' the CO said, 'to find yourselves sharing guard duties with Japanese soldiers. This is purely a temporary measure till the arrival of the Allied forces.'

So that was it for now: guarding the women and kids and breaking up riots.

'I never received that foolscap letter, Harry, probably chasing me from India by boat. The women here are not too bad. Oh, by the way, I was sketched by a war correspondent yesterday holding a tommy-gun. Might see me in the *Mickey Mouse Weekly* or something!'

He was under the frangipani, writing a letter. The frangipani reminded him of women somehow, the petals lying on the grass, thick creamy white, cloying like the scent left hanging on the street after a woman's passed along going out for the night.

In the Hôtel des Indes, the officers were having lunch. Little lads with red fezes on their heads going round with trays. Out in the garden, Bob and his mates smelt the curry on the heavy air. Compo rations, the men had had again, but the officers were eating curry and drinking Bols gin.

Nothing much was doing.

The wireless was on in one of the huts. Australian station. Webster Booth singing 'If I Am Dreaming'. Lovely. Must ask Harry if he knows that one.

'Just think,' Alfie mused, 'all those women in those camps all not seen their fellows for years, all mad for it.'

They were sent out among the crowds in the city, heading off riots. Bellman said we didn't want trouble, our job was to make sure it never started. Anything looked like it was turning into a gathering you had to break it up, nicely if possible. The people seemed OK, not too hostile, usually moved on when you chivvied them, even if they didn't want to. There were Indians and Siamese and Chinese, and small, slight Malays with a prettiness about their features, even the men, all complete maniacs when it came to crossing the road, just dashing out whenever they felt like it, dodging and weaving in and out of the cars and bikes and rickshaws. Bloody mad. Placards jogged about above the heads of the crowds. *Merdeka*. Freedom. And banners. 'We hold these truths to be self-evident ...' He would put this in his letter to Harry.

He liked the sound of the Malay language, the babble of the streams of people flowing by.

You started to see a people as a sea, a flowing, eddying thing, silting up here and there, thickening like treacle sometimes, and you were like the spoon going in and keeping it all stirring, keeping it on the move.

Next day it was the deep end.

Forty-eight-hour guards, getting bitten to death by mosquitoes. You just dozed if you could, now and then, while your mate watched out for you. End of the guard you grabbed a few hours.

They were guarding a camp for women; they'd been liberated but they couldn't come out because there was nowhere for them to go. There were no boats. The Japs couldn't leave the island for the same reason. A couple of Japs guarded the outer perimeter with him and Davy, but they weren't allowed into the women's camp. They were sort of prisoners themselves. This one he got talking to one night, he was OK. He gave him some Jap money. Just wanted to go home, couldn't wait. You heard all sorts of things – you didn't know what was what, really. Mobs gathered and milled about on the margins of the camp. Those placards again, bobbing over the crowds. You were glad of those Japs in a way: they knew what they were doing, and it got nasty at times.

You shot over their heads.

You didn't know what to make of the Indonesians. They looked the same, the people in the streets just going about their business, same as the people with placards, same as the ones shouting loudest, same as the ones reaching down to pick up stones. You just didn't know. Any one of them could be a Black Buffalo, Bellman said. You kept hearing about the Black Buffaloes, extremists, they were everywhere. They tortured informers. Bellman said they'd attacked some camps in the interior and killed everyone, even the babies.

'They'll do anything, then,' Alfie said. 'They'll do anything if they'll kill babies. If they'll kill a baby what will they do to you if they get you?'

'There you are,' Bellman replied. 'Stick together, then. Strength in numbers.'

First light, MacKenna and McDaid came and told them a lad called Price had been killed, another sentry. 'Stabbed in the guts,' said McDaid, who was roly-poly like Humpty Dumpty and made a daft-looking soldier, 'and half his face put away with an axe.'

'Jesus.'

'How?'

It could have been me. Could have been me, Bob thought.

'Morgan found him.'

'Jesus.'

'Christ almighty, what a bloody way to go,' said Alfie.

MacKenna, a big fair-haired lad from Berwick-on-Tweed, looked sick.

Price had been a very short, squat lad with frizzy ginger hair and ginger eyelashes. Hardly ever spoke.

'Come up behind him while he was on guard. Must have climbed the fence. Right mess.'

'Poor old Price.'

'I didn't know him,' Bob said.

McDaid produced a ridiculously thin cigarette and a light. 'Chance said Morgan was shaking.'

'I'll bet he was.'

'Jesus.'

McDaid sucked on the cigarette and passed it to MacKenna.

'Don't mind telling you,' Alfie said, 'I'll be glad to get back in civvies.'

Bob felt stupid, he was so tired.

'He was from Wigan,' Alfie said.

'Who? Price?'

'That's right.' MacKenna nodded.

With a *kris*, they later discovered, the traditional Javanese dagger with the wavy blade. Right in the belly, seventeen stabs.

It was sleep he missed more than anything. It got so you didn't know if you were ever really awake or asleep. You kept getting second winds, and third and fourth winds, keeping going, till suddenly you'd think, Jesus Christ! and everything jerked, like when your head snaps down and yanks itself back up to the shock of reality still being there. All the time they were after looters, down around the docks and the warehouse area, was like that. Yet, in a funny sort of way, things were looking up: 'Well, we have plenty of money, Nell, as you can imagine there is plenty of loot etc. we eat nothing but chicken and can buy the dearest drink in Java which is best Dutch stuff at 70 guilders a bottle, a Jap guilder is valued at 6d, living just like gangsters, talk about Gestapo.'

You had to be tough on looters. For a start, they might be armed, lots of them were, you couldn't take a chance. Seventeen stabs to the gut and half his face put away with an axe. You thought about that poor sod. Poor Price. Some poor bugger from bloody Wigan. Probably got his dear old mam back there saying her prayers every night for him, worrying herself sick like Vi said Mam was. Mam worried anyway. She worried all the bloody time, even if you were only on Mellands with the ferrets. Mellands with the ferrets. Ah! Mellands with the ferrets. The fair fields of Manchester. Impossible, here, this sweltering heat, the haze on everything, the great black knots of flies rising up from heaps of rotten stuff in the warehouse area. That sky glaring and blaring, blue like a headache.

They were after the sugar to make explosives. They'd not think twice about doing it to you. Seventeen stabs in the gut and half his face taken away with an axe. Taken away where?

You weren't supposed to shoot them unless they were armed. The rest were examples to the others. Bellman said: 'Remember. These people we catch looting, these are not the normal law-abiding Indonesians, these are the other sort. They have to be discouraged because the situation is untenable. Obviously you can't just have a population running riot smashing things up and taking what they want. Some of the very poorest people are suffering because of these looters. Your average Indonesian is OK, your average Indonesian just wants a peaceful life. But these looters, some of them, not all, but some and you can never tell which by just looking, some of them will be armed. With the *kris*. A wavy dagger that goes in and makes a hell of a mess coming out.' That's what you'd come up against likely as not. The thought of it makes your hair stand on end. You become used to your hair standing on end. It's true. You can get used to anything. They said you never really knew when you got stabbed. It felt like being hit hard. Then you saw the blood. *Seventeen stabs in the gut.* Don't suppose you'd know much after the first one. Or maybe you did. Seventeen though. One, two, three … Seventeen, and half his face put away with an axe.

He'd never used a knife on anyone. A fish, yes. He'd never been tried. You roamed around the docks in a band. Some you let run away, if they were just kids. But then you got that cocky little fucker with the mouth on him. Bamboo makes a good weapon. Bamboo in your hand. Ugly little fucker too. Nasty eyes. Beat him, Bellman said. He didn't have a weapon, if he had a weapon we could've shot him but no. But he cursed us vilely in Malay, he was bloody mad. Fighting mad. Hold him down, Bellman said, and Bellman always sounded calm, it was like you were just dispensing justice, just doing your job. He told Davy and Chance to hold him down. Then Bellman stepped forward, with his calm face and his bantam walk, and ripped the dirty shirt open across the man's back.

Like flaying a carpet.

Everyone had a go. Bellman insisted. It was important that we all work together, he said. If you made sure this bastard never even dreamed about doing it again, you were doing him a favour. Maybe, even, you were saving his life. Bellman didn't take part, but he supervised. He knew exactly how far you could go without killing a man. The intention was not to kill. Morgan and MacKenna went first. The man clamped his mouth shut so as not to cry out. Bob thought his stomach was getting so that he could take anything. Davy didn't want to do it. He didn't say anything but you could tell because of the look on his face, like someone squeamish who had to kill a chicken. Of course, that only made things worse. Your chicken is actually better off with the hard case who'll wring its neck in a flash. Doesn't feel a thing. Get nervous and you end up torturing the damn thing. He knew. He'd done it. Out with Ralph Brigg on Mellands with Ralph Brigg's brother and the dogs. They nicked a chicken once off someone's allotment. It was OK. Death was just what happened in nature. And a rabbit, he'd done a rabbit. Broke its neck first time. The man wasn't as tough as he thought. When his skin cracked open he suddenly screamed. That bamboo's bloody lethal stuff. Best weapon Nature ever made, and just put there for the taking. You could kill a man easy with bamboo. Nasty, though. In a way the ones who got shot were better off. Bang! Gone.

The man begged and cried. It was extremely disgusting, the state of his back when they threw him out into the sun.

They shot five that day, leaving them where they fell.

Bob lost count of the beatings.

A Dutchman was shot at the Hôtel des Indes. Bob saw it. The Dutchman had come out of one of the camps. The Dutch wouldn't stay in the camps, Bellman said. It was mad. They were free but they couldn't come out. A Dutch life was nothing, like a cat in Hell. But out they were coming, going back to their old places, and out came the mobs, crying, '*Merdeka! Merdeka!*' and slitting their throats and hanging them up in trees. Still, there were more and more of them around, sticking to the main thoroughfares and keeping their heads down, some working at the Hôtel des Indes with the army. What did they think? That somehow everything would blow over and they could all just go back to their houses and jobs and whatever? Look at Surabaya. Some Dutch had hoisted the Dutch flag there. The mob killed them and hoisted the Javanese.

The Dutchman at the Hôtel des Indes was shot on a very still day, under a sky of spectacular clouds. You never saw clouds like that in England, so grand and high, so full of light, such pure colour, such deep canyons, such solid, shaded banks: a whole landscape in the sky. The man was half-way across the yard coming back from the toilet when the crack of the shot rang out, and a dark red stain appeared low down in his white shirt. He went down on to his knees with his hands over the stain. A second shot pitched him forward smack on his face in the dust, but he wasn't dead, he lay in the yard making a noise like 'hoo-ooo, hoo-ooo', like sucking air.

Bob and Alfie were right there.

'All right, chum, all right,' Alfie said, hand on the man's shoulder.

There was a terrible stink. The Dutchman had been going backwards and forwards across the yard all day because he had dysentery – that was the smell, really foul, making your eyes water and your stomach rise up in your throat.

The man retched, there was a kind of slow, exhaling sound.

'Gone,' said Bob.

Bellman and another man came with the medics and a stretcher. One of the medics turned the body. Bloody mess all over the dust. The Dutchman's face was ordinary, nothing, just a man.

'Oh, bloody hell,' Bellman said.

They threw up a cordon round the area and patrols went out after the sniper but they didn't get anyone. Bob wasn't sick. He managed to keep it down, though there was a bitter taste in his mouth. Anyway, there was no time, they were out again, guarding a bank, the biggest bank in Java, and a printing works. The rebels said by telephone that they'd take it by twelve o'clock noon; there was a tip-off. They fixed bayonets and put a Bren at each end of the street, but nothing happened, just the long hot morning and the sound of a wireless playing off somewhere in the distance, a Malay station. Then in the sleepy afternoon a patrol of some office blocks. He didn't want to go in. Neither did Davy. There were reports of knifemen. Bob and Davy went up to the top floor, the others were in twos in other parts of the building, a solid colonial block with petals from the yellow trees flown in the windows and lain and gone brown over a long period of time. No one worked here any more. They prowled, rifles at the ready. They didn't give a fuck, these people, they'd be on you and slice your throat in a second. Let it be quick. But there was no one around, not here. Nothing. Abandoned offices, desks covered in dust. The bins left, overflowing, tipped on their sides as if by dogs. The dim windows dusty. Smelt of mould. A corridor, a bit of old dark green carpet. He opened a door and walked into a room, setting off a swarm of lazy flies, which rose in murmurous protest from a long heap a foot high. The stench. He gagged. Oh, God, it was a man. Crawling with big fat maggots.

The heat.

He'd been skinned, there were his muscles, shiny. Bad meat. The skin in withered shreds, hanging off here and there, arms and legs lurid.

'Davy,' he called.

Davy came in behind him. 'Oh, God, I hate this,' he groaned.

The face was black with flies. He was an Indonesian man, you could tell by what was left of his clothes. Underneath the humming of flies, resettling, there seemed to be some other sound, a small, slight, gentle sound, constant. It could have been the munching of maggots.

Both of them were sick in the corridor. Davy was sick again at the top of the stairs. Davy really made a meal of it when he was sick.

194

'You OK, pal? You OK?'

'I'm OK.' Davy's eyes watered. 'Give me a minute. I'm OK.' He cleared his throat and hawked down the stairs.

They stood looking at one another.

'Phew! Phew!' they said, and unaccountably started to laugh.

A thing like that made you feel light-headed.

Bellman said the man was probably taken up there and cut to pieces by a gang of Black Buffaloes for informing. There was nothing we could do. Send someone in to clean up the mess, or leave him there for someone else to stumble across. This place was getting worse.

This is the way of the world, thought Bob. This is war.

His first kill was in a warehouse. It was easy. The man darted out from behind a pile of bales and made for the door. Bob was the nearest, so he shot. It was a good shot, smack in the middle of his back, and he just went down. They left him there. Bob didn't even see his face but noticed the man's foot size imprinted on the sole of one of his shoes as they passed. He was a four. Small for a man. They were a small people. He went on with the rest, gun at the ready, wary. They came out on the docks and he felt a sense of relief. It was over, he'd done it, and it wasn't that bad.

Bellman said the rains were coming. He said we'd be going in soon to liberate the camps. The jungle was full of armed men. Our lads were opening up the road to Bandoeng but the bastards were coming out of the jungle and slitting their throats. Loads of trouble round Semarang and Ambarawa, lots of fighting, through to one of the biggest camps in Java, but when they got there what did they find? Men and women and children, hacked to death and mutilated. Because they knew the army was getting near. God, how they hated the Dutch. Then a Black Buffalo stronghold just outside Batavia was found, weapons, machine-guns. The army went in. Not the Drummonds. Christy's getting tough now, Bellman said. You wait.

Things died down a bit then. And the rains came.

So you thought Manchester was rainy? Ha. The grass turned to mud. What rain. All day the clouds would pile and pile, burst like bladders, chucking it down in floods. It was like standing under a waterfall. But, God, it was beautiful. And the streets would turn into rivers and all the paths vanish, and the sky would come down so low you felt you could put your hands up and touch it. It went on and on, drumming and thrumming and drumming, till you were going mad, and it rained through your dreams and through your thoughts. Then, suddenly, a beautiful morning. Glorious. Those croaky birds calling. A wild, wild smell rising in steam from the ground.

Christmas morning was like that. There was a big open-air service, where everyone kept silence for those who'd died. The heat still. Rain made no difference. Bob had washed thoroughly and his golden hair gleamed, but the sweat was building up already at the hairline. Later they went in trucks to a beach a few miles out of the city. You could look both ways and see nothing but golden sand going on for miles and miles, look out across the glittering sea towards Singapore, the ocean bright blue and the great white clouds like towers above. There were islands off the shore. A couple of lads stood on guard with rifles while they swam, then lay about under the palm trees and had a smoke and drank their beer.

Davy missed his girl. He lay on his back slowly smoking, staring up at the sky. 'We shouldn't be here,' he murmured.

'Well, we are.'

'For what? It's not our business, is it?'

Little boys from a local *kampong* came out of the scrub. Give them a bar of chocolate and they'd swarm up a tree and throw you down a coconut. Some of the lads made them a see-saw out of some old wood and gave them turns.

'Wonder if they're having snow back home,' said Alfie.

They were standing on the end of an old wooden jetty looking down through deep clear water, piercingly blue, at the soft sand and coral below. Bob laughed. Home. At this moment he could have stayed here. Later, though, he knew, getting eaten alive in the mud by mosquitoes, he'd curse this place. When he was back on the compo; no compo today, though, special treats for Christmas, chicken back in the mess. Never mind that you could hardly see your portion. And after, to the big field in front of the Box Club, where the officers played cricket sometimes. The Drummonds dance band played. They always drew a big crowd, not just the soldiers but all the local people would come and gather, all the children, they loved the bagpipes. The C-in-C made a speech. On the terrace, a man in a white suit with a big hat, and an Indonesian woman wearing a sarong made out of some very bright patterned material. Her mouth was crimson. Then a show in the evening at the Harmony Club, all the officers sitting on chairs with long cane backs and the men on the floor, watching a strange and beautiful shadow-puppet show, with haunting music, all drums and high delicate strings, tinkling and jangling, different from anything he'd ever heard before. He loved it. Beautiful, beautiful music. If only he had his guitar. He'd have loved to get his hands on one of those instruments they played.

There was lamplight on the audience's faces. When he looked around he felt again happy, that he should be seeing these things so strange and far, that the world was such a jewel. They all wanted to go home. Everyone did. He did. But, God, sometimes. When you'd had a few drinks and the smoke from your cigarettes made fantastic patterns in the rays of light.

They got a NAAFI shop and an open-air cinema after Christmas, with films sent over from Singapore. There were women, internees, in the Hôtel des Indes. The curfew was lifted, but it still wasn't safe. It rained. God, how it rained. Thunder and lightning in the dark, the wet trees lit up, quivering with the beating of the rain. It went on and on for weeks, then it was damp and sultry and thundery and the bodies lying around the warehouse area started to smell. You couldn't move for mobs of flies, huge bloody things. Bellman said they'd make the looters work. They caught four and made them carry the bodies to the Molenvliet canal. You held your guns on them and watched their will collapse. One in particular, a round-faced, stony-eyed thug who just stood and stared them all down at first, till Alfie hit him with the butt of his gun and Bellman screamed at him to get down there. He went down, he had to. But you could see from his eyes that he'd kill you without blinking, given half a chance. Chance kicked him up the bum. It was a trek to the Molenvliet. The four, like good donkeys, were hauling some dead clown whose shirt was saturated with blood. His head hung down and his eyes were half open. The expression on his face was ridiculous, imbecilic, unless it was just the angle, the way his head hung and the hair, quite long, formed a tufty black halo. All the way to the Molenvliet, Chance kept putting in a kick, till one by one they all got at it, even Davy. Chance and Morgan kept making jokes. The soldiers hung back when they got to the foul canal, sending the looters on to the very edge, which sloped down into thick brown mud the colour of shit. It probably was shit.

'Heave-ho, lads!' Bellman cried, and with a will the four let go their load. Down slid the corpse, open-mouthed through the mud till it sploshed in and floated away slowly, face down, on the filthy water, its arms outstretched.

There were just one or two people in the back streets around here; the whole area stank from the canal and everything was boarded up so you didn't hang around. One man watched, expressionless, smoking a pipe. Another two on a fire escape. Chance and Morgan kept them covered, just in case. But they were no one.

Coming back they met MacKenna and the others.

'There's one back there crawling,' MacKenna said, and pointed out the way.

God knows how long this one had been dead. The rats had had their share so he was in a pretty bad way and the smell was wicked. They put cloths over their mouths and noses but would not extend the same privilege to the looters.

'Sorry, boys,' Bellman said, 'short of supplies.'

All the way to the canal the four looters vomited. You never saw such a vile mess as those four poor bastards spewing from their mouths and noses all down themselves and all over the corpse, splashing the ground as they trotted in a weird clumsy run, desperate to get rid of their burden.

It went on all afternoon.

By supper time Bob couldn't eat. Just couldn't fancy anything. He sat out on the veranda, smoking to keep away the mosquitoes. Davy couldn't eat either. Alfie ate his, though. All Bob wanted was a drink. His skin was hot to the touch and felt as if it was crawling. There was plenty of beer and high spirits that night in the barracks, but when finally Bob lay down on his bunk and closed his eyes, his mind was in turmoil. Partly it was the drink making his head swim; partly because when he tried to say his prayers in his mind, just the usual pre-sleep quick God–bless–Mam–and–Dad–and–Nelly–and–Vi and so on, nothing happened. He kept not being able to get to the end of a sentence because all kinds of things kept piping up in his head, things like: what about when you die? What if it's true, all those things like Heaven and Hell and everything you'd ever done, no matter how small, all weighed up in front of you in a big pair of scales? He'd always accepted that one day you accounted for it all, far away on the other side of death, what Grandad called beyond the veil. What about this man you'd killed? What about all these dead people? Were they in Heaven or were they in Hell? And how could they blame you when it was war and if you didn't get *them* they'd get you? If they could send you to Hell for that, there'd be a hell of a lot of people going to Hell before this war was over. But the war *was* over. The war was over but everything was still bubbling.

A week later he shot another man, a straightforward execution this time. That was easy too, even though the man was standing there in front of him looking at him. All you did was shoot. That was the trick: don't think, shoot. Anyway, the man had a *kris*. Bloody horrible thing. Could have been a Black Buffalo. After a kill, you wanted a drink. All through the next day the man you'd killed came back into your mind, the way he'd looked at you. He couldn't do anything, they'd tied his hands behind his back. Black shiny eyes, a jutting upper lip. Funny the look in his eyes, you couldn't place it. Not really unfriendly, almost curious. Like: You're the man that's going to kill me. But it was after, at night, or early in the morning listening to the gongs in the dark, the eerie trembling gongs – that was when he really got scared. That was when he thought about dying himself, and remembered the dead men standing solid as real people, alive, thought of them going home and eating their tea and doing whatever it was they did, and having mams and dads and sisters and girlfriends. There was an afterlife. He had no doubt. Stood to reason you couldn't put an end to everything that a man was, all the little thoughts and feelings and weird things in your head ever since you were a baby, couldn't put an end to all that with a gun. No. Just because they were gone for now didn't mean you wouldn't have to face them again one day. He was sure of it. Like they say, you have to meet up with everyone again. Granny and Grandad, think of them, they were somewhere. So these men were too. Maybe if there was a bar up there he could be mates with them, like he was with Davy and Alfie. It might all seem different up there, you could buy them a drink and say, Look, mate, no hard feelings, it could have been the other way round, you know how things were. Maybe if I'd been born in Indonesia … Anyway, he might have been a Black Buffalo, stab you in the gut soon as look at you. And then he thought, What rubbish, he'd broken the first rule, he'd done it now, thou shalt not kill and he'd killed, twice, would again, so he was damned and going to Hell. And was seized with appalling terror and felt what little moisture there was left drain from his chapped mouth, and shook with feverish cold in the tropical night.

I have shot a couple myself, not trying to boast or shoot the shit to you Harry but my conscience is none too good now its easy to shoot a bloke but after you keep thinking about going to heaven etc. no joke. I am quite serious I will be glad when I get back in civvies and out of this army. Dont show this to Nell as she wont speak to me again or something. I have about 200 tootal ties so I will send you and the old man some in letters which might go by boat because of the weight so you might not get them for a while. oh I nearly forgot the biggest laugh of all …

The woman they caught looting, she was a nice-looking girl too, round face, big lips, small but a bit on the heavy side. She was at the end of an alley with an armload of shirts, which she dropped when she ran, but they soon caught her. She didn't struggle. She stood between Chance and Morgan, dead still and stiff, with her head hanging and her eyes firmly on the ground.

Bellman said something to her in Malay, but she was sullen.

'Strip her,' Bellman said.

She did struggle then, but what could she do? She kicked out but MacKenna and Morgan grabbed her legs. Chance got her in an arm-lock, and her fingers went like spiders on his arms. They were all struggling this way and that, while she screamed her head off in Malay, her face screwed up. Her round brown belly appeared, and her chunky brown thighs. They pulled her trousers off her kicking legs, her blouse over her head. Her breasts were small and smooth with big nipples. You couldn't help it, there was nothing you could do. You were excited. You felt sick and excited, and you were scared, but you wouldn't have missed a second, you were scared to blink in case you missed anything. Then she was bare as a baby with her arms around herself, standing in the middle of them all, her skin very smooth, thighs dimpled.

'OK, sweetheart,' Bellman said, 'Off you go.'

She stared at him.

'That way.'

She started running with them all around her, cradling herself, head down. They ran alongside, MacKenna and Morgan grabbed her arms from covering her breasts, one each side of her, marching her along left right left right, at a good brisk pace through the barren streets. Everyone whistling. You'd never seen a naked girl before, apart from pictures. You couldn't take your eyes off her, you watched the way her flesh wobbled as her short legs tried to keep up with them, left right left right.

'You're going for a swim, sweetheart,' Bellman said.

Lacey whacked her across the arse with his bamboo.

She screamed, then burst into tears. They had to drag her the last few yards to the edge of the Molenvliet. She knew what was about to happen and she started screaming and thrashing and trying to dig in with her naked heels, which left bloody marks on the ground. So they lifted her, four of them, each one holding a limb, Morgan and MacKenna and Chance and McDaid, and they did a-one and a-two and a-one-two-three, all jolly as if it was a birthday party, swinging her violently this way and that so that her breasts stood proud upon the air. Then with a great cheer they flung her in.

She flew, spreadeagled, graceless. She stopped screaming, or maybe you just couldn't hear her with the loud cheer going up, then splash: she sank in the muck and came up swimming for the other bank, her sleek head like some water animal all covered in slime. At the far bank she scrambled in the mud, getting covered, falling back twice on the slip before managing to get a leg over the edge and haul herself up. They whistled and hooted. She fell on all fours and retched, then staggered to her feet and ran, hell for leather, a mud monster, away round the corner past a derelict godown.

'Right, that's today's laugh, boys,' Bellman said, calming them down.

Going back, Bob saw one of her shoes lying where they'd flung it, a flat black slipper with a strap over. Tiny thing. You wouldn't go in that canal to save your life. It would be like going into a blocked toilet. She was bound to get sick. She might get something fatal. He kept thinking of her naked body swinging in the air, and then covered in all that filth. He felt sick, sick and excited.

He wanted a drink.

... if we catch women looting we strip them, march them through the streets and then fling them into the canal, rather disgusting I know but these people must be taught a lesson. So. Well I will write again soon Harry, well I hope so, so I will finish now expecting to hear from you soon. Your Brother, Bob.

15

Chell Street

'It's over, Vi! It's over!'

Harry danced with Violet in her back yard, his hands on her waist. Nell stood at the door with baby Jean.

'There's your mammy,' she said, smiling, 'dancing with your uncle Harry.'

She was happy. She loved her house. Peace. No one breathing down your neck. Only Harry, and he was out all day and she could go and sit in Vi's and have a cup of tea and a natter. They passed Bob's letters backwards and forwards, those exciting air letters marked 'On Active Service, 14746716 Pt. Robert Bruce Holloway, A Company, 1st Battalion the Drummond Highlanders, South East Asia Command'; giggled about Mam, sided with Dad. Nell liked walking down the street and all the neighbours knowing who she was because they all knew Vi, who always got to know everyone wherever she lived because she was like that. And waking up in the morning to the cock-crow while it was still dark. She didn't mind it at all, it was nice, reminded her of Morland and Granny and Grandad, both dead now, and the old forge bridge and the path down the side of the church-yard. Old Mr and Mrs Fallowes next door, with their chickens, and their lettuces and radishes growing in tubs of soil. Though nowhere less like the country could you find than the narrow terraced street with its two tiny offshoots, all two-up, two-downs with cobbles at the back. They had a high-walled yard with a coal bunker and privy and a tall gate into the back alley. She wrote to Bob: 'I like Chell Street, it's quite like home in a way. As well as Violet and Stanley there is also Cousin Joey and Berenice.'

At their end of the street a ginnel ran under the railway, which went over high in the air behind a big wall to stop kids getting on to the embankment. People chucked rubbish over the wall. At the other end was Stanley Grove, with the shops and Bee's chippy, and if you turned left it was only a step to Stockport Road, where there was Woolworth's and the King's and Queen's picture houses, and shops of all kinds, and pubs, and a couple of big hotels. The buses went up and down, to and from town, chugging and fuming all day in the back-ground.

Next to the railway line a narrow passage went one way down to Stockport Road; the other way under the long dark ginnel, its mossy dripping bricks seeming to breathe, then out under the railway line at the back of a school and a big church with a wild green garden all around it; and after that, lots and lots of neat little terraced streets.

It was a fairish walk back to Mam and Dad's. She was glad she'd left work now. For a while at home (listen to her, still calling it home) she'd felt depressed about it, but now she had her own house it was lovely. She wasn't a great housekeeper: she whipped round quickly in the mornings after Harry had gone out, then she could do whatever she liked; sit and read if she wanted to, without Mam always nagging at her to get off her lazy arse and wash them pots or sweep them stairs. She could nip down to Stockport Road and go round Woolworth's. She could even go to the pictures if she wanted to. She loved the pictures. Now and again she and Violet left Jean with Sissy Slack up the street, bought themselves a bag of sweets and went to see a film. They loved epics.

She sang as she went about her jobs, then made herself a cup of tea and sat alone with the cat on her knee, a sweet, slinky little black and white female called Chisholm. *He* was at his mam's. She didn't like it when he went to his mam's. I bet the old cow's saying things about me, she thought. She'd been awful when he'd told her they were getting married. Called her a snotty-nosed kid. He'd had a big row with her but he'd started going to see her again.

Things were better with Harry now he could play his trombone all the time. They'd stayed with Mam and Dad for a while after they got married and it was awful, him all jumpy wanting a blow and worrying about making too much noise. This house was full of music whenever he was in. He couldn't stand a silent house. Didn't like being on his own. Always wanting to be doing something or hauling her off somewhere. They went to the pictures on Stockport Road a lot, saw *Hellzapoppin'* and *42nd Street* and *Sullivan's Travels* and anything with gangsters in, and *Cabin in the Sky* with Louis Armstrong in it as an angel or a devil, playing his trumpet in the hereafter. She felt so lucky to have him. She loved the way he looked, and the way he was always so much more serious somehow than all the others. Life was serious. He'd suffered. It was tragic about his dad. And yet he was very brave and strong and just carried on doing what he thought was right. It was important, doing what you thought was right. An honourable man. Like Brutus. He'd never let her down, she knew that instinctively. In fact, odd as it may seem, in some ways she thought he was keener than her. He could be very romantic. A letter he'd sent: *I hope we will be sweethearts in this world and the next.* Funny, he was supposed to despise faith, yet he talked about the next world and believed in ghosts. She kissed the cat on top of its pretty warm head and carried it purring on her shoulder up the stairs, opened the wardrobe door and started going through Harry's pockets. Something in Bob's last letter had upset him. Bob wrote to all of them, but all the real news was in his letters to Harry, letters she'd found neatly folded into fours in inside pockets. Harry, being such an honourable man, wouldn't pass them around since they were private. Bob wrote all the horrible stuff in Harry's letters: he was trying to keep it from the rest of them. All he wrote to *her* was stuff like how the sergeant had complimented her darning on one of his socks, said it was beautifully neat, almost a work of art.

I was very glad to receive your very welcome letter, also the photograph, I thought it was a good one. it was just like seeing you both again when I looked at it, I am glad you sent it me, thanks. Well Nell I am in a good place now, on a mountain pass not far from Buitenjorg on the road to Bandoeng. it is very cold up here. we have just found out that we are higher up than Ben Nevis the highest mountain in Britain so you can imagine. it's a big change from Batavia, where even sleeping on top of a blanket makes one sweat. We have a Dutch swimming pool here. Although it is always freezing we go in a lot because we have nothing else to do.

But there was nothing in Harry's pockets, so she opened the old pot-bellied sideboard that served as his own private place. He kept all sorts of things. Tickets. Travel arrangements. Finances. Harry took care of all this side of things and had all these boring documents in piles with different-sized elastic bands holding them together. Nell was only too happy to leave those things to him. She couldn't stand even to think about them. There were his art books. Rembrandt, Leonardo da Vinci. He had cousins in London and once, down there on a visit, he'd stood in front of Leonardo's *The Virgin of the Rocks* in the National Gallery all day long. He said it was the most beautiful thing he ever saw in his whole life and if he had it for his own he would just sit there and do nothing but look at it for hours on end. There were his books on drawing, his sketch books with the nudes. They were fat, those models. How could they stand there like that? His books about the Mafia, his H. P. Lovecrafts, his *Weird Tales*, a couple of old Everyman Classics, *Eothen* and the works of Edgar Allan Poe. His old stamp collection. The small blue hardbacked pad in which he wrote his music notes, sitting there late at night with it on the arm of his chair, seriously writing. She picked it up and opened it. Neat, rather stern handwriting, on the large side. Artistic. In some ways he reminded her of Dad. That meticulousness. A heading: 'Instrument Selection. Mouthpiece Characteristics and Their Significance'. A numbered diagram. Typically thorough and scientific. In the back he seemed to be writing his own handwritten tutor, with notes.

Note: the term 'air' in this work refers both to the air which is inhaled, and the mixture of waste gases which is exhaled.

More headings: 'Correct Breathing and Blowing'.
'Correct Use of Lips'.
So proper. And yet he was an emotional man. His deep brown eyes had filled with tears when he'd suddenly said, one night in the Gorton Mount pub, 'I'm crazy about you, I think we should get married.'
Nell put the book back.
Then she found the letter.

The extremists called the Black Buffalo organisation who are all murderers will get no mercy from us for we are getting fed up with them there will be plenty of firing squads. the usual method is to kill them about eight at a time stood on the edge of a canal with their hands tied. I have been on a couple and it gives me great satisfaction to execute these men who cut little children into small pieces but who plead for mercy when caught. it makes my blood boil one man about to be shot dived in

*the canal and swam under-water for about thirty yards when he came to
the surface my pal knocked half his skull away with a 303 bullet it came
away just like cutting the top off an egg. I am enclosing a Malay love
song to give you an idea of the music out here. the words will sound very
corny, but they are the nearest you could get to the translation to English
from Malay language. Well Harry I will close now as I cant think of
anything else to tell you at present. Lots of Love. Your Loving Brother.
Bob X*

Like cutting the top off an egg, like Mam used to cut the tops off
their eggs when they were little.

An egg full of blood.

Nell put on her coat, put the door on the latch and went out.
Violet was in Bailey's, talking to Sissy Slack. Vi knew everyone in the
street. Baby Slack was sucking her dirty thumb and solemnly observ-
ing Jean, who was screaming because she wanted a barley-sugar stick.
Vi would give in to her. Vi always did.

'Ey ey ey,' Violet was saying, as Jean wiped snot on her leg, 'stop
it, you naughty girl!'

'She looks a bit peaky,' Mrs Bailey said, rocking forwards on her
vast breasts to look down over the counter. Mrs Bailey was dead
nosy.

'Baby's not been too good,' Sissy Slack said. 'She ran a bit of a
temperature last night.'

'What can I do for you, Mrs Caplin?' asked Mrs Bailey.

'I'll have a small condensed milk, please, Mrs Bailey.'

Mrs Bailey swivelled in her chair. She was so fat that she couldn't
get up easily, and the entire business of the shop was conducted by
means of a long metal pole with pincers on the end that could reach
into every corner and up to the ceiling. Anything this couldn't handle
you had to get yourself. As she turned, her breasts flopped off the
counter like walruses and landed in her lap. 'Hubby gone out?' she
enquired.

'Gone to his mam's,' said Nell. She hated that word, hubby.

'Mam well?'

'Fine.'

207

'Oh, go on, then,' Violet said nowtily, 'give us a stick of barley sugar when you've got a minute. You naughty girl!'

'You don't want to give in to her,' said Nell.

'Where was it you said his mam lived?'

Nosy cow.

'Over the other side of Belle Vue,' Nell said.

'Ah.'

'Oh, well,' Sissy Slack sighed, 'home again home again bumpety-bump! Come on, you.'

Kids. Always snotty. Nell was supposed to be trying for a baby, but she wasn't sure she wanted one. Harry did. He wanted two. Well, she was in no hurry.

'There!' Vi said roughly. 'Nice toffee! Now shut up!'

Jean shut up and sucked.

'Another letter from our Bob,' Nell said, when they got outside.

Vi's face lit up. 'Is he all right?'

Well, what could you say? 'Come and read it. He's fine. It's just all the horrible things he's seeing.'

'She's got to go down for a sleep,' Vi said. 'You come in mine and I'll make a cup of tea.'

Violet had got her house nice. She was well settled now. A fire burned in the grate, and she'd got a couple of glass-fronted cabinets with ornaments in. A brightly coloured oilcloth on the table was smeared with porridge in front of Jean's highchair.

'Here.' Nell passed her the letter.

Vi's face changed as she read. Outside, the sound of a dog barking. Nell went into the kitchen and put the kettle on and stood gazing out at the yard and fingering her locket, a gold one Harry had bought her, with the two tiny pictures she'd put in, one of Harry, one of her dad. A big old black and white stray with notched ears was sitting on Vi's back wall. She smiled at the cat through the window. He fancied Chisholm. You should hear him sing some nights. When she went back in, there were tears in Violet's eyes. She handed back the letter. 'He's still our Bobby,' she said, 'he'll always be our horrible little Bobby.'

'He's too young for all that.'

'Who isn't?'

'You know what I mean. He's only a kid.'

Violet sat very still for a moment, staring straight ahead.

'He sounds hard,' Nell said. 'It's turning him hard.'

Vi blinked and scooped up Jean, all sticky and cross and red. 'It's war,' she said evenly, 'it's just war. Better he gets hard than goes barmy.'

Nell couldn't bear to think of him out there turning hard; in her mind constantly there was a picture of him crying, big lad that he was, when Mam had Jock put to sleep. His framed photograph stood next to Jesus on the sideboard, head and shoulders, slightly touched up with colour so that his fair hair gleamed and his skin had a delicate rosy hue. He looked very handsome, full-lipped and cleft-chinned, his soldier's cap at an angle, his expression pensive. Another of him in his kilt stood on the mantelpiece. She couldn't get that out of her mind, even after she'd gone back to her own house and put the letter back where she'd found it, folded just the same. That and another picture, of Bob the soldier, handsome in his uniform, blue-eyed, pink-lipped, hard. Laughing callously in a big gang of other soldiers. Anyway, what if he goes hard *and* barmy?

A knock on the door.

Cousin Joey asking if he could clean her windows. Cousin Joey lived in the other, longer bit of Chell Street, the bit that continued over the other side of Stanley Grove. He was Uncle John and Auntie Grace's third or fourth, a big strapping lad with dark ginger hair and a morose rectangular face covered with dark freckles from corner to corner. Harry called him a scruff.

'I've got my ladders now, Nelly,' he said.

He was starting up as a window-cleaner.

'I thought I could do this side Tuesday. I've got Barnby and Purcell and all them lined up Monday. Is Tuesday OK for you, love?'

'Oh, all right, then, Joey. How's your wife?'

'In the pink, Nelly.'

Joey had amazed everyone by somehow, during the course of the war, acquiring a stunningly beautiful Greek wife with jet black eyebrows and a big film-star mouth.

'I saw your Ruby yesterday,' she said. 'When's she getting married?'

'July, Nelly.'

'Smashing.'

'Is next-door in?'

'He's in the back with his chickens.'

'OK if I cut through?'

'Course.'

Big rough Joey in his baggy overalls went lumbering through the house to the back door. Harry came in, and started larking around asking for a shirt, standing there in his vest pretending he'd got muscles. Atlas! Him and his thin white arms. 'Come on, Nell. Let's go out.' He just couldn't sit still.

'What? Now?'

'Look.' Proudly he laid out upon the bread-board two pound notes. 'That's from the Dixielanders' job. And the Capri Ballroom do.'

He pulled at the strings of her pinny. 'Get this thing off and let's go out. We'll go to Archie's chop-house.'

'I've just done the potatoes,' she said. Her hair wanted washing.

'Well, they'll keep, won't they?'

'Not really.'

'Yes, they will. Put them in water. Come on! You can have a mixed grill. The mixed grills at Archie's chop-house are supposed to be fantastic.'

She went and put on some make-up, combed her hair, changed into her decent dress, put on some stockings. Sometimes she just didn't feel like going out, all the palaver of having to wash your dial, hair all greasy and him saying you look OK when you know you're a mess. But it was funny: once you were out it was OK. Off they went, arm in arm down to Stockport Road, caught the ninety-two and went up on to the top deck.

'You ought to see yourself going upstairs,' he said. 'You really wiggle from side to side.'

'Ssh!'

He laughed. 'No one's listening. Honest, coming up behind you, you're going ...' He made movements with his hands.

She pushed him. He pushed her back. They were on the back seat.

'Stop it, Harry! Not here.'

His eyes were merry. He rested his arm along the back of the seat and whistled 'Ain't Misbehavin'', full of twiddly bits.

There was still a lot of bomb damage round Archie's, in the old end of town, not far from the Shambles and the cathedral. Where Harry used to come and ride around on his bike when he was a boy, where now he still haunted the second-hand bookstalls on Shude Hill. Archie's was posh. Nell felt dowdy going in, the waiters' jackets were so white and the carpet so red, but Harry walked in as if he was in these places every day. They were given a table for two, with a pale pink tablecloth laid over a spotless white one, sparkling cutlery, folded white napkins in glasses. The menus were white cards with fancy edges, all printed in flowing italic script. Harry ordered wine. She tried to say she didn't want any, but Harry said you had to have wine with a meal like this, it was the done thing. 'Just sip it slowly,' he said, looking around with a satisfied expression. 'My dad always said to me, never be afraid to hold your head up and walk into any of these places. You're as good a human being as any of them. Never forget that all men were created equal.'

Ha! she thought. And our Joey's not good enough for him. 'My dad used to say something similar,' was all she replied.

'"When Adam delved and Eve span, who was then the gentleman?"'

There was a piano in the middle of the room, and a fat man with glasses and dark hair and a big nose tinkling away. Harry started singing along, quietly: 'Walking My Baby Back Home'.

'You're as good a singer as any of them, you know, Harry,' she said loyally. She meant it.

He smiled, pleased. His narrow, delicate nose wanted strength. She didn't care. She thought he was very handsome. The wine came, red. Harry acted like a connoisseur, sniffing the glass and swirling it round briefly before taking a sip, raising his head thoughtfully, taking another. Finally he nodded, and the man poured for them both. She ordered chicken; he had a mixed grill. She forced a bit of the wine down. It was horrible. The food was lovely, though, and made up for it, and so was the sweet – Knickerbocker Glory. She'd never tasted anything so delicious in her life. In fact, she'd only eaten out once or twice before, and never with wine. And then, when it was all over and she was full to bursting, they had coffee. Nice, though rather bitter, even with the sugar she put in. All in all she thought she preferred tea.

She felt nice and sleepy then and wanted to go home, but Harry wouldn't hear of it. They had to go on to a jazz bar, some dark smoky poky place, and of course it was noisy and rowdy and full of people he knew. These jazz people all went to the same places. The trumpeter Paddy Noonan was there. And Andy Fuller, the thin dark one who always got dead drunk, and a strange-looking man called Murray Wells that she'd never seen before. Hideously ugly, poor man, huge bent nose, tiny eyes, big wet slobbery pink lips, great yellow tombstone teeth sticking out all over the place. One of those people who always held liquid in their nostrils. And of course all these people had to crowd in at the table with them, loud and boozy, the talk always of jazz, jazz, endless, one-track, as if there was nothing else in the world to talk about.

Couldn't these people think about anything else?

Soon as they got home, out came the trombone. He stood playing in front of the remains of the fire. There was no doubt about it, he was good. She didn't know the name of the tune he was playing, but it sounded sad and happy at the same time.

'That Andy Fuller was very drunk,' she said, as he pressed the valve that let out the saliva. Disgusting, she thought.

'He's a banjo player,' Harry said, as if that explained it.

'Who was that man with the very gappy teeth?'

'Murray Wells.'

'He seemed a bit odd.'

'He's the manager of the Tailgate Five. Or Six or whatever it is now. Alex's band.'

Harry played some more, soft-mouthed, then said, 'You know, Nell, I could join them. They've got this Roy Finlay on trombone now but he's not likely to stay. Paddy's in. And Johnny Miller.'

'Hm,' she said.

'The Tailgaters really swing,' he said.

She couldn't help it, it sounded a bit daft to her when he talked like this, as if he was trying to sound American.

'They're much more my style.'

'Well, that's all right,' she said, 'so long as I'm not expected to go along to everything.'

'You don't have to go to everything.'

'I don't know where you're going to find the time.'

What with the evening classes and the D Train Seven and the Silver Band, though he was always saying he was giving that one up. A shame, really, because they were a very good silver band, always winning cups. They'd won the Perrin Challenge Shield, the Duckworth Challenge Cup, the Alex Owen Memorial Cup.

'Well, obviously I'd have to cut down on other things,' he said. 'But Murray's a fantastic manager. He lives somewhere out near Alderley Edge. Alex Kirby says he lives in a great big house full of antiques with his old mother. Never got married.'

'I'm not surprised,' Nell said.

16

Spoils of War

It was the night before they went into the jungle to locate a camp that had been spotted from the air by one of the Dakotas. The forests were full of guerrillas, dressed in black, calling from the trees: 'Hey, Tommy! Hey, Tommy!' Sometimes you heard them but didn't see them. It was their terrain. They'd slit you up the middle soon as look at you.

Bob stank. They all did. Same clothes day in, day out. He had this feeling as if he wanted to go to the toilet all the time, only he was scared to go; they all were, because the jungle was all around, huge and black and full of noise. They were in a hut. Everyone telling jokes and having a laugh. You couldn't say you were scared. All sitting about just waiting, a feeling as if he'd got maggots walking around in his stomach. The heat running off him, and the sweat.

A small window, high up, was open to let in a bit of air, though you wouldn't have known. Through it came a little cat, a skinny spiky scrap of a thing, tabby, like Sukey when she was a kitten.

'Ey up,' said Alfie, 'what's to do?'

The kitten miaowed, curious and friendly.

'Puss-puss-puss!'

'Ch-ch-ch!'

It jumped down on to Chance's bunk. Morgan picked it up and held it and it twisted in his hands and scratched him.

'Charming!' He dropped it and it ran along the bunk and sat down suddenly to have a good scratch.

'Well, you're a nice little thing,' MacKenna said, picking it up and tickling its chest. It had a loud purr.

'We've got a cat called Felix at home,' someone said. 'He's just like that only he's got a white chest and white back paws. He sits on the hob even when it gets really hot.'

'Let's look at the little blighter.'

MacKenna passed the cat back to Alfie. Everyone wanted to have a stroke and a pet of the creature.

'Hello, Puss!'

'Puss-puss-puss!'

'Here, Pussy!'

Afterwards whenever he tried to explain to himself about what happened, he couldn't. The only person he ever told was Nell. He knew it was something to do with the fact that they were all nervous and that the jungle was pressing up all round them in the dark. The cat went around the hut from hand to hand, playful, batting with its paw. It sat on Bob's knee and looked up, miaowing into his face with its clean pink mouth and all the rough white spikes on its tongue. He gave it a stroke, tickled it behind the ears. MacKenna took it. They started teasing it. Where did the playing end and the teasing begin?

At some point the kitten put out its claws, and a few of them got red stripes down their arms.

It got a bit rough.

'Come on, give it here!'

'My turn!'

'Puss-puss-puss!'

All of them laughing, my turn, my turn; then it scratched Morgan really badly and he roared and tossed it up in the air and when it came down, landing on its feet as they do, Davy picked it up, but it squawked, lashed out and ran along the wall. After that it was a free-for-all. God knows how. They weren't so much passing as throwing it round, tossing it from one to the other. Its mouth was open but you couldn't hear it. Up, with its legs flailing, up in the air, reminding him of the girl they threw into the canal, and the great gales of laughter, swelling and swelling from the men.

Bellman didn't join in. Bellman just sat there and watched, smoking, shirt off, chest shining, smiling as he watched.

Up, up in the air, from one to another.

'Worrrgh, over 'ere over 'ere!'

Pulled and grabbed and tossed, a tug of war, a game.

They killed it.

God knows who was the first to dislocate a leg or twist its neck – after all it was so soft and small, it was so easily done. They all got scratched. They wore the scratches for days. Bob had a memory of a furry thing yielding in his hand. They were trying to stop it scratching because it had gone lethal; they were trying to finish the job, because it was damaged, quite obviously, you couldn't let it live past a certain point.

They killed it and threw it out into the darkness and the jungle, and the funny thing was, after it was all over, nobody spoke. You could have heard a pin drop in that shed.

Incipient thunder.

No one said a word. No one looked at anyone else. They went straight to bed in silence. He'd never known an atmosphere like it. As if they were all embarrassed.

And nobody ever said a word about it ever again.

★

215

The convoy lurched and bumped slowly along the track. The rivers were in flood. You could hear them, gushing and swirling deep in the jungle. Twice they heard the hollow booming roar of bombs in the distance.

Near midday they came to a place where about half a dozen big tree-trunks had been dragged across the road. Bellman went up ahead to see what was going on. It was going to take a while to shift the blockage, he said when he came back. Several men must have done this. The scouts didn't think whoever had done it was still in the area. He half smiled, his cold, narrow-eyed smile, and said: 'It's all right, boys, I don't think our number's up quite yet.' These dense forests threatened more than the city streets and the warehouses. The jungle played with sound. You couldn't tell if a thing was near or far. There was an echo. This narrow track was like a tunnel. They strung out all along the edges of it, prickly as cats with a strange dog in the street, rifles at the ready. Strange birds called, harsh-voiced, not very near.

It took half an hour to clear the track. The jungle was still. There was a lot of talk between the officers, and a couple of Dakotas flew across, low, slowly circling. Bellman told them the planes had dropped bombs on a terrorist stronghold not more than a mile away. A mile! Anyone there who wasn't dead must be badly injured, but you never knew. We were going in to finish off anything that needed finishing off.

'Chance, Cooper, Holloway, Dickson, Geddes, MacKenna, come with me.'

Let them be dead. Let them all be dead. But if they're not, let me do my job properly.

A scene of peace. The camp smoked mesmerisingly in the noon heat, humming with the murmur of flies. They split into twos. The terrorists were dead, killed by rockets and bombs. Not as much mess as you would have thought. There were eight of them, lying where they'd been thrown, any old way. Some had been running when hit. But two were a real mess. It wasn't as bad as the man in the office block, maybe because they weren't stinking yet, maybe because he was getting used to it, but bad enough. One man's legs must have taken a direct hit, they were just gone from half-way down the thighs, and you couldn't tell where they were. There didn't seem to be anything nearby that could have been them or a part of them. Bob couldn't quite believe what he was seeing.

The other had no face, just something like you'd see in a butcher's shop. Like when you skinned a bunny on Mellands.

Silently they moved through the smoking, humming camp. Then they stood, looking about.

'There's nothing more we can do here,' Bellman said sorrowfully. 'That's it, boys.'

Before they left, they went through the dead men's packs and pockets. They took the guns and ammo and any food or money. Bob found an old brown leather wallet in the inside pocket of a small curly-haired man with even features and a gentle, girlish mouth, lying upon his back with his neck snapped sideways at a horrible angle. His cap had fallen off.

Searching the dead was easy. Your mind snapped a picture as your hands worked, you recorded it but you did not think. Not then. You put the wallet in your own pack with your other things. Spoils of war.

They got through. The gates of the camp were open, no guards patrolled. A dead Jap lay on his face across the threshold. Bob and Davy moved him to one side. The camp was just a few long barrack-like huts in rows, with a bit at the side that looked as if it might have been tended as a garden. Four women dead in the garden. Three in the central area. Throats cut, so deep their heads hung at funny angles, like puppets, impossible. The flies were feeding at the cut throats and the bloodstained sand. Dutch women, he supposed. Black Buffaloes did it. It was what they did if the soldiers got too close to a camp. You can liberate it, sure, if it's worth liberating corpses.

Five of the huts were empty, just a few rough sleeping areas on the floor, neatly folded filthy blankets, tin mugs. In the sixth they found another twelve women and three children, all thrown in a corner together like a pile of discarded sheep's heads in the corner of the butcher's. He'd actually seen that once, a pile of sheep's heads, lambs still with their white curly wool and mildly smiling mouths. The faces of the women and children had been abominated. Their arms had been hacked. Noses, lips, ears cut off. Eyes bloody holes. How could you make that out of a child's face? No grace in death, these women with their splayed hairy legs, splodges and holes for features.

Two of the children were girls. They might have been twins – at any rate, they were about the same size and their hair was the same colour. Light brown and fine, tied up at the sides. How old were they? Bob was no good at judging kids' ages, particularly when they had no faces. Five? Six? Seven? And a boy, about twelve from the size. Scabby little-boy knees, dirty, drawn up to his chest. Clasped in the arms of a woman with the face of a nightmare.

'Christ,' whispered Davy.

Bellman sighed. 'OK, there's a lot to be done here,' he said.

These things change you. Of course they do, it stands to reason. Though reason seemed an odd thing to appeal to here. Bob felt changed, deep down at some profound level, as if his blood had all been drawn out of him and tampered with in some way and then put back different. At night you thought about it. It was beyond thinking. You wondered about those people. You couldn't tell if not seeing their real faces made it better or worse or didn't make a difference. One thing you knew: nothing could be undone. You could wish and wish and not a thing could be undone. It was real. It was true. You stopped thinking. You took out the old battered brown wallet, the one belonging to the curly-haired extremist. There were bits and pieces of worn paper with Japanese writing on. There was a very old Jap guilder, no longer legal tender. And there was the man's photograph, a very good one, very clear, head and shoulders looking straight at the camera. Quite a handsome lad.

Bob threw away the wallet but he kept the photograph.

He couldn't sleep. Very early, before the bamboo gongs began, he sat up in his bunk and began a sleepy moonlight letter to Nell. 'You wouldn't believe how cheap life is out here,' he wrote.

On to Bandoeng, a big place up in the hills fifty miles away. Terrible road. First all the supplies went for a burton. They had the big white cross all staked out in a clearing for the plane as they always did, and it all happened as it always did: the Dakota transport circled round a couple of times before making the drop. You could see the men kicking the supplies out of the side door of the aircraft. Sides of beef. Rice. Jam and butter in tins. Green toilet paper. It dropped into the jungle and they nipped in pretty quick, but the Indonesians got there first anyway. You couldn't blame them. Poor buggers were starving. So, measly rations all the way to Bandoeng, and all the time the planes buzzing back and forth over the dense bushes alongside the road, sometimes firing too close to the convoy.

'Have seen no bread for 2 month,' he wrote when they made camp. 'Substitute oatmeal biscuits. I think my stomach has contracted couldn't eat a good meal now.'

They were taken to an airfield and put on guard near a big medical marquee where the Red Cross were checking over internees from one of the camps. A Dakota waited on the Tarmac to take them to Batavia. Men starved down to the bone, eyes and cheeks sunk in. Stick arms, stick legs. Pleased as punch to be going home.

After a week, Bob and the boys were flown back to Batavia too. All the top brass were there for Mountbatten's visit. A letter from Violet was waiting, saying Mam was worried. So he wrote Mam, then wrote Violet to tell her he'd written to Mam. Then he wrote the one he owed Harry. 'Well Harry, heard on the news that Burma's going independent too. Everyone else is. don't know why the Dutch don't just give it all up here as a bad job. Tell you what Harry there are some of us getting fed up. You should be having some good weather in Manchester now its nearing the summer.'

He looked about and thought of Manchester at this time of year. May, soon be Nelly's birthday. Nice to send her something.

Mountbatten spoke to the troops. He said things were going along nicely and we should all be able to go home in about six months. Christ knows, from what you heard, there were no jobs back home anyway.

The bed hard and narrow. Sweaty. There was a fan in the officers' quarters, but not here. Not that their fan made much of a difference. Nothing made much of a difference. The heat just was. You lived in it. It ran off the end of your nose. Remembered the bed at home, him and Nell in Dad's old union shirts. One night Dad came back from the pub with pies and brought them one each up to eat in bed. Delicious. Hot chip-shop gravy. He pulled a bit of gristle out of his pie. 'Ugh!' he said, 'I'm not eating that!' and flung it wildly. It stuck on the ceiling. They both collapsed in a terrible fit of giggles and couldn't stop. It was the funniest thing they'd ever seen, that bit of gristle stuck on the ceiling. Nobody else ever noticed it and it stayed up there for years and was eventually painted over by Dad when he gave the room a coat of paint. Every time they looked at it, him and Nell, it made them giggle. It was there now, surely, in Fremantle Avenue. At home. He smiled into the thick night. A quick flicker of lightning lit up the wall over his bed. Didn't matter if you went outside, made no difference. Just as hot. Couldn't get any cold water.

He'd have given the earth for some corporation pop from the tap in the back kitchen.

When they got the word they were for Malaya again, they cheered.

Seeing them leave, the peasants along the roadsides grinned and raised their fists.

'*Merdeka!*'

'*Merdeka!*' the Drummonds returned, fists in the air.

17

Home

Marjie and Flo called round together a couple of weeks before Christmas with their boyfriends. Marjie was going out with a soldier from the Gordons, a nice lad called Guy. Flo's was Reg. Flo was dark and slim and smart, Marjie plumper and dimpled. They were good with make-up, hair, that sort of thing, smiling and laughing together in a girly, secret way all the time, accepting lights for their cigarettes, straightening their skirts, talking easily to everyone, turning their smiling heads this way and that. Nell had never been at ease like that in company, but to them it seemed to come naturally. Not to Harry, though. That surprised her. Harry was brave enough in company, but deep down she knew he was more like her. Yes, he is, she realised. In some way he's like me, but she couldn't have said how.

'Well, Nell.' Flo leaned forward and smiled her wide boat of a smile. 'We've been given our instructions. "You are not to return", our mam said, "without making it quite clear to our Nell that she's welcome here in my house for her Christmas dinner with our Bud." Really. She'd *love* to see you both, she's got a present for you, Nell.'

Our Nell. Two-faced woman. Nell half smiled. 'Well, you can tell her thank you very much, Flo,' she said, 'but we've already made our arrangements. We're going round to Violet's, we're all having Christmas dinner over there. My mam and dad are coming round. Tell her thank you very much, though.'

Harry raised his eyes to the ceiling. 'I knew this would happen,' he said. 'I knew she wouldn't last out till Christmas. Didn't I say, Nell, she'll suddenly panic the week before Christmas? Well, she's left it a bit late.'

But in the end, of course, everybody compromised, and it was agreed that after Christmas dinner at Vi's, Harry would go on to his mam's for tea. Nell wouldn't, she didn't want to ruin Christmas Day. She'd go on Boxing Day with him, just for an hour or so to test the water. And she let him write 'From Harry and Nell', on her Christmas present, a big box of New Berry Fruits, the old Dutch's favourites, he said. So, Christmas 1946, round at Vi and Stanley's, Harry with Nell, Mam and Dad, all of them together apart from Bob. Stanley played his accordion and baby Jean sat on Vi's knee and was jogged up and down.

Dad was starting to look old. He always wore the same thing, these days, his uniform, a dark pinstriped three-piece suit, old and baggy. They all had a bit to drink, even Nell had a shandy, more lemonade than beer, quite nice in fact. Dad sang 'I'll Be Your Sweetheart', 'McCafferty' and 'Sam Hall'. Harry sang 'Walking My Baby Back Home' and 'Josephina Please Don't Leana On The Bell'. Harry had a lovely voice.

Boxing Day, when Nell did finally go round to Harry's mam's, it was civil but awkward. His mam made her tea too milky and sweet.

''Ere you are, love.' The anxious little woman pushed a paper bag into her hands. 'A merry Christmas and a happy New Year. You can open it now because it's after Christmas.'

It was a bottle of talc, the sort you got cheap as cheap from Woolworth's. It wasn't wrapped up even, just in the bag it had come in.

'Thank you,' Nell said. 'Look, Harry, lily-of-the-valley.'

'I always say,' said Harry's mam, 'you can't go wrong with lily-of-the-valley.'

Cousin Joey and his lovely Greek wife had had a little boy. Funnily enough, the day Nell first knew she herself was expecting was when she'd just been admiring the baby in Bailey's. It had red hair, just like Joey. And Steffi, with her hair so black, looked funny with this ginger-haired little creature.

'Who's a little smasher, then?' Mrs Bailey crowed. 'Who's my right little smasher?'

Nell held out her finger. The baby gripped tight. Suddenly she felt queasy. At first she thought it must have been because she'd been out late the night before, all those bitter lemons, and what a boring night that was, another jazz session, Harry on stage depping with the Tailgaters and her sitting at a table with people she didn't know, people who seemed to think the only way to hold a conversation was to laugh very loudly at the least stupid little thing. Where was the sense in that? Lighting cigarette after cigarette. Thought they were posh. You couldn't relax with posh people. They were OK but you couldn't relax. Mind you, Kitty could put on quite a good posh voice when it came to it. If Kitty had been there they could have had a laugh.

But of course Kitty was never there any more. She hadn't seen Kitty for ages, not since she'd married that big lug, which was a shame but there you go.

Nell went home and tried to be sick but couldn't. Fancied a cup of tea perhaps but couldn't face making one. She felt quite wretched. That old cat was sitting on the windowsill looking in. Poor old thing with his dirty notched ears. Looked like a chow-chow dog. Harry was out at judo. Another hobby. Always casting about for things to do. Nell ran the tap and got a cup of water, went and sat down in the front room. Chisholm came and sat on her knee. And suddenly Nell thought: I'm pregnant. That's what it is. I'll bet. Not that she knew, it was just an idea. Well, it's likely, she thought. It was what was supposed to happen, what everyone was waiting for. They hadn't talked about children, it was just known that this was what happened. Harry would be happy. She was happy. She must be happy but she didn't feel particularly happy. The street was quiet, the house was quiet, apart from the purring of Chisholm. Stroking the small cat's black and white head, she was distantly afraid. You could die in childbirth. It would hurt. A baby. She wasn't a baby person. Some of them were downright repellent yet their mothers thought they were marvellous. They smelt horrible. You had to wipe their bums.

She sang very softly, thinking her voice sounded nice in the quiet house:

> *Within the woodland flow'ry-shaded*
> *By the oak tree's mossy moot ...*

This and the other songs, all the old ones, these were the songs she loved to sing around the house. Not jazz. She sat and sang for a while till she felt better.

He came home late, all excited. After judo he'd gone roaming round Mazel's and Shude Hill. He had a bag of seventy-eights. 'Look, Nell! Jimmy Harrison! Bix with Paul Whiteman!'

'I've not been feeling too good,' she said. 'Can you make tea?' She wouldn't say anything. Not yet. Not till she was sure. She'd go and see Dr Fowler tomorrow.

'Oh, we'll have chips, shall we, Nell? What is it? Feeling fluey? There's a lot of it about.'

'I don't think I could face chips,' she said.

But by teatime she was fine again, and it was she who went out to Bee's for chips in the end. So it was she who was standing in the queue when a scruffy lad of about ten came in with a small brown pup under one arm.

'Anyone want a dog?' he bawled.

The pup looked at the queue with a brown whiskery old-man face. The queue looked at the pup.

'Me mam says I've got to get rid of it,' said the boy, a poor peaky little thing with a dirty face.

There was a mumbling. Some girls said, 'Aw! Look at it!' and the boy brought it over and let them tickle its head. It went mad licking their faces and making them laugh. Mad black shiny eyes.

'She's got fox terrier in her,' the boy said.

'That and everything else,' said a man.

Everyone wanted to hold the pup, to tickle it under the chin, lift it by its pathetic weak armpits, but no one wanted to take it for good. He was going down the queue, the boy, holding it up into people's faces hopefully.

'She's a nice dog,' he said.

'Can I see her?' Nell asked.

The pup licked her chin furiously, trembling with excited delight. Wild eyes. Nell got a strong whiff of that funny milk and onion smell you get on a puppy's breath.

'I'll have it,' she said. It wasn't a good time with a baby, if it was a

224

baby, on the way. She shivered with fear at the thought.

But she never could resist a pup.

''Ere y'are.' The boy placed the pup gently into her arms and was gone.

'You've got a nice little dog there, love,' said another man. 'Bonny little thing.'

The girls still cooed, peering under Nell's lapels with big smiles. 'Cheeky!' they said, 'Cheeky little doggie!'

She stowed it away under her coat, where it wriggled and squirmed and trembled until it was her turn to get served. She bought an extra fish and rushed off home, keeping the dog warm under her coat next to the chips. She'd be good company. Harry was out all the time anyway.

They called the dog Bonny. The big old tom with the notched ears moved in too. He wouldn't come near you, just sat in the corner and spat if you walked past him. But he slept curled up with Chisholm nights in the chair by the fire, and he was good enough, never peed in the house or worse. They called him Chow.

'Good old boy!' she'd tell him appreciatively. 'Good old boy!' and he'd curl his lip at her.

And Bonny, who certainly must have had some fox terrier in her, the way her whiskers grew so square round her mouth, loved both of the cats and curled up there with them too after a while, and not one of them objected. Bonny was the smallest of the lot. Night after night she'd creep on to Nell's knee while the sound of the trombone went on and on, the same bits over and over again, Harry developing his lip. It's such a loud instrument, the trombone, Nell thought, stroking the sleeping pup's brown wiry-haired head; you can't get away from it. The baby was growing inside, and Nell was getting tired. The noise got on her nerves. Pity he didn't play something a bit softer, a clarinet maybe. But it was just one of those things, like the way he whistled all the time, you couldn't have Harry without it. It was unimaginable. He was over the moon about the baby. He wasn't nervous at all. He couldn't care less if it was a boy or a girl. His child would have the best he could manage. His child would have an education. If his child wanted to go to university, go that child would.

But the one thing about being pregnant that was really good, she could stop going to the jazz sessions. She could stay at home with the dog and the cats. Oh, no, she could say, I don't feel like it, I'm a bit tired tonight. And he'd go on his own.

He was disappointed, she saw that. But then he had to take her as she was, didn't he? And she had to take him as he was.

When she was in bed and she heard him come in and sit downstairs playing for a while alone, she knew what the music meant to him, and sometimes at those times she thought she understood. Sentiment. And tears and things, deep, deep feeling, things he didn't speak of. That of course was what the music meant to him.

18

Jenny Lim

They were posted up-country to Ipoh, out through the suburbs of Singapore, where the big houses stood far back in their brilliant gardens, painted chairs on the verandas; over the Johore Straits on the train, up-country, where things were poorer. The trains were as bad as he'd remembered, heat, dust, flies, bloody mosquitoes. The stillness of the sky when you stopped somewhere for no reason anyone seemed to know, for hours, sometimes two, three, four. It was three days to Ipoh. They saw out the year there in a transit camp. Dusty red roads, bad coffee. The camp was near a small town full of Chinese shops along a straggling main street resplendent with huge hand-painted billboards for Tiger beer and Gold Flake. Outside the town hall were some spiked railings on which the Japs had displayed the heads of Chinese civilians killed in the war. The Japs and the Chinese hated one another. The Chinese liked the British, Bellman said. But then again the bandits in the jungle were Chinese, and they were the enemy, the CTs, Communist Terrorists. So there it was again, like Java: you couldn't tell who was on your side just by looking. It wasn't being Chinese that made them the enemy, Bellman said, it was being Communist. Which again was funny because, when he thought about it, Bob thought he himself might be a bit Communist in a way. They had some good ideas, you couldn't doubt that. Equality. Giving everyone the same. When you thought about it, it was only like Jesus, wasn't it? He was a bit of a Communist too in a way. *Merdeka*. Why should one lot have more than another lot? There was a lot of reading he wanted to do when he got home.

They were given to Nangku, an Iban tracker from Sarawak, to take out on patrol scouting for terrorists. All in jungle green with his hair done up in a bun, Nangku got two dollars a day and two pounds ten pay on top of that to train them. The Iban were famous trackers. They used to be headhunters, Bellman said. Nangku had a lovely, quite girlish face, with big curly lips and deep dark eyes. They set off in the back of a truck, eight of them, a scout car following with a Lewis gun. After a couple of hours they stopped and got out. They were supposed to patrol all this section of the jungle, cutting through to a rendezvous with the trucks at a *kampong* about three days away.

Nangku took out his map and checked the compass. Lucky charms dangled around his neck. He laughed. 'Army map,' he said cheerfully. 'No good.'

He led them out into the *lallang*, the grass with blades like knives, towering over your head, making you feel like Tom Thumb. Big red ants falling down on you as you pushed through. Sweat pouring down. Nangku showed them how to use a *parang* to hack through. He told them to watch out for booby-traps. Then the land turned to swamp, and the water came up to your knees. Above was no sky but a green light, and the trees so high they blocked out the world. Like a time before us. Or like being under the sea. What sound there was, the squelching of the mud sucking at your boots, the call of a bird off in the trees, a solemn strange fluting, hollow, echoey. Lianas in swags. Underfoot, everything rotted.

The swamp went on for hours, then turned into dense thicket, with here and there tracks made by animals. Nangku went down on his hands and knees.

'That's pig,' he said.

Butterflies, red, green, iridescent, the size of birds. They had to move without sound in this place, where to move was to snag on a thorn or do battle with creepers. Nangku, a ghost, slid on ahead. When he held up one hand without looking back, everyone froze.

Nothing. Dead still.

Then a sound like a twig breaking.

Then nothing.

Nobody stirred a muscle for what seemed like an hour.

Everything itched. A fantastic bird, all glowing and blue, flew into a tree above their heads. The branches swayed and swished. It flew away again.

Stillness.

Then at last the signal to go on, then more of the same, more of the same, hour on hour, way past the hottest time of the day, hour on hour till Nangku signalled it was time to stop.

They waited for the all-clear, sitting on their packs till the patrol was sure it was safe, not a sound, not a breath. Bellman posted sentries with Brens. Bob was with Alfie. Alfie had the groundsheet and the mosquito net, Bob a poncho and a blanket. The first thing they did, even before a drink, was get rid of the leeches. Alfie was nearly in tears.

'Anything else,' he said, shuddering all over, 'anybloodything else.'

He hated anything like that. It wasn't so bad for Bob: he used to go fishing over Reddish Vale, he was used to handling bait. These leeches, though, they were bloody horrible things. Stuck like mad. You burned them off with cigarettes. Alfie scratched himself all over. 'I can't fancy food,' he said. But when they'd done that, and unpacked the DDT from the dressing bundles and given themselves a good rubdown, it was his turn to make stew. Just a big glop of compo.

'I bloody tell you, Bob,' said Alfie, stirring, his upper lip trembling a little, 'I don't like this. I don't like this one bit. Gives me the willies.'

'I know what you mean.'

But he didn't, not really. The jungle gave him the willies too, but with Alfie it was something else altogether. Alfie's flesh crawled every second he was in there. He hated everything about it. His eyes snapped about, watchful and scared. He flinched at a sound. Sound carried in the jungle. Anything out there could hear you. Tiger. Panther. Bandits.

Evening, Alfie became more and more strange, his comical face owlish, the eyes rounder and rounder, the plump upper lip swollen with some bite or other. You couldn't connect with his eyes, and he couldn't seem to smile or move his mouth and cheeks at all. Only those pale eyes, darting scared.

At dusk the noise began. It came alive at night. Bullfrogs, cicadas, crickets, other things, clicky, crackly, craking things. It was like the dawn chorus only the other way round. First just one or two in the distance, then a couple nearer, then here, then there, till with the full blossoming of dark you could hardly hear yourself think. It came alive at night. Things that hooted like owls, maybe they were owls, bigger things, things you hardly dared think about, things that screamed and howled and yapped, like the roar from Belle Vue in the early morning magnified a million times. Bloody ridiculous trying to sleep through it. Alfie was on first watch. Under the stick and poncho in the pitch black, Bob lay awake for the noise, wondering if Alfie would go mad and run off screaming into the jungle. But he was there to wake Bob for his watch, so Bob reckoned he must have slept, even though he didn't remember falling asleep.

They were in the jungle three days. What they'd seen in Java was nothing to this.

Every morning Alfie whispered to Bob, 'I don't think I can take this, Bob,' and every day he took it. His face had a haunted look. When he could, he sucked his thumb. He was not a slight lad, but by the time they reached the *kampong* near the camp road where the trucks were supposed to meet them, you could have called him haggard.

Maybe I look like that too, Bob thought.

The people from the *kampong* came out to meet them and made them welcome. There was a spice garden, a tapioca patch. Children played with dogs, just like at home. A small girl carried a huge red squirrel in her arms as if it were a baby. All around the *kampong* grew fruit trees, and big flowers, showy like girls in can-can skirts. They were taken to a hut with mats spread on the floor and fed from a big bowl of sweet potatoes spiced up with something delicious. I could live here, Bob thought. Find a nice girl. Live in one of these bamboo huts on stilts. Listen to the rain in the rainy season beating on the attap roof.

Bob kept thinking of that girl they threw into the canal. The filthy shitty Molenvliet canal. Wicked, that. Wicked. It was coming up to Christmas. Another one – where was the time flying away to? – and he was still here. Getting on for three months now. Nothing was happening, there was nothing to do, they were just stuck in camp most of the time. They did a few patrols. Each time, poor old Alfie went funny in the head. God knows how he'd react if they ever did encounter the enemy. But nothing ever happened. They just got wet and bitten and their feet started to rot. And, anyway, it wasn't the enemy that bothered Alfie, it was the jungle itself.

At last they got leave. Bob went and got blinding drunk with Davy in Kuala Lumpur. They had steak and chips, then went on to a dance-hall, where they started drinking with some Chinese blokes who were playing mah-jong. Bob was mad when he was drunk sometimes; he'd do anything. While Davy watched the red and green dragons on the mah-jong tiles, drunk, mesmerised, Bob was deep in conversation with a man called Lau Chen who ran a bicycle-repair shop. God knows what was said (his memory was hazy), but it resulted in his being approached a second time when leave was over and they were back at base, this time by a small, thin, hatchet-faced man called Lee.

Bob was having a drink in town.

'You know Lau Chen?'

Bob hadn't got a clue who Lau Chen was. Then he got a vague flash of a small fat friendly man in a bar, and it came back. Bob had told him he could get him a jeep if he wanted. He'd had it all worked out. Now that he thought about it again, it still seemed a good idea. Those jeeps were in and out of that compound all the time and the whole thing was a shambles. Those jeeps were easy.

There was a place out by some old spice gardens where they arranged to do the exchange, about four or five miles off base. Lee would come with a friend, So Eng. They would arrive on So Eng's motorbike, then Lee would take the jeep and give Bob the money, and So Eng would run Bob back to camp on his bike. They shook on it and had a game of billiards.

Alfie and Davy told him he was out of his mind. They said that even if he could get away with a jeep, what's to say they wouldn't take the jeep and shoot him? What's to say they'd give him any money?

'No, no, really,' Bob said, 'they're OK, these blokes are. I've had a drink with them. They're OK, these Chinese. They're like us. You can have a laugh with them.'

He was sure. He got a feeling about people. And he could do with a bit of extra, Christmas coming and so on. He could buy some little local things and send them home, something exotic, impress them.

'Have you seen those jeeps and trucks just sitting there in the transport yard?' he said.

Of course they had. In fact, they'd all sat round and discussed how easy it would be to take one about a week ago. The difference was that Alfie and Davy would never have actually done anything about it; with them it was just mucking around. Bob would. Little risk, little adventure. Nothing like it. He was bored silly. And if he got caught, at least he wouldn't have to go back in the jungle for a while. Give his feet a chance to recover properly.

He had a drink or two for Dutch courage before he set out, went into the transport yard, not so late as to arouse suspicion, picked the jeep nearest the gate and drove it away. Simple.

He was half-way to the rendezvous before he realised the police were after him. He could smell the spices perfuming the night. At first he thought it was a coincidence, but then they came right up close behind and started banging on their horn. Bugger it. Bob put his foot down hard on the accelerator. His blood was up, the headlights swung back and forwards over the rutted red tracks, trees and bushes loomed, fell aside; and the other headlights, behind, trying to blind him. All I have to do is outrun them, he thought. The trees whirled faster, the headlights dived.

When he woke up he was in a British military hospital. A nice nurse came and told him he'd come off the road and smashed into a tree and been unconscious for nearly nine hours. His tongue was thick, his head ached, his neck ached, he ached all over. His eyes wanted to close again. She said he was a very lucky boy. He liked the way she said that, and the way she leaned over to tuck him in. The nurse was small and plain with brown hair, but she had lovely friendly eyes and he got the feeling she'd been watching over him and got to like him and was glad to see him come back from the Land of Nod.

'There are two policemen waiting to see you,' she said. 'When the doctor's seen you. Because you've been a very, very naughty boy.'

He was put on a train into the highlands with two NCOs for guards. It crawled for two days. The wooden seats were hell. Then a journey by truck up hairpin bends to a hill station from which there was a view such as he'd never seen, right down to Ipoh one way and the islands out to sea; and very far away on the other side a silver-grey gleaming, the South China Sea, past miles and miles of mountain covered all over with wild jungle like a creeper gone mad. The hill station was an old estate, the bungalows being used as offices. They had red corrugated-iron roofs; one or two had lovely butterfly-fluttering gardens. It was mild, like an English summer. But he was banged up inside straight away and never let out, apart from the odd time he was sent to do a bit of gardening round one or two of the bungalows where they were growing fruit and vegetables. There were lots of tiny lizards and small snakes, and a big iguana that sat on the wall watching him intently. He looked it right in the eyes. At night he'd hear the monkeys chattering in his sleep. Thank God for cooler nights. There were a lot of books up here that the planters had left. He was reading *War and Peace*.

Christmas morning it poured. He'd thought he'd be home by now. He wondered if they were all sitting round there at this moment eating a big turkey, and remembered the taste of his dad's sage and onion stuffing.

The sky turned to lead. For days it went on, right through New Year. The battalion had moved back to Singapore. Jammy buggers, and him stuck here.

232

He did his three months. When he was released it was coming up to Chinese New Year. He had some time before he needed to go down to Singapore and fancied seeing the coast, so he took a train to Port Dickson, where there was an army base and a famed beautiful beach.

It was very late when he arrived and he was tired. He found a room from which he could hear the ocean, fell asleep instantly and woke in the early hours wide awake, desperate to get outside. He'd been indoors for so long. The ocean hissed. Bob sneaked out and headed towards the sound in the dark. He found the beach and paddled, the shocking silver stars in the black sky like a fanfare. The peaceful waves rolled in, silver-tipped. He cried. He wasn't sure why. Home and the East whirled in his head. Blood and beauty. The smell of his dad's pipe and the dark sweet smell of a Chinese cigarette. If someone could have magically transported him home at that moment, he might not even have gone. He walked back up the beach and lay down under a tree and fell asleep.

It was light when he woke up. He felt wide awake, tuned up. His feet had healed up a treat. He sat up. In the daylight he saw that the beach went on and on for miles, palm trees waving all along the coast. Not a soul about, only him. He stripped down to his trunks and went for a swim. The water was warm. He dipped and dived for a while, going under to look at the corals, the red fish swimming in shoals. The sun like knives on the water. At last he came out and stood dripping on the shore. Someone else was in, a dark head far out. He looked round. A long way up the beach, a little heap of things. No one else. He went back to his tree and got dried and dressed and lit a cigarette. The swimmer was going out ever so far. Quite out of sight. But then the black dot bobbed back into view again and began the return.

Bob lay down on his back and smoked and looked up into the trees with their sweeping curves of trunk, to the blue sky beyond. When he sat up, the swimmer had dressed too and was sitting on the sand looking out to sea. He couldn't tell from here if it was a man or a woman. But then, when she stood and picked up her bag and started walking along at the edge of the sea in his direction, he saw it was a girl. Chinese, he thought. Half-way towards him she sat down once more with her back to him and started rummaging in her bag. She pulled out a purple ribbon and started tying back her wet hair. He didn't think she'd seen him.

He took a slow stroll down to the tide-line, not too near her, then paddled vaguely in her direction. She'd seen him by now and watched him approach, sitting with her arms round her knees, staring boldly. She'd lit a cigarette.

He got to within about twenty feet from her. 'Morning,' he said, raising one hand.

She smiled.

He looked at her properly. My God, he thought. Her hair was wet and all pulled back from her face. She wore a big loose shirt over a sarong.

'Good morning,' she called back, in a sharp voice.

He couldn't think of anything to say but 'You swam out a long way.'

She didn't reply but smiled still, looking out to sea. She was too beautiful.

He reached down and picked something out of the sand. A bullet. 'Bullet,' he said.

She waved both arms, one in each direction to indicate the entire sweep of the beach on either side of them. 'Bullets all over,' she said.

She was something you'd never see walking down the street in Gorton. Never. The perfect, serenely upswung outlines of her black eyes, like the eyes of the Buddha in the temple in the jungle.

He skimmed the bullet out to sea. It hopped twice, then sank. Could have done better. He started looking round for another.

'Why you so pale, soldier?' she asked.

He laughed. He'd gone white again in the glasshouse. And his hair was still bleached white by the sun. He thought about saying he'd been sick, some excuse, but instead said, 'Because I've been in prison.'

This didn't seem to bother her. She finished her cigarette, picked up her bag and shoes, black ones with a strap across. 'Time for work,' she said.

'What do you do?'

She didn't answer.

'Fancy being able to have a swim like that every day of your life,' Bob said, amazed. 'Fancy living like this! You don't know how lucky you are. You ought to see where I come from.'

'Aren't you homesick?' she asked. Her English was very good.

'Sometimes,' he said.

Then she suddenly smiled, a big beautiful smile that crinkled up her eyes. 'Of course,' she said. 'All soldiers are homesick.'

He walked up the beach with her, his hands clasped behind his back. She didn't seem to mind. A few more people were appearing.

'I only just arrived,' he said, 'last night when it was dark.'

They reached the road. He wasn't sure if he could recognise where he was staying. 'I think I'm lost,' he said.

She laughed. 'You can't be lost. All roads go to the base. The whole town is full of soldiers.'

'It was very close to the shore,' he said, and at the same moment saw the house he'd started the night in on the other side of the track, its blue door and rickety steps familiar even though he'd only seen them in the dark. 'There it is,' he said.

He felt strange, as if he was going to cry. The heat.

'You OK, soldier?'

'Aye. I'm fine.'

Sweat.

The shops across the way were opening, putting out their boxes on the street.

'Will you come out with me tonight?' he asked her.

She smiled. 'I'm not supposed to,' she said.

'Why not?'

She smiled and shook her head.

'Only for a drink. You drink?'

She shook her head again.

'Shame.'

Neither of them made to go.

'Is it nice where you come from?' she asked.

'It's all right. Not like this, though. I live in Manchester. Big town, much bigger than this. Go on, come out with me tonight. Just for a walk.'

She considered.

'Well, you know,' he shrugged and gestured, half turning away then turning back, 'only if you want to.'

'I'll come if we go to the pictures,' she said.

A night out in Port Dickson with Jenny Lim.

'Jenny?' he said, 'That's not a Chinese name.'

'It's my name.' She laughed.

They were in a bar. They'd been to see *Forty-Second Street*. Jenny loved it. She must have seen it before because she knew the words of all the songs and had sung along with everything in an avid whisper, leaning close to him. She made him go funny at the knees.

He was drinking Tiger beer. She had a coconut drink; she let him have a taste. He was madly in love. He didn't know which was most beautiful, Jenny Lim on the beach or Jenny Lim in the bar with all her make-up on. She sat opposite him, smoking and smiling. She had a white bow on top of her head. Her blue-black hair hung down in a heavy wave, thick and glossy. Her lipstick was glossy too, bright red.

'Now you tell me,' she said, 'why you were in prison. What did you do?'

He told her. He couldn't have cared less: he'd have told her anything. Somehow he knew it would be all right. She drew in her breath but smiled. 'You learn your lesson,' she said.

'I learn my lesson.'

She had to get home. They went outside and he saw her into a rickshaw. He would have kissed her then but she brushed him cheerfully aside. 'Not now,' she said.

'Coming down to the beach tomorrow?'

She shook her head.

'Want to go out with me again?'

'I meet you,' she said casually, then smiled. 'Here. You buy me coffee. *Six*.' She held up six fingers as the rickshaw drew away.

He had ten days. He spent as much of it with her as he possibly could. She got away to see him whenever she could, which was often and erratic. Her father had a shop she helped in. She'd just finished school, a convent boarding-school. That surprised him. The nuns were all French, she said. 'Listen. I speak French.' She said something that didn't sound completely Chinese but didn't sound French either.

When he was not on the beach or in a coffee shop or bar with Jenny, he wandered about the town or stayed on base. There was a sports ground and a swimming-pool, a good market, some nice cafés, but all the time he was just hanging around waiting to see Jenny, sweet Jenny, always ready for a laugh with her huge beautiful smile. Not only was she the most lovely thing he had ever seen, she was more fun to be with than anyone he'd ever known. She was seventeen. She liked a good time, to dance and laugh and play around like a big kid. She said she'd never been out with a soldier before. Her parents wouldn't like it. She was only supposed to go out with Chinese boys. But she didn't seem too worried about it. Her father liked the British, she said. He wouldn't be as bothered by Bob as he would be if she went out with a Malay boy. She knew some Malay boys but she wouldn't go out with any of them.

She loved to talk. She was curious. She wanted to know all about England. Time flew.

Time always flew when he was with Jenny.

Every night, not too late, when he saw her on to a rickshaw back to her house, the sight of her face looking back at him as she waved made his heart bleed with pleasure.

Chinese New Year. The fire-crackers going on all night. A big torchlight procession on the *padang*, huge fishes and tigers, the lion, the dragon shaking and swirling. Bob and Jenny held hands in the crowd. She wore a white suit with short sleeves. She looked sophisticated and she carried herself sophisticated too. But she wasn't sophisticated at all. Not deep down. Deep down she was innocent.

Of course, her family got to know that she was going about with an *orang puteh*, Port Dickson wasn't that big. She turned up angry one night and said she'd had a row with her father. She said her father was worried about what people would say but she didn't care. She liked who she liked. If *she* wanted to sit and talk for hours with Bob, she would. If she wanted to tell him all about home and school and hear

237

all about Gorton and Manchester, she would. And so the days rolled by with talking and walking, swimming and dancing, kissing and cuddling under the palm trees, till a sudden horrible moment of realisation, standing waiting by the Kuala Lumpur bus stop where they always met. Only three more whole days left.

They went down to the beach. The lights of the fishermen shone on the water.

'Do you think we'll see each other again?' he asked her.

'Yes,' she said simply.

'Will you write to me?'

'Yes.'

They exchanged addresses.

'We could get married,' he said.

She laughed.

He'd never find anyone half as good as this. Never. He didn't care how it happened, whether he had to stay here or she had to come back to England with him. He might get killed. She pulled his head down against her breasts. She was wearing a pink shiny blouse with mother-of-pearl buttons that scratched his cheek.

'You will come back?' she asked. 'Will you?'

'Oh, God, yes!'

He rejoined his regiment at Gilman Barracks. Trouble was afoot: they were training hard. It was to do with the strikes in rubber and tin, Bellman said, Chin Peng was stirring things up. Chin Peng was a Communist who used to be with the British but was turning into a trouble-maker.

Back to soldiering. Bob's was the one pale arm among all the brown ones as they marched in formation. Thinking all the time about Jenny Lim, composing letters to her in his mind. Summer passed. How many letters? Shoals. Effusive girly letters covered with a million kisses. 'Always my love, my darling Bob', she wrote. All the little xs filling up the margins. Love, love, love. She sent him a photograph. He sent her one of himself standing proud, the young warrior Scot, looking good in a kilt. He wrote long, tightly packed letters about what he'd been doing and what he'd been thinking. It was easy to write to her. She was like another person sitting in his head sharing everything with him, even when she wasn't there. In a sense he didn't miss her that much because it was as if she *was* there.

People boasted about sex in the NAAFI. People came back from leave with stories of Chinese girls who couldn't get enough, of streets in Kuala Lumpur where you could get a girl of any nationality you wanted. Try a bit of this and a bit of that. You could do anything. Bob didn't talk much about Jenny, just said she was a nice dish who was mad about him. He wrote and told Nell and Vi and Harry: 'By the way I have a girl writing to me whom I met on leave she's a nice dish too. Tell Mam not to worry the war in the east will be over before too long.'

19

Your Old Flame

Mam worried, of course. Mam was incapable of not worrying. She was always sitting around in Vi's or Nell's moaning fitfully, veering into a whine, sometimes weeping. It got so that they dreaded seeing her walk down the street, that heavy tread, the wretched eyes.

'The way she goes on,' Nell said, 'you'd think no one else loved Bob but her. You'd think no one else had a son out there.'

'I know.'

Violet was in for a cup of tea with Jean, who looked like Alice in Wonderland with her Alice band on, very straight fair hair growing long. They were looking at photographs of Harry playing with a jazz band called Bert Hill's Collegians, on stage at Levenshulme Baths Ballroom. Harry looked handsome and serious sitting there on the end of the front row of the musicians, his trombone resting against his shoulder.

'You want to send one to our Bob,' Violet said.

He had to wear a dickie bow for the Collegians. Nell got them ready and starched his white collars. One night he put on his dickie and it wouldn't lie flat, it kept sticking up, curving forward at both ends like a sandwich gone stale. Violet and Nell got the giggles. He was late already, and nothing they did could make the stupid thing lie down. It looked ridiculous. He got more and more frantic as the two of them went weak. They'd get it right, he'd put his foot over the threshold, *boing*, up it popped. In the end Nell had to run into the kitchen and cry with laughter while Vi ran for a needle and cotton and actually sewed the thing down. He couldn't see the funny side of it at all. The D Trains weren't so fussy. He was with them tonight, playing the Palais de Danse, Chorlton. They had a residency there two nights a week. Harry had an agent now, he played all over with all kinds of bands. Letters came, with headings: 'The Larry Clifford Musical Direction. Dear Mr Caplin, Would you please telephone the above number whether you are available for Feb 11th and 14th and if so, whether you could attend a rehearsal at Stock & Chapman, Oxford Rd. on Thursday at 2pm.'

He played Stockport Town Hall with a seven-piece Latin-American band called the Cubanaires. He had to dress up as a Cuban in a frilly shirt and dress trousers. He looked just the part.

He went to Sheffield and supported Big Bill Broonzy.

'Big Bill Broonzy, Nell! Big Bill Broonzy!'

He was like a kid when he was going off to see one of these big jazz people. She could have gone with him. She could have gone out just about every night if she'd wanted to, but the baby was tiring her out. All she wanted to do in the evenings was flop down with the radio on, a book, a bag of sweets.

'Come on! Do you good to get out. Lots of wives go.'

She pulled a face. There was nothing she fancied drinking. Her stomach was off. All she could face was Vimto.

'Pop into Violet's for a bit,' he said.

So she pressed his trousers, fetched him a fresh starched collar, and he kissed her and went off down the street with his black hair shining and his trombone in its big black case banging by his knee.

She yawned, looking out at the yard. Might as well have an early night. She wiped her hands. Chis was on the coal bunker with Chow. Getting fat, probably pregnant.

Well, it wouldn't be him without his jazz, would it?

Could be a lot worse. Some men gamble, some men drink. He's got his jazz. He'll never change.

She opened the back door, called in the cats, poured them a drop of milk, shifted the sleeping dog, and lay down with a yellow-backed Lewis's Library book, a cup of tea and a bag of peanut brittle from Bailey's. Bonny came and settled with her, licking her feet. Chow and Chis snuggled down in the other chair. You could hear the trains from time to time going over the ginnel. Sometimes, if it was very quiet, the sound of a bus revving its engine as it pulled away from the bus stop on Stockport Road. All those people going off to town, the girls with their perfume and make-up, going out after fellows, just like her and Kitty O'Neill used to do. So long ago it seemed now. Here she was, a married woman with a baby on the way. She was scared of the baby. She was scared she wouldn't know what to do. She wanted it by now, though. It was as if there was a great empty hole in the world just waiting for it to slot into. Funny, her and Kitty O'Neill going after fellows. She'd met Kitty once going to Mam and Dad's. She was coming out of the paper shop on Mount Road. Great to see good old Kitty again; she'd put on a bit of weight but still looked lovely. She had a little boy now and was living over Reddish way. 'You must come round, Nelly,' she said, and gave her an address, but there was never time – or, well, yes, there must have been time but somehow Nell knew she'd never get on a bus and trail all the way up to Reddish to a strange house.

Her and Kitty. That was all a different time. And Jimmy Lee too. Harry had seen him.

'Guess who I ran into on Dickenson Road?'

'Who?'

'Your old flame.'

'Who?'

'Your old flame. Jimmy Lee.'

'He was never my old flame.'

'Well.'

He wasn't married. Harry told her. He was still living with his mother and sister over Rusholme way. Harry said the man still looked a bag of nerves. Said he was working in Didsbury.

Jimmy Lee.

Jimmy Lee with the sweat dripping off the end of his nose in the baking hot smithy.

She was so tired she was just one big yawn.

Late that night a cat woke her up, yowling away on one of the back walls as if it was being strangled. Chow growled like a dog at the top of the stairs. Someone somewhere opened a window and it went quiet. Slunk away down the alley. She couldn't get back to sleep and lay there wide-eyed in the dark, listening to the ticking of the clock and waiting for the sound of Harry's whistle as he walked home down the street.

20

Five Days

In September when he got leave he went straight up to Port Dickson, checked in at the base, from there straight to Jenny's father's shop. She was expecting him to meet her at the bus stop at six tomorrow anyway, it had all been arranged, but he couldn't wait.

She wasn't there.

It was ridiculous to feel so disappointed. Why should she have been there? She could have been anywhere. A man with gold-rimmed glasses and greying hair stood behind the counter, measuring out some material for a customer. Her father? It was a shop that sold everything, dried fish, salt fish, newspapers, clothes, spices, shoes, vegetables, shelves up to the ceiling, large glass-covered counters, a long bench for customers to sit on. Bob surveyed cans of turtle soup on a shelf. He'd have to buy something now. Maybe he should talk to her father: *Mr Lim, I know you're worried but honestly, there's no need. I am very fond of Jenny.*

At that moment she came out through a bamboo curtain that divided the front from the back of the shop. She looked far more beautiful than he'd remembered, and suddenly he didn't believe in any of it at all. She wasn't part of real life, not for the likes of him. She saw him straight away. She didn't smile at first or even look surprised. It was a strange look, bold and searching. But then she smiled like before, glanced over at her father counting out change to a tiny old woman, glanced back at him and mouthed, 'Wait.'

He stood awkwardly. Fragrant dust spiralled over the boxes of sweet potato. It was poor stuff. The shop was understocked.

When the old lady had gone, the three of them stood silent for a second. Her father seemed already to know who Bob was.

'Baba!' she said sweetly, walking towards him. 'I would like you to meet Corporal Robert Bruce Holloway of the Drummond Highlanders.'

Bob stepped up to the counter. Mr Lim nodded.

'Pleased to meet you,' Bob said, offering his hand across the glass case.

Mr Lim took it and shook firmly.

'Jenny has an education,' he said very seriously, looking steadily into Bob's eyes. He smiled, yet his face remained serious. 'She has done well. She is going to be a teacher.'

His English wasn't as good as Jenny's.

Bob didn't know what to say. She had told him this. He didn't know why her old man was also telling him. It was obviously very important to him.

'She told me,' he said affably. 'I think she'd make a very good teacher.'

'Baba,' she said, 'may I go for a walk now with Corporal Holloway?'

She asked him right out like that, but he didn't answer her straight away.

243

'What was your school?' he asked Bob.

'Old Hall Drive,' Bob said, laughing. 'It's in Manchester. A lot different from here.'

'Did you get certificates?'

'No.'

Bob had never had any kind of a school certificate in his life. No one he knew had ever had any kind of a school certificate, except for Grandad. And Harry, of course, who was getting his. Mr Lim pondered that, unsmiling, shifting stock about in the boxes on the counter. Then he said something in Chinese to Jenny and, picking up a broom, nodded once more to Bob and disappeared through the bamboo curtain.

'Wait!' She ran in and reappeared immediately carrying a handbag, came out from behind the counter in her sensible dress and sensible shoes. She had a nice ample figure, just right. Her hair was scraped straight back off her face, tied at the back, and she wore no other make-up but her bright red lipstick.

'Is it OK?' he asked. 'With your dad?'

'It's OK.'

They went out and walked along side by side in the direction of the beach.

'Did you miss me?' she said.

'Course I missed you, you daft sod.'

She laughed. 'You daft sod,' she repeated. She thought that was very funny. When she said it, it didn't sound like swearing.

'I missed you,' she said. 'I cry for you every day.'

'Get away!' he said softly.

They went into a coffee shop. He showed her the photograph of Harry with Bert Hill's Collegians. 'Very handsome,' she said, 'but not as handsome as you.'

He was brown now, not pale like before. She'd liked him pale. But she liked him brown as well. He'd got more tattoos on his arms. She liked those too. They went to the beach and walked up it a long, long way, far, far, far away from everybody else.

They had five days to make the most of.

21

Kitty

It was a terrible, hard winter.

Marjie married Guy, smart in his kilt and sporran; Flo married
Reg, a very dark man who looked like a New York Italian *mafioso*
called Louis or Joey or something, with a big smile and a bent nose
and eyebrows that met in the middle. Chisholm produced a litter of
four black and white kittens, and Nell and Harry's baby was born, a
girl, a real beauty they called Georgia, after 'Sweet Georgia Brown'
and 'Georgia On My Mind'. People thought Georgia was a bit of a
fancy name. People didn't call their kids Georgia. Nell didn't mind,
she liked it.

It was so cold Nell really didn't want to go out anywhere at all.
She just wanted to stay in with the baby and the dog and the cats. It
was nice by the fire with the radio on and the rain pouring down in
the street. Georgia was a good baby, the most beautiful ever. Harry
out somewhere with one of his bands. The clock, tick-tock, tick-
tock. Sometimes she was so tired after feeding the baby that it lulled
her to sleep. But she always made sure she was in bed by the time
Harry came home. All quiet. Baby in cot, sleeping peacefully, she on
her side facing the cot and away from him, fast asleep. So that he
wouldn't start. Really, she thought, it's very inconsiderate. What with
all the extra work, and it all fell on her, of course, because – let's face
it – he was hardly ever there – out all day at work, out at nights playing or rehearsing or doing some evening class or another. He'd been
out all over Christmas and New Year with the D Train Seven, all late
dos. The New Year one hadn't finished till four. More exams coming
up. You couldn't tell him he was doing too much, though. Would he
listen? And even when he *was* there, he was always engrossed in
something, poking about up there in his own personal cupboard

where he kept his own special things, or he had his music on much too loud, lost in it, eyes closed.

Anyway, what with all the nappies and the washing and the house getting into such a mess, what did he expect? She had a right to be tired. Drove her mad. She'd be standing there with her back aching and her hands all soapy doing the pots and up he'd come and put his arms round her and want to canoodle. Oh, God, get off! she'd want to say. Expecting you to want it at a time like that. Ridiculous.

His mam and Sid moved to Stovell Avenue in Levenshulme, though God knows why it was called an avenue, it didn't have any trees. It was just a long yellow-brick terrace with red raddled steps. Of course, now she had to keep going there with the baby. Not that his mam came here to see *them*. Nell's mam and dad did, fairly often. Dad always brought Maltesers. Vi was always popping in and out, and now and then Joey or her cousins Berenice and Ruby. And one day, a big treat, a rap on the door and it was her old friend Kitty O'Neill, looking great.

'Kid!' cried Kitty. 'Kid!'

She had her little boy with her, a big boy now, Peter, sitting forward and contemplating the world solemnly, one hand resting on each side of his pram.

'So where's this baby, then, Nelly?'

She grabbed Peter, braked the pram, left it there and came in. She smelt lovely, talcum powder and just a hint of flowery scent, like a rose-garden in the distance. Just as she always did and always had, Kitty looked very smart, very bright and tall and straight. Peter could toddle. She put him down and he stood holding on to her leg, looking round with an earnest air.

'Isn't he sweet?' Nell said, squatting to look at him. He smiled and hid behind his mother's knee. A little darling.

'Where's baby?' Kitty asked.

'Upstairs. She's asleep.'

They tiptoed up. The front bedroom was curtained and dim. Harry and Nell's bed filled most of the room. The cot was next to it, in a corner. Georgia's head was just a faint blob. They peered in. Kitty was holding Peter. 'O-oh!' she cooed. 'Oh, the little thing! Look! Baby!'

'Baby,' Peter said.

246

They tiptoed out.

'They're never awake when you want them to be, are they?' Kitty said.

Nell put the kettle on. She had a bit of cake left that Mam had given her. They sat by the fire and guzzled the tea and gobbled the cake, then Kitty offered a Woodbine and they lit up. It was just like the old days. Kitty seemed happy with her husband. 'And how's Antonio?' she asked, seizing with delight the framed photo of Harry on the mantelpiece, the one where he was wearing his white scarf and looking like a sensitive young poet. 'You got the pick of the Peacock's bunch all right, Nelly,' Kitty said.

'Baby,' Peter said, toddling about happily dropping crumbs every-where, followed by the dog.

'Yes, baby!' Kitty said. 'Baby upstairs! Doggy! "How much is that doggy in the window? Woof Woof!" And how's your gorgeous Bobby?'

Nelly jumped up and searched out all the photographs. 'He's got a lovely Chinese girlfriend,' she said proudly. 'He's sent us a picture. Look! Isn't she beautiful?'

Kitty gasped. 'Golly!'

'This is my Chinese girl', Bob had written on the back. 'Not too bad, is she?'

Kitty stayed for at least three hours. Georgia woke and had a feed, Kitty played with her and walked her up and down, Peter went under the table and played with a box of old bobbins. It rained. They had to drag the pram in. All the time, they reminisced about the larks they'd had, doing each other's seams, checking each other's hems, the dances they'd gone to, picking up lads at Belle Vue, going on the Bobs. You got on, a pair of girls with a pair of boys behind, went round once screaming all the way up and over the big dips and round those terrible curves, till it pulled back into the platform. Then one of the boys would climb forward and one of the girls would climb back, and the boys would pay, and they'd all go round again, and by the end you'd have made up your mind whether you were going to say goodbye and go your separate ways or pair up for the night. That's how it was done.

But after Kitty left, while she was getting the potatoes on as well as she could with Georgia under one arm, Nell began to feel sad.

She probably wouldn't see Kitty again. It took such an effort. Or if she did it would maybe be one time, or two, and then they'd drift and drift, and one day realise that that was it.

22

The Jungle

He was in Singapore, wishing he could have brought Jenny Lim there with him, thinking what a time they could have had, when the letter came.

They'd be off up-country again soon. Things were bad there. He read the letter in the mess and said nothing about it to anybody all day. At last he went and had a word with Bellman and said he wanted to see the CO.

Bellman's cold eyes flickered. 'You're not the first it's happened to,' he said.

Alfie and Davy knew something was up but they knew him well enough by now not to say anything. He'd tell them when he wanted to.

'It's his girl,' Davy said. 'He got a letter.'

Alfie whistled. 'Bet she's in the club.'

The CO's office was neat and shiny. A big glass jug of iced water and some glasses were on the table, under the desk a dark red Indian rug. He could see golden petals falling past the window. The CO was brisk and firm with a rich, well-modulated voice. He clasped his hands and muttered, 'Mm-hm, mm-hm,' from time to time as he listened, his expression never changing. Bob explained first that he wanted leave to go and get married, then that the girl was Chinese and pregnant. 'It's quite important that we do it sooner rather than later,' he said, 'before she starts to really show. I don't want her getting looked down on.'

The CO thought for a moment, rubbing his thumbs together, then said, 'You know, Holloway, I think we should take this very slowly. When did you receive this letter?'

'This morning.'

'Ah ... Not exactly a great deal of time to mull things over, then.'

And the CO went on to point out, very seriously, that marriage was a big step and one not to be taken lightly. He said that sometimes we all do things under pressure. In the heat of the moment. 'Think. Supposing you marry this girl and then she doesn't give birth. What if she were to miscarry? Try for a moment to imagine how you would feel if you married this girl and then found there was no baby after all. If for one moment you feel that you would then regret having taken this decision to marry, I would strongly advise you to take time and think. Remember, you're both very young. Supposing you were to take a step now that both of you might live to regret? Have you thought about where you would live? Would you be planning to settle here? I wonder if you realise quite what it would be like for you if you lived over here. You'd be a pariah. The British community would have nothing to do with you.'

They wouldn't anyway, Bob thought. Bunch of nobs, they didn't want anything to do with the common soldier.

The CO said the rights and wrongs of the social mores of the British community in Malaya were not his concern. He was simply giving the facts. His concern was purely with the welfare of his men. If you stayed in this country, in all likelihood you'd end up with the Eurasians in the Chinese quarter. Neither side accepts them.

'She can come to England,' Bob said.

'Have you thought about how she would fare if you took her to England? Have you really considered how it would be for her to have to adjust to living in a completely alien community, away from all her family and friends and everything she's ever known?'

'But, sir,' Bob had a horrible feeling in the pit of his stomach, 'she's pregnant.'

He was no good at holding his own against authority. This man would talk over everything he said. He *had* thought about it, all day. He was certain he'd never ever as long as he lived find anyone else like Jenny. Her smooth-lidded eyes. You'd never see the likes of her in England, a dream, something you thought in the deep of the night, impossible. The gypsy campfire at night, your head full of some strong drink the gypsy ladies let you sip.

'And I am very fond of her, sir.'

Bob was not easy with the word 'love'.

'No one's underestimating your strength of feeling, Holloway.' The CO sighed. 'This is a sad business whichever way it turns out, Holloway, it's a sad business. What we have to do is choose the most sensible path, the one that's best for everyone in the long term.'

'I'm trying to think of her,' Bob said.

'The Chinese look after their own, you know, Holloway. From what you say, she's from a good family.'

'I want what's best for her. I don't want to leave the girl in the lurch. She's a nice girl.'

The CO looked solemn and nodded. 'Something worth remembering, Holloway.' He leaned forward, linking his fingers. A big gold ring gleamed on one of them. 'All this out here, you know, this isn't your real life. This is a different world. And when your time's up you'll go back to the real world. You mustn't confuse the things that happen out here with your real life.'

Bob said nothing.

'Think about it. That's all I'm saying. Don't do anything rash. Go away and mull things over. In any case,' he consulted some forms on his desk, 'I'm afraid there's no question of leave at the moment, or for some time to come. We simply can't afford to let you go, Holloway.'

He stood up. Bob stood too. The CO shook his hand.

'These things happen, Holloway,' he said. 'Be careful. You might make a terrible mistake that will affect not only your life and the lives of all your family but also the life of this young woman. Come back and see me when you've had some time to think and we'll talk again.'

Bob had the strangest, most uncomfortable feeling of relief as he walked away from that meeting. He didn't want to think about it. But if it was relief it was a poor kind, very heavy about his heart. He wanted a drink.

Bob wrote to her and told her not to worry. We'll get married, he said, but I'm afraid it can't be for some time. The CO won't give me leave. The army are very funny about this sort of thing and they are not being very helpful. Don't worry, I'll come back as soon as I can. Tell your parents I am responsible and I will be back soon. First we have to go back up-country ...

'You know your mistake, don't you?' Chance said. 'You gave her your address.'

Chance would get a thump if he wasn't careful. Everyone knew Bob had got a Chinese girl pregnant, but they also knew he was smitten with the girl and wouldn't talk about her. But Chance always had to stick his bloody great oar in.

There was trouble all over. The bandits killed some planters up in Perak, near where they used to be in Ipoh. They were murdering people on the estates, slashing rubber trees, attacking mines, laying ambushes and shooting at the police. A state of emergency was announced. The Drummonds were sent to a transit camp deep amid endless rows of rubber. Nangku was there with the other Ibans, all sitting round in loincloths outside their tent, hair loose down to his waist, body heavily tattooed.

Nangku grinned and stepped over to them, greeting them like old friends. He was to lead them on patrol again. That was good. He was OK, Nangku, the best there was.

They patrolled. Endlessly. Their feet turned spongy again with the wet, and the bloody leeches sucked them dry along with the heat. Alfie still cried sometimes, getting the leeches off.

They never encountered the enemy.

Bob saw Jenny Lim two more times before the baby was born. He went to her house. From the way she talked, he'd realised her family couldn't be short of a bob or two, but not until he saw the house did he realise quite how well-off they were. They had a big garden and a garage, and the house had trellis all over the front of the veranda, covered in orange and pink flowers. Her parents had been very upset about the baby. She'd told them they were getting married. Of course, they had to agree now, but they weren't happy. Her mother, a tight-mouthed woman who never cracked a smile the whole time he was there, completely ignored him. Her father took him into another room and talked seriously, asking for Bob's intentions.

'I intend to marry Jenny,' Bob said.

Her father wanted to know when.

'As soon as I can,' he replied, and went on to explain the problem with the CO. It simply wasn't possible at the moment. He'd talked it all over with Jenny. They would marry and live in England.

Her father's eyes went misty. Bob felt awful.

She said she wanted to get married now. She couldn't live like this. Soon everyone would know.

'You can tell everyone we're married if you like,' Bob said. 'It doesn't make any difference because we *will* be married anyway. It's only a matter of time. I don't want to get married till I've told my mam and dad. I don't think they'd like to think of me getting married and them not being there or at least not even being told. I think I ought to tell them first.'

'Write to them,' she said.

'I will.'

This would all be over soon. He'd be demobbed, out of the bloody army for ever. He put his arm around her childish shoulders. She could come to England with him. It would be OK. They could live with his mam and dad at first.

His mind stopped at that. It was impossible to imagine.

Jenny looked at him for a long time as if she was trying to make him drop his gaze.

'Jenny,' he said, 'I promise. I promise. I just can't get permission yet.'

She smiled. 'OK,' she said.

She was tough.

The second time he saw her she was showing. She carried the baby high. She'd put on weight everywhere, even round her face. She still looked lovely. She seemed quite happy, laughing and smiling a lot, showing no signs of worry. She'd told everyone she had married her soldier in Singapore, her name was now Jenny Holloway, and after her baby was born she was going to live with her husband in England. In Manchester. Her parents knew the truth but they weren't letting on. They loved her, she'd always been their favourite. She'd had a good education and was going to be a teacher. She couldn't do that now.

Bob received news of his child's birth at the camp the day they were given their orders for Sungei Tenak. A boy, eight pounds twelve ounces. Mother and baby doing well. He wrote at once that he'd be there as soon as he could. Davy said they should celebrate. They had a drink and raised their glasses to Bob's son. But the CO said there was no chance of leave. The CTs were burning out factories, laying ambushes on those lonely estate roads. They'd held up a bus, killed everyone on board and set it alight.

Bob's unit was to go up to Sungei Tenak and guard it until the Specials could get there, then push on through the jungle to a police post miles from anywhere. Any enemy encountered on the way were to be destroyed. Not that they ever did encounter the enemy. It was getting ridiculous. But off they went anyway.

Sungei Tenak was the strangest thing you ever saw: in the middle of the swamp and the sombre rubber groves, suddenly sandbags and sentry posts, barbed wire, a tall chain-link fence, as if you were approaching a concentration camp; but behind it all, just the planter's house, its verandas with their rattan chairs, lawns, English flowers, the garden with a golden drift of angsena petals and a paw-paw tree. The mem, a tall imposing woman in a blue embroidered dress, came out to meet them. She wasn't particularly friendly. She was alone out here with just three big dogs and a couple of servants, an old Chinese couple. You'd think she'd have been pleased when the soldiers arrived but she didn't seem it. Turned out she'd had things nicked from the house when she was in Singapore, and she blamed the army. After three days, her husband arrived in an armoured Ford V8 with a steel visor that could be wound down over the windscreen. He had a couple of other men with him, all carrying guns. Then a day or two later the Specials came, Malay lads in berets, and the patrol was up and off again, through the silver-grey mottle of rubber, into the jungle. The base they were heading for was supposed to be four days away but you could never tell.

The first night out, they made camp at a cave in a rocky outcrop. When the jungle chorus started up, Alfie still went rigid. Bob was used to it now. He was quite content to be on watch with Nangku. Being on watch here was a strange affair. You sat very still in the pitch black and the jungle went on all around you. They sat upon a slope. The jungle was alive, full of rustlings and voices. You could distinguish the separate voices in the dark, some far, some near. Strange language. He thought of Jenny and the baby. A son. How could he have a son? Then a silence came walking down the slope from above. Nangku put his hand on Bob's arm and gripped. The grip said: You do not move, you do not speak, you do not breathe. The silence was a band of air with a different quality, passing like a flow of slow lava down the slope. As it came closer it brought with it a stench. Nangku's grip tightened. It came by them. It breathed over Bob's right shoulder with the breath of a charnel house. He wanted to gag but daren't.

He felt the heat of the tiger passing. Not a thing in the jungle stirred.

Nangku showed him the pug marks in the morning. He said there had never been any danger. It had eaten already. That was the smell.

They hacked on through fronds of nipah palm. The *parangs* slipped in their sweating hands, the snagging prickles cut their arms. Occasionally, off in the jungle, something heavy fell to earth. A stink rose through the dim green light, all the earth putrefying beneath their feet. The light quivered. There were snakes, more than Bob had ever seen before. Big ones, some huge, coiled high in the trees. You had to walk under them. Smaller ones slithering away underfoot. He was in a kind of dream, Alfie behind, Chance behind him, then Davy. Alfie's terror was palpable, in his sweat, attracting more of the horrors to him than to anyone else. Every flying, crawling, stinging, disgusting thing loved Alfie. The hairs on the back of his neck were on permanent alert.

The land sloped steeply upwards. You couldn't have a smoke till you got to the top of the hill, and that was always miles away and you were practically crawling. You couldn't move. Hack on and on. Soldier ants running across the roots and creepers.

It rained, poured buckets, soaked the men through.

When it stopped, the heat dried them. Then it rained again.

It took the rest of the afternoon to reach the top. In two days they covered seven miles. Alfie had gone into a walking coma. He should have been on watch but Bellman let him off and Davy volunteered to take his place. Davy had turned into Jungle Jim. After Nangku, he was the best of them. Next day it was swamp, foul-stinking swamp all the way.

It rained. They waded.

Sometimes the jungle did strange things. Bob wondered if he'd fallen asleep. He thought he saw a great green curtain flapping over to the left and a little ahead, but when he looked it was just the endless trees and the lianas hanging tangled, or snakes, they could have been snakes, bigger and higher than it was possible for a snake to be. Sometimes he got a glimpse of how it was for poor old Alfie.

That night when he took off his boots they were full of blood from burst leeches. He burned off thirty-odd from all over his body. Blood from them, his own, ran down his skin and mingled with his sweat. They got in anywhere, through the lace-holes of his boots, the fibres of his clothing even, he didn't know how, they were diabolical. He powdered his feet and changed his socks. Next day they followed a riverbank. Thick bamboo, the butterflies sailing. Davy saw a kingfisher. They spaced out crossing the river. The kits got wet but everything was in rubber bags. There were no crocs down here, Nangku said. Only a million leeches. Something had made tunnels in the undergrowth on the other side. Nangku got down on his hands and knees.

'Men,' he said.

Everyone froze.

'Four men,' he said, 'two days ago.'

'Bloody hell,' Chance said.

'They made this?' Bellman asked.

'No. Pig made this.'

They crawled on hands and knees after Nangku through the pig's tunnel. After a while it was crossed by another. Nangku considered. At last they moved on, deeper and deeper into an endless maze. It was like being an insect crawling in a carpet.

Just before sunset they reached a place in the *lallang* where they could pitch silent camp and settle down for the night. They were experienced by now. They could eat and shit and clean their guns in total silence.

This was always the time when Alfie most wanted to scream and scream and scream, but he never did because he knew that if he did they'd have to shoot him. Of course they would, and he understood why.

'That was this morning,' Nangku said.

They were down in the *lallang*. They moved on, flattened, crawling, slower and slower. Nangku was listening, pausing every knee-step. He raised a hand for silence. The men were still. They had learned to be still, even when the flying things were all over them. They could hear the river. Nangku signalled for them to stay, and crawled ahead. They couldn't see him any more. Ages later he returned, crawling backwards, looking over his shoulder and motioning for them to follow.

It was a camp alongside the river, recently abandoned. Huts on stilts, linked by catwalks. A pot with the remains of rice lying on its side by a dead fire. Cigarette ends littered the ground, footprints passed to and fro. Six bamboo beds, a Communist flag.

They waited while Nangku sniffed around. Eight of them had set off together, he thought. He moved ahead and they trailed him, mile on mile.

'Here,' he said, 'they separate.'

Four one way, four another.

'It's as broad as it's long,' Bellman said.

They chose a path and went on, following Nangku. They walked and then they crawled. Sliding on his belly, Bob realised he was exhausted. He couldn't remember a time when he hadn't been exhausted. Ahead, Nangku moved slower and slower, till at last he stopped altogether and looked back. Grinned. Mimed a man smoking.

Bob's blood went up. A man. The enemy. Any enemy encountered were to be destroyed. Silently, they gathered in the undergrowth and peered through the leaves. A man in jungle green sat looking out of his *basha*, smoking a cigarette, his face calm, slightly humorous, eyes quite clearly visible. He had a Bren-gun and three stars on his cap. You could smell sweet Chinese tobacco.

Bellman gave the signal and they all stepped out at once. Chance and Bob shot, got him in the stomach and chest. He'd registered them, was rising when they shot, fell forward, slumped over on to his side. The cigarette burned on the ground a little way from his outstretched fingers. There was a moment of silence, then a skinny demented girl came screaming in Chinese out of the *basha*, a tommy gun in her hand. She shot straight at Bob and the bullet grazed his right arm, a hot lick.

Shots rang, she ran, firing behind her. They ran after.

She hid in a patch of beluga fern. They shot into it again and again, then Davy went in with Bellman to get her. The back of her head was smashed to bits by a bullet but her face was OK. Her eyes were closed. Bob and Chance had to carry her back to the *basha* where the body of the male bandit was, plonk her down next to him and lay them out together. Her hair was cut chin length and she wore a sweatband round her head and an Aertex shirt with huge sweatmarks under the armpits. The man had very high cheekbones and his arms were sinewy, rippled with thick veins. Bellman and Nangku checked their boots for money, the rest emptied the haversacks, all apart from Alfie, who just sat there gawping. Vitamin tablets, Paludrine, cotton wool, Bovril, a Chinese pin-up – that must be his. Plasters, a compass, a snapshot of a Chinese family standing together in front of an official-looking building. Hand-cream, hers.

All they'd had to eat was tapioca root.

They just had to follow the river now, Nangku said. The river had many rapids. They put together a bamboo raft, tied the bodies on and floated them downstream. It was the quickest way. They had to get the kills to a police post. Every time they came to rapids the bodies bashed about against the rocks and would have been smashed to pieces and swept away if they hadn't been tied on. River water soaked them and drank the blood from their wounds, especially his. He'd bled like mad. Bob could see the girl's face, upside down. The back of her head sloped away from the crown at a horrible angle, collapsed. It looked as if someone had taken a scoop out of it with a big spoon. Her mouth was set hard. She wasn't very old. Nineteen? Twenty-one? She'd bitten her nails. Fancy a young girl like that running around out here in this terrible place getting shot. Where were her mam and dad? He thought of Nelly, and of Jenny Lim. Jenny and her baby, waiting for him. His heart had been aching so long he thought it might be going hard.

On and on they went. Nangku consulted the compass. He never bothered with the map. He studied the ground and the leaves all around. It was time to leave the river, he said, the camp wasn't too far away now. They fished the raft out of the river and hung the bandits from poles by their hands and feet and carried them along. Bob hated to see the girl like that, the place where her sex was, visible through her trousers because of the angle at which she hung. What a way for a young girl to end up.

They relaxed a little. The jungle was thinning out a bit. Nangku was ahead. They were fanning out slightly, Bellman going wide. Somewhere not far behind, Bob heard Alfie sniffling softly.

Then Bellman got it in the leg.

Bob heard it, it was all over in a flash. Pure bad luck. Heard the rush and thwack of the spear. Bellman's scream, high and horrible. The branches shook. Nangku was there in a second. Bellman went on screaming. It was bamboo, sharpened to a point, a long spear that had gone right through his thigh from front to back. The point stuck out about three inches behind. Chance gave him a shot. Nangku pulled the spear out.

'Trip-wire,' Davy said.

Aboriginals. The spear had been tied on to a long thin branch. Bellman swore solidly, crying with the pain.

'Oh, no,' Alfie moaned thinly, as if he were standing at a bus stop and it had just started to rain. 'What next?'

'How far are we?' asked Bob.

Bellman's blood soaked all down his leg. 'For fuck's sake, do something!' he sobbed.

They set about staunching the blood, but it kept coming out through the pads. Nangku did a tourniquet. Bob felt sick. Bellman went on weeping, sighing, trying to control it. His teeth chattered and his face was wet. They made up a stretcher of bamboo and Chance dragged him. Bob and Alfie hauled the girl on her pole. Nangku went ahead with Davy, carrying the male bandit. The heat was hideous. The girl's head hung down, swinging with the movement of their progress. Bob thought of Jenny Lim and her baby. The boy. Bruce Robert Holloway. The jungle spoke soothingly around him. There was a terrible smell. If I ever get out of here ... he thought. If I ever get out of here ... But he never finished the sentence. Would he ever get home? See Belle Vue racetrack, go out with a dog and a ferret over Mellands? Would he take Jenny Lim back to that? She'd feel the cold.

Would she mind not having much of a house? Maybe he could get a house in Chell Street. The thought depressed him. Jenny Lim and Chell Street, he couldn't put the two together.

Bellman had gone quiet, though he moaned in soft agony once in a while. Chance had given him some morphine.

'He was lucky,' Alfie said suddenly. 'Bit higher and he'd have got it right through the heart.'

The jungle dragged on, still thinning. The last few miles through the rubber trees they started talking properly again. Laughing, even. Even Alfie, who was crying sporadically. At last they heard music, then they came to an aboriginal village with huts on stilts, fishing nets laid out to dry. A brass gong hung in a window. A Malay song played from a crackly gramophone. Three naked children hung on a rope swing.

The men of the village, barefoot, in loincloths, came forward and talked to Nangku. They carried blowpipes. The headman came out. Bellman was put into a hut out of the sun, while a boy ran to camp.

These Aboriginals were OK. It was like everything else out here, you never knew what was what. Just as Bellman had always told them, you can't tell by looking. The Indonesians, the Chinese, the Aboriginals. Some are OK, some aren't. You can't tell by looking.

These seemed very friendly. The women were bare-breasted and wore bangles all up their arms. The men laughed with Nangku. The dead man and woman were laid down with their poles on the edge of the village. No one took any notice of them. The children brought water and splashed it over the soldiers' heads, laughing. The soldiers laughed too. Then the trucks arrived to take them back to camp and the medics carried Bellman out, motionless, dead-looking on his bamboo stretcher.

'I'm going to get blind drunk tonight,' Bob said to Davy.

Davy grinned.

Alfie slumped in an old charabanc seat by an open fire, sucking his thumb.

'Blind blind blind bloody drunk.'

Bellman lost his leg. They never saw him again; he was taken out by helicopter. Could have been worse, Alfie said, a stake through the heart.

He laughed and lit a fag.

Bob was granted leave to go and see Jenny Lim and the baby. He got off at the station in Port Dickson and took a rickshaw to her house. There was a path through a small garden, to a gate with a latch. A door stood open on to the veranda. Her mother would not look at him. Her sisters were shy. Her father came anxiously towards him.

'Not here. Not here,' he said, and led him out and round the veranda.

Jenny was living in the garage with the baby. They'd made it as nice as they could for her. She had mats on the floor and a rug, a stove and a kerosene lamp.

When she saw him she ran at him and threw herself into his arms, laughing and crying. She was fatter. 'I knew you'd come back!' she cried.

'I said I would.' He was full. Full of unbled emotion. He couldn't speak. He saw the dark head of a sleeping baby among the tumbled sheets.

'Yes,' she said, 'your son. Bruce Robert Holloway.'

He laughed. Tears filled his eyes. He hovered nervously over the baby, a brown snub face, the eyes crinkled.

'Do you think you'll like England?' he asked.

'I can't wait.'

'What if you don't?'

She snorted.

For three weeks he lived in the garage with Jenny and the baby. The three of them slept together, baby in the middle. In the very early mornings he'd wake to the sound of wooden shoes going *toc-toc-toc* on the street outside.

She'd be sitting up, feeding the baby at her breast, long black hair hanging down. Then her father would get up and do his exercises in the garden, and after a while she'd hand Bob the baby and get up with her plain white shift wrapped round her and make *gula malacca*; later her sisters brought food over from the house and took it in turns to hold the baby and walk about with him. Bruce Robert Holloway had almond eyes and a soft black shining head.

Bob hardly saw Jenny's parents and never spoke a word to her mother. The days unfolded in a dream of a dream. They slept, they ate, they never went out. The sisters brought food. Her father exercised. The baby cried, fed, threw up, sucked his thumb, smiled. He had a big wide-open smile, and a fat dimpled brown hand that lay along Bob's neck when he carried him.

He left early one morning before her father was up. She came out with him as far as the gate, carrying baby Bruce. They kissed each other, he kissed the baby.

'The next time I see you will be in Manchester,' he said.

She crinkled her eyes. 'My Bob,' she replied.

He looked back twice before the end of the street. Each time, she was waving the baby's hand. He turned again at the corner and raised a hand. She waved, blew him a kiss from her palm, waved the baby's hand again.

I'll never see her again, he thought.

PART FOUR

Stormy Weather

23

Green Grove

Once upon a time, far, far away, there'd been a jolly daddy, who'd disappeared. There was a jumper: blue-green with a dark brown and yellow stripe down the sleeves and round the neck. He wore it with his shiny black Brylcreem hair when he used to be jolly. When Harry did zombies and Frankenstein's monster to make the kids scream, and tickled and wrestled them, and made them giggle so much they sometimes wet themselves, clambering over his knees, falling on the floor, laughing, climbing up again. Once, in the fray, one of them scratched his nose. He felt a right fool going into work next day, everyone asking him what had happened to his nose and him having to say he'd got it scratched in a wrestling match with his kids.

He hardly ever wore that jumper any more, and when he did it was like a ghost of before.

Now he was a great mystery, a formal man. Nell never sang when Harry was in the house, and the children were subdued. Ease went out when he walked in. The funny atmosphere had always been there, lurking, like intermittently smelly drains; but it had got worse and worse, been left to fester, taken over. It was something to do with his mother not liking to be touched. Jack knew about it even though he didn't understand, because Jack knew everything: everybody talked in front of him. And the girls knew because Nell had started confiding in Georgia, and Georgia always told Joanne everything, and he always listened. He knew that the funny atmosphere was because his mother did not like to be touched, and he knew that his mother couldn't stand his father: she said he talked to her as if she was an idiot and, anyway, he was a real snob.

Jack was on her side, they all were. She and the kids were all together on a mainland and Harry was off on his own over there, out on a spit of land. His life was jazz and the Tailgaters. Everything was jazz, even Jack's and Georgia's names. He whistled jazz all the time, he couldn't help it, it just happened. His life was blowing on the *Royal Daffodil* from Tower Pier to Margate on a hot summer day with all the other bands, playing the Albert Hall, making records for George Martin at Parlophone, profiles in the *Chron*, radio, TV even, meeting Dizzy Gillespie and Coleman Hawkins and Ella Fitzgerald and Count Basie, drinking with J.J. Johnson and Kai Winding in the artists' bar of the Free Trade Hall, chatting backstage somewhere with Johnny Miller and Oscar Peterson about the modern jazz scene in America.

That was real life.

He'd picked up Jay D. Smith, Jack Teagarden's discographer and biographer, on a point of personnel, and Jay D. had written a long letter from Washington DC; now the two swapped records backwards and forwards across the Atlantic regularly. Jay D. wrote: 'Jack has left Armstrong and will form his own group in California. He proposes using the family, Norma on piano, Charlie on trumpet and Clois on drums.' As if they were distant family. A transatlantic jazz family of Teagarden and Armstrong, and the Tailgaters travelling all over the country in the old twenties Rolls Royce they called the Hearse, eating Chinese food, driving on through the dark lanes at night and stopping whenever they felt like it to get out Johnny Miller's telescope and look at the planets and the stars. On warm nights they'd sit for a while and drink coffee from a flask at the side of the road and talk a little drunkenly about the vastness of the universe. And one night in Newcastle he met a clarinettist called Ernie Tomasso, who knew Jack well and gave Harry a picture of himself and Jack and their wives taken outside the Hôtel Negresco when they were playing the Nice jazz festival in 1949. Jack's wife was wearing a big fur coat, and Jack had his arm round Ernie and they all looked happy.

Every morning, somehow, he was up and off to work on the bus, clean shoes and shirt, the jazz still in his head, while a world evolved at home without him, a cosy, inturned world of Nell and the kids and the radio and the cats and the dog.

*

266

In the new big house on Green Grove, in the parlour, on the wall above the fireplace was a large painting of a Chinese woman with a serious green face. Her hands were hidden under big sleeves. A Russian artist, Tretchikoff, had painted it. Nell loved that picture. It always made her think of Jenny Lim. She missed Jenny Lim even though she'd never met her. So did Violet.

Jenny Lim never came.

They'd got so used to hearing about her through Bob's letters, he'd even sent them photographs of her and they'd studied her heavy-lidded fun-filled eyes, admired the gloss of her hair. They'd grown so used to the idea that she was coming. She'd bring colour and change into their lives. They'd never met a Chinese girl before. They could show her around. She could tell them all about Malaya. It sounded so beautiful.

But she never came. It *could* have happened. Bobby couldn't blame anyone but himself. Mam and Dad said they'd welcome her. Violet and Nell said they'd make a friend of her. There was never one straight reason why he didn't bring her over. He wasn't sure himself. At first he was going to. But as time passed, maybe she just began to seem more and more unreal. There'd been a time she both was and wasn't family. She'd written to Mam and Dad, and to Violet and Nell, very nice letters. She'd written 'To my dear sister Nell' on a birthday card.

First the delay was because of immigration red tape on account of the fact that they weren't actually married. She needed to get all sorts of documents, and at this end they were all supposed to sign something to say they would provide her and baby Bruce with a home. But then after a few weeks had passed with nothing happening, and then somehow a few weeks more, he seemed less sure. You'd ask him straight out: 'Look, Bobby, are you serious about this girl?'

'Oh, aye.'

He'd stick his cigarette among the pegs at the top of his guitar. 'I'm in the middle of writing her a letter.'

He played the same few notes again and again.

'It's dead complicated, Nell. Immigration. It doesn't just happen, you know.'

The same notes over and over again. She watched his fingers. It didn't get on her nerves as much as the trombone. Not as loud.

267

It was cold the day Nell realised Jenny wasn't ever coming over, cold and windy with a blue sky and rushing white clouds. She'd put on a headscarf and pulled the wide lapels of her coat up round her neck and taken the kids and walked up Stanley Grove and cut over the allotments by the Red Path. On Pink Bank Lane, they passed their dog Tim, Bonny's successor, trotting purposefully towards Stanley Grove. Tim always went out on his own. He barked at the door to go out. He barked when he wanted to come in. He flicked his eyes quickly at them in acknowledgement but did not break his pace.

Mam and Dad had moved again, still on the estate, to a smaller house on Darras Road. A ship with sails of horn stood on top of the wireless. On the wall by the front door was a coloured ceramic plate with a raised scene of a fishing village, steps and a cottage. Jesus was in his old place on the doily on top of the sideboard. Dad had the Dura-glit out and was polishing the brass. He wasn't well. God, he was thin, thin as a rake. He'd always been a small man but not like this. He'd taken down the big plates from the walls, and the horse brasses from the leather strips that hung on either side of the kitchen door. The candlesticks stood on the fender. Dad polished the fire-irons meticulously. He was back on cigarettes again, one was stuck on his lip, the smoke curling upwards and making him squint.

'Garden's looking nice, Dad,' Nell said.

His daffs were out. Georgia played in the garden, the gate was closed.

'Our Bobby's at the pub,' said Mam. 'He's after a job at Jackson's next week. Can't seem to settle.'

'Takes time,' said Dad, 'stands to reason.'

'It'll take him a bloody sight longer if he can't shift himself out of the pub.' Mam sat with her hands folded on her big round stomach. She wore a cross-over pinny with small flowers all over. 'Another bleeding drinker in the family. Takes after you.'

'Oh, bugger off.' Dad buffed up a brass plate like the sun.

'He's stinking the house out with curry all the time,' said Mam. 'Gets in from the pub and starts making curry in the middle of the night. He even curries eggs.'

'How does he do that?'

'Buggered if I know.'

'I've put some golden rod in the back,' Dad said.

'Has he said any more about Jenny Lim?'

'That lass is never coming over here, Nell,' Dad said. 'If he was going to bring her over he'd have done it by now.'

'I've told him,' Mam said, '"It's not fair on her, Bobby," I've said. "You've got to make up your mind."'

'He's scared to tell her,' Dad said. 'I think he's been hoping it's all just going to fizzle out.'

'Fizzle out? She's got a child,' Nell said.

Dad sat back and sighed. 'Maybe it's all for the best, Nell. He's been worried sick she'd get over here and then not like it. It's not like where she's from, is it?'

'Anyway, he's met this Eva,' said Mam.

'Eva?'

'And you've got to remember,' Dad said, 'she's with her family. They're not hard up, by all accounts.'

'Eva Harris. You know Doreen Harris that used to knock about with Berenice? Her sister.'

'This place'd seem very cold to her,' Dad said.

'Sam! That child's pulling up all your best flowers!'

Nell had seen herself going round town with Jenny Lim, her new friend. She'd seen them sitting together having a cigarette and laughing. Jenny Lim talking in that funny chopped way they have. It was never going to happen. Jenny Lim would stay out there all alone with Bob's baby.

'A little baby!' Violet had hugged herself and rocked with delight. 'A little Chinese baby!' She dandled Edward, who had one green eye and one brown. 'With those little slitty eyes! Aw! He'll be gorgeous! I can't wait to get my hands on him and give him a cuddle!'

I bet he's the only Malayan Bruce in existence, Nell thought. My nephew. And I'm his auntie Nell and I'll never see him.

Dad stood on the front step in his slippers. 'Picking Grandad's flowers, love?' he said kindly. His hair was nearly white.

★

269

Nell was gone, visiting her dad, and she'd left Harry on his own with the kids. The atmosphere was strained.

He was losing touch with them. It was OK when they used to play and he'd pull funny faces and hang his head upside down to show them how a face seen the wrong way up could look like a whole other person. What was happening? He didn't know. He couldn't even place when it started. All he knew was it had been all right once. It was all right in Blackpool with Nell's mam and dad and that wasn't long ago. They'd gone on the beach and he'd helped the kids make a giant sandcastle. Sam, flat cap, waistcoat, fob watch, hands in pockets of his pinstripe suit, thin old man watching the flat, wrinkled sea. That was just before they knew he was ill. The kids kept wanting hot-dogs. Grandad made jokes about the word. He took them along the prom and sat them on the wall to look at the sea, holding on to them so they wouldn't fall in. Sam frowned at the glare, eyes watery and narrow, gold gleam of a fountain pen in his top pocket. The girls wore blazers and gingham dresses, red sandals and white socks, hair in bunched plaits tied with broad red ribbons.

Everything had been all right then. Everything had *seemed* all right. But it wasn't at all. Sam had lung cancer. He'd been in the hospital for a long time, but now he was home.

The table was up against the back wall and they were playing Snakes and Ladders. It was always dark in the room. There was a fire in the grate. He was in a bad mood anyway because she hadn't been impressed by the photographs of their holiday in Silverdale he'd had developed by a man at work. It might have cost next to nothing but they all came out pink.

'Why are they all pink?' That was all she said.

Pink was all right. What was wrong with it? They were still decent photographs.

'Why is she looking like that?' he asked Georgia, who was shaking the dice in a cup.

He couldn't get anything out of Joanne.

'She's wet herself,' Georgia replied, rolling the dice.

He was never any good at these situations. He didn't do anything for the kids, not in that way. He could fight with them and tickle them and take them for walks round town but he'd never changed a nappy and he couldn't talk to them. He was shy with them. They looked at him in an odd way, as if he was a stranger. He stared at Joanne in despair. Why had she done that?

'Why has she done that?' he asked Georgia.

'She's scared to go to the toilet,' Georgia said.

Joanne, struck dumb and paralysed, looked terrified.

'Don't be ridiculous. Why are you scared to go to the toilet?'

'I don't know.'

'Don't be ridiculous, you must know. It doesn't make sense to say you don't know. Think about it.'

'I don't know.'

'What's she scared of?' This to Georgia. His eyes angry.

'She doesn't like going upstairs on her own. She's scared.'

'But there's nothing to be scared of. What is there to be scared of?'

'I don't know.'

He didn't know what to do. Why did she have to do it when she was with him? Nell was better at dealing with this sort of thing.

'Shall I go up with her?' Georgia suggested.

'It's a bit late for that now.' His tone suggested some serious calamity. Joanne's eyes were starting to fill. He glared at her for a while, and she stared back. Georgia sat awkwardly between.

'Well,' he said at last, 'I suppose you'd better go and sit in the back kitchen.'

Joanne went immediately.

'Close the door,' he called after her.

He didn't know why he'd done that. She had to be punished for wetting her knickers at her age. She was much too big for that sort of thing. But then when Nell came back she said, 'Didn't you tell her to take the wet knickers off? They've dried on her,' and went into a bit of a sulk. He sulked at her sulk. She sulked back. The girls escaped to the big front bedroom, which was now their own. He didn't like you being scared. He didn't know what to do about it. Once, years ago, he'd taken them up to the attic to watch the fireworks at Belle Vue. There was no light in the attic. He'd left them up there on their own by the window just for a couple of minutes while he went downstairs

271

for something he'd forgotten. It was OK at first but then Joanne realised he wasn't there and panicked.

'Where's Daddy? Where's Daddy? Where's Daddy?'

'He's coming back!'

Joanne, terrified of the dark, screamed.

'Ssh! Ssh!'

Georgia flapped her arms. He hated anything like this. Fuss. Noise. Georgia was frightened not of the dark but of his anger.

He came running back up. He was big and angry in the dark room. Outside, the fireworks fizzed and crackled in the night sky. 'There's no need for that!' He slapped Joanne on the leg, hard. She went hysterical and had to be hauled back downstairs and it ruined everything of what was meant to be a big treat. It took her ages to calm down. No one spoke. Harry sat down in his chair with a terrible look on his face.

Georgia kept out of it.

'You've made a mark on her leg,' Nell said, in a low, strained voice.

Georgia looked. There was the mark. Red fingers.

He didn't respond. Everything went quiet. Nothing more was said about it. Everything was ruined.

Dad was worse. He was on morphine. It kept him peaceful, rocking in his chair with a blanket over his stick-thin knees. He'd feel for his pipe, reaching out but muddled by the drug, unable to locate it at first. On fine afternoons they'd move his chair to the front door so he could sit and enjoy the fruits of his work, the small red roses that rambled around the front window, the daisies and snapdragons and his favourite pansies. Bob had taken over the gardening. He'd got a dog, a mad fluffy thing like a smaller version of an Old English sheepdog. Danny, Dan, Dannyboy, that mutt, a mad thing that liked to race madly about the house and garden irritating Mam.

Joanne was terrified of Dan and screamed whenever he came bouncing furiously out of the kitchen.

'He won't hurt you, chuck,' Dad said. His cheeks had fallen in and his eyes were bright and old and watery, his silvery hair like clumps of wire.

'Just bash him, Nell,' Bob mumbled through his cigarette, sleeking back his quiff, darker now, at the mirror. He was going out with Eva. They were getting married in September.

He could have brought Jenny Lim and his child over, could have left England for ever and gone back to her, made a life out there. Easy to say. When all was said and done he didn't love her enough for that. He didn't know what he would have done out there. He had no money. He was only a soldier. The Brits out there classed him somewhere with the ayahs and amahs. Back home he'd slotted easily back into all of his old habits. He was handsomer than when he'd left, grown-up and hardened. Eva had lived on Sutton Estate all her life but she was exotic-looking, with slashed ink-black eyebrows like Katy Jurado's in *High Noon*. She must have always been around. Her older sister Doreen used to knock about with Berenice. He bumped into her in Sivori's one night. It was all Teds down there these days. They'd got a jukebox. She was with one of her sisters and he was with a mate or two. She worked in Kendal's on Deansgate as a shop assistant and was very down-to-earth, knew him instinctively and wasn't taken in for a second by his charm. He was just a big soft daft spoiled thing as far as she was concerned, and she could see right through him. Her own father drank, she knew all about that. It was in Bobby's family. Look at that cousin, that Joey, gone all to seed since that wife of his took off with the little boy. Well, she wouldn't stand for any of his nonsense. She'd sort him out. He wanted her to. He wanted to get away from his mam and dad, branch out on his own. He didn't have to put anything on for Eva, he could muck about and be stupid and be himself. She knew about Jenny Lim and the baby. She'd given him a good telling-off: 'That poor girl. Have you thought about what you've done to her? You wouldn't pull a thing like that on me. I'd kill you. You don't get a damn thing from me, not with what I know about you. If I was her I'd be on the next boat to England by hook or by crook, and I'd bloody kill you. And have you thought about that poor child without his dad? Well, you've given him a great start, haven't you?'

On and on.

'I'm thinking of marrying Eva,' he said to Nell. 'I mean, Eva's all right, isn't she?'

'Of course she's all right. But if you're thinking of marrying some-one, you should think they're more than just all right, Bobby.'

He smiled.

'Beautiful picture that, Nell.' He was standing in front of the Tretchikoff.

It was the same tone in which he'd say: 'That's that Segovia, Nell. Beautiful that. Beautiful that, Nell. It's that Los Paraguayos, Nell. That Jimmie Rodgers. That Harry Belafonte.'

He gazed at the picture for some minutes. He's thinking of Jenny Lim, Nell thought, his real true love in Malaya.

He married Eva, thin Eva with her hollow face, bushy black hair and bright brown eyes. They lived with Mam and Dad and argued all the time, as much as it was possible to have a decent argument with Mam and Dad always there. Bob sat around all day playing 'Yellow Bird' and 'The Banana Boat Song' on his guitar. He read *Anna Karenina, Tales of Mystery and Imagination* by Edgar Allan Poe, and the works of Harold Robbins. At night he pressed his trousers (just so, he wouldn't let anybody else do them for him), combed his hair sleekly back, just so, and went out with Eva. He wouldn't talk at all about Jenny Lim any more. It was as if she'd never existed. When he'd first come home, that's all he'd wanted to do, sit around in Nell's or Violet's drinking tea and eating dripping and toast, telling them all about her, all about everything. Everything. He always had a conscience about the things he'd done in the war, even the things you couldn't blame him for. It was war. That's what everyone told him. It was war, Bobby. Things were different in war. It's another land.

He'd always drunk, but he drank far worse when he came back from Malaya.

Once or twice he wept, telling Nell and Violet about the things he'd seen and done. He never lied. 'We did these things,' he said. 'Everyone did them.'

He got a trophy from the army when he was demobbed, a Japanese bayonet in its leather scabbard, with a leather strap and a metal encasement for the handle. He would withdraw it and hold it across his palms. It was dark pewter grey, not very large. The encase-

274

ment, of darker metal, was all pocked and mottled. Nell shuddered to look at it. Eva never liked it either. The first time he brought her round to Mam and Dad's and showed it to her she scowled at it. 'I don't want to look at that,' she said brusquely. 'It's been used.'

'Aye,' he said, 'it's notched.'

It was kept in its box, high away in a cupboard with the scrapbook he'd made of his time in the East. In it was the photograph he'd taken out of the dead bandit's wallet back in Java. 'Extremist', he'd written under it. And there was one of Nangku. 'A great lad, that Iban,' he'd tell everyone. 'Asked me to come and stay with him and his family when the war's over. In Sarawak. You know, I just might. They used to be headhunters, the Iban. But he was a great lad, that Nangku, headhunter or no.'

He was still writing to Jenny Lim and she was writing to him. They'd fallen into penpalship. Eva didn't know. Jenny was living in Kuala Lumpur, working as a housekeeper. She sent him photographs and wrote about them on the back. 'I was fat then. xxxxx forever, my darling Bob', and three rows of tightly packed kisses. Kisses all up the margins of her lovely girlish effusive letters. 'A hundred kisses for my darling Bob.' He'd told her he was getting married. 'You broke my heart,' she wrote, 'but you are Bruce's daddy. I am always yours.'

Bruce wrote too: 'Dear Daddy Bob, How are you? I hope you are very well. I am going back to school tomorrow.' Clever little lad, he seemed. Wrote beautifully. In a funny sort of way Bob hated seeing the letters arrive because they made him feel so sad.

Sometimes he closed his eyes and thought of Jenny, under the palm trees, in the white sand, singing 'Forty-Second Street' with the silver light of the screen on her face in that little flea-pit. Later, softer, fatter, with her baby in the garage. The baby. Little brown thing, black hair. The smell of spices. It was all real, still happening, bringing a lump to his throat and tears to his pale blue eyes. He'd open them and see Jesus on the sideboard and the cat on the windowsill, and his mam cooking his tea, like waking from a dream or looking up from a book; he'd pick up his guitar and fiddle about and think about getting ready to go down the Essoldo with Eva. How easy that would be. Eva, thin, tall, wiry, good legs, hair a black bush, mouth a rosebud, carefully coloured dark red when she went out.

She was realler.

Bob fastened his tie, cigarette waggling up and down on his lip. 'Hey, Nell,' he said, 'have you heard that Elvis Presley?'

'No.' Nell sat down and lit a fag.

All the doors were open to let in the nice fresh summery air. Mam was making tea. 'Sterrer or ordinary?' she asked.

'Sterrer,' said both the girls immediately. A treat, sterilised milk in its different-shaped bottle with a cap you pulled off with a bottle opener.

Two weeks later Dad went back into hospital.

He grew weaker and weaker, thinner and thinner, shrivelled up like a winter leaf and died just as the big clump of Michaelmas daisies he'd planted at the side of the front path was coming into bloom.

He was profoundly mourned. His three children adored him. His grandchildren adored him. Nell couldn't fathom it. He was the one abiding love at the back of it all, constant, unconditional. His walking-sticks rested by the door. His old rocking-chair stood empty and still. She took as keepsakes one of his pipes, the spyglass he'd used because his eyesight was getting bad, and a pair of old opera glasses that had belonged to Auntie Bennet. She didn't cry in front of the children. Ever. Violet did. Violet's eyes were forever filling. Jean and Georgia took it hard. Georgia wrote a poem. The teacher called Nell into school and showed it to her and said she'd never seen such maturity of style and feeling in a child of nine.

> A Lament
> ... *when I go to Grandma's house*
> *And see your empty chair*
> *My heart feels heavy, my eyes are full,*
> *I wish you were once again there ...*

Unbearable.

'She takes after my grandad,' Nell said.

Bessie was equable. She wasn't alone. She still had Bob and Eva. The time she shed tears was not at the funeral, but later when going through some old drawers with Nell, when she came upon her birth certificate.

'Look,' she said, whispering pitifully, 'I was illegitimate.'

Nell had never known. None of them had ever known except Sam. It said on the certificate: 'Altrincham Union Workhouse, Knutsford Nether, Cheshire. Mother: Harriet Williams. Father: no one.' Nell wanted to know all about Harriet Williams but Bessie didn't know anything.

'Well, it's nothing to be ashamed of,' Nell said, but Bessie shook with tears, and Nell tried to imagine that time, the last decade of Victoria's reign, and what a shameful thing it was to be a bastard then when it was a millstone, a heavy word, a word to be whispered as Bessie had whispered it before she wept, lifting up her glasses to wipe the wetness that had gathered in the cracks under her eyes.

None of her adoptive family had stayed in touch with Bessie.

24

Holidays

He did not complain to them about their mother. Hers was the voice they heard: 'Did you see that? Did you *see* that?'

He made her shake with fury.

'Mortified. By a headscarf. I wouldn't mind but it was a load of old rubbish anyway, that podgy blonde woman trying to pass as a young girl. Stupid. And they weren't very good. Just because it's opera it's supposed to be good. Not opera, he says, operetta. Thinks I don't know anything. Anyway, he doesn't even like opera, he just wants the people he works with to think he's cultured. I hate snobbery, I really do. Hateful sod. It was a freezing cold night too, I got the most awful earache. Swine!'

They'd gone to an amateur production of *HMS Pinafore* at his works. When they came outside she'd started putting her headscarf on. He nearly hit her across the back of the head in his rush to dash it out of her hands. 'Get that thing off!' he hissed. There was something horrible in his voice. Shame. Bitterness. The children saw their mother turn silently furious. Nothing else was said. She folded the scarf and put it back into her bag. They didn't speak all the way home. But that wasn't unusual. Parents didn't speak to each other. Parents didn't touch. Parents didn't like each other. Parents just didn't.

Nell told her daughters this about sex: 'Well, I know it sounds horrible, but you shouldn't have sex with someone unless you really love them, and then you don't mind. And then after that, you don't have to do it as much. Well, now and again you have to. But you make the best of it.'

After tea, they argued about a holiday. Nell wanted to go to Rhyl at the same time as Mam and Bob and Eva, who were getting it all booked up and wanted to know whether she and Harry and the kids wanted to be included. Harry wasn't keen on the idea of going with Nell's mam, to be honest. She got worse. She just moaned, all the time, she'd lost the ability to relate to the world in any other way.

Your grandma won't be around much longer.

I might not be here next year.

You get weary, you know.

You get old, you know. You'll find out.

It's old age creeping on.

Nobody bothers with you when you're old.

What do you mean, awkward? Who's being awkward? I'm not awkward!

And to complicate things still more, he'd been having driving lessons and was booked in that particular week for the test.

He didn't want them to go and he didn't want to stay at home on his own. He hated being on his own. She'd only been away once with the kids, just overnight, when her dad got sick. The house had seemed like a tomb. You could go out but you had to come back to the cold empty house and the listening silence. You could play your music softly but sooner or later you had to stop.

So they argued. Here's how. No one shouted. No one swore. It was strangely formal. They spoke in low, grudging voices and between each exchange there was a silence. Their faces were drawn and long, their brows knitted, their eyes downcast. He had a book on his knee, she was sewing. She'd sit up late tonight and finish the dress with its pattern of yellow flowers and blue ribbons. She'd never used a machine in her life. She even made clothes for the soft toys and knitted them all little jumpers.

They could keep this up for days.

Weeks.

They couldn't have been further apart.

He lost that one.

They left him on his own and went to Golden Sands Holiday Camp, and it was a disaster. Two big caravans, side by side in one endless row of hundreds of endless rows, stretching as far as a child's eye could see. Among the rows were roads, where you could ride three-wheeler hire bikes. Loudspeakers pumped out music all day long, mostly skiffle, Lonnie Donegan singing 'Last Train To San Fernando', Tommy Steele singing 'Little White Bull'. In one caravan was Bessie with Bob, Eva, little Robin and the new baby; in the other, Nell with Jack and the girls and Eva's teenage sister, Patricia.

By the third day Bessie was alone in the first caravan with everyone else living squashed into the second, the kids and Patricia sleeping on the floor next to the sink.

Bessie wasn't talking to anyone. No one really knew why any more, it could have been any one of a number of things, she took umbrage every five minutes. But it was probably something to do with Robin, Bob and Eva's eldest, a dimple-kneed toddler with long, silky black hair cut in a dead straight fringe. Whenever Bessie looked at him, a daft smile appeared on her face and her eyes were painful with love. She wanted him. She sulked if his parents tried to take him off her. Whenever he fell asleep she enforced total silence on everyone, making the children play in mime. They became practised at falling out in whispers. She took all the children to the beach but wouldn't let them buy a lolly even though their parents had given them the money and said it was OK; she said if Robin saw, he'd want one, and he wasn't allowed because he was too little. So nobody could have one. That's what she said. Then when they got to the beach she wouldn't let them take their socks off, even though it was a scorching hot day. She said they'd catch cold.

'For God's sake, Mam, stop interfering,' Bob said.

Now she wouldn't come out.

Joanne was sent as ambassador.

Her grandma opened the door, tight-lipped.

'My mum says, do you want some dinner? It'll be ready in ten minutes.'

'Tell them they can bugger off.'

Slam.

Joanne returned. 'She said, "Tell them to bugger off."'

Auntie Eva, slicing bread, shook her head. 'She's not right, is she?' she commented mildly.

'We've had it all our lives, Eva.' Nell laid the table. 'You can't please her.'

'She's sitting in the caravan crying,' Georgia said. 'I saw her through the window.'

Nell heaved a great sigh up from her chest. 'Oh, God, I suppose I'll have to go over.'

When she did, of course, it ended in one of their big squawking rows. The children listened, giggling. Auntie Eva laid out slices of cold meat on a plate. Patricia, the big girl, joggled the fractious baby. Louder and shriller the voices rose. Grandma was obscene. 'Don't shit on me and rub it in!' she shrieked.

Auntie Eva drew in her breath sharply. '*I've* never known anything like it,' she said. 'Imagine what it was like living with her. I did, you know. For a few months when I was first married. Never again.'

Patricia laughed.

There was a slam, another slam. Nell returned, rolling her eyes. '"I know when I'm not wanted!"' she mimicked, screwing up her face.

'She makes herself not bloody wanted,' said Eva.

But they made up, sort of, and by the end of the week they'd all changed round again so that it was Bessie, Nell, Jack and the girls in one caravan, and everybody else in the other.

At night Nell and Bessie held whispered conversations.

'He's still writing to her, you know. She sends letters care of Violet.'

'Does she really? Well, they say love'll find a way.'

Bessie was outraged. 'It's not fair on Eva, him writing to another woman. He should put all that away now. He's a married man with responsibilities.'

Nell snorted. Responsibilities! Bob was still down the pub all the time, out over Mellands with Dannyboy. Still a big kid. 'I knew Vi was writing to her,' she said, 'but I didn't know Bob was.'

'Our Vi shouldn't do that, you know. It's none of her business. I've told her. Of course, no one listens to me.'

'I think Vi just feels like they're family,' Nell said. She'd let her own correspondence with Jenny Lim trail off. There hadn't seemed much point in it after he'd married Eva.

'Well, it's wrong.' Bessie's final word.

Harry met them on the doorstep. 'I've chucked the L-plates away!' he cried. 'Come and see our car. Our car, Nell! Come on!'

They hadn't even put the cases down.

'Let's get in,' Nell said, damping down the dog's ardour, but he made them dump the luggage in the hall, shut the dog in the back room and come straight back out with him and round the corner to where the new car was parked in the side street. It was beautiful, an old Riley, shiny and black with a grey top and a running-board. The inside was leather. They all got in and sat there, Nell and Harry in the front, the kids in the back. It smelt very strongly of petrol. They sat there for ages in wonder, stationary, while Harry pointed out the speedometer and the windscreen wipers and the orange indicators that flipped up on either side. Then he revealed an even greater wonder. He'd bought a TV. 'It's fantastic!' he raved. It was like Christmas. They all piled out of the car and ran in, and as if it wasn't enough that a brand new TV was sitting in the corner of the room, he'd decorated and bought two little round pouffes, red and green leather on the top.

'Oh, it's great, Harry!' Nell wondered how much it had cost and why they could afford all this when they couldn't afford for her to have any new clothes. He'd say it was a matter of priorities. *His* priorities, of course. And a little flame of rebellion came licking, again.

Harry turned the TV on and they sat looking at it, fascinated. The test card. He gave the children an excited little lecture about how fortunate they were to be living in a scientific age, an age of wonders. 'Think,' he said, 'if you showed this to medieval man, it would be mighty magic. Incredible. Anything could happen in your lifetimes, anything. It's the age of miracles!'

To top the lot he suddenly announced they were all going to Silverdale in the car, driving up Friday and coming back Monday for work Tuesday morning. He'd checked it all out with the farm. The kids were over the moon.

Nell was so weary. 'What, this Friday?' she said. '*This* Friday? I've only just got back. Everything wants washing.'

'That's all right. We don't have to take too much, it's not for long.'

Fine to say that if you didn't have to do the washing, mounds and mounds of it in the steamy dungeon underground, working the mangle till your hands were sore and the cloudy grey water no longer crawled out, with the damp making your hair go flat and the wet coal-dust smell in the air. If they were going Friday she'd have to get cracking first thing in the morning. And, of course, she'd have to pack for everyone and if anything got left out it would be her fault.

'Are you sure we can afford it?' she said.

'Oh, yes,' he replied suavely, 'I know what we can afford.'

He had charge of the money, she had no idea what went on. All she knew was that she never had enough and was living on tick all the time and getting stuff from catalogues and wearing horrible old clothes that made her feel awful. And now suddenly they could afford to go to Silverdale. It didn't make sense. No point in saying anything, of course. Pompous pig.

Priorities.

She sighed and assumed a patient, waiting expression.

Later they watched *Wagon Train*. He was right, it *was* a miracle, unbelievable, like being at the pictures, only sitting in your own house.

Silverdale was on Morecambe Bay. The caravan was small and green, almost completely like a ball, with a window that pushed up, a stable door, a chemical toilet in a privy outside. So many wasps, they put out a jam-jar with jam in the bottom to trap them. The jam was always covered. Nell hated to see the poor things struggling away there with their legs and wings all stuck up, very cruel it seemed to her, but what could you do? You couldn't have the kids getting stung, could you?

They had a table outside with an enamel jug and a bowl for washing-up. The sun, the green smell of close ancient woodland surrounding the wild, ragged field. Red squirrels appeared on the old ivy and moss-covered walls of the perimeter. There were apple trees here and there, and a big gate on which the children swung, a hen-house under a tree in the field, a venerable, formidable old bull of massive girth, with a ring through its nose, pigs, cattle, geese, a farmer's daughter called Eliza, sturdy and rosy-cheeked and dependable.

Almost like Morland. Almost. Wild strawberries in the woods, tiny pink flowers, white flowers, red clusters of berries that stood up on thick stalks and looked dangerous, all kinds of weird fungi. You had to be always watching the kids. Miles of saltmarsh along the coast about a mile away, the landscape changing all the time.

Morland was not so far, as the crow flies. Straight up and over the Lake District mountains, north towards Penrith, Carlisle and Scotland, not far away at all.

They used to go up on the train, a big black steam train from the high platform at London Road station, but now they went in style in their own car. The leather seats of the Riley burned your legs. The smell of petrol was very strong in the back. Jack was sick twice, Joanne three times. Harry said they were doing it on purpose.

Georgia just felt extremely nauseous and kept her face turned away from the other two for the entire journey. But once they'd arrived and parked the car in the field next to their caravan, which had been freshly painted in green and cream and had a white picket fence put around it, once they smelt the flowers in Eliza's garden and saw how everything was the same, Bluebell the cow, the red tractor in the shed, the tang of the whitewashed haybarn with the slit at the top where the white owls lived, and the stile over the ivied wall to the wood going down to the field where the hens and geese scratched – then everything was OK again.

There were calves in one of the sheds. Eliza, a bucket under her broad red arm, took the children in to pet them. The smell of their hot baby breath was sweet, the lick of their pink tongues warm and rough. Their noses glistened black and soft pink, the shade of sugar mice. At teatime, yellow mugs and plates bright on a red-checked tablecloth. They ate ham and tomatoes in the window, and a red squirrel came and sat on the wall outside. Everyone kept very still till it had gone.

Late at night the field filled up with toads, great big grey warty ones that just sat there waiting to be stepped on, so that when you went to the toilet after dark you had to pick your way very carefully. They weren't at all frightened of people. Harry brought one into the caravan, into the light, so that they could all get a good look at it. It sat on his palm, perfectly calm.

'Aw! Poor little thing!'

Nell tickled the back of its neck. Its throat blew up and down like someone playing about with their bubble-gum. 'That's why they became known as witches' familiars, you know,' she said. 'Because they got tame and used to come in the house, and some old lady would start having one as a pet, so they got the reputation.'

She'd read about it. She thought it would be rather nice to live all alone in a little cottage somewhere like Morland or Silverdale, with just a cat and a dog and a toad for company. Idyllic. She could have a small garden and keep a cow for milk. And she'd have a barn where she'd let tramps sleep. A big pot of her broth would always be ready, simmering. Poor tramps, down-and-outs. I'll look after the tramps, she thought, and saw their romantic figures, toe-rags wrapped round their feet like the cloths of mummies, wandering country lanes on sharp nights of frost towards the curl of smoke in the darkening blue sky from the chimney of her cottage, a yellow light from the barn, the aroma of a good thick broth like Dad used to make, with every vegetable you could lay your hands on, butter beans, barley, lentils.

But then you always had to come back down to earth.

After the country, the town. The dirty house always wanting cleaning. Marlon Brando on at the pictures. One of the first things her kids had learned was how to behave in the pictures. They saw everything. When she saw westerns she wanted to be carried off by a Red Indian. They were much nicer than the cowboys. Compared to Marlon Brando, Harry was nowhere. What a laugh, Marlon Brando and Red Indians; and look at my life, she thought, waiting in a damp old playground, dragging her blue-eyed boy about everywhere with her. What a pair. Her with her bare white hairy legs and cigarette, her eternal headscarf; him with his long grey socks falling down around his skinny legs. A biddable boy.

25

Louis Armstrong in Longsight

Murray Wells ordered up a bottle of champagne at the Bodega and ran about shaking it up and cackling, waiting for the cork to pop and the spray to go everywhere before he finally spilled the news: Louis Armstrong All-Stars, May, Belle Vue. Satchmo. Old Pops. Dippermouth. Genius. The Tailgaters were to open both first and second houses. The programme would say: 'THE LOUIS ARMSTRONG ALL-STARS', and then, in much smaller print, 'The Tailgaters' Jazz Band'.

Their names would be together on posters plastered on walls and the sides of theatres. It did not even seem real when Murray called them together a week later and showed them a telegram he'd received, addressed to the band: '*Old Pops is happy to hear that you are working on the bill with my All-Stars. We have got a wonderful show and my boys are playing greater than ever, and I know from your tremendous reputation that you boys will help us to give the local cats a good evening's music I will never forget.*'

There'd never been anything like it in Manchester. The *Evening News* ran big spreads on all the Tailgaters, the local lads chosen to play with the King of Jazz.

Harry rushed home from work, bolted down his tea, then into his stage suit and off to Belle Vue for the first show at six fifteen. They just had time to meet up at the King's Hall and dash out on stage, no time to look around, no time to think, just get out there in the bright lights and the heat and do it. The crowd cheered. Everyone was out there, everyone they knew, but not Nell. Dust in the footlights. A garden of flowers before the stage, the air heavy with their scent. They swung straight into 'Sweet Georgia Brown'. Harry blew with his eyes closed. For a month he'd been practising four or five hours a night on every night he didn't have a gig. Nell was sick of it but she hadn't said anything. You couldn't argue about a thing like that, not when it meant so much to him. You just had to let him get on with it. What Harry could *not* comprehend was how she, how anyone, given the opportunity, could choose not to go and see Louis Armstrong play the King's Hall. It was history, Louis Armstrong in Longsight. Harry had been born less than a mile away. His sisters were out there with Guy and Reg. Bob and Eva were out there somewhere. People had come from all over the place. Humphrey Lyttelton was up from London specially.

The Tailgaters played for an hour and it seemed like minutes. The crowd stomped and cheered.

When they came off, Louis was there. They were all there, tiny Barrett Deems, the only white man in the band, the great Trummy, Billy Kyle, all of them. The wings were packed.

'Some real hot breaks there, boys,' Louis said. His teeth flashed. He had his trumpet in his hand. It was too real. Not a photograph, but flesh and blood. Beads of sweat at his hairline. Face shiny with it. He carried a big white handkerchief in his hand, and a white silk hand-kerchief poked out of his breast pocket. There they were, in dark suits ready to go on, Edmond Hall, Billy Kyle, Jack Lesberg.

'Boy, that's some horn you play,' said Edmond Hall, clarinet in hand, to Alex.

'Thanks,' replied Alex.

The others went on first, then Louis marched onstage and up to the microphone, raised his horn to his lips and started blowing, play-ing in softly with 'Sleepy Time Down South'. Harry stood in the wings with the others. There were tears in his eyes. No one in his life was important. No one was great. *He* would not be great. But he'd been here. After this, nothing mattered, everything was possible. So gently and surely, the way the man's fingers slid over the valves. The skill. He played round low notes, graceful and easy in his move-ments. The crowd went wild. The music ran up and down Harry's spine and through every little vein. They played 'Basin Street Blues', 'Clarinet Marmalade', 'Margie'. Trummy cakewalked across the stage. Louis hit top C, effortless. He shook hands with all the band after every number. 'Bucket's Got A Hole In It'. 'The Gypsy'. 'Mack The Knife'. The blues singer Velma Middleton joined the Tailgaters in the wings. Slitty eyes, big fat smiling face. Shaking her shoulders, she rushed out on to the stage, an enormous woman, was fondly greeted by Louis and launched with him into 'That's My Desire'. Not much of a voice, but she jumped about all over the place and made Louis laugh. What a sight. Louis applauding. They sang 'Baby It's Cold Outside', crooning together.

After all the encores, after the screaming, shouting, whistling, whooping, stamping, cheering, after the smiling and bowing, Louis walked offstage, wringing wet, beaming.

Then it all happened again, only this time the place was even more packed and heaving, and everyone went wild from the start, and then wilder. Everything the same, only better because this time Harry was wide awake and knew he was really here, that this was his life for real and what he'd been born for. To play. It didn't matter about going pro or Nell not going along with it, the only thing that mattered was playing what he wanted. Then it was over again, an hour like minutes, and they were watching from the wings and Louis danced, wiping the sweat from his face again and again. Dripping. How those men in those big suits sweated. Velma Middleton shouted out and sprang in the air and came down crash in the splits, unbelievable, a woman that size doing a thing like that. Everyone was bopping about, singing, beating out time on something. Billy Kyle smiling at the piano. Over it all, the music. Filling up the air, high in the smoky light and the dust.

When it was just about over and the whole place was screaming and shouting and stamping for more, Louis turned with a grin and summoned Alex Kirby from the wings and brought him onstage, to a huge cheer from the crowd. They had a discussion about keys away from the mike; then the band launched into 'When The Saints Go Marching In', in G, Alex playing upfront with Satchmo.

Alex Kirby playing with Satchmo!

Anything was possible. Harry would have given the world to be on that stage now, to be a part of that sound, making it. *He* was there, in that number with the Saints, marching in. Alex Kirby from Ancoats played with Satchmo and the All-Stars, played as he always did, with all he'd got.

The crowd exploded. In the wings the Tailgaters and all the backstage people exploded. Louis shook hands with Alex, grinning that great big grin. 'A fine musician,' he cried, applauding Alex. He applauded Alex, and Alex applauded him. Harry's arms ached with clapping. No one wanted it to end.

But it ended.

'Hey, boys.' It was Jack Lesberg, the All-Stars bassist. 'You care to join us?'

Louis's dressing room. Louis in his shirtsleeves standing in a slouch, hands clasped in front of him, white handkerchief hanging down from them. He came over and greeted each one of them in turn, shaking hands. Harry shook hands with Louis. Louis clapped him on the arm and grinned and thanked him. Thanked *him*, personally. 'Thank you, Harry,' he said.

'It's an honour,' Harry said.

Louis's face shone with sweat. He looked tired.

Trummy said, 'Hi, Harry.'

They talked shop, the Tailgaters and the Louis Armstrong All-Stars. They drank bourbon and smoked. Louis was quiet but very friendly. He sat easy, his face so famous it was magnetic. You had to make a special effort not to look at him too much. He wiped his face again and again with his white handkerchief then wrapped it like a bandanna around his head. Billy Kyle was next to Harry. Harry mentioned he'd just bought a disc of Jack Teagarden's Big Eight with Billy playing piano on it, a 1938 recording.

'I remember that,' Billy said. 'Barney Bigard was with us. He was with Duke Ellington at the time. We did Saint James Infirmary.'

'"Shine",' said Harry. '"Dinah". "Big Eight Blues".'

Billy laughed. 'That's right. You've been playing that?'

It hadn't been off the turntable.

'I remember once we played a dance on a Hudson River boat,' Louis was saying, 'me and Joe Oliver ...'

Listen. Drink all this in.

Smoke pooling above their heads. The lights on the mirrors.

That night Harry was a happy man. He glowed. His eyes filled up with joy.

Home. All over. Downstairs alone. She hadn't waited up. She never did.

He looked down: in his hand an artist's pass for the Louis Armstrong All-Stars Concert, Belle Vue, 14 May 1956. His souvenir programme with the All-Stars' autographs: Edmond Hall (clt), Jack Lesberg (bass), Trummy Young (tmb), Barrett Deems (dms). Not Louis. Somehow he hadn't asked Louis. Work in the morning. Had to get to bed. But he was all churned up inside.

It was worth living for that. It really was.

26

Belgium

They went to Belgium, flew on a Dan-Air plane with a grey and red stripe down the middle, stayed in Ostend, where the sand was hot and white and the girls in their gaily coloured shorts and T-shirts rode ponies along the beach, led by a plump woman in a dress. No one had ever been abroad before, apart from those who'd gone to war, but Harry had been saving for ages. No one had ever flown. It would have been all right if the kids hadn't been sick on the plane.

There were waffle stalls everywhere. Horse-drawn gigs lined up at the side of the road, the lovely horses champing. At their hotel they had a nice young waiter, a boy called François. The soup smelt different from English soup. They went down to the front, Nell with her blue straw bucket bag, Georgia with a beach ball in a string bag. Outside tables on all the streets. Adverts for Cinzano. The sand was full of red and white striped windbreaks and bright beach umbrellas, pink and green and white bullseyes. Nell sat in a deck-chair in her navy-blue polka-dot sundress, the kids played with the beach ball, Harry made a castle and sent them off collecting shells with their buckets. There were a lot of sailors in town. A lonely one sat on the beach, arms folded among the deck-chairs and sandcastles. At nights some of them came into the bar of the Coq d'Or for a drink.

My God, it was hot, that summer. All of them peeled. There was a flower festival, bank upon bank, row upon row of glory, the colours blazing in the sun against one another, bright yellow and red, orange and purple, white and pink. The kids were wonderstruck, sitting at a round white table with red metal chairs, under an umbrella on the cobbled street outside a café. They had bottles of Coca-Cola with straws in. Nell burned badly, her shoulders and the tops of her arms. Her face, which always tanned quickly, was deep brown. Her hair was nearly black, thick and bushy. Sweat gathered on the bridge of her nose under her glasses.

They were lying on the bed in the Coq d'Or, where they were staying, relaxing. Harry staring at the ceiling and thinking what a terrific team that was, Bechet with Tommy Ladnier and Mezz Mezzrow the reefer boy on *Really The Blues*. Nell was reading a book, her arms bright red and scaly, shiny with the cream she'd rubbed on for the sunburn. The kids were mucking about playing.

'Ssh!' he hissed, sitting up sharply on his elbows. 'Remember where you are!' His thunderous brow and deep serious voice.

They were getting scared of him. In awe. They did as they were told.

He was jumpy as a cat. God knows what was the matter with him. They'd been traipsing round all day and she was exhausted. She said something as they lay side by side on the bed in the room in the Coq d'Or while the children played as quietly as they could with French comics and crayoning books. He said something and she answered, and she couldn't even remember what it was, just words, nothing, they didn't matter at all. Words about nothing.

'Are you being funny?' he shouted, turning and half hunching over her, gripping her by the arms, shaking.

She was frightened. 'That hurts!' she cried. 'I'm sore!'

He kept the grip for several seconds as they looked into one another's eyes, full of hurt and hostility. Then he let go.

Big fingermarks on her sunburn. The pig. The *pig*.

The children, quiet, watching.

He jumped up and took them out for a walk with him, ambling round the back streets. They walked through a beautiful square with a large garden on one side, through which nuns progressed in a long silent crocodile among the twilight trees, two by two, into a street of square cobbles and very old buildings with strangely shaped gables and tiny windows, curly tiles and stepped roofs. Small shops with gay metal advertisements all round the doors. It was very peaceful.

It was too dark for photographs, otherwise he'd have made them stand in one of those little doorways.

★

291

On a coach trip into Holland (they were sick again) he tried to put his arm round her. She didn't like it, didn't want him to touch her. Touching only ever meant one thing and she didn't want it. Well. Why should she? And why should she like jazz? So what if she didn't? She had a right not to, didn't she? That was the trouble, he expected everyone to be like him.

They went to a Dutch market. People were walking about in Dutch headdresses, wearing clogs. And there were windmills. A strange, flat country, oddly beautiful. Harry was driving her mad with his camera. Stupid, stupid things he made you do.

'Go and stand over there and link that Dutchman and I'll take your picture.'

What kind of a fool did he think that made her feel? She wasn't a jolly woman who could walk up and link any old stranger.

'Look! Go on, look, that woman's linking him, go on, you go and get on the other side of him, go on.'

You couldn't argue with Harry.

27

Jack

But of all the wonders of the time, nothing came near the one great light: not the Louis Armstrong show, not playing with Bechet, not being named among the greatest names in British jazz in the *Melody Maker*, but meeting Teagarden backstage when the Jack Teagarden-Earl Hines All-Stars played the Free Trade Hall.

Harry watched both shows out front and went through to the artists' bar with his pass in the interval. Jack Lesberg was on the bill; he was in there drinking, he remembered Harry straight away from the Armstrong show, bought him a drink and introduced him to

Cozy Cole and Peanuts Hucko. There was no pulling rank.

'You better watch it, Harry,' Cozy Cole said nasally, 'we're all down with this here Asian flu. This is medicinal.' He raised his glass.

'Jack's got it bad,' added Peanuts Hucko. 'And I'm getting a sore lip.'

Out front you'd never have known they were half dead on their feet. Maybe the sweat they worked up helped. And they were all going back to London by coach after the second show.

'You gotta meet Jack,' Jack Lesberg said, taking Harry by the arm. 'Good thing you came by.'

Tea's wife Addie, a big woman, let them into the dressing room.

'Hey, Harry Caplin, you play trombone, I've heard of you,' Tea said.

Of me. Jack Teagarden's heard of me. Of me. Harry Caplin.

A big man, a wrinkled face, large and flat and broad. Used. Deep brown smiling eyes. He looked very tired. His illness was apparent. Harry didn't want to intrude but Jack said, 'No, siddown, Harry. You still in touch with Jay D. Smith?' Deep South drawl.

'Not for a while. Has he still got his radio show?'

'Oh, he's still going strong.' Jack's instrument, with a plastic mouthpiece, lay across two chairs. A railwayman's hat hung on the back of one of them. Jack opened his trombone case and took out a bottle of whisky. 'Want some?'

'Thanks.'

He poured two shots straight and handed one to Harry. Addie didn't drink.

'Helps with the nerves.' Jack smiled.

'Do you still get nervous?'

'Always,' said Jack, 'till I'm out there. You?'

'It's part of the kick, I suppose.'

Jack nodded.

They talked about the trials of touring. Harry showed Jack the picture of himself and Addie standing outside the Hôtel Negresco with Ernie Tomasso and his wife. Jack beamed.

'Hey, look, Addie, remember this?'

Addie looked. 'I sure do,' she said. 'That was in Nice?'

293

'Nice Jazz Festival,' Jack said. 'Nice guy, Ernie. We had a good time. When was this?'

''Forty-nine,' Harry said.

'Long ago as all that? Haven't seen Ernie in years.'

A knock on the door. Addie went. 'It's the doc, honey,' she said.

'I gotta have a shot of penicillin,' Jack told Harry.

'I'll go back out front,' said Harry. 'It's been terrific meeting you, Jack.'

'Nice knowing you, Harry.' The doctor came in. 'You know, I'd very much like to come back here one day. Maybe we'll really get to jam one of these days.'

He held out his hand and they shook.

When Harry got home he put on 'Peg O' My Heart', lay back in his chair and smoked a slow cigarette, gazing glassily at his work shirts hanging drying on the rack over the range. Here he was again, alone in the small hours, a sleeping family upstairs, the dog leaning blissfully against his leg, panting; open across his knees a souvenir programme, autographed by the stars: Max Kaminsky, Cozy Cole, Peanuts Hucko, Earl Fatha Hines himself, but somehow not Jack.

Somehow he hadn't asked Jack.

28

Some of These Days

They thought he couldn't hear. His mother talking to Auntie Violet in Auntie Violet's front room, the patterned carpet and the glass-fronted cabinet with fancy tea-cups in.

'I'm sick of it, Vi. By the time I can afford to buy anything nice to wear it'll be too late. I'll be old.'

'Well, ask Harry.'

'He's got no idea. He's dead mean.'

Then they drop their voices and whisper for a bit till they forget to, and the conversation pops up again, audible:

'I tell you, Vi, there's times when I could wring his neck. He's such a pompous sod, he makes my blood boil.'

'Poor old Harry,' said Vi.

'Oh, poor arseholes!' Nell replied.

Or she sat in their own house having a cup of tea with Auntie Jill, who wasn't really an auntie at all but a woman called Jill Hood who lived at the back on the other side of the croft. 'He wants everything his own way, Jill.'

Making a dress for one of his sisters, tiny fairy stitches.

'He doesn't even speak when he comes in, these days. I get fed up looking at his miserable face. Wants waiting on. I do, I do, I feel really angry sometimes. He's like a big kid with his sulks.'

Auntie Jill was brisk and teacherish, with brown hair in a ponytail and narrow dark eyes in a flat brown face. She wore trousers like a man and was always coming or going in a mac. 'Well, they are big kids,' she said, unsmiling.

Jack was sitting under the table with Mary Hood. Mary Hood had a quiet way of bossing him. She sang, 'Jackie boy,' and he was supposed to reply, 'Master.'

'"Jackie boy."'

'"Master."'

'"Sing you well?"'

'"Very well."'

> Hey down ho down derry derry down,
> among the leaves so green-o.

Under the leaves of the elderberry trees that hung over the roof of the adjoining garage. The boughs were horses. Next door's garden was a big wild green tangled place all shaded by trees. A grotto. It wasn't theirs to play in but they got over the wall, and nobody ever came down there from the house on the other street. Looking back, it wasn't bossing so much as treating him like one of the kids, one of the constant runny-nosed population of nappied humanity that made up the Hood household. Mary always had charge of at least one adenoidal, faintly reeking scrap of it. 'Wipe your nose,' she'd say. 'Don't do that, that's rude. Don't you pull that face at me. Put it down. Sit there. If the wind changes your face'll stick like that and serve you right.'

The stripy edge of the tablecloth hung down around them. Mary Hood's house was even scruffier than his. She lived in one of the terraces on the other side of the croft, with the row of outside toilets that served for all. You saw her lining all the kids up to go to the toilet. The baby with its nappy hanging down round its leg. Round here was full of scruffy people. One day as his mum was down on her knees in her green dress, her face grimy and nowty, he'd said, the realisation dawning: 'We're scruffy, aren't we?'

She'd been very angry. By that time he'd been in one or two other people's houses and seen things such as ruched curtains and little glass Bambis, proper salt cellars on the table, jugs for the milk, lace at the window. Their house wasn't like that. Their house had a big black range covering all of one wall, a rack above the fire for hauling the clothes up and down. The gramophone had a special corner, and the wireless stood on a bamboo table. The back room was where they ate and played, where the fire burned, where the dog snored, where the gramophone played:

> He had to get under, get out and get under
> to fix his little machine ...

and:

> Josephina, please don't leana on the bell,
> When you mush please don't push on the bell,
> I heard Mrs O'Leary tellin' Mrs O'Flynn
> Somebody keep ringing but nobody come in ...

The rug was threadbare. There was a small back kitchen attached, where Nell cooked and washed the pots and bathed the children in

the big white porcelain sink, and hung the towels to dry on the two
pipes that stuck out of the wall, one with a peculiar bulge in it as if it
had burst one time and been fixed. Their house had a bare lightbulb
in the room where they lived. The ornaments were confined to the
parlour, a crinoline lady and a pot dog with a place to grow a
hyacinth. The parlour, that strange, solemn, tidy room, was Harry's
special place. He'd taken over the end near the window. His pile of
copies of *The Ring* was shoved away under the table. On top of the
table were mutes and mouthpieces, music books, arrangements he
was writing out. And, safely laid away and tucked up in its hard
black case, lovingly cleaned and polished, his trombone. His voice,
more his voice than his real voice. More and more that was how it felt
to him. They dropped him off at half past one. *T'ra, Ed!* Door slamming. He came in, softly whistling: 'I Found A New Baby'. Very
softly. Sat downstairs for a little while, soulfully playing his trombone,
quiet as can be. He could make it whisper and croon. He painted in
the parlour; he'd erected an easel. He collected art books. He took
the kids round Manchester Art Gallery. They'd have everything.
They'd have culture. They'd be educated. The book cases were full.
All his favourites would be there for them. *The Ragged-Trouser'd
Philanthropist. Eothen. Love on the Dole. The Small Miracle.* He'd take
them to the ballet, to the theatre, to the Hallé Orchestra at the Free
Trade Hall.

Not opera, he drew the line at opera.

They'd have better than he had. If they wanted to go to university,
go they would.

Their house was chaotic, with a peculiar unused middle room full of
packed things, boxes, stuff no one knew what to do with. This was
called the playroom, and sometimes Jack did actually play in the
smoggy highways that had evolved between blocks of unused and not
quite yet unwanted things: some grim dark game of war and hiding
with Mary Hood. Mary smiled a lot, with her head held down in a
peculiar way that somehow made him think of how the calves in
Silverdale, where they always went for their holidays, lowered their
brows and butted their soft bony topknots at your hand if you

dangled it over the half-door into their pen. Her straight brown hair was held back by a clip on one side. When she was smily she seemed like a simpleton. When she wasn't, which was less often, she was old and very serious. They played with gas masks and old wellies and a box of bashed-about wooden cars. A lot of time was spent sitting under tables and in tents made of sheets slung between chair legs. Good listening posts. When she sat under tables, Mary Hood stuck her knees under her squarish chin and pulled her old-fashioned home-made long print dress down over them. Her face was big and overdone, her eyebrows met in the middle.

'Men are funny buggers,' Auntie Jill said, standing with one foot crossed over the other and her hands in the pockets of her beige mac.

'Our Violet's husband now, he never speaks. You go in and he doesn't speak.'

Auntie Jill raised the thin startling pencil lines of her eyebrows. 'Doesn't he speak at all?'

'Not at all. He used to, I think. Or did he?' Nell tried to think of the last time she'd heard Stanley talk. Then she tried to think of the last time she'd seen Stanley play his accordion. She had to cast her mind so far back. 'Mind you,' she added, 'they seem happy enough.'

The room was full of smoke. Both Auntie Jill and his mother smoked all the time. Mary Hood and he were trying to stare each other out and not giggle. He always won. His eyes were big and blue and watery and bright, and could stay open indefinitely, swivelling here and there like a reptile's. She couldn't do any of that.

'I feel sorry for that poor mite,' his mother said, when they'd gone. 'Jill doesn't treat her fair.'

It was something his mum had a bee in her bonnet about. He knew this because his sisters said so. Auntie Jill wasn't Mary's real mum. In fact, of all the mighty Hood clan that lived across the croft in the *really* scruffy houses, only three were Auntie Jill's own and Jack didn't know which three. The rest were fostered. Auntie Jill's was where children got left. Grown boys came and went, sons and foster-sons who'd left home. Mary had been fostered then adopted. Jill used Mary as a little skivvy, Nell said.

'I've told Jill,' she said. '"She's too little to be looking after babies,"
I've said.'

'She's such an *old* little thing,' Georgia remarked.

The girls were back, Georgia from the grammar in her green uniform, Joanne, black gymslip and white blouse, from the rough,
snot-nosed raucous school down the road. Georgia talked grown-up
and wore shoes with little heels over her white socks. She kicked
them off on the red rag rug in front of the fire, where the dog
scratched amiably, an affable smile on his silly face, his leg thump-
thump-thumping.

Nell put down her sewing in a heap on the settee, needles and pins
sticking out all over the place. 'Take him!' she ordered, meaning
Jack, going into the back kitchen to get started on tea.

Georgia grabbed his hand. Through the house they took him, past
the cold black cellar door, the playroom, the parlour, up the towering stairs that mounted into darkness. They let him into their big
room and gave him some plastic scissors and set him to cutting pictures out of an old catalogue. 'Look,' they said, 'you can make
jigsaws.' They pulled all the clips and rubber bands and ribbons from
their plaited, severely scraped back and battened-down hair, the
fringes cut very straight and high and far back at either side as if a
stray wisp was a sin. Still, there were always stray wisps. Shaking out
their fair-brown locks, like dogs after a bath, they threw themselves
down on the bed and read the American comics their dad brought
home for them: *Little Lulu*, *Jughead*. And the old French comics: *Gus
and Gerry*, who said, '*Hein!*' a lot. Downstairs their mother's deep,
rolling voice throbbed along, 'You Are My Lucky Star', as she fried
onions. Now and again they heard her talking to Tim. Cars hissed by
in the road, squealing as they reached the crossroads.

Once when he was out with his mum, Jack had seen Tim crossing at the lights on Stockport Road, standing waiting with everyone
else and seeming to know exactly when to go, a perfectly safe,
responsible dog. Once they'd passed him with his friend Patch and
he'd wagged his tail at them as if to say hello. Patch lived round the
corner. They'd palled up and started calling for each other. You could
tell when Patch was in the yard because Spike, the cat, sitting on the

windowsill, would turn into something resembling Dennis the
Menace's head. When Patch barked, Nell would open the door and
Patch would look through her legs to see if Tim was coming. Then
off they'd trot down the street, side by side.

Tim was a good dog. Tim always knew who was at the door and
never barked when Harry came home. He jumped up now, eager as
a pup, scrabbling open the kitchen door and running down the hall
in greeting, wagging his whole body and making little throaty excla-
mations of pleasure while the rest of the house turned solemn and
heavy. Harry was home.

She'd been grumbling all morning about having to slog right up
Slade Lane for the hardboard for his dad's oil painting. It looked like
rain too. She was going so fast he had to keep breaking into a run. He
saw Joey, who used to come and do their windows, all dirty, lying
down the full length of the bench on Stanley Grove near the corner
of Stockport Road. The rain was just beginning to make big black
blots on the dusty flagstones. Joey looked as if he was asleep but his
eyes were open. He looked straight through them. Nell hurried on
by, dragging Jack by the hand. They had to go right up near
Crowcroft Park. The wood shop was next door to Wojtaz the
Woodcarver, outside whose shop hung ornately carved clocks and
plaques and signs to stick on your door. The pavement in front was
crowded with chairs and benches and bird-tables. Wojtaz was a Polish
Jew, Nell told Jack, who'd got out of Europe just in time. All the Jews
were being put to death just for being Jewish and it was a terrible
thing, she said. But it was all over now and we were all friends again.

'You've got Jewish blood in you,' she said, 'from your dad's side.'

Nell had a scrap of paper with the measurements for the hardboard
written on it. She showed it to the man and he went to cut her a
piece. This one wasn't too big fortunately. Once when Harry had
been feeling particularly ambitious it had been three foot by three
foot and she'd moaned about it all the way home, shifting it about
constantly and never finding a good way to carry it. But this one was
reasonable and she could stick it under her arm. Harry would trans-
form it into a painting. His easel was in the parlour, standing on a

sheet of newspaper to save the rose-patterned carpet. It was always cold in the parlour because the fire was hardly ever lit, only at Christmas or something special, say a birthday party full of girls in big bright party dresses, bowed and flounced. But Jack liked to go in and watch his dad paint sometimes. He even liked watching him prime the board and paint it white, carefully getting it smooth and even, not a trace of a brushmark anywhere. Over time a picture would evolve: a bowl of fruit, a mountainside, a street scene. The bowl of fruit was all done in blues and dark greens, laid on thickly with a palette knife. Nell thought the greens on the mountainside were too bright, not like you really saw in nature.

This new one was a departure. Harry, in a brown overall that made him look as if he was serving in a grocery shop, was painting the profile of a grotesque gaunt head with livid red eyes, a hooked nose and long tongue lolling wolf-like down a spiky chin. The face emerged from darkness. Four or five squat little demons with tiny pitchforks clambered about the head like rock-climbers. One stood wide-legged on the droop of the long pink tongue and thrust its pitchfork right through so that it came out the other side. Drops of blood dripped down.

He'd been studying Hieronymus Bosch, the Brueghels, Goya.

'Note the brush I've chosen,' Harry said. 'Now, why do you think I chose this one instead of, say, that one?'

'Because it's thinner.'

'Good. Now watch what I do ...'

His dad liked having him there as long as he was quiet. As he painted, Harry would explain what he was doing. 'This is Veridian Green,' holding up the tube. 'Now I'm going to mix this,' dabbing it deftly on to his big wooden palette with the hole for his thumb, 'with Burnt Sienna. Watch what happens ...'

When Jack started school, that horrible rough school down the road, Nell was bereft. She couldn't let him go, pined for him at the school gates, timing her trips to Stockport Road for playtime so that she could watch him wistfully through the bars. She missed him jogging along beside her, sitting next to her on the bus when she went into town to Lewis's Library. Still she had more time to browse. She couldn't have too many books. She always took out her limit and one unofficial. She'd always been quite open about it. 'Stand there. Good boy. I'm getting this one out unofficial.' There was nothing wrong with it, she explained. It wasn't like stealing because she always took them back. It was just borrowing an extra one, so she always had enough reading to tide her over till next time. John Steinbeck, Howard Spring, Mazo de la Roche, Jean Plaidy, Norah Lofts, hour after hour, lying on the settee eating sweets and idly twiddling the dog's ear, totally engrossed.

A week at Butlin's Pwllheli. All the family plus Bessie, Harry's mam and Sid. It was the only holiday anyone could ever remember Bessie going on that she didn't ruin, which they put down to the fact that she had someone of her own age around. Harry invited her out of guilt, after hearing how she stood on her doorstep and cried every time Nell and the kids left after a visit. They said they had to keep turning round and waving till they turned the corner, and she'd wave back with her handkerchief, occasionally using it to dab at her nose or eyes, and they'd all feel terrible.

Bessie actually enjoyed this holiday, but Nell didn't. Everywhere she went she was flanked by grandmas carrying coats over their arms, and in Bessie's case an umbrella, no matter how clear the blue sky. She kept finding herself stuck in a deck-chair with one on either side, in front of the big four-tiered fountain, full sun. Look left to right and see all the fat legs sprawled like so many hams, Bessie's mottled purple and brown, a permanent effect from sitting too close to the fire in her cold house. Or three in a row, the old ones snoring in front of the pink and blue hydrangeas by the chalet door. Sid in a short-sleeved white T-shirt, sharp nose, little thin mouth, black-rimmed glasses. (Joanne had to sit opposite him in the hangar-sized dining hall where they ate all their meals. He put her off her food. She didn't think it was very nice watching old people eat. It would be better if they could do it separately.) And Nell. More sedate, awake, alert, legs together. Don't you dare come and take my picture, she is thinking, seeing Harry saunter into view among the rows of chalets in his lightweight stone-coloured jacket, a camera slung round his neck.

Inevitably he is whistling. 'I Love Paris In The Springtime'. He's been thinking about a rough diamond called Minnie Graham on and off all week. Minnie Graham was Miss Lula Dupree, who'd turned up at the Bodega one night with her brother Chester and asked if she could sing. Minnie and Chester flogged carpets all over the North-west with their father and mother. She was short and tending to dumpiness, with a round face and bubble curls. Harry thought English girls couldn't sing jazz. They were either rubbish or, very occasionally, just OK. But they were never great. But Minnie Graham was great. When she opened her throat the people at the front recoiled. The first thing he ever heard her sing was 'Careless Love Blues', and in so far as a foghorn can be a soulful plaintive thing on a dark and stormy night at sea, her voice was like a foghorn. They trained her up at the Bodega and she sang with them at the Cleethorpes' Empire. She wasn't allowed to speak onstage. As long as she stuck to singing she could have been from New Orleans, but as soon as she spoke, it was Wigan with a speech impediment. She went down a storm everywhere and Harry was teaching her musical theory.

There's Nell, a book on her knee. No smile for him. His marriage is not a happy one. So be it. They have nothing in common. She never wants to do anything he wants to. But they're married and that's that. They have kids. There's nothing to be done about it, they'll have to scrape along. He's taking them to London for a three-day break later in the summer. They've never been, and he has. He'll show them around. They'll see everything. He'll make sure they have a good time.

It was all right for him, Nell thought, resenting his sauntering, whistling approach. He was off doing things with the kids all the time. He took them to the children's zoo and on the chair lifts, took them horse riding, which caused a sulk from Georgia because she thought she was too old to have to go on a leading rein, but Harry insisted; and, anyway, look at the clothes she had to wear. She was fourteen now and in love with the Fabulous Fabian. It was absolutely incredibly ridiculous that she should have to go on holiday in her school uniform. Was that fair? Was that reasonable? That she should have to sit astride a horse in her pink and white and grey striped school summer dress, with the green blazer with the school's crest and motto on the pocket? Wearing white socks with pointed-toed white shoes because she wasn't allowed stockings? With her hair like this? She'd had it cut and permed and it had been a terrible mistake and now it was half grown out and all flat on top. But you had to wear what you had. Her father insisted. Georgia hated all her clothes without exception. Nell got sick of her mithering.

'*You* ask him,' she'd tell her. 'He's less likely to say no if *you* ask him.'

But they hated asking him. He was stern and had a look that could wither. Asking him for things was something you had to pluck up courage for. Something you could be about to do all night long but somehow not do. So Georgia, sultry and sulky, slouched about Butlin's feeling stupid in her hideous clothes, blaming her mother. It was *her* fault he was like this, she should have stood up for herself more, should have trained him better. Ridiculous state of affairs. Endlessly moaning about him but never saying a word to his face, just sulking. Sulk sulk sulk. Sometimes it felt as if this whole family was just one great big disharmony of sulks, a kind of silent cacophony.

Bessie and Harry's mam went in for the Glamorous Grannies Competition together, after much pestering from Gordon the Redcoat, who sat at their table. They were given numbers to hold and went up on stage with two other old grannies, none remotely glamorous. Grandma Caplin was probably the worst, Georgia and Joanne decided. Grandma Holloway was a toss-up with the others. But there wasn't much to choose between any of them at all. Old age was just hideous, with its terrible chins and thick ankles and its fat: Grandma Caplin's saggy and droopy, Grandma Holloway's solid, impacted. What a strange thing it was, putting them all on stage like that, practically forcing them on, just so everyone could laugh at them.

They went down on a chara to London Victoria and walked to the hotel, which was in a street not far from the coach station. Harry had been poring over maps and guides for days, making out an itinerary. It rained intermittently, sometimes heavily, for most of the three days following. Nell and the girls wore plastic rain-hats with flowers on. They walked everywhere to save money. They saw Horse Guard's

Parade, Trooping the Colour, the Changing of the Guard, Pudding Lane, the pelicans in St James's Park, the pigeons in Trafalgar Square, Poet's Corner in Westminster Abbey, where Browning and Tennyson were buried.

'Tennyson was my father's favourite poet,' Nell said. (He needn't think he's the only one with any education around here.)

They went right up to the top of St Paul's and all round the National Gallery, where Harry stood mesmerised in front of *The Virgin of the Rocks* and Nell sat down and rested her tormented feet. She had blisters on the back of both heels and a burning sensation completely covering both soles. They walked round the Tate and a good part of the British Museum, went to the Tower and saw Traitor's Gate. The itinerary could not be deviated from under any circumstances short of total collapse. They stood in gloomy little clusters being photographed in front of the Monument, the Albert Memorial, Big Ben, *The Burghers of Calais*, the Peter Pan statue, and the sign which said: 'On this site stood a scaffold on which were executed Queen Anne Boleyn, Margaret, Countess of Salisbury, Queen Catherine Howard, Jane Viscountess Rochford, Lady Jane Grey, Robert Devereux, Earl of Essex. Also near this spot was beheaded Lord Hastings, 1483.'

'He's the one that was going with that Jane Shore,' said Nell. She knew all about it from Jean Plaidy books. Also, she'd taken them to see the film with Laurence Olivier at the Regal. It showed you the blood running down the block.

'Go and stand with that Beefeater,' Harry said.

They stood. Harry made Nell and Georgia link him, one on either side. Joanne and Jack stood in front raising mirthless smiles.

They went on a boat on the Thames, and to London Zoo where the sky turned black and the heavens opened with a heartrending crack. They saw Guy the Gorilla.

'Poor little thing,' said Nell.

He had to make a decision. This marriage was more and more barren. Some day, maybe not yet, maybe not soon, there would be a chance to err.

There were other things, life outside the family, Harry the jazzman his family never saw, Harry at work talking to the girls in the typing pool, with his social ease, his tapping foot and whistle, his music, the soundtrack of his life. Together with his underlying seriousness, he had a certain charisma. Some women found him attractive. He thought perhaps Minnie Graham did. She wasn't his type, far too common, always threatening to give him a punch up the belly, but she was great. A laugh. Mad about the music, she had it like he did, that feeling, whatever it was. 'I heard Louis Armstrong on the radio singing "Basin Street Blues"', she said, 'Vat was it. Oh, yes, vat was it for me.' That feeling. Oh, that feeling. You couldn't put it into words, you just knew when another person had it the same. It was in the air.

'But ven,' she said, 'when I heard Bessie Smith ...'

Something was in the air with Harry and Minnie Graham. Not that anything was ever said.

She said, 'Me and you should sing some duets.'

One-night stands. Scarborough, Nottingham, Wolverhampton, duetting with her on 'Some Of These Days' and 'Bucket's Got A Hole In It'. He couldn't match her voice. She could hardly read words let alone music, but what an ear! Sharp as anything.

There was a fantasy he ran through in his mind occasionally, in which he went pro with the band and Minnie, and they were up there with all the greats, Harry Caplin with Teagarden, Minnie Graham with Billie Holiday and Bessie Smith. But you couldn't count on Minnie. Sometimes you'd be all booked in somewhere and the programmes done, and off she'd go flogging carpets in Cockermouth. Totally unprofessional. She could never have been a pro or even a semi. She just wanted to sing when she felt like it. She sang on her market stall while she sold carpets, she said, harmonies with Chester. All the people would gather round. Lucky people of the markets of the North-west, to have a world-class singer for free. Harry was perfectly happy to give up a whole night of vocals to her because he knew she was a real singer and he wasn't. She left him way behind. So when Kid Ory came to Bradford, and the band and their wives and girlfriends and Minnie and Chester went over in the Hearse and Mert Rosenblum's car, he was glad Nell never came to these things. That made him feel less guilty about the slant of his mind, listening in the Hearse to Minnie and Chester on 'Heart Of My Heart', gorgeous harmony.

They went to the Students' Cellar after the show with some of the Ory band, and everybody had a lot to drink. Afterwards they had a Chinese meal with Kenny Baker and his new girlfriend. Harry ended up sitting between Minnie and Alex. Chester was completely sozzled on the floor, well out of the way, and Minnie kept putting her hand on Harry's shoulder when she talked to him; she was very bright and vivacious. You never could tell with Minnie because she was friendly with everyone and it was in her nature to put her hands on people. But for whatever reason, he became excited by the realisation that if he were to make a pass at her tonight she'd respond.

'What we should do, Harry,' she was saying, 'is we should have a go at some real blues. "St Louis Blues". Ooh, vat song really gets me. Now the trombone is a really good blues instrument. It gets left out it does, the trombone, Harry, but it's a really good instrument, I fink. We could do a two-hander, me singing, you playing. I can really see it.'

She rambled on.

Alex leaned across and started raving about the fantastic disc they'd cut with Minnie, a classic recording. He'd been giving this some thought. 'Careless Love Blues' would be on it. 'Lazy River'. 'Ain't Misbehavin''. 'Stormy Weather', he said. He had a yen to hear Minnie sing 'Stormy Weather'.

She did it there and then.

Everyone fell silent for Minnie's big, tender voice singing without a trace of self-consciousness. The whole place erupted, whistling and applauding when she finished.

'I want to do "St Louis Blues" with Harry,' she said at once.

'Fine, fine.'

'Who's going to pick my brother up off the floor?'

Harry was thigh to thigh with Minnie in the Hearse. His arm lay along the back of the seat. Paddy Noonan snored on his left.

'How many kids is it you got, Harry? Free, is it?' she asked.

'Three.'

'I love kiddies, me. I'm having seven, me. Seven's a good number.'

'Three's enough,' he said.

'Free's not enough. You not having any more, ven?'

'No.'

'Seven at the very least. I'm a good Cafflic, me.'

Then she told him she was moving to Canada to flog carpets over there.

'For good?'

She had family over there, she said, she'd always been intending to go. Of course. How could it be real?

'Me and Chester,' she said.

Chester woke up at the sound of his name and said he thought he was going to vomit.

She smiled and patted Harry on the cheek. 'Will you miss me, Harry? Will you miss me?'

Nell didn't go to the Tailgaters' tenth birthday party at the Bodega, which was just as well: she wouldn't have liked it at all. They started with a fantastic multi-coursed meal and the wine kept coming, bottles filling up the tables. Harry never got to the bottom of his glass. It kept refilling as if by magic, like something in the *Arabian Nights*. After the wine, he drank beer. Johnny Miller played piano. Harry and Johnny sang close harmony duets on old evergreens from the twenties. Harry got drunker than he'd ever been in his life. He sang 'Come Landlord, Fill The Flowing Bowl', a thing from his schooldays, in his deep *basso profundo* Paul Robeson 'Massa's In De Cold Cold Ground' voice. 'Deep river, my home is over Jordan.' What harmonies! Singing, drinking, dancing. The sound of smashing glass. Anarchy. For every glass that was broken, the manager of the Bodega raised another above his head and dashed it to the floor, till people were walking on broken glass. Pure good luck no one was injured. Acker Bilk arrived with a bunch of people that included two leggy models leading a pair of huge greyhounds. They hadn't been invited, they thought it was an ordinary Jazz Club night, sat and watched for a while then left.

Harry woke up in bed. He couldn't remember getting there. When he went back for the souvenir menu everyone had signed, he found out that Johnny Miller had been locked in the ladies' toilet all night with a large flagon of gin, and that the vomit all over the pavement outside was Clarence Brown's. He ran into Alex and Ed at the bar and learned how, while Alex turned the coloured spotlights on him, he'd indulged in a show of eccentric dancing on the stage till he tripped backwards and crashed right through the plywood wall at the back of the bandstand, only to appear a few seconds later round the side and resume the performance on the dance-floor in the middle of the broken bottles and glasses.

'You should have seen him,' Nell said, for the umpteenth time. It was so unlike Harry. He wasn't much of a drinker. 'Can't take it, see,' she said to Auntie Jill. 'Our Bob now, you never ever see our Bob in that condition. Our Bob can drink all day and you'd hardly notice the difference. I suppose that's worse in a way.'

'Of course it's worse.'

His mum was picking him up from Auntie Jill's where he sometimes got left. Mary was in the kitchen buttering round upon round of thick toast, her socks thin and grey, her green print dress hanging lower at the back than the front. He'd been at the Hoods' all afternoon. Auntie Jill had not been there at all, apart from about the first ten minutes. Mary was in charge, which was a funny thing really as she wasn't any older than him, maybe six months at the most, and yet somehow she was in charge, and the littlest one she was in charge of, Colinette, she was only one. Colinette was called after Colin, the eldest son, who was married and lived in Droylsden. Afternoons round at the Hoods' meant games, Mary's games. Ian and Gary, sort of twins, not identical, sevenish; Sally and Gillian; Edward in his unravelling brown top. Colinette. Old records on the gramophone. All the kids dancing around like maniacs, waving their arms about and yelling. Mary had such a big smile. They'd play a game where she stood in the corridor with her arms out and they had to try to get past her, under her arms or between her legs or something, but she always won, that was part of it, they'd keep running at her, but she just kept throwing them back on to the chair cushions and all the cushions off the settee that lay around the floor in the living room.

There were times during those long late hours alone below the sleeping house when Harry would cry and not know why. Minnie Graham had never been anything more than a possibility. He was, first and foremost, an honourable man, and he'd made a free choice when he married Nell. He didn't do things lightly. He had children. He was nothing if not responsible. To lose that, to be feckless, would so agitate his grain that life would not be bearable. Responsible. He must be responsible. Responsible. So the decision he came to at last was to carry on as normal but keep in a corner of his brain a little space where he could indulge his whims: later, that's where he had quite a serious fling with the actress Claire Bloom; Marilyn Monroe appealed to him in some way similar to Minnie Graham; and there was that plain little blonde chanteuse whose gimmick was to weep real tears while she sang.

He no longer thought in terms of love, romantic love. He was with Nell. That was it. Nell and the shy kids. He did, however, keep something in reserve: a possibility. Just that. A possibility of a future something, after the kids were grown.

He sat downstairs alone listening to Teagarden sing blues.

> *Blues in the mornin'*
> *Mis'ry in the evening,*
> *Wake up crying like a child of two ...*

Jack Teagarden's voice was rough, with an understated quality that made it all the more moving.

Long runs on country lanes, getting out the telescope: the rings of Saturn, the mountains of the moon. Dawn coming up on one side. Sheffield, Nottingham, Birmingham, Stoke, Derby, Liverpool, Sunderland, Glasgow, Liverpool again.

They went down well at the Cavern Club and were invited back again and again. They played twice in December, topping the bill with Micky Ashman's Ragtime Jazz Band, the White Eagles Jazz Band and a guitar band called the Beatles, four leather kids playing rhythm 'n' blues. Johnny Miller went down a storm in the Cavern. After the show the Beatles gathered round the piano, clapping their hands. Johnny was great. You could feel that double rhythm through the soles of your feet, coming up through the floorboards, Johnny stomping the loud pedal and those kids stamping, their big toothy grins. God, Johnny could play. He was with them in February when they played with the Beatles again. And Johnny was on the recording of 'Ostrich Walk', one of the best things they ever did, the recording that prompted *Jazz News* to call them 'an experienced band reaching healthy maturity'. But Johnny didn't live to see its release. He was stroked by the fairies, Paddy Noonan said. He didn't die straight away; he went into a coma and died two days later in hospital. Harry was expecting the news. It came just after tea, a knock on the front door. Harry went down the hall.

Nell looked up intently. 'That'll be his friend dead,' she said softly.

Everyone fell quiet. They heard the solemn mumble of voices before the door closed and he came down the hall, stopping for a long moment half-way and blowing his nose.

The memorial concert was held at the Bodega. The tickets cost four bob. The Saints, the Merseysippis, the Yorkshire Jazz Band and six other bands played. Acker Bilk's bowler hat was raffled and they raised two hundred pounds for Pam and the kids.

29

Twinkletoes

They were in Blackpool for a few days, Nell and the kids, Bessie, Bobby's two, Robin and Wendy, and Georgia's best friend from school. It was cold, the sand wet and clammy. Bessie wore her big black coat and carried a black umbrella, strolling thoughtfully through the bright thronged Pleasure Beach.

'Hang on a minute, Nelly.'

She wanted to consult the gypsy palmist. She'd gone to work in the canteen at Granada TV, where she'd become very highly thought of and, to the great awe of everyone, received a proposal of marriage from the head chef, Mr Pink. Bessie herself expressed no surprise and seemed indifferent, as she did to nearly all of the famous stars whose autographs she got. The girls had both got autograph books with different coloured pages, which they gave to her to take to work, and she'd come back with the very scrawly signatures of people on TV, some of whom they'd never heard. 'Yours sincerely, Duncan Lamont', for instance. The name was familiar, but no one could put a face to it. But they had Yana, and Alma Cogan and Dickie Valentine and Billy Fury, and later she got Freddie and the Dreamers, Billy J. Kramer and the Dakotas, and the Animals. Anyway, she'd been toying with Mr Pink for a few months, not quite going out with him but allowing him to pop round for a cup of tea now and then, and once letting him take her to see a dog race at Belle Vue. So she thought she'd see what the gypsy might say.

She came out of the booth solemnly impressed.

'She told me I was a widow.'

'Oh, well, you know, Mam,' said Nell, who was with her at the time, 'she'll have looked at your wedding ring and taken into account your age, and made a good guess, and then the fact that you're all dressed in black ...'

'She said: "You've got rid of a devil". "What do you mean?" I said. "You know," she said, "you know."'

'What do you mean?' asked Nell sharply.

'She said: "You've got rid of a devil."'

'That's a horrible thing to say!'

'She said, "You've got rid of a devil. You know what I mean," she said. She said, "You don't want to go replacing one devil with another."'

'I've a good mind to go back there,' Nell said, 'and tell her what I think of her.'

'Well, I'm not having him.'

So that was that.

'It's like your grandad always said,' Nell told the kids. '"It'd take a bloody good 'un to please your mother."'

Bessie got home and discovered two orange-and-white striped deck-chairs missing from her back porch. She didn't notice till she'd been back a day or two, and then in passing with a shovelful of coal she suddenly thought, I wonder where those deck-chairs have gone. Violet had had the key, she'd been feeding the cat. It was too late to go out now but she worried about it all night and couldn't get to sleep for the niggling annoyance. Bit of a cheek, really, borrowing her deck-chairs without asking and then not putting them back. I bet the whole bloody lot of them have been in and out all week helping themselves to whatever they fancy, she thought, peeved, and so bothered was she that she got up in the middle of the night and had a good look round to see what else was missing or out of place, but she couldn't find anything.

First thing in the morning she was round at Vi's. It was a Sunday and Jean opened the door, dolled up to the nines already as if she was going out, blonde hair bouffant, backcombed, tightly curled up by the ears. A full flowered skirt with loads of petticoats, flat white shoes with pointed toes, an open cardigan. 'Oh, hello, Grandma,' she said, 'come in.'

Bessie stomped in.

'Have you got my deckchairs, Violet?'

Violet was sitting in a many-pocketed pinny, eating toast beside the radio. *Easybeat* was on.

'What deckchairs?'

'*My* deckchairs. The deck-chairs in my back. *You* know what deckchairs I mean. *You*'ve had the key, *you*'re supposed to have been looking after my house. My deckchairs have gone!'

'Oh, Mam. Mam, calm down,' said Violet.

'What are you all dressed up like a dog's dinner for?' Bessie looked sourly at Jean.

'I'm going to church.'

'Church?' cried Bessie, in an offended tone.

'I've been going a while.'

Adjusting her hair as if adjusting her head, Jean set off down the path with her big skirt swaying like a fairground ride, simple white shoes displaying shapely ankles to their best advantage. She said she'd fetch Edward, he'd got the key. Bessie exploded. 'The key! The key! What's he doing with the key? A kid?'

'He's twelve,' Violet said. 'He's old enough to pop round and feed Tiger.'

Edward didn't appear after ten grumpy minutes, and Bessie said she wasn't hanging around here all day waiting for him to decide to come back, she had better things to do with her time, and she couldn't stay in bed all day like some could either. She walked away down the path grumbling to herself. Nothing was safe these days. That Edward was turning out a right bad lot, mucking about all day long in the road with his yobby little pals. Kicking footballs.

Sunday roast. Edward said he didn't know anything about any deck-chairs. Stanley's dinner was always kept warm for him on Saturday and Sunday, the meat in a slow oven, the potatoes and vegetables in hot water on top of the stove. Weekends he didn't get up till two, sometimes three in the afternoon, then sat in front of the TV and ate his dinner. He was mashing his spuds into the reheated gravy when Bessie returned and stood blocking the light from the window.

'There weren't any deckchairs, Grandma,' Edward said. 'I don't think so anyway. I wasn't looking. I only let Tiger in and changed his food.'

'You've been in there with your mates, haven't you?'

'What are you saying?' Violet got to her feet and put her hands on her hips. 'Are you making accusations?'

'They were there when I went to Blackpool.'

'Well, I don't know,' Edward said. 'I only went round to feed Tiger.'

Stanley finished his dinner and put his plate down on the floor.

'Where are they? Where are they? You've taken them! You and them yobbish friends of yours. And you can take that smile off your

314

face, you cheeky little bugger! You'll laugh on the other side of your face when I call the police and they take your fingerprints!'

Stanley jumped up. 'Right, that's it,' he croaked. 'Out.'

'Who do you think you're talking to?' Bessie screamed.

'Out. You don't come in here calling my son a thief. Out.'

Bessie's watery blue eyes filled with tears. 'You take his side!' she cried. 'You *would* take his side. You're all the same tribe!'

'Out!'

Stanley moved across the room, lanky, lurching, stiff–legged, big-beaked.

Bessie lumbered to the door, threw it open and turned. 'And you'd stand by and hear your own mother talked to like that, Violet.'

'You're not my mother,' Violet said.

Bessie hurtled down the path like a tank, her wide nostrils pumping. At that moment she hated the world. All of it was against her. She was nearly running, such a heavy elderly woman, short of breath because now her tear ducts and nasal passages were also filling up with fluid, spilling over. She got home and sat in her chair and wept with Tiger on her knee. Poor cat purring, not knowing what's wrong, just liking to be stroked, liking her hand moving shakily over his fur. How could they do that to her? How could they speak to her like that? How could they all be so horrible to her? It was because she was just old now, old and pointless. Nobody wanted her any more. Well, they weren't getting away with this. Oh, no, not this time. This was the injustice too many. Stealing from an elderly lady, your own grandmother. The lack of respect. The sheer gall of it. And then to insult you and call you a liar when you go round.

They wouldn't hear the last of this. Oh, no no no.

She went over to see Bob and Eva in the slummy place where they were living now. They were in the middle of a big row when she arrived, as per usual. Bobby was scrubbing out the insides of some electrical contraption he had the back off.

'That's my toothbrush you're using,' Eva was saying.

'Well, you never bloody use it anyway.'

'You cheeky sod!'

A shivering whippet huddled like a little fawn in the corner of the settee, thumping its tail neurotically. Hawaiian guitars played in the background.

Bessie told them Edward and his friend had stolen two deckchairs out of her house while she was on holiday. 'What kind of a child would do that to his own grandma?' she asked. 'He'll have sold them on. That's what he's done. Celia over the road says he was round all the time, him and his mate, hanging round the back with their bikes. Of course, they closed ranks. That's what it's like these days. You can get away with robbing the old. Called me a liar and ordered me out.' Tears pouring. 'Stanley did. Ordered me out of the house. I'm not going back there again. Not after being treated like that. You don't know what it's like! You don't know what it's like.' Bessie rummaged in her big black leather bag for a handkerchief and pulled out a crumpled white one. 'Everyone thinks they can rub dirt on you!'

Bob and Eva exchanged a glance.

Eva sighed.

Bob tutted loudly, shaking his head. 'Terrible that, Mam,' he said. 'Don't get yourself upset.'

'You'll have to go and have a word with Violet.'

'Me?'

'You can tell her. Say you're not having your mother spoken to in that way.'

Bob's confrontation with Violet ended in a cup of tea and a chat about the relative musical merits of Elvis and Cliff Richard. Nell was there. Nell said she found Cliff Richard a bit pobby. As for the deckchairs, it was all a load of nonsense. All in her head. She was barmy, obsessed with trying to set the family against each other.

'I'd lay bets,' Violet said, 'she chucked them out ten years ago.'

'She had them when Grandad was alive,' Jean said, 'but not for a long time.'

Bessie sat in her house and wept, burning her legs by the fire. She said they'd all find out when they got old. She said Violet was not her child. Blood was thicker than water. No one was to go round and see

Violet. She told Celia and Mrs Brocklehurst across the road and all the people in the local shops and in the chippy that Edward had stolen from her and that Violet and Stanley had called her a liar. Anyone who sided with Vi would get no more of her. She'd finish with them.

Everyone went on visiting Violet as normal but in secret, and all the kids were given strict instructions never to mention in front of Grandma that they'd even seen Auntie Vi and Uncle Stanley and Jean and Edward. Every now and again there'd be a big scene when a neighbour or someone would mention having seen your Nelly and the kids walking down Sutton Road, and Bessie would storm round to Green Grove straight away and weep and moan and spit at Nell that she was finished with her. They'd squawk for a while till Bessie cried: 'I know when I'm not wanted!' snorting a great wet sniff up her big round nostrils, gathering up her umbrella and bag and lumbering down the hall.

Everyone felt awful. That's how it was now with Bessie. She made everyone feel awful, all the time. For a visit to Bessie you girded up your loins, and always you came away depressed. Her misery seeped out of her eyes, constant. Still, Nell and Bob and their kids continued to visit her, regular as clockwork, Bobby twice a week and Nell once. 'Still,' they'd say, 'she's had a rotten life. She was born in the workhouse, you know. Like Oliver Twist.'

Violet went once but Bessie didn't open the door. Jean tried too but got nowhere. After that they didn't bother.

His grandma favoured him just as she did Robin, so after one particular stormy encounter, Jack was sent as a sort of peace-offering to get round her. He knocked on the door but no one answered. He looked in the window. The house was all locked up and empty. He went round and sat on the back doorstep waiting for her to come in. The golden rod was high. After about twenty minutes he heard the gate go. He went round the front and met Grandma coming heavily up the path with her wide feet spreading out of her slippers and a shopping bag hanging over one arm. She walked past him up to the front door.

'Who's sent you?' she asked.

'No one,' he said, which wasn't strictly true. 'I just thought I'd come round.'

She looked sour. In the house, she put more coal on the fire, and he sat down in the chair across from her.

'So,' she said, still in her coat, her massive bust like a breastplate, 'would you like a chucky egg?'

'Oh, yes, please, Grandma.'

First she made him a chucky egg, then went out into the back garden and picked some rhubarb and made him rhubarb and custard. They watched TV and every now and again she sent him for a shovelful of coal. She asked if he was staying for tea. She didn't cry or moan or anything. He said OK, and Bessie sent a message with a kid over the road that she'd bring him back in the morning. For tea they took a couple of pudding basins and went to the chippy. When they came out, a drunk was staggering about at the fifty-three bus stop over the road.

'Don't you ever drink alcohol when you grow up,' Grandma said. 'It makes people stupid like that. Don't you ever do it. You don't want to end up like poor Joey.'

'Who?'

'Your cousin Joey. No, not your cousin, your mother's cousin. Joey. He died in a brick kiln on Jackson's.'

'Joey the window-cleaner?'

'That's right. He did clean windows for a while.'

Bessie pushed open the front door. Jack laid out the plates and knives and forks and got out the salt and vinegar, while she tipped the puddings and their gravy out of the basins and divided up the chips and peas.

'I didn't know he was dead,' Jack said.

'Last year.'

Joey had taken to the drink and gone bad and ended up dying dead drunk in a brick kiln on Jackson's one very cold night.

'They think he'd climbed in there to sleep,' she said, 'because he used to sleep all over the place. Terrible state for a man to get into. And then he just died because it was too cold, I suppose. He was Uncle John and Auntie Grace's. He was nice when he was a little lad.

318

So don't you ever go drinking like that when you grow up, do you hear? It ruins people.'

She paused, then added: 'It's in the family.'

The food was delicious, hot and crisp and salty. The peas were a purée. But his grandma's tea was horrible. She couldn't make a decent cup of tea, it was always weak and too milky. She turned on the radio and there was music. 'Would you like to look at the pictures?' she asked, when they'd finished eating, and got out the photos and started telling him about them, who all those people were and some of the things that had happened to them. Auntie Bennet with all her hair. 'That picture,' she said, 'that was on the cover of a chocolate box. They used to have pictures like that of pretty girls on chocolate boxes.' His grandad looked stern but he was as soft as anything, everybody knew that. She got on to his religious views somehow. 'He had some funny ideas,' she said, 'he thought this world was Hell. He used to say, "All this talk of Hell and we don't realise we're already in it."'

'What do you think?' Jack asked.

'I don't know,' Bessie said. 'I don't think anybody does, really. But you can't do anything about it whatever it is so you might as well not think about it.'

Then some particular music came on the radio, something jolly and jazzy and very old, and Grandma smiled and grew sentimental. 'I used to dance to this,' she said. 'I bet you never knew your grandma was a very good dancer once upon a time, did you?'

Quite suddenly she was on her feet, dancing for him with an imaginary partner, complicated footwork deft and fast and perfect, a portly old woman with toffee-coloured waved hair, amazingly light on her feet. Bright-eyed, darting her eyebrows up saucily, a smile set brightly on her face. He'd never seen his grandma like this before.

'Do you know what they used to call me?' she said, breathless, laughing, as the tune ended and she sat down in her chair across from him by the fire. 'Twinkletoes.'

30

The Yellow House

Jazz was going down. All these new guitar bands coming up, the ubiquitous groups. 'Five Foot Two Eyes of Blue'/'Sweet William' by the Tailgaters was released as a single in the pop catalogue rather than jazz. Everything was pop now rather than jazz. You bought the *Melody Maker* or the *NME* these days and they'd nearly all gone over to it. Not that the Tailgaters had any less work. That was the trouble, they had more than ever. They could always pull a crowd. But Harry was tired. He'd been thinking very seriously. Wanted change. Move on.

Leave the Tailgaters.

He'd been thinking about it for a while. He was in his forties now. He supposed tiredness was something to do with age, but he was sure all the travelling didn't help. When you were a young man you could manage it. You could manage it now if you didn't have the day job too. He could keep his lip in. He'd still play.

First he cut down on the travelling, and the band used deps in his place. He played local, Manchester, Liverpool. As well as the jazz clubs, it was the thing now to play on long line-ups in big venues, variety shows, pop shows with the odd jazz band thrown in for good measure. The Tailgaters were billed fifth in a line-up of six at the Opera House, after Adam Faith, Craig Douglas, Cherry Wainer and Eden Kane. Bob Miller and the Millermen completed the bill. After finishing his act, to dodge the screaming crowds, Adam Faith rushed from the wings right through a quickly opened side entrance to a waiting car with the engine running. But there were only about six little girls out there after all. Harry laughed about that. He couldn't wait to tell the kids. He loved putting down pop. He wanted them to appreciate proper music. He wouldn't let them listen to all this pap.

Once when they were sitting watching some pop show on the telly, some rubbish, he walked in, switched over to the other side and walked out again. No one dared switch it back.

'There's no point,' Nell said sourly, looking up from the square she was crocheting. 'He'll just go into a mood.'

They listened to the radio in bed at night, under the bedclothes, soaked themselves in pop.

'He's a snob,' Nell said. 'He thinks he's the only one with any taste. I've always thought that to be a true music lover you have to appreciate different types of music. Not just think there's only one kind and that anyone who likes anything else is stupid. That's not being a real music lover.' She wielded the crochet hook angrily. 'He makes me furious.' Her brows knitted.

'Tell him,' said Georgia.

'You tell him.'

It was the same with the TV. You could only watch what *he* wanted to watch. That meant you got all the comedy shows, *The Army Game*, *Sergeant Bilko*, *Hancock's Half-hour*, and you got all the variety shows and game shows and cartoons, and as many old Hollywood musicals as you could take.

But you couldn't have pop.

A new start. A new house. A better area. Both the girls were at the grammar school now. The boy was very bright. They had to move up. They found a house miles and miles and miles away from Gorton and Longsight. So far out, past Stretford and Salford, past the motorway, closer to Trafford Park, where Harry worked. The kids would have long bus rides to school. Bessie was horrified at Nell moving so far away, particularly now Bob and Eva had finally been rehoused in Reddish, but Nell and the kids still went once a week, getting three buses. The only ones still living near Bessie now were Vi and Stanley and she wasn't speaking to them.

Ely Road was very long. They lived at 143. There were trees all along the pavements. The houses were bow-fronted semis with square-cut privet hedges and well-kept small gardens front and back. Lots of smaller streets ran off Ely Road, laid out symmetrically to a plan. These in turn fed into other big roads, nests of crescents, cul-de-sacs, further offshoots and tributaries, all of bow-fronted semis with small gardens front and back, all of the same design. At first they got lost quite often.

Where you caught the buses into town the houses ended, and a main thoroughfare ran down to the motorway, under it and along the lengthy drag towards Stretford. The bus stops stood alongside a big open field, hedged round, in which nothing ever seemed to happen. Beyond this were a few more houses and then the motorway.

The new house had yellow and black paintwork. It seemed terribly small after Green Grove, like a doll's house. The back garden had a flat square lawn, a small garden shed, a bit of crazy paving and a birdbath, and, wonder of wonders, an apple tree. There were rosebushes in the front, reds and various pinks, and a garage at the side, though they didn't have a car any more. The Riley had got too expensive to run. Still, the garage was very handy for putting stuff in.

There was no doubt it was a move up and away. There wasn't so much room for painting here. Harry took up golf. His clubs stood looking important in their leather bag by the coat-stand in the cramped hall, with the brand new two-tone green telephone on a little table. Whenever it rang, Harry leaped up with a shocked look on his face and dashed out to it as if it was timed to blow up the house if you didn't get there by the third ring.

In spite of the move, in spite of the rambles with Jack all around the hills surrounding Manchester, in spite of the day trips with them all to Fountains Abbey and the Blue John mines, to Chester Zoo and Gawsworth Hall, things got worse.

Things got so unutterably worse. Silences fed on silences. The little yellow house was hell.

Jack had the boxroom. He didn't sleep. Somewhere over the dark stairwell his consciousness hung each night, half in and half out of his body. Things changed. The mineral man no longer came. For years he'd brought them one limeade, one cream soda, one dandelion and burdock every week. No more. But some things stayed the same: his father whistling down the late-night street, long, quiet, leafy Ely Road. Because, of course, Harry still played, with this band and that band. Played with the Sid Lawrence Orchestra and the BBC Northern Dance Orchestra. Still did the odd gig with the Tailgaters now and then. Like old times. Keeping his lip in. At home he played all the time, just here and there around the house. He even played in the bath. The sound of Harry's trombone, picked up and doodled on, sometimes only for a cracked second or two, sometimes at length, was by now so engrained into the soul of the family that it was hardly noticed. It just was. But now there was other music. Harry had been unable to keep back the tide. The girls were buying records with their pocket money; they played it in their rooms. The Beatles had made it big, the Cavern band, the lads who used to love Johnny Miller's boogie-woogie piano. Little girls all over the country were screaming their heads off. But not his. His were much too repressed. His had been told to pipe down ever since they were born. His couldn't have screamed with abandon if you'd paid them. He was glad about that. They had all the Beatles' records, though, and played them over and over again. He let them go to see the Beatles and the Rolling Stones when they came to the Apollo on condition that they did not make exhibitions of themselves. There was no danger of that. Joanne went to see the Beatles in socks and her school shoes because they were all she had. When she got there all the other girls from school were in high heels and stockings. And then it was Bob Dylan, Bob Dylan blasting out continually. It didn't matter what it was, Harry hated it all.

He was not a happy man. This hit him most strongly some time after the move. He looked around and thought: I am not a happy man. So he climbed Great Gable in the Lake District and took up woodcarving, encouraged by the fact that, bizarrely, there was a woodcarvers' supply shop on the one row of shops on Ely Road. He made a horse with wild eyes and a neighing open mouth. He made a pond in the back garden. Still he was not happy. The pond was not a success. He had kids he could not communicate with, a wife who sat around with a long face all the time. He would have felt worse if he'd known what she was thinking: Look at him sitting there with the newspaper on his knee, fat sod, white shirt, elephant-grey trousers, hair a mess, fluffed out and greying at the sides. Starting to look old. Round about the waist. Lips vanished. Cheeks fat. Nose pinched like his mother's. God. And that pond, God, trust him to make a complete mess of it. The black plastic lining had lost its shape and gone all wrinkly and leaky, so it was always half empty. It was like an open grave in your back garden, all clogged up with slimy green algae. It was supposed to have lily-pads and goldfish and tadpoles. Him and his grand ideas. Like when he tried to grow cypress trees in the back yard in Longsight. Cypress trees in Longsight, I ask you. Anyway, other men do things like that. Our Bob would have been able to do a little thing like that, make a pond.

She didn't know anyone round here. No one knew anyone round here. The people next door were posh. The woman wore stockings and proper shoes every day. The man was weedy. They had a plump, clean-cut son. Nell talked to the woman over the back fence but it was all just silly small-talk; she preferred to go back home and sit in Jill Hood's tip of a place, with the back door open on to the croft with its straggling yards and the toilet block and the old wash-house. They were supposed to be pulling all this lot down. Jack, hanging on the gate idly swinging, scraping his toe along the ground, watching one of Auntie Jill's big lads up a ladder doing something to the guttering, could hear the women inside talking about Uncle Bob and Auntie Eva.

'Mind you, she goads him, you know. She doesn't know when to stop. You don't goad our Bobby when he's had a few drinks.'

Auntie Jill tutted. She was feeding the baby. 'Nell, there's never any excuse.'

'No, of course, you're right.'

A bunch of scruffy kids, coming over the croft with a bicycle.

It was Mary, surrounded by children. Colinette was hanging on to her skirt, pulling her back as she pushed the bike. Colinette sucked her thumb, always. It looked all pink and raw and unnaturally clean compared to the rest of her dirty self. Ian and Gary, two interchangeable almost-twins, plodded along behind, deep in conversation, hands in pockets, shoulders hunched, eyes to the ground, tough little coves. Then those other two girls, the ones whose names Jack always got mixed up, the babyish ones, squeaking and squawking like mice; and then Titch, whose real name was Terry, a boy born with a weakness of the heart, small, bull-headed, bright blond. Jack raised a hand in greeting.

Mary waved back.

'Colinette,' she said, '*will* you stop pulling me back?'

He trailed in after them, in and upstairs to the big central bedroom, where the silly girls set about trampolining from bed to bed. Titch laughing, delighted. When Titch got excited he laughed till you thought he'd choke. Colinette running about looking like Snufkin in the Moomin books in a triangular white dress, slightly soiled. The big boys, Ian and Gary, off in their own side-room, playing Subbuteo. Football chants. The hammering in the guttering. The struts of the ladder going past the open window. The door was open on to the landing, a public thoroughfare, huge and brown, which children traversed constantly. Jack and Mary got out all the old Toby Twirl and Bobby Brewster annuals. These books went back all the way with them. They had become more than just the silly stories and bad rhymes. All the spare bits were coloured in. Each child that had passed through the house had added its graffiti to the pages over the years. The games on the inside front and back covers had all been played a million times: shake of the dice in the cup, the round plastic counters, red, yellow, blue. *You Have Dropped Your Toys – Miss Two Turns. Lost Map! Go Back To Start*. All the spines were broken, all the edges scuffed. Whenever in later years he thought of that landscape, that land where Toby Twirl and Bobby Brewster and Rupert Bear and even Noddy and Big Ears lived, sort of Toytown-cum-Storyland, he saw it as if Mary Hood was there: she looked like Tiger Lily, her straight chin-length hair darker than before, eyes dark and narrow. Her face was broad. She was heavy round the middle. They found a nature crossword that hadn't been done. It was too hard. They couldn't get anything. Yes, they could. Hedgewarbler. Is there such a thing? A crowned frog wearing a purple cloak leaped down the margin. The Dillypuff chuffed along, blowing its blue and yellow funnel:

Dilly-puff-puff-puff, Dilly-puff-puff-puff, Dilly-puff-puff-puff-puff-PUFF!
He grabbed her wrists and they started to wrestle. They fell on the floor and he got her in a headlock.

'Submit,' he said.

'Gerroff, you pig!'

'Submit.'

'No.'

Then, of course, it never went any further because he'd never have hurt her, so they just rolled around and fought and giggled for a while more. She had breasts now, small bumpy ones that banged against his arm.

Old Tim died. The next dog was a pain in the arse called Pal, a plain short-haired black and white runt of no distinction, with chronic flatulence and a twitch in his head. He caused havoc when they took him round the Hoods'. Nicked toys, barked at the caretaker, who aimed a kick at him, jumped over the wall into the bit round the side of the wash-house where the communal ladder was kept, along with buckets and brooms and cloths and sundry cans of dried-up paint. He cocked his leg and peed on some old dust-sheets. Then he galloped furiously round and round the croft, in and out of the house, up and down the stairs, making the children scream and chase after him. Colinette ran round the back of Jack's leg and clutched his knees. He looked down on the top of her white sparse head, wispy fair hair coiling about it like down feathers. He had a soft spot for Colinette because he'd nearly knocked her on the head with a swing when she was a baby. She'd been so bald and narrow-eyed she'd reminded him of a maggot, in a nice kind of way, if that was possible. He'd been mucking about on the swing, a blue swing that used to be out on the croft, and Auntie Jill had called out of the window: 'Mind the baby's head!'

He'd looked up and seen the baby, brought the swing to a halt, sat very still as Colinette crawled by, that strange white head, that odd name. Her head looked so breakable he had to feel sorry for her, and at that moment she'd smiled at him, flashing her one tooth.

'It's OK,' he said now. 'The doggy won't hurt you.'

She smiled round her thumb, looking up and crinkling her eyes.

'Bloody dog!' shouted Nell, finally trapping the bugger behind the settee. 'Calm down, you fool!'

It was to save on boarding-kennel costs that Harry didn't come to Ireland.

'My mam's booked a cottage for a week. She's paying. She's taking our Bobby's kids. Do you want to come?'

Well, of course he didn't. Stuck in a cottage for a week with Bessie? So off they all trooped and left him on his own again, and he spent the week encouraging the dog and cats to sleep in the bedroom with him.

Banlough Bay. A long beach, rocks, rowing-boats. Kiosks. Shops selling sunhats and fishing-nets and postcards. A hot and steamy August. Their bungalow, Willow Cottage, was a mile or two inland, on a winding leafy lane, with a high crag at the back. Nell, Georgia, Joanne, Joanne's posh friend Fiona, Jack, Grandma, Robin and Wendy. Georgia and Joanne couldn't stand each other. Georgia swanned about in a denim skirt and red top, flouncing her long dark-brown hair with her fingers and whistling through her teeth. Joanne had had *her* hair cut, disastrously, and slouched around with a false tight-mouthed smile, greasy-haired and sallow. Her posh friend Fiona was very much taller than everybody else and had strong square talons painted silver.

It was the holiday on which boys happened.

The first day, everyone promenaded at Bessie's pace along the sea-front by the shingle beach. Then Nell and Bessie bought some cold meat for tea and set off home to make a salad. Joanne and her posh friend took off their shoes and rolled up the legs of their jeans and clambered over the rocks that went on for miles, full of pools and slippery seaweed. The kids trailed after. Georgia didn't know whether to go with the kids or the oldies. In the end she went off by herself, bought a sunhat and a big Mr Whippy ice-cream and sat on a bench at the foot of a large green cliff to watch the sea, hoping to get a tan on her legs. She wore white sandals and a minidress with a large purple check design, and she kept adjusting her sunhat to sit more becomingly on her long dark hair. Below on the shingle the rowing-boats were dragged up and tethered, colonised by gulls. A little further along there was a small jetty where the boatmen waited to ferry people out to a famous rock where a huge colony of seabirds lived. She had to walk past on the way back. One of the boatmen stood on the end of the jetty, about to cast off. 'Room for one more?' he said softly.

She smiled and shook her head. She was afraid she might get sick and look a fool.

'Another time,' he said. He was a dark stocky boy with a handsome shifty face.

'Maybe.'

'On holiday?'

'Yes.'

'Going to the fair tonight?'

'Maybe.'

He nodded significantly, cast off and jumped down into the boat.

In the end the whole bunch of them went down to the fair, much to the annoyance of Georgia, who walked off alone as soon as she could. The boy from the boat engaged her in conversation by the Test-Your-Strength machine. He smoked a cigarette and leaned against the side of the candy-floss stall.

'Don't look,' Nell said. 'Act natural. She's talking to a boy.'

After a while, Georgia came over with him and told Nell she was just going for a coffee at the café on the front. 'This is Dominic,' she said. The boy smiled and said hello. Nell watched them go with a strange sinking feeling. Her type exactly. The way he stood. The way he walked.

'Are you letting her go off like that with a complete stranger?' asked Bessie, appalled.

'She's OK,' Nell said. 'It's only over there. Look, I can see them from here. They're sitting at a table near the door.'

Joanne and Fiona got chatted up on the Waltzer by two boys. Bessie went mad about that too.

'There's no harm,' said Nell. 'It's all right, they're only kids. Let them have a good time.'

'Well, *I* wonder what Harry would say if he was here,' Bessie said righteously.

'He wouldn't say anything.'

'Oh, wouldn't he?'

Well, maybe he would. Who cared?

Every night the girls went down to the fair and met the boys. By the third night Fiona was seeing her boy on a regular basis, while Joanne had been jilted by the other and was crying bitterly in her room. Georgia and Dominic had decided on that first night in the café that this was true love. Like Romeo and Juliet, he said. He was from Dublin, a student, up for the summer to earn a bit of money. The kids were running wild in the woods. Bessie complained loudly about everything to everyone in sight. As for Nell, she spent much of the time out on the patio, lounging in a deck-chair with her book (*Royal Road To Fotheringhay*), cigarettes and matches on her knee. Her short, thick hair was still black. Her figure wasn't too bad, her legs were OK. She wore a Crimplene dress in chocolate and cream. She thought: If I were twenty years younger. He was very nice, this Dominic Crohan. A sweet mouth. One of those mouths with brackets. He talked so easily to her, looking deep into her eyes for rare still moments that now and then occurred in all the nervous dartings of his eyes.

'What's the matter with his eyes?' asked Bessie. 'I don't like his eyes.'

'It's not his fault,' Nell said. 'It's because he had a very bad accident when he was sixteen. He told me all about it. He was in a car crash. It had a terrible effect on his nerves and now he can't keep his eyes still. He can't help it.'

One night towards the end of the week, Georgia had not returned by half past ten. Bessie had already gone to bed, but she got up and came out of her room in her long winceyette nightie, teeth out, hairnet on, and stormed up and down in front of the television for twenty minutes till Jack announced from the window that Georgia was outside, kissing. Everyone rushed to the window. Georgia stood talking to Dominic at the gate.

'They *were* kissing,' Jack said.

'There you are!' cried Bessie.

'So what?' said Nell. 'What would you expect them to be doing?'

'He could be anyone!'

'No, he couldn't.'

'Well, I wonder what Harry'd have to say about all this!'

'He wouldn't say anything. He's not stupid. You're the only one making a fuss.'

'Well, I'm going to tell him!' Bessie ran for the door. 'He's no right to bring her back at this time! She can get in here right now!'

'Mam!' Nell ran after and grabbed her by the arm. 'Don't you dare!'

For a terrible second they grappled in the doorway.

'Don't you dare! She is not your daughter, don't you dare to tell her what to do. You cause so much trouble, you do!'

'Listen to the way she talks to her mother!' Bessie's eyes filled up. She addressed the goggle-eyed children. 'They've always taken sides against me!'

'Oh, Mam!'

'I'll make sure Harry hears about this!' Bessie swept away into her bedroom and slammed the door so that the walls shook.

'She's gone mad,' said Joanne.

The kids started to giggle.

Bessie opened her door and stuck out her head. 'And don't you go talking about me while my back's turned. I know what you're like. Can't wait to sling shit!'

Slam.

Georgia arrived at the door.

'Get in, quick!' said Nell, starting to laugh.

Bessie opened her door. 'I'll have you know I'm sixty-eight years old! Sixty-eight years old! And pushed about like a piece of furniture! Change rooms!'

Slam.

'And don't blame me if she gets in the family way!'

'What?'

Slam.

Joanne and Georgia leaned together, giggling, helpless. Nell joined in and the three of them sank to their knees and laughed painfully, silently, convulsing more and more with each diatribe. Fiona watched, laughing slightly uneasily.

'Go on, go on!' screamed Bessie. 'Ignore me!'

Nell went to the door. 'Mam! Don't be so ridiculous!'

'Don't you dare call me ridiculous!'

'Shut up! Shut up!'

They were off.

It went on all the next day, and the next. Bessie ignored everyone but Robin and Wendy, whom she commandeered to be on her side. The garden was full of wasps. Dominic Crohan was there all the time. He seemed able to give himself time off whenever he wanted to. He and Georgia walked hand in hand up and down the banks of the little bubbling rill that crossed the track in the woods. Jack and Nell went down to the beach. The girls washed their hair and dried it on the patio. Bessie was out there but she went in as soon as they came out. 'Fucking wasps!' she said, loudly and defiantly, as she passed them.

'Your grandma swears a lot, doesn't she?' Fiona said thoughtfully.

'She does.'

Joanne imagined Fiona going back to the house around the corner and telling her posh prissy mum and dad all about this.

On the last day Dominic came to the cottage to see them off. When the minibus arrived and they all clambered in, and Wendy had been made to sit upon a piece of brown paper and given an arrowroot biscuit to prevent travel sickness (Grandma swore by it), the boy who'd been squiring Fiona about turned up, and Fiona had to get out of the bus to kiss him goodbye ostentatiously. Then they were off.

Dominic walked to the end of the road. He raised his hand to the bus as it passed, winking when he caught Nell's eye.

'He's coming over,' Georgia said. 'We're going to meet half-way. Somewhere like Bangor. Unless, of course, he could stay with us. Do you think Dad'd mind?'

'We'll see,' said Nell.

Georgia opened her magazine. *Honey*. Nell sat with a secret smile on her face. Joanne looked out of the back window, crying.

331

'What's the matter?' Nell asked her.

'Nothing.'

Every five minutes Grandma turned to Wendy and said, in a loud voice, 'Do you feel sick?' till Wendy was sick.

Georgia was writing to Dominic. It went on for nearly two years. From time to time she took day trips to Anglesey to meet him, when she could get time off. She was training as a nurse. Two or three times a week he phoned. Now and again it was Nell who picked up the phone. He would always keep her talking a little. So sweet. So easy to talk to. You didn't even have to try. He seemed to like her in a very natural way, in spite of the age difference. Of course Harry knew about him. He hadn't said much. He never did say much. You never knew what he was thinking, unless you could read his face, and his face was always closed, these days. Closed or worried.

Dominic wanted to come and see Georgia, stay in Manchester for a week. Of course, it was obvious that he must stay at the house. He could have Georgia's room and Georgia could go in with Joanne. Georgia asked Nell to ask Harry if it was all right. Nell didn't like to. He'd been sitting there with his miserable face for days. They were hardly speaking. She couldn't really remember why any more. No one knew, it was just the way things were. Everyone swam around in the atmosphere, taking it for granted. Nell was terrified Harry would say no. She wasn't going to let this opportunity go by, the chance to have that lovely boy in her sight for a whole week again. Just to see him. Just to see him, that was all. That was enough. She wasn't stupid enough to think anything else was possible. She didn't mind that. It was just that she thought about him so much, almost as if she had a son living away from home; just that she kept track of all his letters, and the letters Georgia wrote to him, that she got a lovely soaring feeling when she came down in the morning and saw his familiar handwriting on an envelope on the mat.

He was so good. He wrote regular as clockwork.

He was so good and Georgia was a sod. She'd sit there with her knees up, picking her toes, watching telly when she should have been writing to him. Nell would have to keep reminding her. She'd end up nagging. Georgia wouldn't write then, just to spite her. Do him good to wait, she'd say. Then Nell would get frantic, and walk around in a bad mood kicking the dog when he got under her feet, snapping their heads off if they asked what time tea was ready.

'Don't worry about your dad,' she told Georgia, and went ahead and made arrangements for Dominic's stay, and sorted out dates, and one night at teatime, boldly but awkwardly, Nell said, 'Oh, by the way, Harry, that lad's coming to stay in a couple of weeks. That Dominic. You don't mind, do you? Only for a few nights, about a week.'

Harry's head jerked up from the paper, a stricken look on his face. 'You what?'

'Dominic's coming to stay for a few nights. Two weeks on Friday.' The look on his face.

All he said was, 'Well, it would have been nice to be consulted.'

Then he went behind his paper and there was a horrible silence.

Georgia went into the kitchen to do the pots. It was all ruined now. All spoiled. There was no point in Dominic coming now, it would be horrible.

Her dad came in and saw her crying into the suds. 'It's all right, love,' he said kindly. 'I'm not annoyed with you. It's your mother. It's all right, I don't mind him coming, it's just that I would have expected to be consulted about a thing like that, that's all.'

'I'm sorry.'

'It's all right, it's not your fault.'

He was embarrassed. He was always embarrassed by emotion.

Anyway it was too late, he was coming. Nell scrubbed the house happily. Just think, if Georgia married him he'd be in the family. He'd be there, in her life, for ever. He'd come and live here in Manchester and she'd see him all the time. They'd be close, all that mother-in-law stuff was rubbish, she'd get on really well with him. And even if he didn't come, if Georgia went over there to live, then Nell could go over for holidays. Regular. And they'd come over here. It wasn't that far away. He'd still be there, in her life. Part of things.

*

Harry didn't like Dominic.

Jack could tell because as soon as Dominic came into the house, his father stopped sleeping. Jack, doing his homework late at night, or unsleeping, heard him in the room downstairs, quiet, then moving about, opening a drawer, playing a soft phrase of music, muted, yawning, opening the back door to let the cat in, opening his cupboard, taking things out. Harry's cupboard, the necessary place all his own. His books. Music. His stamp collection. His chess set.

The house was restless. Jack didn't like Dominic either. He was a big-head. Whenever anybody said anything, he always had to know something about it, and he was always steering the conversation back to himself. And what he said was actually quite stupid really, he just sort of made it sound as if it wasn't.

But Nell fell so hard. She couldn't keep her mind on anything but him. She wished she was young again. She looked in the mirror. No one's ever going to fall for me for my looks, she thought. I can't compete. What I have is what I have. Anyway, none of that mattered, she wasn't a fool, just having him around was enough. It was lovely. Every morning when she woke up there was something to look forward to. She shaved her legs. She didn't care any more about Harry grumping and sulking about all over the place with his fat angry face. She could put up with that and still have some happiness for herself.

She sat and smiled, just sat and smiled in the middle of the day.

Even when he'd gone it didn't matter so much: he was still there in a way, still in her life, her son away from home calling up regularly. She often had a chat with him these days. They talked about the crocuses opening up. He asked her what she'd been doing that day. Which, of course, was never anything much, but it didn't matter. She was planning next year's holiday in Ireland. He was doing the boats again. They could go back to the same cottage. How could she stop Harry coming? She'd have to invite Mam. Great. Oh, well. Dominic said she should book soon, things got full. He said he would really look forward to seeing them all again.

'This time,' he said, 'you must come out in the boat to the rock.'

Georgia was hovering, waiting for the phone. This was expensive.

But Nell always let Georgia ring him back so they could share the cost of the call.

'Hi, sweetheart,' he said, 'God, your mum goes on.'

Then Georgia met Les Tong, a patient in the hospital who'd had his sinuses scraped. Les was tall and thin with frizzy fair hair, a plain, long, big-chinned face and an adenoidal voice. He was twenty and worked in an accountant's office. Georgia liked him very much straight away. He was much more fun than Dominic − not so moody, just a nice easy person with a nice easy manner, and funny, always fooling around and making her laugh. He was her favourite patient and she was his favourite nurse. When he was discharged, he asked her out and she said yes.

Nell was horrified. 'He's so ugly. I don't know how she can bear to let him kiss her. And have you seen his teeth? They're horrible. Filthy. Looks as if he never cleans them. Ugh! I couldn't kiss that!' She ranted. She lectured Georgia on fidelity and responsibility and loyalty, and how you shouldn't mess people around.

'Mum!' said Georgia. 'It's not serious. I only went to see a film with him. It doesn't mean anything.'

'Oh, yes. So what do you think Dominic would think?'

'He won't know.'

'That's not the point, Georgia. You just don't do that. You just don't do that to people.'

Georgia marched upstairs. At the top, she smiled, licked her thumb and rubbed it on her collar, caught sight of herself in the bathroom mirror and tossed her hair.

She broke it off with him again and again. He rang every night and they argued. He pleaded. She explained and reasoned and prevaricated. He wept. She relented. Nothing was ever resolved.

Nell was furious. She stormed silently about the house with a savage line between her eyes. Harry just sat behind his paper all the time. Everyone else stayed in their rooms or went out as much as possible. No one came to the house. Georgia went out more and more with Les Tong, becoming a fixture round at his place and marvelling at the difference between his household and hers. The first thing she couldn't believe was that his mum sat on his dad's knee, even though they were just an ordinary podgy little old couple. That his mum and dad walked arm and arm and chatted and laughed together when they went out. That Les and his five brothers all dashed about the house saying whatever they liked and nobody minded. That everyone talked all the time. Why couldn't she have grown up like this? Why were her mum and dad so stupid? Why was all her family so stupid?

Dominic took to ringing up in the afternoon and catching Nell on her own. He was quiet, polite. He said he just wanted to talk. Was Georgia all right? He just wanted to know.

'I'm so sorry it's not going so well at the moment, Dominic,' she said. 'I'm sure it'll all work out in the end. You can't rush her, you know. Remember she's not as old as you.'

'I care about her very much, Mrs Caplin,' he said. 'I hope you don't mind me ringing. I sort of like to keep in touch.'

'How can she be so cruel?' Nell raged to Joanne. 'That poor boy, she's broken his heart. You can't treat people like that.'

She sat for ages after tea, after Harry had gone out playing somewhere, just sitting, brooding, the telly on but not really watching it.

'Are you feeling all right, Mum?' asked Joanne.

'I'm worried,' Nell replied. 'I'm worried about what he might do.'

'Mum, it's not really your problem.'

'Of course it's my problem!'

She wouldn't speak to Georgia at all. Then Georgia stopped messing about and announced one night after Harry had gone out that she'd been having a good think and there really was no point in dragging it on any further now that she was going out with Les. She was ringing Dominic that night and finishing it once and for all.

'Oh, no, you are not,' said Nell. She was darning the elbow of Jack's school jumper.

Georgia put her head in her hands. 'I don't believe this.' Her hair was greasy. She wore a grey pinafore.

'Georgia, you just can't treat people like this!'

'Like what?'

'You must be completely insane. Look at the difference between them. How can you compare that ugly streak of water with *him*?'

'Who's going out with him, Mum? Me or you?'

Georgia got up and went out into the hall where the phone stood on its round table, closing the door firmly. The television quacked on. Nell put her head down over her darning, right down. Joanne pretended to watch TV. Georgia came back five minutes later.

'I've told him,' she said.

Nell did not respond.

Georgia went upstairs and into her room, closing the door quietly. She lay down and sobbed. The phone rang. Nell got it. It was him. His voice turned her over. She could hear him holding back the tears.

'Mrs Caplin, what have I done?' he said. 'Please can I speak to her?'

Nell marched upstairs and flung open Georgia's door. 'You speak to that lad now!' she ordered. 'He's in tears.'

'Mother!'

'You speak to that lad now!'

Georgia leaped up, ran downstairs and grabbed the phone. 'Leave me alone, Dominic!'

She listened for a second then slammed the phone down.

'There!' She pushed past Nell, back upstairs. 'There's your precious blue-eyed boy! Do you know what he's just said to me? Do you know what he's just said to me? Fuck off, you common bitch! That's what he's just said!' Tears streamed down her face.

There was a shocked silence. Georgia, who was so nice she called her knickers Ks because she thought knickers was a vulgar word.

'Oh, no!' cried Nell.

The phone rang again.

'Leave it!' shrieked Georgia, running into her room again and slamming the door.

'Will you stop slamming this bloody door!' screamed Nell.

'Oh, God,' said Joanne, downstairs, turning up the TV.

That was when the house became Hell. No one could live in it but everyone lived in it. Nell and Harry were not speaking to each other. Nell and Georgia were not speaking to each other. Joanne and Georgia formed a sombre truce. Jack kept out of everything. For three days Dominic rang Nell in the afternoons and talked. Sometimes she thought he was crying. Once or twice she suspected he'd been drinking. Poor boy, he was devastated.

'I can't tell you how sorry I am,' she said, and added impulsively, 'You'll always be welcome here, Dominic, as far as I'm concerned. You're a friend of the family.' She coloured as she said it.

'Thank you,' he said softly. 'That's very kind of you.'

After that, he rang sporadically in the evenings, putting the phone down unless he got Georgia, who'd been waiting for Les to call. She just kept hanging up. Then he didn't call at all. Two days, three days, four, five, six. Nell thought about ringing him. She had the number. But she was too scared. She knew when she was being ridiculous. This is madness, she told herself.

And then he called, and she picked up the phone, and he was sweet and sober and wanted to know if she could say to Georgia that he was sorry for all the stupid things he'd said and the swearing; and tell her he was sending a letter, and please, not to tear it up but to read it and think of him. It was very important.

'Of course I will,' Nell said.

That teatime there was a big row between Nell and Georgia. It ended with Nell flouncing away into the back room, saying, 'I miss him!' in a strangled voice, banging the door.

'God!' said Joanne, slipping out of the front door.

'That does it,' said Georgia. 'I'm moving into the nurses' home.'

The letter came. It was huge and thick. Nell felt it, turned it over and over in her hands, sat motionless with it on her knee for a long time, looking at his writing on the envelope.

Georgia tried to tear it in two when she came home but it was too thick, so she had to go into the kitchen and get the big kitchen scissors and cut it up into lots of tiny pieces so that no one would ever be able to put it together ever again.

Nell didn't do anything. There didn't seem any point. In all her life there had never been anything as bad as this. Not even when her father died could she remember such absolute hopelessness. How stupid she'd been. She'd thought she could have that feeling back again, that thrill. It didn't matter that she knew she'd never have him. It didn't matter at all. Just as long as he was somewhere there. But now even that was gone and she couldn't stand it. She wanted to

338

do something, change something, kick something, scream. There was nothing she could do. It was like being locked in a black box with the lid tight down and the air slowly seeping away. She didn't cry, she just sat there, day after day, doing nothing. Sometimes she sat in the front room. Her eyes roamed about, over and over the things in the room, the settee of dirty cream plastic with a cracked, crazed-effect finish and maroon bias binding. Harry's trombone and a couple of mutes standing in the curved bay of the window with two hard-backed chairs piled with sheet music. Flowery curtains. Harry's trombone. The Chinese lady, who for ever would be Jenny Lim in Nell's mind, beautiful Jenny Lim who never came. The painting of a Dutch yard over the settee. A spindly plastic chair.

Then she'd get up, go into the next room, sit there for a while. A table with drop leaves. The mantelpiece of brownish marbled tiles, the gas fire. A huge pile of higgledy-piggledy old papers and maga-zines under a table in the corner, with the radio on it, a small transistor. Harry's chair. One of his paintings leaning up against it.

She'd sit there for a little while then go and stand at the window looking out at the back garden. Harry had installed a rustic seat on the flagstones under the window. Sandy, the big orange cat, curled asleep under the hedge. Everything still.

It was worse when all that lot came back. Weekends were a night-mare. Joanne and Jack tried to talk to her.

'Don't talk to me,' she snapped.

Things just went on.

The TV, the papers, everything was full of the Moors Murders. She couldn't stand it. Those poor children. It made her cry. Life was just horrible. People were just horrible. Horrible things happened, and there was loneliness. Everybody hurt. And then you died. Pointless. Terror lay beneath. The universe. What the hell was the point of all *that*? And him. Him, sitting there night after night in that chair, hateful ugly fat sod, I hate him. Hate him. Stuck with him. Stuck with him. Always got catarrh these days. Snorting it down the back of his throat, disgusting. When you live with someone you have to live with all their disgusting habits. Their snot, their smells. She shuddered. Look at him, his mouth a stern line. Miserable sod.

And Mam complaining she hadn't been. Who wants to go and see *her*, miserable old bugger? Still moaning on about those bloody deck-chairs. Look at him, bacon grease on his chin. I could throw up.

'So what is it now?' she said loudly, defiantly. 'What are you sulk-ing about now?'

He looked up from his paper. Horror and disbelief. 'Are you mad?' he said faintly, indicating with his eyes Jack, finishing his tea in front of the TV.

'Well,' she said, in the same loud voice, 'you don't wait till they're out before you go into one of your sulks, do you?'

'I'm not talking about this now, Nell,' he said.

Jack got out quick.

Harry said she was imagining things, he wasn't sulking. She was the one who was sulking. Pointless to talk, really. He went out. Nell sat there. Pots to wash. Sod them. Everything breaking up. No more Dominic. Georgia making enquiries about moving into the nurses' home. Joanne never there. Jack moody. Awful kids, moody little buggers, as if they're the only ones who can feel anything, they're the only ones with hearts that can break.

Week after week.

Week after week, a broken heart.

To live in that house, it was necessary to withdraw. Everyone had a withdrawing place, but Nell had the whole house to roam about in all day long. It took on her mood and incubated it like an illness.

Week after week.

The kids were going to see Bob Dylan at the Free Trade Hall. Everyone knew he'd gone electric and was getting booed for it. Everyone was expecting something to happen. Joanne couldn't care less if he'd gone electric, she loved him whatever. They wandered in and out getting their things. Nell told them all to stay together like she always did. She was harassed, looking for the scissors. They were always going missing, and it drove her mad. Even worse, Harry had somehow enlisted himself in the search for them and was scrabbling around in the drawers. All three of them, and the big cupboard, were wide open: years of official forms and certificates, balls of wool, old jars and bottles, things that needed mending and hadn't been got round to, old envelopes with things written on, shoe-shine and brushes, bits of wire, dog and cat toys, some slightly chewed.

'This is ridiculous.' Harry tugged on a tangled clump of green wire that lurched slowly out of the top drawer pulling with it a horrible clot of string and wool and a half-untangled bit of failed knitting with a squashed soft-centred chocolate stuck on it. 'When was the last time all these were cleaned out?'

'How do I know?' said Nell.

'Oh.' Harry started piling things on to the table. 'Well, I beg your pardon but I thought you might. It just seemed to me that might be feasible.'

'We're off now,' Georgia said, sticking her head round the door.

He went on piling stuff out of the drawers on to the table. 'This is ridiculous,' he said again. 'The only way is to take everything out and work through the lot item by item. Now. Is this needed?' He held up a small bent silver spoon with some kind of coat-of-arms on its handle.

'I don't know.'

'Well, is it?'

Nell bent down, put out both her arms straight, pulled a face like a terrified chimpanzee and swept everything off the table on to the floor.

There was a moment of stupefied silence.

Then Harry said, 'Well, that was clever, wasn't it?' and walked out.

The kids sneaked out, caught the bus into town. They hardly spoke of it. Why should it ruin their night? They'd been looking forward to this for months. Seeing Dylan was big. Bigger than the Beatles and the Stones and all the others. Living in Manchester was great for bands. Everyone came there, usually to the Apollo or the Palace. Dylan at the Free Trade Hall was funny, though, because that was where they had their speech days; for ever it would be associated with the heavy scent of flowers, real but so perfect they didn't look it, of heavily powdered old ladies, men of office, of lady mayoresses awarding prizes to girls in striped dresses.

Dylan was tiny. He walked on past the people sitting on the

stage, just him and his guitar, and sang. They had seats in the front row overlooking the stage on the left-hand side. So close you could see the sweat shining on his face, catch the nervous little movements of his hands. Joanne had been dreaming scenarios all week whereby she bumped into him in some odd fated way, the gods having brought him all this way from America and deposited him here less than a mile away from her school, less than three miles from her birthplace. Fate. She'd go with him. Her and Dylan. Soulmates.

And there he was standing in front of her in pointed boots singing 'She Belongs To Me'. If he'd looked up he would have seen her.

Harry and Nell sat in awful silence. The TV was on. Harry was reading a paperback, in gaudy red letters on the cover: *The Untouchables*.

They didn't speak for an hour.

Nell took the dog out. When she came back she made tea. She put his mug on the arm of his chair.

'Thanks,' he said.

They sat for another hour in silence.

'This marriage is a sham,' Harry said. 'It's over in all but name.'

'What are you saying?' asked Nell.

'In about six years' time they'll be old enough,' he said, refusing to look at her. 'They'll all be out in the world. More or less. That's when we should divorce.'

'Fine by me,' said Nell.

'Good.'

She thought about it for a moment. 'Well, if you're only staying because of the kids, you might as well go now,' she said.

'Didn't you hear what I said?' That tone she hated, as if she was a fool. 'I said we'll wait until the kids are a bit older. We're not the only ones to consider.'

'No,' she said, determined. 'I'm not staying if you feel like that. Oh, no, I'm not staying in a thing like that, it's too demeaning. What do you think I am?'

★

Joanne leaned on her arms on the balcony. It was hard to hear the music for the shouting. Poor boy! Sweat pouring off him. Most of the trouble was in the front of the circle: catcalls, whistles. Slow hand-clapping. He just kept on. Little man, frail, in a check suit. You couldn't tell at first what the songs were, but as he sang you worked it out. This was 'One Too Many Mornings', only it was nothing like the old 'One Too Many Mornings'.

'Well, he's made a right hash of that,' Georgia said.

He played 'Ballad Of A Thin Man' at the piano, and things got worse. Joanne could look right down on the back of his head. 'Oh, why don't they just shut their faces!' she whispered, through gritted teeth, and the noise went on and on and on, rising, till he was back at the mike, and the band were just waiting, not knowing what to do, the guitarist smiling, and the audience shouting and booing and chattering and laughing, just like being in a rowdy bar. Then a man's voice yelled, 'Judas!'

Dylan backed away from the mike, mumbling softly on, no one could tell what he was saying, till he called out in a hoarse voice, 'I don't believe you!'

A great cheer went up.

'You're a liar!'

Another cheer.

He turned to the band. 'Play fucking loud,' he said.

Great rolls of sound came swelling, welling from the organ, crashing over everything.

When they got home the TV was off. Their parents were talking seriously in the back room. There was no pretence of normality. The three of them sloped off upstairs, elated, disoriented.

'You didn't *really* like it,' Georgia was saying. 'You're only being pretentious.'

Joanne went into her room without a word.

Jack had had a great time. It was momentous. Joanne had been telling him that for days. It was the noisiest thing he'd ever experienced and his ears were still ringing. He replayed the concert in his head, sleeping fitfully, and in the morning his father wasn't there and his mother wasn't talking. When he came home from school that night his dad was back as usual for his tea. No one spoke. Late that night, from his bed, Jack heard them talking again. They talked for hours. Around two, he heard his mother come to bed but instead of going into her own room, the one she shared with his dad, she went into Joanne's. Ten minutes later, his father went to bed alone, and in the morning got up before everyone else and went off to work very early.

His mother came into his room. 'No school today,' she said. 'Your dad and I have decided to get a divorce. We're all going to stay with your grandma for the time being. Don't worry, it won't be for long.'

That night there was one of the occasional appearances of the Tailgaters at the Astoria Irish Club on Plymouth Grove: 'Personal appearance of the fabulous Tailgaters Jazz Band. From ABC Granada, BBC Television, Stage, Radio, Parlophone Records.'

Harry still played with them now and then. He'd taken his trombone with him and gone straight from work. It was a good night. He told Alex he was splitting up with Nell. Alex had split with Kathleen two years ago. You should have seen the bird he was with now. Black hair in a chignon. Spiky high heels. Thick make-up, short skirt. Thick acid perfume like a punch in the nose. Alex said he didn't regret splitting with Kathleen. 'In a way,' he said, 'you never get over it, but I wouldn't go back. You get another chance, Harry,' he said. 'Another stab.'

Another stab.

When he got back, they'd all gone and he was alone with the dog and cat.

They were stuck at Grandma's.

Getting to school was a nightmare, two buses. Joanne kept crying.

'Why?' asked Nell unsympathetically. 'You didn't like him.'

Joanne couldn't tell her mother she was crying because she'd faced the awful truth that as long as she lived she was never going to go away to America with Bob Dylan.

'I bet it's another woman,' Grandma kept saying in a sour voice. 'That's usually the way.'

Jack sneaked round to Auntie Vi's to tell her what had happened. She was sitting happily listening to her Donovan records. Auntie Vi loved Donovan. She said his lyrics were so wise for his age. 'Out of the mouths of babes and sucklings,' she said wonderingly, listening to 'Universal Soldier'. 'Out of the mouths of babes and sucklings.'

She cried when he told her Harry and Nell had split up. 'I remember Harry on VE Day,' she said, blowing her nose. 'He was dancing me round and round the yard. "It's over, Vi," he was saying. "It's over, Vi." And you're staying at your grandma's? Oh, you poor things! Where are you going to live?'

No one knew.

Next day Uncle Bob came to Grandma's. He'd walked over from Reddish. He was looking out for a flat for Nell, he said, but he wished she and Harry would get back together. His eyes were sad. He'd pulled a muscle in his back carrying a hod and was on the sick. He took off his shirt. Nell rubbed his shoulder with Deep Heat. He was thickening out a little now with age but there was not an ounce of fat on him. He had an old scar on his upper arm, where the Chinese girl had shot him in Malaya. He didn't talk much about Malaya or Java. Just now and again, like once when *The African Queen* came on the TV, the bit where Humphrey Bogart has to keep going down under the boat and getting covered with leeches. He said that was just what it was like, the leeches, horrible things, the leeches in Malaya, and how they drove his poor friend mad.

After a week, Harry knocked on Bessie's door and asked if he could have a word with Nell. She went out and talked to him on the path. He started crying. He said he couldn't stand being on his own. He missed them all.

'Please come back,' he said. 'Please come back, Nell.'

Oh, God, it was going to be so hard getting a flat and sorting everything out on her own and the kids and everything. She'd won. She didn't know what but she'd won something. 'I'll come back if you change,' she said.

'What do you mean?'

'You've got to stop sulking. You've got to stop dominating the TV. You've got to stop scoffing at their taste in music.'

He promised.

'Tomorrow,' she said. 'It's too late for tonight.'

He said he'd come for them next morning in a taxi.

It was a great relief to be going home. Jack couldn't wait to see the dog and cat. His father, arriving with the taxi, was shy. Everyone was shy. Everything was now supposed to be different. The taxi sped down Darras Road. They passed Auntie Vi and waved wildly to her surprised face. Harry chatted to the taxi driver. Nell hardly said a word, but she appeared to be in a reasonably good mood. By Hell, she was thinking, he'll do what he promised. He'll do what he promised. I've got this over him now. He knows I can do it. She wouldn't expect happiness. She'd learned her lesson. She was cured. There had been no great passion in her life and there would not be now. There was no Jimmy Lee. There was no Dominic Crohan. There was no one else but Harry and her dad, the two in the locket, a little gold locket that, now she thought about it, she realised had been lost in the chaos somewhere along the line. Probably in a drawer somewhere.

PART FIVE

Flying Home

31

Mary

Jack got his guitar in Soho. His dad knew the man in the music shop. His dad always knew people in music shops, it was like the Masons or something, a secret society of men in music shops all over Manchester and now London too, and probably other cities all over the place. His dad and the men in the music shops always talked very knowingly together. His dad would refer disparagingly to the musical tastes and abilities of Jack and his sisters. They were all a dead loss when it came to music as far as *he* was concerned. The rubbish they listened to. Anyway, Jack took the guitar home on the train and spent all day playing 'Green Onions'. It was summer. He had the house to himself. Joanne had dyed her hair black and left home and gone to university and was in London with friends for the summer. Georgia was at work. She had not gone into the nurses' home after all. She'd changed her hair from dark brown to copper-gold, finished with Les Tong, gone out with posh Roger from Alderley Edge, finished with him, and was now going out with Andrew, a trainee teacher.

His mum was at work too. She worked in a home for old people till two. She came in, tired, flopped down on the settee. She could-n't care less any more. She was dumpy. She wore any old thing. She shoved her flat, short hair back any old way.

'Jack, please,' she said, 'don't just sit around playing that thing all day.'

She lit a fag. Her matches were on her knee. One big brown hand held the fag, the other was limp on her knee next to the matches. She wore a brown two-tone nylon overall. Her new glasses were oval and black-rimmed, like Nana Mouskouri's. The smelly little dog's unprepossessing twitching head nudged its way on to her knee, next to the hand and the matches, his snotty eye gungeing up again. He had some sort of infection; she was putting drops in at regular intervals. She must wipe them again. Her spare hand went to his head and fondly caressed his twitching brow.

'You'd better go and see Grandma,' she told Jack. 'She's moaning you haven't been near.'

So he went.

It was about six miles through town on his bike. But he was used to it: he went miles on his bike. All his friends lived miles away because of school. He'd never gelled with the new place, not like his sisters. His life was outside it. He had a couple of good friends at school. He met them down town regularly and they just hung about. He hardly ever visited the family now. The last time he'd seen Uncle Bob and Auntie Eva, Uncle Bob had shown him how to play 'Me And Bobby McGee' on the guitar. The last time he'd seen Auntie Vi, she'd been nursing her first grandchild: Baby Max. Max was the child of Edward and Sally-Anne. Edward was fifteen. Sally-Anne was fourteen. Sally-Anne was a pretty little blonde thing in white miniskirts. Edward was just a big daft lad who liked kicking a football around in the road with his daft mates. Jean had been there. Jean was blonde and backcombed and lacquered. She'd been sort of engaged to a bearded man called Dennis for about ten years. Jack didn't really have anything to say to any of them. He felt himself not of this world. His soul yearned backwards, to antiquity. He looked upon the landscapes of his childhood and thought: Where does this stand in time? Why am I, this speck, speckled here on this particular speck of time out of all of it? What the fuck's going on? Where have I awoken?

And woke up.

His grandma he still had a soft spot for, not because she was any good, not because she had any hidden wisdom that only he could see. Only because he felt so sorry for her. She was ridiculous, a granny in a cartoon, a joke. 'She gets more and more like the Giles grandma,' that's what Harry always said, and she did. She looked worse than Les Dawson. Yet sometimes, sitting with her late at night out of kindness, with the telly drawing to a close and her sitting there by the sleepy fire in her shapeless creamy tent of a nightie, her teeth out, hairnet on, something in him would burn with pity for her. Poor old bag. Never loved or wanted in all her life. What was all that about? So it was always him who ended up going, in crisis, in times of weeping and distress, and Bessie was full of them.

She'd left Granada. The doctor said the pains she'd been getting were angina. She worried. 'Your grandma won't be with you this time next year,' she said.

Visits to his grandma were not sunny occasions. She got him to turn her mattress. It smelt stale. Her bedroom smelt stale. Jesus Christ. He was reading Camus, Sartre. What the fuck is all this about? She had a metal bucket full of wee in one dark corner of the room. Oh, sacred life. Jack's head whirled with the enormity of it. What was the point of his grandma?

That day, coming home, getting off one bus to get on another, he suddenly saw Mary Hood near Belle Vue. Hadn't seen her for ages. Must be, what? Six months? More. She was at a bus stop on the other side of the road. He crossed over.

'Mary,' he said.

She turned. 'Oh, hiya, Jack.' She smiled.

She looked older, completely different. Skintight white trousers, long hair, no make-up.

'Going home?' he said.

'Uh-huh. Been to your gran's?'

He nodded.

'How is she?'

'Miserable.'

She nodded. 'You never come to see us any more.'

'Well, it's a long way.'

'So?'

He shrugged. 'How's everyone?'

'All right.' She pulled her bag up on her shoulder. Her bus was coming.

'Do you wanna go out some time?' He didn't want it to sound too much as if he was asking her out.

'All right.'

'Meet you at the front of Lewis's tomorrow. Two.'

'OK.'

*

351

Jack and Mary never made their minds up about each other.

They went out together for over a year, spending most of the weekends together. They were doing their A levels, him a year ahead of her. All they did was walk. That was all. Just walked and sat in cafés drinking coffee. All about town for hours. Over the moors, over the scrublands where hairy ponies grazed in fields full of humming pylons, and great stone reservoirs lapped against the sky. And they talked, hour on hour. Scarcely a thing that came into their heads they did not say.

Sometimes he went to her house. Apart from the fact that Auntie Jill was always upstairs very tired, and a baby called Susan now crawled about like Swee'pea, one-toothed, everything was more or less the same. Square-faced Titch with his dazzling glinty-eyed smile. Ian and Gary in and out, bullet-headed, grunting, barely distinguishable. Colinette grown into a smily pixie. Mary still looked after them all. Everyone came to her for socks. It was an easy place to hang about in. The mess was cosy. It was funny with Mary. He couldn't really say he fancied her that much, though they spent a lot of time snogging in places like bus shelters and doorways. He kept getting an urge to cuddle her but it was a bit like how he'd felt about his teddy bear when he was little. You wanted to cuddle your teddy bear but it didn't give you a hard-on. Well, she was like that. So they more or less resumed their earlier relationship, mucking about, wrestling, rolling around, only now they were bigger. Anyway, she wouldn't let him do anything. He was a *Penthouse* and *Mayfair* boy, a stainer of sheets. His fantasies were not of Mary.

One day she said to him, 'Jack, do you think we're just going around together because it's safe?'

They were walking around Salford Docks, their arms round each other.

He thought about it. 'Well, yes, there's an element of that,' he said, 'but it's not the only thing.'

'Isn't it?'

'Well, not for me.'

'What is it, then? Why do we keep going about together? Do you ever think about it, Jack?'

352

'Of course I do. I go about with you because I want to. Because I like being with you. I don't know why you go about with me. What do you want to analyse everything for?'

He leaned his back against a wall and she leaned up against him, holding him round the waist. 'I keep thinking,' she said, 'if I wasn't always with you all the time, maybe I'd be going out and finding the love of my life.'

He laughed. 'But then again, maybe not.'

'No, seriously, though, when you think about it we really will have to split up. Otherwise how are we ever going to meet other people?'

He drew back his head, frowning. 'Don't you want to see me any more?'

'I do.'

'Well, what are you going on about?'

'I just mean, like, taken that we're obviously not going to stay together long-term, that means that one day we're going to have to split up. Obviously. I'm just thinking long-term.'

'Oh, shut up,' he said and kissed her. After a while she broke away, took his hand and they walked along in the shadow of the cranes.

'I've always liked your hands,' she said, stroking her thumb against his palm. 'You've got lovely hands, Jack. One of the nicest things about you.'

'Better than my face, you mean?'

'Oh, infinitely. Let's walk into town.'

They set off, hand in hand.

'Just think, Jack,' she said, 'one day we won't know each other.'

'Not necessarily. You always look on the sunny side, don't you?'

'Oh, yes,' she said, with a deep sigh, 'that's usually how things go.'

'Stop thinking. We're here now, and it's OK, isn't it? For now? What do you want?'

She had no answer.

Next week when he rang her up, she said she couldn't come out.

'Why not?'

'I just can't.'

353

She sounded funny.

'Don't you want to go out with me any more? Just say it, Mary, it's no big deal.'

'Oh, thanks.'

'No, I don't mean ... Anyway, it's not me that doesn't want to go out, it's you.'

'I don't feel well.'

'Well, just say so, then.'

'I've got a spot,' she said, 'I can't come out.'

'You what?'

'It's a really big one. I can't come out.'

He burst out laughing. 'Where is it?'

'On the side of my nose.'

'I'll come round anyway.'

'No!'

'Don't be stupid. It's only me.'

'No!'

But he went round anyway. Titch let him in. He banged on her door. She was playing very loud Jimi Hendrix. The door was locked.

'Let me in!' he shouted.

She came and unlocked it but retreated straight away to the far side of the room. The curtains were drawn. 'You're not looking,' she said. She sat on the bed with her left hand covering all one side of her face. He ran over and wrestled the hand away from her face. She had a big spot, red and angry.

'Oh, my God!' he cried, bursting out laughing. 'It's hideous!'

'Stop it!' She hit him.

'Oh, Mary, that is so ... Agh!' He made as if to vomit over the side of the bed.

'Pig!'

Jack rolled her over and got on top. She struggled.

And then suddenly she started to cry, big hot tears all down her flushed face.

'What's the matter? Hey.' He rolled over beside her and put his arms round her. 'What's the matter, Mary?'

She didn't answer, just gave her head a shake and wept against his chest for a minute or two while he rubbed her shoulder. Then she pushed him away and sat up. 'I'm all right,' she said, wiping the back of her hand under her nose.

'No, you're not.'

'I am.'

He lay with one hand behind his head, stroking her back with the other.

'We're just too ordinary with one another,' she said. 'You're just Jack. I do actually love you in a kind of a way, but not like that. It's like you're one of the kids or something.'

Jack was shocked. She'd never spoken intimately before.

'Mary,' he said, sitting up, 'you're getting too serious. Much too serious.'

She looked him in the eye. 'I feel awful, Jack,' she said. 'I don't know how I feel. It's all right, it's nothing to do with you.' She stood up quickly, went to her kidney-shaped dressing-table and wiped her face with a tissue. 'Bloody hell,' she said. 'Isn't matter bloody disgusting?' She shook something out of a bottle on to some cotton wool and started dabbing vindictively at the spot.

He didn't know what was wrong with her. He thought perhaps she wanted to finish with him and couldn't bring herself to say so. He could see her face in the mirror. In the dim light her lips looked heavy and swollen. Her eyelashes were stuck together in spikes. He felt a surge of tenderness, moved beside her in one step and took the cotton-wool ball out of her fingers. 'Don't worry about this,' he said, pulling her on to the bed and hugging her against him as tight as he could. For a moment he was overcome. 'I've never had a friend like you, Mary,' he whispered, right against her ear.

She put up her smeared face and kissed his lips. 'I know why I keep going about with you,' she said. 'It's because your face is so familiar in my mind I can't imagine the idea of being without it.'

He blushed.

He looked terribly angelic, she thought, with his soft, fairish-brown hair curling round his ears. She kissed his cheek. 'You're so sweet,' she said, 'so, so sweet.'

355

'I thought I was odd. You're always telling me I look odd.'

'You do look odd,' she said. 'I like you to look odd.'

The time came when he wanted Mary. It had crept up on him. When he could no longer lie down beside her without his leg sliding between hers, his hands seeking entry through some unguarded fold, some musky tunnel into her clothing or her body. She wouldn't let him touch her down there; but she stroked him through his jeans, smiled, undid the buttons of her cheesecloth shirt and let her breasts hang out for him. They were plump and round, filling his hands, with small pink nipples that swelled when his fingers teased them. Mary's breasts became his obsession. When he was with her he couldn't leave them alone. He sucked them by the hour and made them sore, sometimes in her room falling asleep cushioned against them, jerking awake, snuggling in again, between. And when they were not together, he thought about them. They got him to sleep at night.

'Here you are, love,' she'd say, spilling her bounty for him. And he would sigh and sink into it, as into a soft bed after many a battle.

Georgia was marrying Andrew in October; Jack was leaving for Durham. He'd done well. Four As. He was doing Classics. Couldn't wait to get away from the poky little box of a house that had never been home, from the deadly atmosphere. Things hadn't changed too much since his mum and dad's big break-up. Ha! Big break-up! They'd gone home and nobody had ever openly referred to what had happened; everything went on the same as before, only now everybody accepted nothing was going to change and just put up with it.

Harry and Nell still didn't talk. When Harry wasn't out playing, they still sat largely wordless, TV on, smoking, drinking tea, reading books. Nell knitted. Now and again she'd make cheese on toast and they'd eat it while watching the telly.

But maybe something did improve. Maybe the silences, though just as pervasive, became a fraction less tense. For the first time in years, Nell and Harry went on holiday together, to Killarney with Georgia. They rode on a jaunting cart round the lakes, and at some stage

Georgia snapped a picture of the two of them sitting on a fallen tree on the banks of Lough Lene. It had been a beautiful day, and Nell had bought herself a lovely jumper from some nuns selling knitwear.

'Take your big coat off, Mum,' Georgia said, copper-orange hair in bunches, orange minicoat, black stockings.

Nell wouldn't. There was a nip in the air towards evening. Harry had his mac over one arm, a fag in his hand. Suddenly, just as the shutter clicked, Harry kissed Nell's cheek. Nell smiled.

Nothing like that ever happened. They weren't that sort of family. Everyone smiled, gobsmacked. Georgia wound the film on. They stood up and walked back to the jaunting cart.

'It was weird,' Georgia told Jack later. 'I mean, they just don't do that sort of thing. What got into him? It was surreal.'

Jack was removing himself more and more from the family. He looked upon all things with a detached eye as if he'd already gone. October lay, uncharted, ahead. Once he'd gone he wouldn't return. Not really. Any returns would just be visits.

Mary said, 'You know when you go away? You don't have to stay faithful or anything.'

They were drinking coffee, a snack bar in town. He picked up her hand over the table. 'I know that.' He smiled and thought, I am too soft. Altogether too soft. It scared him. He had to go away from everything. Had to leave and start all over again. Some things would be a wrench.

'Jackie-boy,' she said.

'Master.'

'Sing you well?'

'Not particularly.'

She laughed.

'You know, Mary,' he said, 'I'm not coming back. If you still want to see me, you'll have to come with me.'

'You'll come home for the holidays,' she said. 'Everybody does. What you do when you're away is up to you. What I do when you're away is up to me.'

'You know what you'll do,' he said. 'You'll lose your virginity to the first lad who asks you out after me. That's what you'll do.'

357

She didn't say anything.

'Do you think ever in the annals of recorded time you and me'll sleep together?' he asked.

They looked closely at each other. 'Probably not,' she said. 'You're my brother, Jack.'

He felt a lump in his throat. This is me and Mary finishing, he thought. Or at least the beginning of it. He couldn't see her properly any more, she was too familiar. He didn't even know if she was good-looking or not. Looking at her face was like looking into a mirror. He swallowed the lump and grinned. He wasn't having it, lumps rising up in throats, a little lonely voice in his chest. Not having it.

'In the long run,' he said, suddenly vindictive, 'none of it matters anyway. I can cut off from you, Mary. I can go and not look back.' As he spoke, his conviction grew. 'I can. I can cut off from everything in my life up to this second and start all over again.'

He was still holding her hand across the table. Suddenly it was inappropriate. He let go, but she grabbed his hand back and held it in both hers and stroked. 'Stop acting hard, Jack,' she said.

'I'm not acting anything.'

'You are. You're not hard. You're soft. I know you.'

'You don't.' He stared her down. He always could. His big watery blue eyes swam. 'You don't,' he said.

There was granite inside, somewhere at his core, growing.

'I don't know what we are,' she said. 'I've never known what we are.'

'No. But you always thought it mattered. You always wanted to analyse it. I didn't. It just was. Is. But I can leave it. I can leave anything. I can leave you.'

'You're not hard, Jack.'

'What do *you* know?'

A shutter came down over his eyes. Nothing there. He was aware of it, a shade behind which he sat quietly watching, experimental.

'I don't know anything,' she said drily. 'Not a bloody thing.'

But when they got outside in the street it was just so natural to sling their arms around one another as they always did; if it was cold, for him to take her hand and put it into his pocket where it could be warm with his own. This was how they went about, each the other's teddy bear, bashed about and grimy, taken for granted. The time was coming when they must put each other on the shelf, in storage. Away with childish things. Ahead, real life. His mother was getting stuff ready for his leaving. She could darn a hole in a sock so that it was a thing of beauty. She was rushed off her feet, also getting ready for Georgia's wedding. It was going to be a big one. Church, bridesmaids, big car, reception for three hundred in a big hotel.

'Let's finish it, Jack,' Mary said. 'Let's try not seeing each other. For an experiment.'

'Fine by me.'

In two weeks they met up to compare notes.

'Of course I missed you,' he said, 'but it's only like a headache or something. You take an aspirin. It goes.'

'I don't know if I missed you,' she said. 'It was hard to tell because it didn't really feel as if you'd gone.'

'I missed your tits more than anything,' he said truthfully. They went back to her room and he caught up with them for ten minutes.

'Now go,' she said. 'It's like weaning, see? You get less and less each time.'

The week after, when he rang, she said she couldn't come out. Some excuse. Headache, something. Fuck you, he thought. I'm not calling her, she can call me. She didn't. He thought he might ring her Friday if she didn't call before. But then on Thursday came the phone call, at ten o'clock in the morning. He was still in bed so his mum took it. She came into his room and woke him up. 'Jack,' she said softly, 'something horrible's happened.'

Early this morning, half five, six.

The fire started in the kitchen, they said. Probably the cooker. Someone had gone down to make toast in the early morning, probably the boys, Ian and Gary, who always got up early. The grill was left on after the toast, the grease in the grill pan caught fire. This was speculation. The fire spread via paper bags and carrier bags, tea-towels, aprons, a pile of laundry, a wall of wooden shelves filled with packets and jars, to the door-frame, the floorboards in the hall, the stair carpet, the piles of stuff sitting at the bottom of the stairs waiting to be taken up, clothes, magazines, toys. He could see it all. It must have shot across these things and through an open door, to where the fat settee and overstuffed, cushiony chairs, comfortably leaking their highly flammable innards, waited in the living room.

Mary's mum and dad and Edward had jumped from the first floor and were more or less OK. Mary got off lightly, breaking an arm, an ankle and a collarbone and grazing herself all over. She had two black eyes from a roof-landing. She'd told the kids to stay under the window, she'd be back with the ladder, but the ladder was gone. Must have been stolen, it never turned up. Not that it would have made any difference: you couldn't have got a ladder past the flames at the downstairs windows. They were past saving, Ian and Gary, Colinette, Titch, Susan the baby; as was the house, even before Sally and Gillian first woke up, raised the alarm and got out of their ground-floor window. It was burned out to a blackened shell, utterly consumed.

Jill Hood's hair fell out. She had to wear a wig.

Nell went to see her, after a reasonable interval, in her new house. What could you say? Nothing. Mary was making macaroni cheese. Everything was new. New and strange.

'You know, Nelly,' Jill said, the thin-fingered hand holding her cigarette trembling, 'I keep dreaming about them. Every time I go to sleep I dream about them.'

'Oh, Jill!'

'Last night it was the one about the bus again. I'm on the fifty-three going up Mellands Road and it turns the corner into Levvy Road and goes on up to that bus stop just before Darras Road, opposite the shops. You know where the big wooden fence is? And it pulls up and there they are, standing at the bus stop at the end of a big queue, waiting to get on.'

'Oh, Jill!'

'All of them. Colinette's holding Susan's hand. Colinette, you know, in that little white dress with the blue flowers round the hem. And Titch just like he was, and Gary, and Ian. But then just as they get to the front of the queue, the conductor rings the bell. And we go off without them.'

'Oh, Jill!'

What could you say?

Jill Hood's fingers knocked against things, clumsy. A bag of nerves she was, though you didn't see her cry.

'I want them, Nell,' she said. 'I want them.'

The neighbours got up a collection. They went all round Longsight, all over Sutton Estate.

'They never thought to have a collection for me when I got robbed,' Bessie said sniffily. Somehow she'd come to associate the theft of the ladder with the theft of her deck-chairs. It was as if she resented the fuss made of the Hoods, the collection on their behalf.

'I can't believe you sometimes, Mam,' Nell said. 'I just can't believe you'd say such a thing.'

Jack was there, doing a job for her, fixing up her new curtains.

'Grandma,' he said, 'that is really near the mark.'

'Nobody sympathised with me when I got robbed,' she said. Another sniff.

He was furious. She can do her own sodding curtains, he was thinking, but he went on doing them.

'I don't know what you're looking at me like that for,' Bessie said, martyred.

'Grandma,' he said, finishing the job, 'how you can possibly equate the loss of two old deck-chairs with the loss of five children I cannot possibly begin to imagine. You don't know what they must have gone through. You don't know what Mary's gone through.'

'Oh, well, yes, you were always thick with that one,' Bessie said nastily.

It was too much, particularly as he was feeling guilty and jumpy about Mary anyway. He sprang down from the windowsill and walked out without another word. This bloody family. Had to escape. Had it to here with them all. Oh, God, all this! Leave. Far, far away. Mary too. How can Mary leave it behind? She can't. Not ever. To leave it behind he had to leave her. I can leave anything behind, he thought. Whatever it is, whatever, I can leave anything behind.

Nothing will ever get me. Nothing I can't do without. He couldn't wait to get away from her, inextricably bound as she was with it all, family, childhood, everything. Seeing her now was excruciating. He only did it because he was too guilty not to. He had to go through the motions for decency's sake, but he knew that to survive at all he must be there with Mary and feel nothing. It was his ultimate test, one that taxed all his mental powers. But he'd do it. He had to live, had to go forward alone, find something better. Panic fluttered in his chest if he even contemplated staying.

He saw her a few times more. They just walked about town, same old stuff, but she was different. It was as if she'd gone a bit stupid since the fire. You couldn't get much out of her. The last time he saw her before he went to university, they sat on a bus in the rain. She put her head on his shoulder and he put his arm round her. She looked awful. A cold sore was forming on her lip. There was dirt in the corners of her eyes and her hair was stringy. He kissed her forehead. Then he flooded. Tears poured down his face into her hair. All his good resolutions were gone. 'Oh, Mary!' he gasped.

'Ssh.' *She* ended up comforting *him*. Right there, on the bus, one last time, she flipped out her breasts and gave suck. But she couldn't smile, poor Mary. She couldn't laugh. She was so tired.

If I can leave this behind, he thought, I can leave anything.

Coming home for Georgia's wedding only stiffened his resolve. Already he felt like a stranger, the eye of a camera. Look at them, the family gathering in the churchyard in their finery. It's the women you notice. They are so colourful. Auntie Violet in bright orange, hair blonde and styled, big white handbag, white gloves. White handbags are the order of the day. His cousin Jean, backcombed, stiff-lacquered, sky-blue minidress with white accessories. His mother, legs pretty in rare high heels, white coat with cerise trim, cerise hat, handbag. The girls have made her wear eye make-up and she looks fantastic. Grandma in a very pale pink two-piece suit with a hat made up of lots of tiny pink petals, or maybe they are feathers, in spite of which she has not a hope in hell of expressing elegance. And there's Auntie

Eva, gaunt in dark shiny blue, black hair up, swirly. Grandma Caplin in donkey brown. Pretty Auntie Marjie with a huge royal-blue hat, Auntie Flo in scarlet, scarlet-lipped.

The men all look the same. Suits with white carnations. Uncle Bob still smart and handsome. Uncle Stanley absent. Uncle Stanley never goes to anything. There are children running about all over the place; Jack hasn't got a clue who most of them are, though many are obviously from the groom's side. That pretty girl with long blonde hair, looking about twelve, is Sally-Anne, who'd married his cousin Edward and now had her second baby at the age of sixteen. The boy with the flowery tie, that's Joanne's boyfriend. There's Andrew's mum, quite sexy. And the woman who is so obviously very important, the one in the big hat with the very high white stiletto heels, that's Patricia Phoenix, who plays Elsie Tanner in *Coronation Street*. She's related to the groom in some way Jack's not too sure of. She's providing her holiday cottage in Cornwall for the young couple's honeymoon.

Mary wasn't there. She'd been invited but she didn't come. He didn't see her again. They'd written to each other a few times but it was clearly over. Nothing was said and nothing was analysed. He didn't think that much about Mary, though now and then things that reminded him of her got stuck in his head. Those old Toby Twirl and Bobby Brewster annuals that had gone up with everything else in the fire. Round plastic counters, red, yellow, blue. *You Have Dropped Your Toys – Miss Two Turns.* A crowned frog wearing a purple cloak. The Dillypuff chuffing along, blowing its blue and yellow funnel: *Dilly-puff-puff-puff, Dilly-puff-puff-puff, Dilly-puff-puff-puff-puff-PUFF!*

The photographs his mum sent him later showed Jack in there with them all, one of the family, smiling for the camera. Georgia very beautiful in white dress and veil, Dad in a grey suit, Joanne looking awkward as chief bridesmaid in yellow satin, chiffon sleeves, tiara of yellow flowers, bouquet of big-faced daisies trailing slender white ribbons. Three little girls dressed the same, Wendy, someone from Andrew's side, and Denise, Flo's little girl with beautiful gold ringlets cascading over her shoulders. Andrew small and dark in a black suit; his best man tall with a black Beatle mop. They all had to stand on a kind of stone podium thing at the side of the church for photographs. All different combinations of people. And then, for some reason, Pat Phoenix stepped up for the photocall with the happy couple and the grannies. There were no grandads. Women lived longer than men. Dressed as if for a day at Ascot in a pure white short-sleeved coat-sort-of-thing with a lacy pattern round the hem and sleeves, her huge straw hat with its masses of spun-sugar pale flowers a grand thing like a full-dressed ship in sail, Elsie Tanner, brocaded, elegant, strode centre-stage in her six-inch stiletto heels, clasped her white-gloved hands loosely in front of her, positioned one leg in front of the other and slightly at an angle and completely stole the thunder from the bride and groom's poor fat dumpy wrinkly little grandmas in their donkey brown or pastel pink suits, their hats like sleeping birds upon their heads. The expressions on the faces of those grandmas, knowing that they were standing there with a big television star and knowing this was something special they could tell all their friends about, yet also resenting the fact that she had gone and got right in the middle as if she took precedence over all of them, when really she wasn't as close a relative as any of them and didn't have as much right to be there as them, did she? And she wasn't very talkative, was she? Not like she came across in her articles in the *TV Times*, like a good homespun northern woman who went around calling everybody love all the time, well, she wasn't a bit like that really. She was really quite grand.

32

Yellan's Knoll

All the kids had left home; it was time for a move, the last one, to the Yellan's Knoll house, east of town, where you could smell the clearer air coming in off the moors. It was a much nicer house, up steps, yellow and purple clusters of flowers hanging over the front wall, tulips and polyanthus and a silver birch tree in the front garden. Opposite was the bus stop into town, a field with cows and two or three horses, a distant pylon, distant houses. The back garden was long and raised up, two apple trees and a pear tree. There was a golf course at the back and a little wood they called the Spinney. The kids came to visit. Georgia was nursing and having kids, grandchildren for Harry and Nell. Joanne was making a mess of her life, going precisely nowhere in the eyes of everyone apart from possibly God; and their clever son, Jack, who turned up now and again with friends from the university.

It seemed to him they'd shaken down reasonably well together at last. Harry played in this band or that. Nell made friends with the neighbours as she'd never done at Ely Road. Next door's kids ran in and out of the house and played with the dog, the last dog, Moss, a sweet-faced, sweet-natured collie, who loved to sit quietly in the windowseat with Nell, red cushions, red curtains, big glass vase of bulrushes, looking out over the big field. She kept a pair of binoculars there for the wildlife in the field, the birds and rabbits and this strange bird she kept seeing very far away on the other side; she wondered if it could be a heron as it was very boggy over there.

'Oh, yes, I go to bingo now with Dor down the road,' she told Jack, dimping her cigarette in the ash-tray and lighting another one straight away. 'And once a week Marjie takes me shopping in her car and we always pop into Tikko's and have a cup of coffee and some nice little snack. They do these lovely vanillas and chocolate éclairs. We'll go down there tomorrow if you like.'

'OK,' he said, 'but I was going to do the rounds tomorrow.'

'Oh, well,' his mother said, 'we can do it the day after. When are you going back?'

He'd do Grandma first, get that over with, then Auntie Vi, have his tea there, finish up at Uncle Bob's for the evening booze-up. His mother told him the latest. Uncle Bob's son in Malaysia had written to him, very friendly, wanting to know all about his family in England. Bob had written back, but he didn't want to get involved.

He didn't see the point, it was all just raking over the past, he'd got a different life now. Eva didn't know he'd written.

'Auntie Violet still writes to his mother now and then,' Nell said. 'Jenny Lim. Our Bob doesn't know. Auntie Violet's got agoraphobia, you know. It's a weird thing. She's done very well, by all accounts, Jenny Lim has. She got married, you know, to the man she was keeping house for. I think he's dead now, I think he was a bit older than her maybe. I'm glad she did well in the end. He must have been a very good man because he brought up our Bobby's boy as if he was his own and had him very well educated. He's very clever apparently. He'd be in his twenties now. Oh, *easily*. Let's see, what would he be?' She started counting on her fingers.

His grandma was just the same as ever only deafer. She said it was getting terrible round here, rough as can be, you daren't go out at night. Nobody came near her. 'Your mam doesn't come. Our Bob doesn't come.'

Jack knew this wasn't true.

'I don't see your Georgia or Joanne. The last time Joanne came she had this horrible-looking lad with her. You know, she's a pretty girl, Joanne, I don't know why she can't get herself a decent fellow. This one looked like the wild man of Borneo. I suppose you're going to see Violet.'

'I'll pop in,' he said.

She looked offended.

'You know, it really is silly, Grandma, you and Auntie Violet not speaking all these years. She's only round the corner. All these years, you could have been friends.'

'Oh, don't you start.' Bessie snorted loudly, took off her glasses and started polishing them vigorously. 'Everyone's against me.'

'OK, Grandma. Sorry.'

What the hell? Poor old bat.

'That Edward, you know he's broken up with his wife?'

'I heard.'

'She's gone back to her mam's. She's got the boy, but the girl's living at Violet's for some reason. I don't know.'

'They were too young,' said Jack.

It was amazing they'd stuck it as long as they had. Edward was selling cars now, he'd got another girlfriend. Sally-Anne had another boyfriend. The little girl living at Violet's was called Sarah. She looked about six but he could never tell how old children were. Could have been anything. Very thin. Quiet.

Auntie Violet made a big fuss of him. 'Ooh, look at him,' she cried, gritting her teeth with pleasure as she hugged him, 'my lovely big boy. Oh, you're frozen, sit down, love. Here, next to me. Been to your grandma's, have you? Silly old moo. What did *she* have to say?'

Uncle Stanley smiled and grunted towards Jack, then said no more. He was watching TV.

Jean said she really fancied chips. A great big pile of them. 'Fancy chips, Jack? With chicken?' She went to heat up the chip pan, brought the potatoes into the living room and peeled them into an old copy of the *Daily Mirror* so that she could talk to Jack. She was thirty-five, a dental nurse. She'd never left home. She'd had a few boyfriends, one for years, and a couple of offers of marriage. But whenever it came to the crunch, she'd look around and think, This is my home. Why should I leave home? And suddenly the man would look like a stranger and she'd just know she couldn't go through with it. And, anyway, she was Auntie Jean, nearly a mother to Edward's chickens, little Sarah and big gruff lovely Max, who was in and out all the time.

Chicken and chips and peas. Individual sherry trifles in little pots. The gas fire roaring and the fat corgi called Ben gasping in front of it. Jean's hair longer, blonde and silky, and she was putting on a bit of weight. Always made an effort, Jean did, wore a nice scarf, put on pink nail varnish. Violet was severely agoraphobic, his mum had said, but he'd had no idea it was this bad. She talked to him quite cheerfully about it, laughing at herself even. 'I did go to the gate,' she said, 'last March. The daffies were out. I couldn't enjoy them. Still,' she smiled, 'I always think I've got a lot to be thankful for, really. When you look about you.'

Once, she'd said to him, 'Whenever I feel sorry for myself, I think of poor Jill Hood losing those kiddies; then I have a little weep and realise I'm really very well-off.'

Uncle Bob gave him a gin on the rocks as soon as he arrived. Uncle Bob drank gin in the day and beer in the evening. Auntie Eva had given up trying to stop him long ago. He was out of work, had been for years. His voice was permanently slurred, his manner mellow. His skin was getting ruddy but he was still handsome. They walked down to the pub on the edge of the odd concrete maze of an estate where Uncle Bob and Auntie Eva lived. Jack got completely pissed trying to keep up with Uncle Bob. Coming back, Uncle Bob got lost. All the doors looked the same. When they got home Auntie Eva made him a huge plate of scrambled egg on toast and pulled out the sofa-bed. In the morning he felt like death. Uncle Bob appeared at his bedside with a glass of gin on the rocks in one hand and a cigarette on his lip. 'Hair of the dog,' he said.

Jack figured he couldn't feel any worse.

He could.

After that, it was really just news from afar. Onwards and upwards. Research Fellow, Cultural Anthropology, oh, yes, sounded grand for Nell and Harry to tell people. University of Durham, then London, a whole other life, a whole other story, another twig on the tree. His dad on the telly with the Sid Lawrence Orchestra. Him sitting watching it with a whole load of people in someone's room in Notting Hill. Passing a joint around. 'Hey, look, that's Jack's old man, hey, looka that, he's sitting there saying, "Hey, pass the joint this way, man."' Everyone laughed.

My old man. News from afar.

Then beyond, to Italy, where the news came in from time to time like muffled bells.

The bells tolled for Grandma Caplin, but he didn't go home. The last time he'd seen her she'd turned into a bewildered little bird with a sheepish air. They tolled for Uncle Sid. That one hardly registered. They tolled for Uncle Stanley, whose family were plunged into a long period of deep mourning. Let it be recorded that not a word was ever spoken against Stanley by any of them.

When she was young, Nell had never dreamed she'd go and see all the places she saw with Harry on their holidays, now that the kids were gone and they could afford it. He'd been promoted: chief met-allurgist and product manager. He had a printed card.

Cyprus, Florida, the Rhine, Milan. Harry took hundreds of snaps, his camera always on his chest. They toured Romania in a coach and saw a poor huge brown bear in a cage, gnawing the bars. They vis-ited Bran Castle where Vlad the Impaler used to live. They toured the cities, Luxembourg City, Nancy, Ghent, Bruges. They made friends on the coaches. They visited the Great War Museum at Ypres, and Nell saw the trenches where her father had fought. They did Rome–Florence–Pisa–Venice. The Colosseum, the Vatican.

'Go and stand next to that Swiss Guard over there.'

'Oh, Harry!'

'Go on!'

They stayed with Jack, who was quite shocked at how old they suddenly looked, his mum homely in a long red wool cardy, his dad in a yellow-brown one with big buttons.

Over the Alps. The bus nearly fell over the Swiss–Italian frontier. Lugano, St Gotthard, Luzern, St Lary-Viella-Encamp. Andorra. Wild horses in the Pyrenees. Giant candles at Lourdes.

And Harry travelled the world with his work, sent to Russia, Japan, Singapore. To Pennsylvania to examine a hundred-and-seventy-five-ton alloy steel rotor forging. To Finland in November, Japan in December, via Anchorage, Alaska. There was a stuffed polar bear standing on its hind legs in the airport. He flew over the mountains of Alaska, over the icefield. To Tokyo, where he was fed by a geisha and saw a Shinto shrine. To the Japan Steel Works, Hokkaido. He was photographed in a kimono with a big group of English and Japanese business-men at the Hotel Takinoya, where his room was most pleasant and simple: a low table next to a window, two low comfortable chairs, a large futon, rush matting, screens. There was snow outside. He saw Mount Fuji from the air, flew over the desert, over Tehran. To Argentina. To Buenos Aires to the El Chocon power station to take X-rays. The cowboys drove their herds to pasture right through the power station.

The more he saw of the world, the more strange it all was, the more absurd, that all this should exist for no apparent reason, just some mad organism gone sprouting off in all different directions like a bacterium.

Suited Nell, him being away so much. She never liked having him about under her feet. He'd drive her mad when he retired; it was something she didn't like to think too much about. Watching bloody sport all day. Golf. Endless football. Tennis. More golf. He was still a pompous sod. He was getting very grey suddenly. He'd started wearing glasses. Anyway, she felt quite happy alone. Taking the dog for his walks. Going to the shops on the bus, sitting in the Black and White Café waiting for the bus back, having a coffee and a sandwich, save her having to muck about when she got back. The Black and White Café was nice because it sold proper sandwiches with plain white bread and you could smoke. She hated all this health stuff: half the places you went in now didn't even do white bread at all, it was all wholemeal; stuff with great big lumps in. Felt like a brick in your stomach. They're infringing my civil rights. If I want to eat white bread I should be allowed to. It really annoys me, that does. Well, she wasn't going to be dictated to by the health police. And what pleasure was there in a sandwich and a coffee if you couldn't have a fag afterwards? Made her really angry, it did, people telling her what she should eat. None of their bloody business.

Harry had a heart attack.

Spring snow in the Spinney. A rainbow on the golf course. People came out with toboggans. Out in the back garden on the buried lawn, a mound of dirty snow was all that remained of the snowman their grandsons Adam and Josh had made with next-door's kids a couple of days ago on one of Georgia's visits. Harry had been out there helping, all wrapped up, woolly hat on his head, the dog beside him looking up at the progress with apparent fascination, tail wagging. Now he stood looking out at it, whistling briskly, some daft old thing, 'Ukulele Lady', jovial. He was putting in a bit of time on his trombone with a local brass band and was in costume. Peaked cap like the Sally Army. She did love a Sally Army band, she could still remember so clearly hearing them in the snow on Cross Street when she was a little girl, the Christmas carols and the tambourines, and everyone's breath coming out in clouds.

Harry turned away from the window, stopped whistling and sat down in his chair. 'I feel really tired,' he said. Then, 'Oh, Nell, I feel weird!'

He took a strange deep breath, put his head down on the arm of the chair and groaned.

It wasn't one of those dramatic heart-attacks you see in films, where someone clutches their chest as if stabbed and drops. It was just a deep, deep pain, a huge bottomless ache. His face turned to putty.

Harry never groaned, never. It had to be bad for Harry to give way and groan.

They kept him in hospital for a week, and he came home with medication and a huge sheaf of stuff to read about what he should and shouldn't do, could and couldn't eat. The main thing was to stop smoking, they said. And she had to start buying all this *low-fat* stuff, which she resented, but what could you do? Obviously, Harry had to watch it now. It wasn't as if he was that old. Fifty-six. They told him to lose weight. Well, that happened anyway, of course, with all this low-fat stuff. And sugary stuff they had to watch too, like lemonade, which he'd always loved. Now he had to have it diluted. Poor old Harry, he made the best of it. The worst of it was bacon. He loved his bacon. Once a fortnight he was allowed it on a dry butty as a special treat. It was worse than the cigarettes, and that was terrible. Sometimes he'd lie awake and fantasise about bacon and egg, toast and dripping, a pork chop. If he passed someone's house and the smell of frying bacon wafted out, he'd salivate. Cutting out the cigs was easy compared to that. He did it gradually, cut it down over a month or two, then went on to cigars for a bit, Hamlets, which he stayed on for about a year before he quit.

He thought a lot about death, ordering his affairs in his usual methodical way, just in case. He didn't talk about it. He and Nell just carried on as ever, watching the telly, taking the dog for walks, holidays, business trips, playing the odd gig with this band or that. They never had talked about anything much, and they certainly weren't going to start now. Actually he was feeling very healthy, but Death was always there now, an imp sitting on his shoulder, neither bad nor good, simply there. He picked up the Lethbridge stuff at a sale on gala day at work. They reminded him of a book he'd been fascinated by years back, *An Experiment With Time* by J. W. Dunne. Now, what had happened to that? It had the same sense of seriousness. You felt these were not just loonies but rational men conducting rational enquiry. And they made him think hard about the truth that his death was a fact. But he wouldn't tell anyone. He'd feel a fool. All these things were behind his curtain. His pendulum made out of a cork. He could play with it, doing experiments (sometimes it seemed to work), late at night as long as he wanted, because Nell had moved into the other bedroom permanently now. His snoring was too much for her. Anyway, he liked to read for a long time in bed with the light on and it kept her awake. She was glad to get away from him. Many a time he'd come in late after playing and just get straight into bed, didn't even bother to clean his teeth. Well, what sort of consideration was that? Who wanted to be bothered sleeping with men when they got old and baggy anyway? Even Marlon Brando put on weight. It was too hard to hang on to your looks. She'd never liked hers anyway. Squinty. Glasses. Leathery skin. Easier just to give in. Eat those choccies. Put your feet up.

Jack was at home for the christening of Georgia and Andrew's third child, another boy, John. Everything was strange and distant, so far removed now from his real life, which in these years was intricate and lurid and secret. He just sort of floated in and hung about on the edges.

Both sides of the family were there, mingling with Georgia and Andrew's friends. Georgia's house was very modern, full of dark red Habitat furniture. Grandad's old rocking-chair, which she'd received upon her marriage, had been painted purple and upholstered in blue.

His mum had gone completely grey. She wouldn't try the dips, she thought they were unhygienic, everybody poking bits of carrot they'd already bitten into the same pot. Quite disgusting, really. Ugh! No, she couldn't!

'I suppose I'll have to go and sit with your grandma,' she said, 'or she'll sulk. Look at the face on her.'

Grandma never moved from the red Habitat sofa all afternoon. When Nell sat down next to her, she said, 'Have you seen how much that one over there's had to drink?'

'What one?'

'Her over there.'

'That's one of Georgia's friends.'

'Well, that's her fourth glass of wine already.'

Jack looked around. Andrew's mum still slim and sexy. Joanne all dressed in black as if she was at a funeral, looking uncomfortable. His father grey, roly-poly and jolly, sitting chuckling with the baby on his knee. 'Oh, you are a Rabelaisian fellow!' he was saying to the baby. A long white christening gown trailed on the carpet.

'He was never like that with us, was he?' Joanne said to Jack.

'Never.'

'How's things, then, Jo?'

'Great. Really great. When are you going to come up?'

She was living with her boyfriend in the middle of nowhere somewhere, keeping ducks.

'Some time.'

As the afternoon wore on, Bessie sank further and further into the sofa, seeming to widen and spread as if she was melting. Her eyes disappeared behind her glasses. Her *cheeks* seemed to widen. The thin line of her mouth sank deeper and drooped down on either side of her chin. All in black, her black bag at her feet, the black stub of her umbrella extruding, radiating ill-will.

'The Giles Grandma,' Harry whispered to Jack.

They laughed.

Every time a passing child washed up against her legs, Bessie made clumsy stamping movements, her face appalled.

They had a new car, a yellow budgie called Cheeky, a hedgehog that lived in the garden. The dog was starting to look old. They grew marrows and tomatoes, photographed the hedgehog in the brassica patch. They were very proud of their vegetables. They grew King Edward spuds, spaghetti marrows, blackberries, *huge* cabbages, courgettes. They'd just had a lovely holiday in Malta. Goatherd and goats went past their flat every night a little past sunset. A nice little flat. Deckchairs outside. Cacti across the road. Gozo. They hired a Mini.

Then Harry has to go and have another heart-attack. After all that giving up smoking, and grilling the bacon, and low-fat this and polyunsaturated that, he goes and has another heart-attack.

Well, now, he wasn't really supposed to play after that. But Harry stop playing? He could still hit G. He couldn't do the all-night runs, the big jobs, but there was many a band around falling over themselves to have Harry Caplin guest with them. And at home he still played in the bath. The trombone still sat ready, faithful at his feet by the side of his chair, like a big golden dog, ready to be picked up at a moment's notice. He couldn't fly this year, so they booked a cottage with Georgia and Andrew and the kids at Quernmore near Lancaster and took the dog. It was a pretty cottage on an old estate. Harry played with the kids in the garden all the time, a jolly grey-haired roly-poly little grandpa. He loved his grandkids. He was always picking them up, sitting them on his knee. Much too soft with them.

It wasn't too far from Morland. Nell and Georgia had a day there. Georgia had to bully her into it because she was too nervous, scared to spoil it somehow, it meant so much, she couldn't explain; just it would be so awful if they'd ruined it, you know, the way places got ruined? But they hadn't ruined Morland. It was all there. Well, more or less. It was a lot bigger, of course, some grotty new houses, a big clump of them. But when you got into the middle it was the same, the ford was still there. The ducks swimming. And the old church and the gravestones and the old dark path where Bobby used to frighten her. And Granny and Grandad's house, on a corner, a white porch on the front, black and white painted windows. Four windows. A neat, good-looking, well-maintained house. Trees on one side and a wall around it. She just gazed. She daren't knock. She photographed the unmarked graves, two long grassy mounds, side by side. Around them, weathered old headstones and a Celtic cross. Behind them, the old stone wall, ivy-clad. She took a photograph of the Morland sign on the way out.

It was their last holiday together.

Harry died.

374

He got very tired. Started sleeping in late. That was unlike him. Once or twice she became anxious and went up to check on him. It was then she found out he'd started locking his bedroom door at night. 'Do you think that's sensible?' she asked him.

'It's just a precaution,' he said. 'The number of break-ins these days.'

'No, I mean with your heart.'

'Oh, you can't be always worrying about that.'

Till the night came when she was going up to bed, and heard a sound. He'd gone up for an early night. Earlier she'd been moaning about taking the dog out, she didn't feel like it, so he'd taken Moss out for his last walk of the day down to the postbox and back. Then he'd felt tired and gone up. It was only about half past ten, quarter to eleven now as she passed his door, but there was nothing on the telly, might as well go to bed and read her book.

Sounded as if he was moving around the room.

Then: THUD.

'Are you all right, Harry?' she called.

A pause. 'Nell!'

The door was locked. 'Open it, Harry.'

Sounds. Harry, crying. 'Nell!'

Stupidly, as if anything was going to change, she kept trying the handle. 'Harry! Open the door, Harry!'

Sounds. Harry. Pain. Thud thud.

'I'm trying to get to the door,' she heard him say.

'Harry!'

'I'm having a heart-attack!'

'Hang on, Harry, I'm getting help!'

She ran downstairs, picked up the phone, dialled.

They were coming. People to make it right.

'Harry! Harry!'

It had all gone quiet.

Bloody door.

Stupid, stupid man! Locking his bloody door. What does he think's going to happen? 'Harry!'

Nothing.

And Harry was gone.

Harry was gone.

The house was full of people. Such upset. She did hate all this, people tramping up and down the stairs, all looking serious. Oh, please. She was so tired. Can't I just go to bed? I was on my way to bed. The doctor. The police. Mrs Livesey from next door came in and offered her a drink of brandy.

'No, thanks,' she said, 'I don't like it.'

'Go on,' said Mrs Livesey, an elderly woman who'd been widowed for about twenty years. 'This is not an ordinary occasion. It's for your nerves.'

Even the smell of it made her want to heave.

There was a horrible tight feeling across her chest. 'I feel awful,' she told the doctor, this dreadful sinking, sinking, sickeningly sinking feeling inside. Oh, Lord God, don't let it. Not now. Please. Much too tired to deal with this now.

'Drink it,' the doctor said. 'That'll do you more good than any number of pills.'

Nell sipped. Hideous.

Forced it between her teeth, nearly gagging.

She couldn't understand why Harry wasn't there. In any sort of crisis he'd know what to do, or at least he'd pretend he did, which amounted to the same thing as far as she was concerned. He was never a man for putting his arms round you in a crisis, not for a long time anyway; all that had gone out of him years ago. But he would have been strong. His brown, bloodshot eyes would have remained steady. 'Calm down,' he would have said, in his deep, obey-me-I-know-what-I'm-talking-about voice. 'Calm down. That's the first thing to do, isn't it?'

She stood in the kitchen. On the back windowsill was a set of red scales and some paintbrushes in a jam-jar. She was putting the kettle on. Mrs Livesey appeared. 'Don't you do that,' she said. 'Come in here and sit down. Do you want me to call your Georgia?'

'I'll do it,' Nell said.

She handled it. Her voice cracked up.

Georgia said she was on her way. She'd tell the others.

Nell sat on the settee. The dog lay on the rug.

Harry, I don't know what to do.

I'm all alone.

He's not in Russia. He's not in Argentina. He's not in Japan. He's not in Amsterdam, he's not in Chile, he's not in France, he's not in Pennsylvania or Canada or Singapore ...

She played this game for a while.

He wasn't coming home.

He wasn't on an aeroplane.

He wasn't getting up and going to work.

There were his shoes, a sock stuffed in each one. By his chair. There was his mug with the dregs of his tea.

What did it mean?

They all came. Georgia first, then Bob. He said, 'I'll come if I have to walk.' Mam gave him the money for his fare because he was on the dole. My lovely little brother, she thought, seeing him walk up the path. My lovely horrible cheeky little brother. His hurt eyes all wrinkled and bewildered.

'All right, Nell?'

'I'm all right, Bobby.'

A quick hug. They weren't a hugging sort of a family.

He did the carpet for her. Down on his knees scraping the dog hairs off the red carpet with a rubber thing. The house was such a tip and all these people coming. Georgia and Joanne were both there. Jack flying in. God, everything changed too suddenly, nothing the same ever again. What now?

Jack came home. A hug at the door.

Jack was shocked again at how old his mother looked, how frail she felt, her sloping shoulders and light bones, and yet she was putting on a lot of weight, getting thicker and rounder, fatter round the shoulders. Just different. An old grey woman in glasses and baggy clothes, always her eyes full of strange humour, a smile summoned easily.

A young priest came to visit. So lost he didn't know what to do. Afterwards Nell made fun of him. 'Poor little bugger!' she said. 'He felt awful, you could tell. He hadn't got the foggiest what to do. He doesn't know me at all. He didn't know Harry. I mean, what can you say? Poor thing, he's just been told he's got to come here and be sympathetic and he hasn't got a clue what to do. I mean, it's not as if we even go to church, your dad didn't believe in any of that. He just sat there, looking at me like this.' She leaned forward earnestly over the arm of the chair, a watery smile on her face, grey eyes moronic. 'Just looked at me like that, not knowing what to say. Poor sod!'

Everyone laughed.

Adam, who was nine or ten, said, 'I feel as if Grandpa's got there now.'

'Look at this,' Joanne said, showing Jack a cutting from the local rag, last Christmas. 'It's the last ever picture taken of Dad playing.'

Harry was playing Christmas carols with a brass band in the rain in the market square: 'Members of the Yellan District Brass Band who played Christmas music in the Market Square on Saturday.'

The picture showed the band standing in a semi-circle playing, a crowd listening under umbrellas: a mixed bag of men in caps, children, a girl in a poncho and miniskirt. Dad, standing there with his mac over his uniform. Harry Caplin, who had once received a telegram from Louis Armstrong. 'Old Pops is happy to hear that you are working on the bill with my All-Stars ...' Who'd wowed them in the Cavern Club when the Beatles were lads and played support to the Tailgaters.

Harry Caplin, trombonist.

Jack remembered a time when he and his father had driven down to a jazz club in Wolverhampton. Everybody knew his dad. In the break, the band came over one by one to say hello, and the trombonist, who was drunk, leaned close to him and said, 'Your dad taught me everything I know. Everything. If it wasn't for your dad I wouldn't be a jazzman. Your dad? Brilliant! Brilliant jazzman, Harry Caplin!'

No jazzman's funeral for Harry, though. No solemn soulful procession through the streets of New Orleans, with Louis, and Joe Oliver playing that glorious lament. No tolling bell. Harry was cremated in the little concrete chapel at the crem. The whole family came, both sides, and an army of men from work whom no one knew, all standing together looking sad. Joanne in a shabby coat, the collar unconcealably frayed, a dress borrowed from Georgia, feeling she'd let him down. All that money he'd put into her education. She was remembering a letter, a long time ago, when she first left home. It shouldn't have been anything, it wouldn't have been anything much in some other families: a letter from your father in which he says he loves you. But in this family it was a hushed, peculiar thing, one not to be acknowledged openly but received in silence. It said, right at the end, after all the ordinary stuff, 'We are very proud of you and, although we never say it, we love you very much.'

It had shaken her. It shook her now.

Auntie Marjie weeping. Auntie Flo saying, 'I'm glad our mam died before him. She couldn't have coped. She thought he was a genius, you know.'

His cousin Jean came over and stood beside him as he stood outside waiting for his lift back to his mum's house for the do. 'You'll never guess what, Jack,' she said. 'Don't laugh, I know how it sounds. I've become a Jehovah's Witness.'

Jesus.

He smiled. 'That's OK, Jean,' he said. 'Just don't try and convert me, right?'

'I'm not daft. I'm serious, Jack. Don't laugh. It's the most significant thing that's ever happened to me. It's as if everything's fallen into place at last.' She chuckled. 'Poor old Jack. Oh, my God, he thinks she's a nutter. Well, I'm not.'

She's not.

'Well, I can't follow you, Jean. It's just not my thing, but good luck with it.'

'I can see how it looks,' she said, 'the magazines with all the pictures, they're just to make it all look attractive to people initially, obviously there's a lot more to it than that ...'

'No, no, Jean, it's the pictures that put me off ...'

'But really, Jack.' She looked at him, right in the eyes, very deeply. 'You mustn't worry. Because you *will* see your dad again. And he's OK. I promise you, Jack. I know. I *know.*'

'Thanks, Jean. Thanks.'

'Nothing really ends, Jack. It's fantastic.'

The card on her flowers said: 'Good night, God bless, Uncle Harry.'

None of the Tailgaters came to Harry's funeral. Nell had not thought to inform any of them. It simply did not occur to her. All that was so long ago. She didn't know even where they all were. Maybe some of them were dead, like Harry. Poor little Johnny Miller died. Nice quiet man. It was left to the Manchester jazz community to pick up Harry's death from the press. The local Gorton rag:

TROMBONIST DIES AT 60.

One of Gorton's most successful musical sons, Mr Harry Caplin, has died aged 60. Mr Caplin, a well-known jazz trombonist, was born in Clowes Street and played for the Tailgaters Jazz Band. He died of a heart attack. He leaves a wife, Nell, also Gorton-born, and three children, Georgia, Joanne and Jack.

Jack had to stay on a couple of weeks. Had to accompany his mother to the Social Security or wherever it was she had to go to sort out her pension, and then, oh, God, all the stuff with the will and the money, a fucking horrible nightmare. Had to accompany her to see his grandma, still there in the same chair at the side of the fire but looking much smaller and older and far more sorrowful, if that were possible.

Nell had just explained to her that Harry had left her five hundred pounds in his will.

'For me?' Bessie's eyes filled up with tears. 'Oh!' she cried, bursting into a full flood. 'Oh, isn't he a good lad?'

Only Bessie had a good open cry over Harry.

33

A Legacy

And who will be there tomorrow, at Nell's funeral?

Mary Hood, for one. They delighted in telling him.

'Guess who's coming to the funeral. Your little girlfriend. Weren't you two sweet?'

He'd laughed. All such a long time ago.

Georgia said Mary Hood was living somewhere out past Ashton. 'Did you know she'd kept in touch with Mum? Funny, isn't it? Well, she didn't live that far off, really, I suppose. She's a teacher.'

'Is she OK?' he asked.

Mary Hood could quite easily not have been OK.

'Seems to be.' Georgia's tone had been mildly surprised. 'Well, that'll be funny, won't it, seeing *her* again?'

'Funny seeing all of them,' he'd replied, and yawned.

In the back bedroom at Georgia's now, all spread about on the spotless cobalt-blue duvet, Jack's spoils. Nell's diary. His dad's things taken from behind the curtain in his mum's back bedroom, a secret musty place, the smell of the mouthpieces and mutes, dust-covered, the musical notations beautifully written in his father's fine flowing handwriting. The autographed programmes, Louis Armstrong, Jack Teagarden, Earl Hines, Ella Fitzgerald, Oscar Peterson, Peanuts Hucko, Dizzy Gillespie. A home-made pendulum and the books of T. C. Lethbridge. His dad had been dowsing for the afterlife. So strict and straight and solemn, yet secretly dowsing for an afterlife before he died. His atheism had been only skin-deep. He believed in ghosts. Jack remembered his dad telling him about the case of Jimmy Lee, who was haunted by his brutal father, how he'd encountered him again many years later in a pub one night after a gig. Jimmy Lee had married and had kids. But his nerves were shot, his dad said.

Jimmy Lee had told him that after they'd moved out of the house the haunting stopped, but that his father had attacked him one more time years later, at the top of St Paul's Cathedral when he was on holiday with his family. He'd felt the old man standing right behind him, felt the malice; then he was gripped and lifted and slammed against the parapet. His father was trying to throw him over. Those standing nearby saw a man struggling desperately against an invisible force. He survived, of course, because he was there to tell Harry. But he was always scared. Always knew the evil old bastard was still out there somewhere. Only Harry hadn't used the word bastard when he told Jack, because he didn't swear in front of his children.

'I wish my dad could have come back,' Harry had said. 'I'd have loved it if my dad could have come back from the other side and seen me play.'

A strange occasion. A small self-effacing tear had appeared in the corner of his father's eye. Jack only ever saw his father cry, if you could call it that, twice. The other time was when he was watching a film on TV, *Never Take No For An Answer*, about an Italian peasant boy and his dying donkey. The boy was taking the donkey to church to be cured. A tear rolled down his father's face and was wiped away. Two times only. His mother he'd never seen cry, it was beyond imagining. She just developed a very deep line between her eyes instead.

Downstairs he heard his sisters' voices, back and forth. 'I'm doing shepherd's pie for tea, so it's easy,' he heard Georgia say.

Jack turned his attention to another pile of stuff. His great-grandfather's Archbishop's Certificate in Scripture, some poems handwritten in ornate script on brittle blue paper, 'On The Death of George Acklington, died 13 January 1927. On Those Who Perished In The Ship *The Ellen Vannin*.' By S. J. Holloway.

On Those Who Perished.

A scrap of paper: 'Private S. B. Holloway. 8767. C Company, 3rd Cheshire Regiment.'

And Grandad's spyglass, a pair of old opera glasses, dark wine-red, and a little locket, oblong gold, with two pictures in, Grandad and his dad when young.

A card for Coral Bingo and Social Clubs.

An old postcard. Four fluffy Persian kittens all looking one way. Up in the corner the words 'Was that a mouse?' He turned it over. 'My dear Nell and Harry hope you are well not so bad myself. Love from Dad xx'. Funny writing he had. Square, with big gaps in odd places. Fancy sending a postcard just to say that. It was from Rhyl, all yellowed and stained. Someone had scribbled a circle on it with a pencil. Letters, likewise stained and yellowed, delicate. From a time before the ubiquitous biro, the uneven, faded textures of ink. The writing so like her own. '... we have taken all our flashes down I am sending mine home I might not be able to get any when I come on leave ... Tell Mam not to worry the war in the east will be over before ...' Uncle Bob. Georgia and her friend Dhani had met him one day in the post office quite by chance. Stocky old man in a muffler. They'd had a little hello-how's-so-and-so kind of chat, and Georgia had said when he'd gone, 'That was my uncle.' Her friend had been horrified. She couldn't believe it when Georgia said she hadn't seen him for about fifteen years, even though he only lived about three miles away. She kept saying, 'Your uncle? Your uncle? And you haven't seen him for fifteen years?' in a tone of absolute horror.

'You know what Asians are like about family,' Georgia said.

A letter: Jay D. wrote from Silver Springs, Maryland, he'd received his Tailgaters discs and they were even better than he'd expected. 'That's some mighty fine horn you play, Harry.' He'd given them a spin already on his new show and the response had been warm. Says he's mailing a package of dubs. Bix. Tea. He'd been waiting for 'Melancholy Baby' from *Birth of the Blues*. He's been in Columbus, Ohio, spending a wonderful few days with Jack, Charlie, Ray Bauduc, and Jack's sister Norma, who is now playing piano with his group. Thanx for the dope. Keep pitchin' with that horn.

Thanx for the dope? My dad?

And photographs, a crammed box file. Nelly and Harry's foreign holiday snaps all mixed up with old stuff, his long-haired self in the seventies, Whit Week Walks, the May Queen and her train, his sisters' school photos, Grandma on the waterlogged Blackpool sands; there are no photos of Bessie till she is already an old woman, or looks it at least, graceless and portly, wide-faced, standing with legs apart, feet firmly planted on the ground with those flat, sensible shoes. Chin wide and shiny. Nose bulbous.

Auntie Bennet and Auntie Molly, the one where Bennet is standing behind Molly's chair. Bennet was young on this, about fifteen, hadn't learned to do the hair and make-up thing. His cousin Jean had the good one of Bennet, the big one where she's laughing vivaciously at the camera with all her dark cloudy hair bushing out around her small pointed face. Auntie Bennet was mythology, like Helen of Troy, legend, like Marilyn Monroe.

Photograph: cracked tombstone: 'Here lyeth ye body of Mary Walker. Late wife to Randle Walker, of [something indecipherable that looks like Herne vry Rexall]. She was buried the 20 day of September 1671. And mary Walker there daughter was here buried 25 years before her mother, being a virgin. As You Are Soe Ware Wee. But As Wee Are, Soe Shall You Bee.'

He'd liked that, Harry. He *would* photograph a thing like that.

He never had gone back. He'd visited, of course, many times. He was a good son. But he never went back to Manchester to live, as his parents would have wished. Life went on without him.

34

Rain on the Swannee

Funny, really, given the early reversal of roles she observed in her parents, the woman controlling the finances, the man at home cooking and looking after the kids, that the feminist revolution so completely passed his mother by, Jack thought. It all came too late for her. She couldn't see much in it, really, though they had a point or two about housework and so on. But she didn't want to work. The idea of having to get up and go out there every day horrified her. She had wanted Harry to take care of all that. He was supposed to look after her, like her mam and dad had done before. She didn't want to know about money. She refused to learn to write a cheque. Each of them tried patiently to go through it with her, step by step. Half-way through it: 'Oh, no, this is not for me. Not for me.'

She got rid of the car, even though she was well on with the lessons. Not for me. Not for me.

Jack, on the plane going home at last, flicked here and there in her diary: 'I go in with Marjie now. Shopping is less of a choir.'

He smirked.

How had his mother become Nelly the inebriate woman? How was it that her writing deteriorated regularly throughout the book from her usual neat curly script to a large sloppy scrawl? How many times had her children tried to puzzle it out, together occasionally after a few glasses of wine? If Mrs Livesey had never come in at that moment with that brandy. If that doctor hadn't said, and he was a doctor so he must know, '*That* won't do you any harm. Far better for you than pills. It'll help that tight feeling in your chest. Don't worry, that's only nerves. Perfectly natural to feel like that at a time like this. Terrible shock to the system. This will soothe your nerves. There, you're doing very well, just sit tight and drink this.'

I can't write much about my poor old Harry. Nothing can make up for him. People are being good. Des sent Darren round to see if I wanted any gardening. I've been asked to Dor's for Christmas dinner. Now that was nice of them wasn't it? Terrible weather. Hope we are not in for a horrible snowy winter.

I find I sleep very well with a small brandy at night.

I can't describe it. He was half of me. I don't feel whole. 37 years is a long time. It's like half dying yourself. It's awful. I suppose time makes it better I don't know. I always knew I had a good one. Deep deep down I always knew. Not that he was perfect, of course, oh no. Well, who is? Still so much hassle with red tape, I'm sick of it. All this horrible money stuff, I hate it. I must go a bit careful until things start coming in. In my mind, you know Harry, I'm always talking to you. I would love you to have seen New Orleans just once. You should have gone, you know. You should have. Life's not long, you're here and you're gone. You should have gone.

Getting colder. Rang Mam. She's annoyed because I'm not going to Georgia's at Christmas. Said she'd miss Harry for that. So mad I had a little weep. Raining all day. No post. Rang Vi. She seemed a bit untalkative, I think it's because I'm not going to Morland with her and Jean but I'm not putting old Moss in kennels. He's got rheumatism. Must ring our Bob about going to Joanne's with me. I'm not going on my own. Violet's not well. Dreamt of Harry last night. I miss him so much. I'm not having my brandy tonight. Yes I am. Rain rain rain. What's happening with my pension? Still waiting for my marriage certificate to arrive. Endless red tape. Last night my brandy made me sick so I'm not having any tonight. Marjie came in for a cup of tea. Looks like it might snow.
Snow.

Marriage certificate came. Looking at my marriage certificate took me back to when we were young, me and Harry. I hope he's in a musical paradise, meeting all his old jazz idols. Please let him be somewhere like that.

Let him be happy. More snow. Coldest night for thirty years. The pipes froze up, Pete from next door had to come in. No water. Rotten night. I'm writing out my Christmas lists. Thursday a horrible day. Thick blizzard. Poor old Moss doesn't want to go for his walk. No papers. I'm having my brandy tonight, I don't care. I put the tree up, I'll do a few balloons, make it look festive for the kids. Feels really horrible writing Christmas cards just from me. Not supposed to send one to Jean, Jehovah's Witnesses aren't allowed them. Daft, if you ask me. It would have been Harry's birthday tomorrow. And I am hating the thought of wrapping their presents up, because Harry was with me, and chose most of them, and we both carried them home.

What is this?

The plane was shuddering. They had to put on their seat-belts. He sipped his coffee.

Who was this happy couple? What was this, the deep missed content of a strong marriage? I'll take you home again, Kathleen. When you and I were young, Maggie. Dear old Dutch.

He remembered that time after the death of his father. The looks exchanged between himself and his sisters. What's she talking about? Because from the moment he died, Nell fell in love with Harry, and as far as she was concerned she always had been, and never again as long as she lived would she refer to him with anything less than total and unconditional affection as the best of men.

'So what was all that?' Georgia demanded behind her back (no one had dared challenge her to her face). 'What was all that misery they put us through? If it was all so marvellous and wonderful, what were all those horrible silences? All that moaning, *endlessly* moaning, your bloody father this and your bloody father that. Why couldn't they just have got on together and given us all a bit of peace?'

'It's guilt,' Joanne said. 'She realises he wasn't such a bad old sod after all, and now it's too late. All that time they wasted being horrible to one another when they could have been nice. She can't face it, so she has to make this fantasy.'

'I always thought,' said Jack, 'that she'd have been quite glad to get rid of him in a way. She loved it when he went away.'

'I know. Couldn't stand having him under her feet all day. She was dreading him retiring.'

'Poor old Dad! He was really looking forward to his retirement. He'd have made the most of it, you know what he was like, always some hobby on the go, he could potter for hours. And he never even got there.'

'Poor old Dad!'

Jack yawned. The air was tight in his lungs. Strange life, him stuck up here in the sky in a shuddering bus with wings, reading his mother's diary. Why did people write things down? To talk to you. Whoever you were who got to read the pages, for whatever reason. To leave a trace, though where that trace would travel remained a mystery.

He was sleepy. He put on his headphones. Jazz. 'Clarinet Marmalade'.

He took out from an inside pocket a poem he had written, a
screwed-up bit of paper, and read:

> *Sleep is taking my soul*
> *Sleep is drawing me down.*
> *Sleep the ravelled sleeve that knots up care is smothering me.*
> *Sleep wants me.*
> *Sleep is my secret lover, whispering seductive sweets in my ear.*
> *Sleep is jealous, clawing me back.*
> *Sleep is my final resting-place, my ultimate end*
> *Bravely I go down armed into sleep, my sword upon my hip.*
> *Sleep is endless labyrinths, dead ends, fearsome beasts.*
> *Sleep is moments of glory, and wonder, and the awe of the*
> *   ineffable.*
> *Sleep is a madness.*
> *Sleep is an eagle soaring with my eyes from a wild peak out into*
> *   endless air.*
> *Sleep is an impossible drop.*
> *Sleep is a fathomless step.*
> *Sleep pulls. Pulls my arms and legs and eyes.*
> *Sleep is my illness.*
> *Sleep is where we all end up, alone, higgledy-piggledy levelled,*
> *   sucking our thumbs.*
> *Sleep has no respect.*
> *Sleep has no shame.*
> *Sleep's honest and a sadist.*
> *Sleep says look your fill, like it or no.*
> *Sleep is my vice and my addiction,*
> *My whisky in the jar.*
> *Sleep is where I go down into the pit and discover the devil within*
> *   and the devil without.*
> *Sleep is bliss.*
> *Sleep is my conscience, and*
> *sleep has no morals and no mercy and takes no prisoners.*
> *Sleep is another shore.*

'You get it from my grandad,' she always said.

Harry's birthday. I think of you always. I always will. Very lonely. Some of the money has come through. Christmas Eve, wrapped up presents. Had a job blowing up the balloons. Hope I'm not spending too much. Met one of his pals from work in town and he upset me talking about Harry on his last day at work. Getting the house ready for the kids. I'm having too much brandy tonight — I don't care. Night bless Harry. I miss you. My best mate. God bless you, Harry. I love you. Lonely, Harry. I love you Harry. Always. No one else for me. No one.

If Marlon Brando came and fell on his knees before her and asked her to marry him she'd say no. She'd choose Harry. She always would have done. Marlon Brando would have been completely wrong for her. Anyway, look how fat he got. Worse than Harry, far, far worse. Dear old Harry wasn't that bad!

Mam says Bob's not well. He had a pain in his back and had to go for an X-ray. I worry about him. I don't think Harry need have died. I think I should cut down on my smoking, I keep getting a tickly cough. God bless Dad, God bless Harry. I must take care of our grandchildren. Thick snow all over the fields and the poor lovely horses out in it. Something terribly lovely about all this snow. Look after my family. Let me stay well.

Every night she said, 'Night-night, Harry. Night-night, Dad.' She needed to feel them both still there with her somewhere, holding her hands in the darkness. But maybe it *was* all just nothing. Oh, God, she wasn't clever, she didn't know. It wasn't fair. It wasn't fair that people should have to put up with this separation, that it should be written into the pattern. Why? Why should that be?

Strange feelings. She broke a bulb in the light, trying to change it. Bob's X-ray came out good. The money came through.

Poor old Harry if he'd lived could have gone to New Orleans, I always wanted him to go. It's no use saving for old age, you may never reach it.

*Harry, thank you for remembering me after. Bless you for money.
Awful, simply awful time. Moss ran off up the golf course. Came back
all cringing. Some man just rang for Harry, he didn't know. Violet's in
hospital with heart trouble and lung trouble. Coughing blood. Rang
Mam. She harked back still to Edward and the deckchairs. Toothache in
my front bottom tooth. Quarrel with Mam. Dor says the brandy's good
for me. Perhaps he's with his dad, who he loved dearly. Moss's legs are
stiff. Give my love to Dad. How good he was, Harry, how well-off he
left me. Good and kind. He put up with me. I was never demonstrative
but he always knew that.*

I'll give 500 each to the kids.

Brandy was nice with Tizer. The trick was to use a beaker, so you
could use loads of Tizer to mask the taste of the brandy. That way
you could get it down and it was even rather pleasant.

*I'm watching celebrity golf on the telly, Harry, before I go to bed, it is
Jerry Pate and Lee Trevino, remember how we used to enjoy it especially
Lee Trevino, he's always funny. Wish you were here with me watching.
There's an old couple in the crowd. Why couldn't it be us? My best
mate. You had to go, just when things were right. We were better off
than we'd ever been. I've had my tooth out. You would have a laugh at
it. But it's not too bad. As you used to say, I'm no chicken, am I?
Georgia's on at me all the time to go and live with them. Well, not with
them but near them. She keeps going on about these flats just round the
corner going down to the shops where she lives but I don't fancy living
round there. Not knowing anyone.*

The nights got lighter, the weather improved. She went to bingo
with Dor and Sheil and Marjie, and she looked after Pam's kids for an
hour each night while she went to work. It was OK. 'I have a feeling he is happy now,' she wrote one day. She didn't know where the
feeling came from. But then one night calling down at Dor's for
bingo, waiting for her lift, she heard Dor and George bickering in the
hall. Stupid. They don't know. Why do people waste time falling out
and having rows? It was a dull night. They didn't win anything. Dor

and Sheil moaned on all night about their husbands, stupid things, like he never washed the surfaces down after he'd done the pots, or he hogged the good bits of the paper, or he only ever wanted one thing and hadn't he got it through his thick head by now that she'd rather have a cup of tea any time?

Tactless, going on like that in front of her.

I don't know, she thought, getting back that night to the dog and the budgie, what's the point?

'Even the little budgie greets me,' she wrote, drinking her brandy and Tizer.

It's no fun coming in to an empty house. He should be sitting in his chair with his trombone on its stand. She would have given anything to hear him play it now.

Quiet. Listen.

She could almost hear it, again, that sound, Harry playing his trombone. And it was sad like rain on the Swannee, drifting grey, and it was beautiful too. Oh, God, it was just so beautiful! Tears came into her eyes. The lovely sound. Where had it all gone? Home and Bobby and Violet and Mam and Dad, Peacock's and Harry and Morland and Jock. It was as if the reel of life rushed backwards in the twinkling of an eye, till she was looking through a door in Peacock's, she and Kitty O'Neill, and there were two young men in the lab eating their sandwiches, one dark, one fair, both OK. And the dark one looked up at her and smiled.

> Oh, oh, Antonio, he's gone away,
> left me on my ownio
> all on my ownio . . .

This was it. This was getting old and lonely with a bottle. Here, pushing sixty, old and grey, softly wrinkled and alone, she burst into tears.

My God, she's aged, Jack thought, next time he saw her. This is terrible. She was completely white with an old-lady frizzy perm, looking more and more like Bessie. He couldn't believe her rounded shoulders and podgy middle. Look at Andrew's mum, about the same age, still trim, does her hair nicely, wears nice clothes. She got married again and went to live in Chicago. You couldn't see Nell marrying again. She just wasn't up for that sort of thing in her cream-coloured padded jacket and baggy red Crimplene trousers with a crease down the middle. She was boozing. She'd stopped getting the *Daily Express* and started buying the *Mirror*. She watched the real lowest-common-denominator stuff on the telly, avoided depth or challenge of any sort. She hated unhappy endings. She stopped bingo, stopped knitting, stopped reading.

She did crosswords, head down in the heat of her crowded house, the living room a hotch-potch of crocheted rugs, the red carpet always matted with Moss's hair, the paintwork sandy-brown and the walls, where they were not plywood, a brownish wallpaper consisting of starburst patterns. Harry had had a phase on woodwork towards the end of his life and built the network of shelves around the gas fire, for books and ornaments, the black pottery candle snuffer from Waterford in the shape of a bird, the china shepherdess who used to have a partner, an old man reading a newspaper, Darby and Joan sitting on a bench, all the little Chinese things she collected. Wally dogs. A couple of fancy plates. A framed picture of a cat sleeping in a window. Etching of Highland cattle Joanne brought back from Glencoe. A few dried bulrushes in a brass jug. Moss on the crocheted cushions on the windowseat looking out over the field.

Sometimes she fell asleep in the chair and dreamed. Daytime dreams were more vivid. Harry came. 'I've had a heart-attack, Nell,' he said.

The next time she saw him he was looking young and well.

The girls nagged her continually about her drinking and smoking. She went on to vodka, so they wouldn't smell it on her breath. She chewed orange peel, a tip remembered from her auntie Lal.

'I think Harry may be annoyed at me,' she wrote in her diary.

He hated drunkenness in women. And she was spending too much.

'It's really bad, Jack.' His sisters on the phone. 'Honestly, I'm not kidding, we were there last weekend and the amount she was knocking back. She thinks you can't tell when she's pissed and it's so bloody obvious. Swears blind she's only had Orangina.'

'I thought her voice was slurred last time I rang her.'

'Of course it was. *God* knows how much she's spending on booze each week. And she lies. "Oh, I know my voice sounds a bit funny, ha ha, it's because of this gap in my teeth." When you know damn well she's been knocking it back all afternoon. There's no other explanation for it. And it's getting earlier. Typical drunken self-deception, she thinks it's not really drinking as long as you put enough Tizer with it.'

Well, you're well out of it, Jack. What can you do? Your work is important. You are a keeper of the flame. You work among the archives, you are a scholar. The god Lugh looks down upon you. You are important. Of course Jack had a life so far away, another place altogether with no points of contact. There were other stories in that life, other people, enduring friendships, affairs that lasted for years, dramas, triumphs, disasters, of which his family knew nothing.

News from afar: Georgia had had a little girl. Photographs were sent.

Moss died, causing another flurry of phone calls from the girls: 'I'm really worried, Jack. You know how stupid she was about that dog. What do you think? She says she won't have another one. Do you think we should just go and get her one anyway? She says this one's irreplaceable.'

Auntie Violet died. She'd been very ill for a long time. Jack didn't go over for the funeral. Later he heard how his cousin Jean, now living alone after a lifetime of looking after her parents and nursing her mother through her final illness, had been burgled a month or so after the funeral, and how the burglar had turned out to be Max Mulcahy, Edward and Sally-Anne's first child, now aged eighteen and in with a really rough crowd. Edward and Sally-Anne were both married to other people now, both with other children. Max had been staying with his auntie Jean for want of anywhere else to go. He'd tried to make it look like a proper break-in, only it had seemed a bit suspicious that the whole house had been ransacked apart from his own room, which wasn't touched. Also, the window through which the burglar had gained access had been broken from the inside. He wasn't a bright lad. Word went round that he'd been flogging a stereo system in a pub on Hyde Road. But there was no solid evidence. What really hurt, Jean said, was that in order to take the stereo, he'd first had to remove the framed photographs of his grandparents, Violet and Stanley, that were sitting on top of it. Did he not realise how hurt she would be? At a time like this?

'He is not my son,' Edward said.

God knows what had become of him, Jack never heard.

Grandma, who had not attended Violet's funeral, died about six months later at the age of ninety-four, from falling off a stool she was standing on to reach up to the top bolt on her front door when she was locking up one night. The meals-on-wheels people raised the alarm when they got no answer the next day. They had to go in the back way because Bessie's body was blocking the front door, filling the tiny lobby where she'd lain all night. It was winter. The house was icy. The stool lay beside her.

God, please, thought Bobby, first of the family to be summoned, let her have died straight away. Don't let Mam have lain there all night knowing she was never getting up again, feeling the bitter cold creep through her bones hour upon hour.

Everyone wanted Grandma's old Catholic statue. Her Jesus statue. It's just so kitsch, Georgia said. It's kind of so bad it's good, sort of thing. But it was Jean who got it, which was exactly as it should be, as she was the only one to whom it meant exactly what it was meant to mean. Bob didn't mind. He thought it was nice that Jean wanted it, a kind of posthumous reconciliation of the warring factions. Anyway, Eva wouldn't have had it in the living room.

Bob and Eva were divorced now, but not so that you'd notice. They still lived in the same house and sent out Christmas cards from Bob and Eva.

And now Nell.

When Georgia and Joanne arrived, they found a half-empty bottle of vodka on top of the fridge in her narrow, messy kitchen. Little stashes of booze around the house, after the fashion of her auntie Lal.

35

Too Quick

Waiting for the funeral. Sitting in his grandad's rocking-chair, now nice dark old wood again, its upholstery wine-red. Thinking of all the things that were no more. The Tretchikoff had gone. Where did that Tretchikoff go? You used to see that picture around a lot but you don't any more.

'It was definitely the booze,' Joanne said. 'You can't just go from being teetotal to hitting the bottle like that. Too much for the system.'

'Well, *and* the fags,' Georgia said. 'She never even made an attempt to stop, you know. Even after my dad died.'

Jack stood up and looked at his face in the mirror. His hair was receding a little on his temples. He'd been thinking about Mary Hood on and off all night. She'd be there. He'd heard things of her over the years. That she'd gone to college. That she'd got married, had a daughter, and was now divorced. That she was a teacher. Had she let herself go? Of course, he was always seeing her as she was when she was sixteen. The trouble was, he hadn't got a place for Mary. She was more than a friend. She'd never been a lover. He didn't know where to put her. He had two old photos of her, taken when she was about fifteen. In one he was giving her a piggy-back down Green Grove. In the other she was standing in Albert Square, wearing a striped scarf and clutching her shoulder-bag. In the first she was smiling. In the second she wore a come-on-get-on-with-it kind of face. The nearest he could get to describing the feeling whenever he encountered one of these pictures during an infrequent clear-out was that it was like looking at himself a long time ago. Strange. Very fond. But not in a missing kind of a way, although every now and then over the years, he'd experience a terrible deep pang of loss. But never anything he couldn't handle. He had not pined. He knew her almost too well for that. She just was.

He thought now that he'd loved her then but not realised it, and that if he'd had any sense he'd have hung on to her for dear life. But it was too late. Whatever close childish love they'd had belonged to that time. The thought of meeting her frightened him. He almost felt they would be obliged, given the right circumstances, to go to bed with each other. It was certainly a possibility. What if she looked awful? What if she thought *he* looked awful? But then again, no, it was a stupid way to think. They were no longer the same people.

'Ready, Jack?' said Georgia.

He looked around in the chapel. All the old faces, Uncle Bob and Auntie Eva, Jean, Edward and his wife, Robin and Wendy. A lot of the neighbours had come. Auntie Eva's hair thick still, once so black, now so grey. Her large dark eyes looked kindly out from a pale, sunken face. Incredibly, Uncle Bob was still handsome, hair close-cropped and greying on his craggy head. He had a bald patch at the back. 'Bob got all the looks,' that's what Mum always used to say. 'Poor me and poor Vi got none, he got the lot.'

No Mary Hood.

Obviously she hadn't made it. What had Georgia said? It hadn't been definite, had it?

Then he saw her. For God's sake, she didn't look any different, it was Mary. She saw him. He waved. She waved back. They smiled.

Then it all started, the same as his father's, the pointless little talk from a priest who'd never known his mother from Adam, the tears slowly slipping down his sister's faces, the surreptitious sniffing, all eyes drawn to the coffin with its lovely burden of flowers. My mum is in the coffin. My mum.

Little Nell.

Nelly the inebriate woman.

She asked in her diary: 'What's it all about?'

I'm watching a play on the telly about the First World War, Harry, I know it is only a play. But what is life all about? Young soldiers dying horribly at eighteen, life cut short, and even if you live to a ripe old age, it's still short. It flies. You may as well make the most of it while you've got it. It doesn't seem long since me and you were first courting, and you said you were crazy about me and would I marry you. You were twenty-two with black curly hair, and I said yes. Then we had our babies, and they grew up and we grew older and greyer and became Nana and Grandpa. You died, and now I'm on my own. It was too quick. Much much much too quick. Oh, use the time you've got! Use it!

A tear slid down his own face. He wiped it away with his hand.

So what was it for, Harry? Why did we live? To keep the earth populated so mankind doesn't die out. But why? Ants don't know why they make an anthill, but they do it. They have to. The one thing that makes it worthwhile is love. Why do people waste time falling out and having rows? It's a waste of living. But it is life.

Outside, they all stood about waiting to get into the cars. A football coach (Robin), a car salesman (Edward), a Jehovah's Witness dental nurse (Jean), a woman who looked like Tyne Daly in *Cagney and Lacey* (Wendy), a nurse (Georgia), a gardener (Joanne), and a teacher (Mary Hood).

There she was. Mary. Of course it was her. The girl he'd left because to look at her was to be reminded of sorrow. He walked straight up to her.

'Hiya, Mary.'

'Hello, Jack.'

They both laughed. Close up, of course, she was older, a few crinkles round the eyes, just a look. Her hair was dark, bobbed.

'Sorry about your mum,' she said. 'She was always my auntie Nelly.'

'You look fantastic, Mary.'

'So do you, Jack.'

He wanted to hug her but it seemed too late now.

'Are you coming back to the house, Mary?'

'Can't, Jack, I'm afraid. Got to go and pick my daughter up. I'm a taxi service. She's fourteen. You know what they're like.'

'Not really.'

She grabbed both his big hands in her small ones. 'But you're not going back just yet, are you? Joanne told me. You must come and see me. We can go for a walk on the moors.'

'Try to stop me,' he said.

'Good. Georgia's got my number.'

Then they did hug, a close hug that could have gone on and on if she had not broken away and said, 'See you, then,' and walked off in her long grey coat and boots to say goodbye to his sisters.

Back at the house, the neighbours were drinking sherry.

'Well, she was a good friend to me,' said a young woman with short fair hair.

'My kids loved her,' said another.

Uncle Bob stood staring out of the window, a fag in his hand.

Jean came over and touched his arm. 'Uncle Bob,' she said. Her hair was cut short and neat, her clothes were smart. Her eyes were raw. She was a crier, like her mother.

'Hello, love.'

'How are you, Uncle Bob?' She gave him a hug.

'I'm not so bad, love.'

'Uncle Bob, can you come round to see me tomorrow night? I've got some things for you.'

'What's that, love?'

'Photographs and things. Some of Auntie Nelly.'

'Aye, love, I'll pop round some time.'

'Tomorrow, Uncle Bob? Tomorrow night? Because I've been doing a lot of sorting out and I've got one or two things I wouldn't mind a hand shifting. There's a cupboard in my mam and dad's old bedroom ...'

'All right, love.'

'Aw, thanks, Uncle Bob. I'll get you some beer in.'

She was starting to look just like Violet when she smiled, he thought. She'd take over now, all the old family stuff Vi had always kept, the pictures and letters and cuttings. She'd keep the archives.

Georgia and Joanne were washing glasses and giggling in the kitchen.

'Perhaps we should have given them brandy and Tizer,' Joanne was saying.

'Vodka and Orangina!'

Jack wandered about with a glass of wine.

'Look what we found,' Georgia said. 'Little stashes of sweets all over the place. In drawers. Really kiddie-type sweets.'

'M&Ms. Revels. Jelly beans.'

'What was it like seeing Mary again, Jack? I notice you fell into one another's arms pretty quick.'

He smiled. 'It was … strange. I'll tell you what it was like, I just realised. It was relief. I'm just glad she survived. She looked … fine.' He ended on a note of surprise.

'People do survive,' Joanne said. 'Mostly, anyway.'

'It's Uncle Bob I feel sorry for,' Georgia said, hanging up the tea-towel. 'He's the last.'

36

Two Sons

Granny and Grandad, Mam and Dad, Violet and now Nelly. All gone. When Bob walked into Jean's house on Sutton Estate, for a moment it all came back. His dad's walking-sticks, which it seemed had absorbed a fragment of his father's soul, were in the umbrella stand in the tiny lobby. He remembered getting home from Malaya, how the first thing he'd noticed was that Dad had taken to carrying a walking-stick.

Ben, the fat corgi, barked and capered.

'Come in, Uncle Bob, come in,' Jean said softly. 'Thanks for coming. Cup of tea or a beer?'

He said he'd have a beer. When she'd settled him by the fire with a pint mug in his hand and a plate of fancy cakes and biscuits on the coffee table, she sat down opposite and leaned forward, looking steadily into his eyes and speaking very earnestly. At first he thought she was going to try to convert him.

'Uncle Bob,' she began, 'I'm sorry I fibbed to get you here. I *have* got a couple of pictures for you of my auntie Nelly, but that's not the real reason I wanted you to come.'

As what she was saying dawned on him, he began to feel afraid, in a peculiar exhilarating kind of way. All the symptoms of nerves started up in his body.

'You know your son in Malaysia? Bruce?'

He knew.

'What's this about, Jean?'

'You know after all these years, now he's, what? forty?, if you were given the opportunity and you knew it was what he wanted, would you want to meet him?'

Bob sat with his hand slowly stroking the fat corgi, which was pressing against his legs. 'You know, Jean,' he said, 'I think I would.' He swallowed.

'Well, he's here, Uncle Bob.'

'You're joking.' But he knew. 'You're joking.'

'He's upstairs. He'll only come down if you want him to.'

'Jesus,' he whispered.

'Shall I tell him to, Uncle Bob? Shall I? I'll leave you both alone for a bit. It's up to you, but he'd *love* to see you. He'd *love* it.'

Bob said nothing for a long moment. He remembered his son. Small brown curled fingers, a podgy hand, the arm lying along his shoulder.

A strange tight feeling across his chest. He swallowed. 'Don't leave him sitting up there,' he said.

She beamed. Her eyes danced. She got up, went to the door and left it open, her feet pattered upstairs. Muffled voices. Sounds. Bob stood, ready, waiting. Then the creaking of a floorboard on the landing, footsteps softly running downstairs.

A small Malaysian man stood in the doorway. A suit, tie, white shirt.

'Daddy Bob,' the Malaysian man said, and laughed.

Bob laughed too. 'How you doing?' he said.

Bruce came into the room and Bob stepped forward and grasped him by the hand, clapping him on one shoulder. 'Good to see you, good to see you,' he said, and the tears started up in his eyes.

'It's all right, Dad,' Bruce said, a tear running down his nose. 'It's all right.'

It was achieved. Jean was upstairs having a little weep. It had become possible now that her cousin had attained such prominence in the business world of Kuala Lumpur that he now travelled on a regular basis between Malaysia and England, and had written once more to his auntie Violet asking if she would approach his father on his behalf with a view to meeting, but his auntie Violet was dead. Jean had replied.

She knew Uncle Bob. If she approached him directly he might say no. Anything for an easy life. Wasn't that the family motto? Hadn't it always been? Don't strive. We are little people, destined only for little things. Take the safe way. No risk. No way was she giving him the chance of backing out. This had to happen, and she was going to make it happen whether he liked it or not. She was going to intervene. In the end it clashed with her auntie Nell's funeral, but who could have foretold that auntie Nell would die?

She went down after a while. They were drinking beer, the two of them, sitting on the settee. Jean took photographs and cried, communing with the spirits of her mother and father, Violet and Stanley, whose photograph smiled down from the sideboard. Sometimes she just filled up with the goneness of everything. But I've done this, she thought, I've done it, I've changed things now, for ever, and I don't care. I'm glad I'm glad I'm glad. Do it. You have to. You only have one life. Change things. Change things for ever. What I've done is right. What they do with it, that's up to them.

★

401

Bruce Robert Holloway. He was rich. He had another half-brother from his mother's marriage, a wife, a beautiful daughter called Rose, who was nine. He showed their photographs proudly. His mother, Jenny Lim, died a year ago, of breast cancer. She'd been very happy in her marriage, he said. He seemed to bear no resentment towards Bob at all for abandoning him. His mother, he said, had held her head up high and taught him to be proud of his birth. He had always kept his father's name.

Over the years he would visit Bob and Eva on their council estate every summer, lavishing presents upon them, offering to buy their house outright for them, though Eva refused. Once, watching TV, he said, 'That set's not good enough,' went out and came back with a new, bigger, better one. They went out for slap-up meals anywhere they wanted, anywhere at all, the whole family and Jean. He offered to pay their fares out to Malaysia. But they didn't really want to go. This was home. They were little people now. They didn't go far.

Bob went to the Chinese takeaway one night with Bruce. Bruce was saying something in Cantonese as they went in. Bob had been in and out of this Chinese for years. The woman was aghast. 'You never told me you spoke Cantonese,' she cried accusingly at Bob. 'I been talking in front of you all these years.'

'I don't.' He smiled.

'Who's this?' she demanded.

'He's my son.'

I have two sons, two sons. I have always had two sons.

37

Tourists in Heaven

Something Mary said that day when he told her about his mother's diary, about her inarticulate musings on the meaning of it all.

'I'll tell you what's pointless.' They were standing in a room full of birds, pigeons with food poisoning and mouldy beaks, ducks who'd got fish-hooks caught in their webbed feet, a blackbird with a broken wing. 'Looking for a point is pointless. And that's a cliché. And everything your mum said was a cliché; like what's it all about, Alfie, and love is all you need, and make hay while the sun shines and you never miss your water till your well runs dry.'

Half asleep, half here, half there. Half-way to anywhere. Flying home. Last night he had been in Mary's house, in her room full of birds.

She laughed and lifted a scabby flea-ridden pigeon from a cardboard box, checked the splint on its leg. 'The meaning of life is a cliché!'

'Mary,' he said, 'are you all right now?'

'Of course I'm all right.'

'No, I mean – are you *really* all right? After the fire, I never really talked to you about it, I always felt too …'

She pushed him. 'Shut up, Jack,' she said, settling the pigeon back in its nest, leading him back to the living room, a tip, the whole house was a tip. He was glad she hadn't cleaned up for him. Any thoughts of sleeping with her had soon been scotched, everything said that: the door left wide open, the continual flow of teenage girls coming and going up and down the stairs, in and out of the kitchen, the constant interruptions from neighbours, window-cleaner, cats. Mary's life was crowded.

They'd drunk coffee. She said Auntie Jill was still going strong. She said she loved teaching. She taught primary, kids about eight or nine. She had a daughter called Amy who was fourteen.

'I still see them, you know,' she said.

'Who?'

'The kids. Colinette. Titch and Susan. The lads. Oh, don't look like that, Jack. I mean, I really do see them. They're still around.'

She jumped up. 'I have something for you.'

She returned and placed in his hand a familiar object he had not seen for so many years, maybe all the years of his life, maybe he'd never seen it, and yet he knew it at once. A brooch, gold filigree, the letters N-E-L-L-Y intertwined.

'She gave it me ages ago. I always thought it was pretty and she gave it me. I think you should have it now.'

Jack looked at it lying on his palm. 'Tell you what,' he said, 'you keep it for now. You can give it to me when you come and see me.'

She smiled. 'I would very much like to see Rome,' she said.

Come soon.

Oh, sleep, come soon.

Following a curve of the earth, sailing above the brilliant snow of cloud, the ridiculous truth dawned: that his parents had loved each other after all. His eyes closed. His mother's stories, his father's music. That's what he'd come out of, that much was true. Sleep gathered up the lights and the sounds around his head and whirled them wildly with a strobe of images. Violet danced in black stockings, kicking her thin legs wildly. Summer's wing sheltered a Morland garden. Grandad let a German soldier go. Stories. Just stories.

Therefore he could tell more, tell the one where Nell goes into that lovely garden and meets her dad and Harry.

Therefore he could give his father a jazzman's funeral the like of which the world had never seen and would always remember; and Pops and Tea are there, blowing like they've never blown before.

Therefore he could tell the one called Tourists in Heaven.

There they are, his mum and dad.

His dad has his camera round his neck.

He's saying, 'Go and stand next to that angel over there. Go on, link him, he won't mind.'

She's saying, 'I can't, Harry, I feel a fool.'
'Go on! He won't mind. He's used to it.'
She turns and speaks directly to camera.
'Your dad,' she says, with a faint smile, 'he drives me mad.'